The Wolf's Song:

A Blood of the Wolf King Novel

Caleb the Writer

Thank you for purchasing this book! I hope you enjoy the story and world of *Blood of the Wolf King*.

Special thanks to Kristian Popec for the soundtrack.

God Bless all of the artists that helped make this world come to life, and to you, the reader! Have fun on this journey across Gotheca!

Contents

Prologue _____ 14
Chapter 1 _____ 19
Chapter 2 _____ 76
Chapter 3 _____ 91
Chapter 4 _____ 110
Chapter 5 _____ 117
Chapter 6 _____ 128
Chapter 7 _____ 138
Chapter 8 _____ 160
Chapter 9 _____ 177
Chapter 10 _____ 194
Chapter 11 _____ 202
Chapter 12 _____ 210
Chapter 13 _____ 221
Chapter 14 _____ 228
Chapter 15 _____ 239
Chapter 16 _____ 253
Chapter 17 _____ 269
Chapter 18 _____ 290
Chapter 19 _____ 306
Chapter 20 _____ 320
Chapter 21 _____ 327
Chapter 22 _____ 332
Chapter 23 _____ 342
Chapter 24 _____ 354

Chapter 25	362
Chapter 26	365
Chapter 27	368
Chapter 28	375

The official soundtrack of *The Wolf Song*. Scan the QR codes below!

Code of the Road

Leave Her Johnny

Mary My Dear

Bold Riley Oh

Hoist the Sails

The Derby Run

7

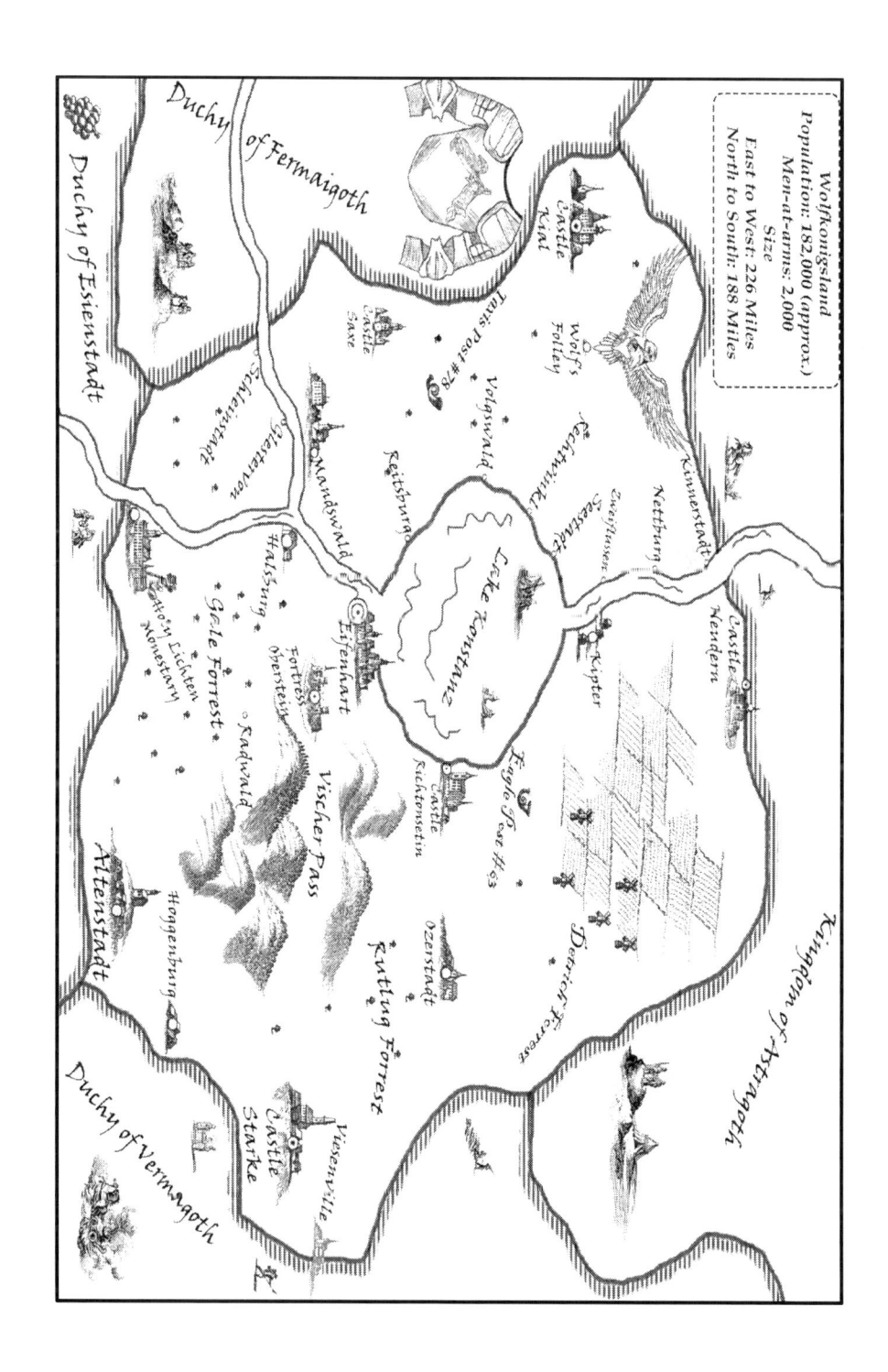

Map of the Duchy of Eisenstadt

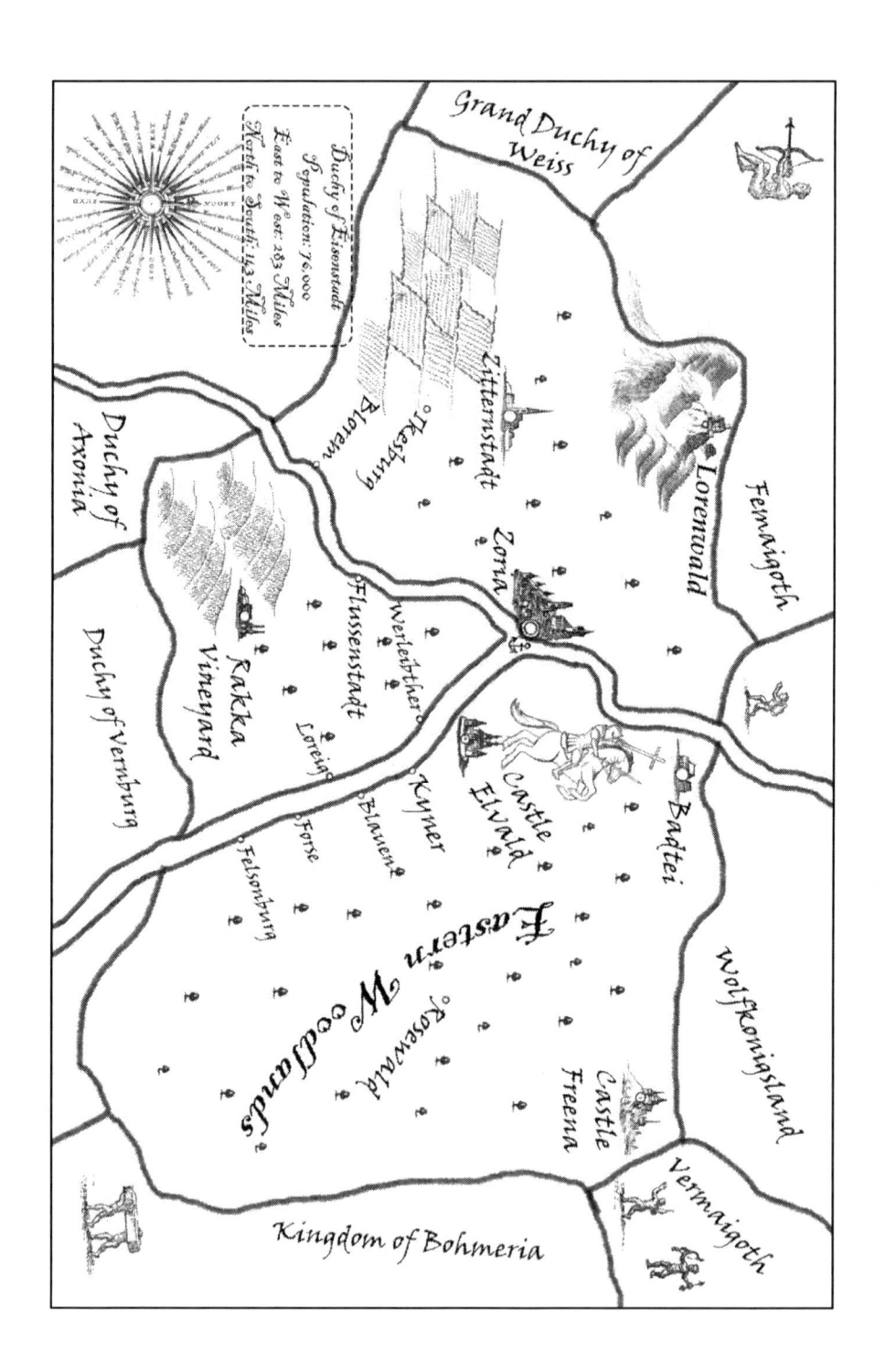

Duchy of Eisenstadt
Population: 76,000
East to West est. 283 Miles
North to South 142 Miles

- Grand Duchy of Weiss
- Duchy of Axonia
- Duchy of Vernburg
- Femaigoth
- Lorenwald
- Zitterstadt
- Hasbrig
- Ploten
- Zona
- Fussenstadt
- Werlerthor
- Loreig
- Kyner
- Blauen
- Forse
- Felsonburg
- Rakka Vineyard
- Castle Elvald
- Badtei
- Rosewald
- Castle Freena
- Eastern Woodlands
- Wolfkonigsland
- Vermaigoth
- Kingdom of Bohmeria

8

The Great Channel

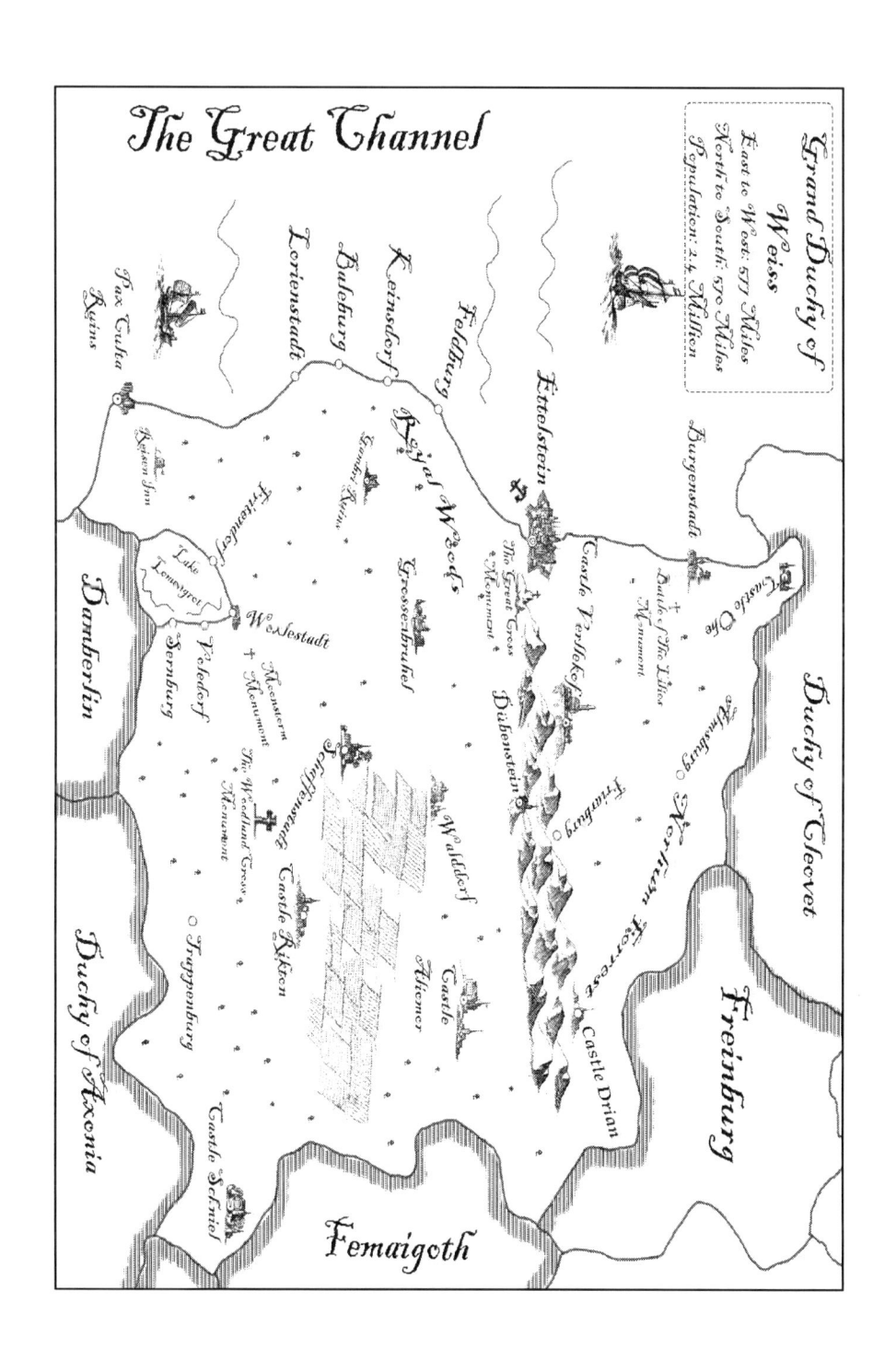

Grand Duchy of
Weiss
East to West: 577 Miles
North to South: 570 Miles
Population: 2.4 Million

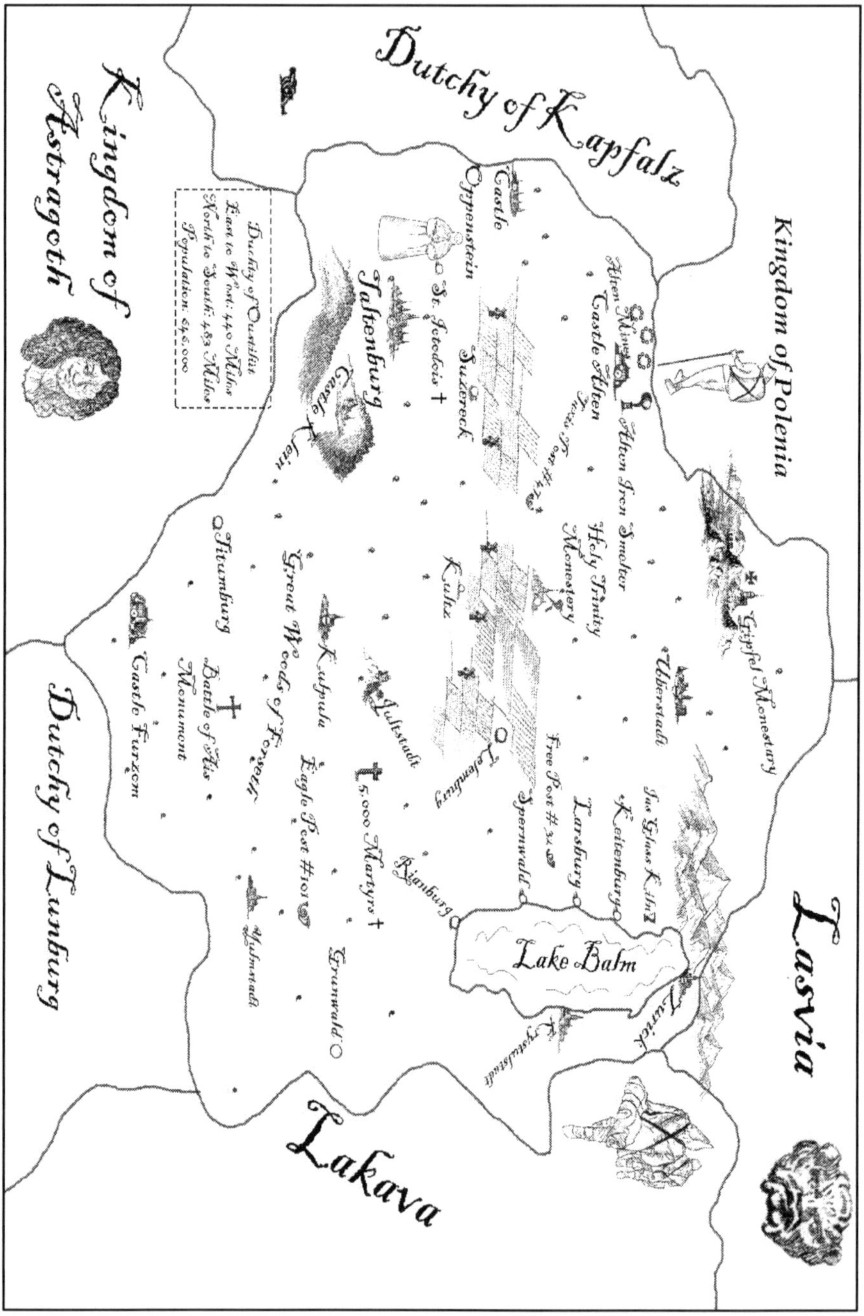
Dutchy of Kapfalz
Kingdom of Polenia
Kingdom of Astragoth
Lasvia
Dutchy of Lunburg
Lakava
Lake Balm
Castle Oppenstein
Taltenburg
St. Jetedois
Suzereck
Alten Mines
Castle Alten
Alten Iron Smelter
Holy Trinity Monestery
Gipfel Monestary
Uberstadt
Kultz
Free Post #32
Sperrwald
Larsburg
Keitenburg
Rianburg
5,000 Martyrs
Eagle Post #101
Kulpula
Great Woods of Forseth
Fitumburg
Battle of Ais Monument
Castle Furzom
Gramwald
Duchy of Oustilit
East to West: 440 Miles
North to South: 483 Miles
Population: 646,000

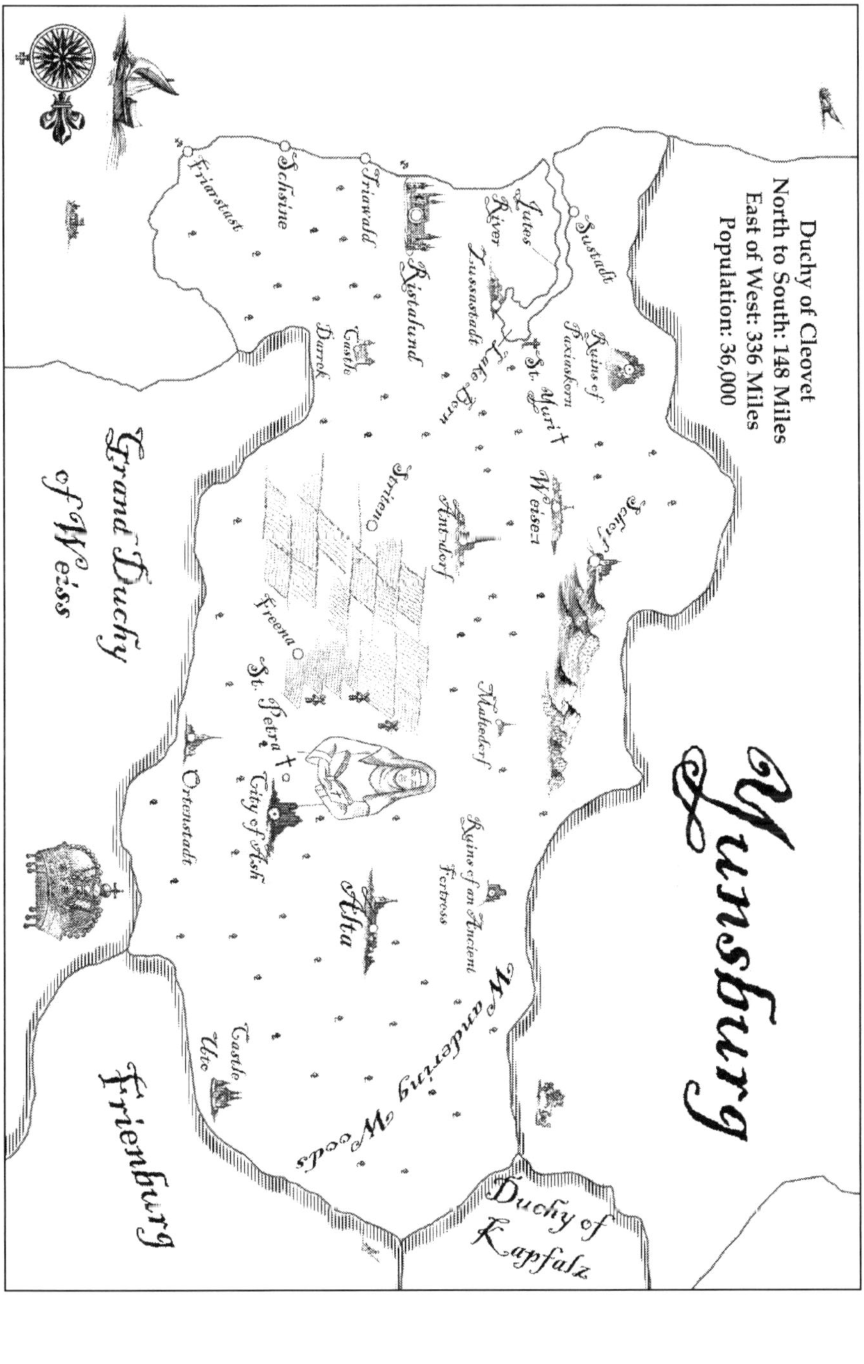
Yunsburg
Duchy of Cleovet
North to South: 148 Miles
East of West: 336 Miles
Population: 36,000
Grand Duchy of Weiss
Frienburg
Duchy of Kapfalz
Wandering Woods
Friarstast
Schisine
Triawald
Ristalund
Lutes River
Lussastadt
Sustadt
Ruins of Paxiaskorn
Lake Bern
St. Yurit
Castle Darrek
Weiser
Schorf
Amtdorf
Strrien
Freena
St. Petra
City of Ash
Ortenstadt
Malsdorf
Ruins of an Ancient Fortress
Alta
Castle Uric

Reaper's Sea

Knight's Isle
Zimstadt

Free Post #14
Castle Gunther
Gunther Lumber Mills

Kingdom of Polenia

Großhenburg
St. Basilia, Lady of The Water
Gretstadt
Balentei
Meltdorf
Pleunburg
Taxis Post #89

Galeburn Mountains
Srick Gold Mines
Srick Gold Smelter
Castle Srick

Leechwald Woods

Hackelbeckum Forrest

Holy Monastery of The Trinity

Frunlock Lumber Mills
Castle Frunlock

Saint Basilia Holy Monastery

Outtendorf

Bahrensburg
Eagle Post #55
Redenves

Lozia Forrest

The Great Channel

Elmsenburg
Bad Rukburg

Castle Ruz

Duchy of Kapfalz

Apsburg

Yunsburg

```
Duchy of Nummelund
Population: 230,000 (approx.)
East to West: 363 Miles
North to South: 451 Miles
```

12

Months and days of Gotheca

Month of Lupus (Wolf)	January	Mornday	Monday
Month of Gemini (Twins)	February	Seconday	Tuesday
Month of Aquarius (Water Bearer)	March	Middleday	Wednesday
Month of Virgo (The Virgin)	April	Thunday	Thursday
Month of Corvus (Crow)	May	Ritterday	Friday
Month of Orion (Hunter)	June	Sutterday (Sabbathday)	Saturday
Month of Norma (Carpenter, Builder)	July	Sumaday (Lord's Day)	Sunday
Month of Leo (Lion)	August		
Month of Aquila (Eagle)	September		
Month of Taurus (Bull)	October		
Month of Sagittarius (Archer)	November		
Month of Pictor (Artist)	December		

Each month is celebrated by local festivals called "Constellius". Although not every place celebrates every month, some larger towns may have a Constellius every month. Lupus is often celebrated with games like chess and the selling of various wolf-pelt clothing. The wolf is seen as a great leader and strategist. Gemini is celebrated by pranks and gags to represent mischievous twins. Aquarius is celebrated with water games. Virgo is celebrated with a large feast hosted by nuns and monks, and they start each feast by venerating the Mother of God. Orion is celebrated by hunting competitions and great feasts where everyone shares their game. Corvus is celebrating with a game of opposites- since the crow is seen as a liar and mischievous, people are encouraged to say and act opposite of how they normally would- within reason of course. Leo is the month of bravery, and is celebrated with tournaments and tests of courage (like seeing how long someone can last in a pit full of scorpions). The month of Aquila is usually celebrated by the upper class, as the eagle is seen as honorable and rich. The celebrations include fashion competitions and feasts. Taurus is celebrated with tests of strength. Sagittarius is celebrated with archery competitions. Finally, Pictor is celebrated with art and sculpture displays and competitions.

Prologue

"I suppose this is the end. Our empire survived two thousand years, brought down by a mere horde of peasants. We crushed countless rebellions, defeated entire countries, all for us to end up here. I'm sorry I couldn't have done more, my emperor."

Those were the last words angrily uttered by a high-ranking centurion fighting for the Aeternian Empire. His lorica segmentata armor was practically torn to shreds. Metal strips hung from the torn leather, holding the armor together. His arms held his innards back from spilling out the gaping hole in his abdomen. As the light in his eyes left him, his arms relaxed, and his guts fell over the cold stone ground. A large man with a thick gray beard stood over him. He wore a wolf pelt over his shoulders, covering the ornate gold pauldrons of his metal armor. He was Tiberius Belasarius, the usurper of the last emperor, the man known to history by the nickname, the Wolf King.

In the year 26 of the Ancient Era, known as 1093 of the Imperial Calendar, Tiberius Belasarius was born. His distinctive red eyes, the likes of which no one had ever seen—at least in recorded history—made many believe he was a demon born of the flesh. Perhaps that prediction was accurate, or the scorn he faced growing up became a self-fulfilling prophecy. He was part of a noble house of the Aeternian Empire, an empire so old its true name was lost to time. He'd become an accomplished general and gain the favor of his legions. Eventually, he usurped the throne, massacred the Senate, and completely took control of the Empire. His men fought beside him for decades, supporting his rule, but uprising after uprising made control all but impossible. One particularly talented general, who history would record as the hero general of Prussia, rose in the eastern half of the Kontinent. After ten years of rebellion, the hero general trapped the Wolf King in a modest ruined temple abandoned in a small swamp for centuries. It was there that the Wolf King's Centurion's and Praetorian Guard's, his most loyal and elite troops, made their last stand for the dying Empire.

The Wolf King looked at the night sky. Clouds passed in front of the moon, darkening the battlefield. He anxiously listened to men screaming and metal clashing. The Wolf King knew the rebels would soon be upon him. He'd fought in many battles and seen many wars. He always felt he was ready for the end, but as certain death approached, he couldn't truly brace himself for what was to come.

The sound of footsteps running toward him broke his thoughts. He hadn't realized it, but the battlefield had been quiet for some time. The smell of blood and smoke wafted through a light breeze. It was a scent the Wolf King was all too familiar with, but it revolted him, unlike previous battles. Men wearing patchwork leather armor approached from the far side of the ruined temple. They were visible only by the moonlight reflecting off their spearheads. The Wolf King smiled a devilish grin.

"Come at me, men of Gothica! That's what you're called now, aren't you? After you so brazenly threw away your true nationality! You are nothing but ants. Come at me already, if you think you can best the Wolf King of the Aeternian Empire!" he shouted as loud as he could, mustering all the strength he had.

The approaching men stopped, their bodies gripped by fear.

"D-don't stop, we can beat him! He's just one man!" a lone soldier shouted from the crowd.

The troops moved forward again. One particularly brave troop charged at the Wolf King, spear in hand and ferocity in his eyes. His bravery was commendable, but it was all for naught. As the soldier charged, the Wolf King stepped aside and unsheathed his gladius. He avoided the soldier's strike. The young man gritted his teeth and lunged forward for another attack. The Wolf King parried and, with incredible speed, plunged his sword into the soldier's neck. He tried to scream but his voice came out only as inaudible air bubbling up in the blood spilling over his patchwork leather armor.

The Wolf King laughed. "Is this all you can muster? You pathetic wretches are nothing."

The men once again stopped with fear. As they shook nervously, loud footsteps came from the darkness. A tall man in metal armor approached. He held a long pike in his hands. Blood, from deep fresh wounds carved into his skin, covered his face. Presumably his helmet had come off during the fighting.

"Finally, the hero general makes his appearance," the Wolf King said. "It's been a long time."

"Yes, and now it's time for your empire to end," the hero general shouted.

The Wolf King knew he had a disadvantage in fighting a spear with a sword. Spears had more reach and power behind them, and he wasn't sure if his sword could even slash through the hero general's armor. His best strategy was to aim for the hero general's head, since he was helmless. The Wolf King didn't want to fight on the defensive. He charged at the hero general, attempting to close the distance between them quickly, his sword held pointed at the hero general's neck. The Wolf King's strategy was nothing more than a half-baked, adrenaline-fueled attack with little chance of success. The hero general pulled back and raised his spear. He gripped the rear of the shaft and pulled the spear upward at a ninety-degree angle. He brought it down with enough raw power to knock out even the strongest of men and struck the Wolf King's shoulder with the shaft. The Wolf King quickly recovered and swung his gladius. The hero general brought his spear back up and used the shaft to deflect the blow. He then brought his weapon parallel to the ground and jumped forward, plunging the spear into the Wolf King's chest. The hero general pushed the Wolf King into the broken walls of the temple and forced the spear head deeper into his chest.

"Ah-ha, so you got me," the Wolf King said as he spit blood onto the ground.

Before he could speak further, a bright light appeared in the sky. Everyone looking up saw a truly terrifying sight. Something struck the moon, shattering it to pieces. They watched in shock as the moon tore into two pieces. Tiny shards soon plummeted toward the world.

"Wh-what happened?" a soldier in the back of the crowd of troops asked.

"Yes, yes!" the Wolf King shouted as he laughed maniacally. "You see this? It's a divine symbol from God himself! Yes! You may kill me now, but this isn't my end! Someday, I will return. I will come back to this world! When I do, I'll bring about the end of this new era you've strived so hard to create. I'll bring about the end of everything!"

"Quiet, demon! We always knew you were evil, but this is all but proof you're nothing but a creature from the Netherworld! I'll exercise you from this realm!" The hero general screamed.

The Wolf King smiled.

"Maybe, but I'll be taking you with me."

His red eyes were menacing, almost glowing in the dark. He lunged forward, growling like a furious wolf. And, with unbelievable speed, he plunged his sword into the hero general's neck. They fell to the ground, having lost their strength, and would soon be gone from the world.

That was the biggest turning point in the history of Gotheca. The vast and rich land split into two halves, Westlichtenhalfen and Ostenhalfen, with a massive channel known as the Great Channel between them. In the many years since the fall of the Aeternian Empire, Gotheca had become divided. Government fell to local counties and small duchies.

The Wolf's Song

The days of empires were over, and constant conflict and strife replaced them. To stop the violence plaguing the land, a man from the great Wolderan Kingdom, a nation he formed through conquest, met with the pope of the Western Church to form a new empire. Then, they founded the Holy Aeternian Empire (HAE), and many states would sign the Imperial Charter. Unlike the Aeternian Empire of the past, the HAE was a collection of states tied to a loose set of ideals. Eventually, the whole of Gotheca signed the Imperial Charter and joined under the HAE.

History would once again take a new, terrifying direction many centuries after the Wolf King's death. In the central region of Ostenhalfen, known as Öustria, sat a small duchy on the same lands the Wolf King made his last stand. The year is 1475 of Divinum Regnum (D.R.) and a baby with red eyes is born. Soon, the entire world will once again fall to its knees.

Chapter 1

Snow drifted onto the wooden roof of a modest manor sitting atop a hill overlooking a small village. A woman screaming in pain broke the silence of the winter night. She was in her bed chambers, surrounded by midwives, biting down on a small oak stick as she gave birth. One midwife gripped the woman's hand as another wiped her forehead with a wet rag. After a moment, a baby crying replaced the pained screaming of the mother. The oldest midwife held the babe firm in her arms. She approached the mother cautiously.

"Lady Adelita, it's a boy! But..." the old midwife began.

"But what? Is he okay?" Lady Adeltia asked, panting.

"Yes, it's just... he has red eyes. Strange, I've never seen that before."

"Let me see him!" Lady Adelita said as the midwife wrapped the babe in a cloth.

The midwife handed the child over to Lady Adelita. His crying stopped as soon as he was in his mother's arms.

"What a nice boy. He clearly loves his mother!" the old midwife said.

The Wolf's Song

The heavy oak door to the bed chambers slammed open. A large, hulking man in plate armor and an ornate velvet cape stepped in. Mud and blood covered him, but he had an enormous smile on his face. His thick beard partially obscured a large scar extending from his chin to just past one of his dark blue eyes. The sound of the door opening caused the baby to cry again.

"Honey, you upset our son!" Lady Adelita whispered.

"A son? Yes, another fine boy in our house!" the man proudly said. "I heard the screaming stop, so I figured you were done. I'm glad to see you're both okay!"

"Sir Welter, you were supposed to wait for us to get you," the old midwife sighed. "I'll leave you and Lady Adelita," she continued as she left the room with the other midwives.

"Let me hold our new son, my wife!" Sir Welter said as Lady Adelita tried to quiet the child.

"My dearest husband, could you not have at least washed up before coming in? You have blood on your beard."

"Oh, I think that's mud. Besides, there was another Visigoth raiding party entering the border. Taking off my armor and washing up would take a couple of hours, and I couldn't wait to see our new child!" Sir Welter said as he motioned at the child.

Lady Adelita handed the boy over to her husband.

"What a strapping young lad. But those eyes. That's worrying." The smile on Sir Welter's face disappeared as he stared into his son's red eyes.

The baby stopped crying and laughed.

"Ha, but you're an adorable little one."

"What shall we name him, dearest?" Lady Adelita asked.

"Those eyes... something about them. Hm." Sir Welter paused for a moment. "Let's name him after a traveling wolf, Wolfgang."

"Why that name? Why not after a Saint?" Lady Adelita asked.

"I can tell by looking at him. In a world with sheeps wearing lion's skin, barking and growling, fighting over scraps of land, he shall be a wolf."

"That poetic side of you is coming out again, dear." Lady Adelita smiled.

"Ah, sorry. I am getting ahead of myself, aren't I?"

The baby cried again.

"Sounds like he beckons for his mother once more."

"Ah yes, here." Sir Welter handed Wolfgang back to Lady Adelita. "I'll go wash up and prepare for bed. This young boy will be a strong one. I can feel it."

Lady Adelita looked at her son and rocked him until he was calm. Wolfgang was the newest member of House Coburg. He'd join his two brothers and three sisters in their small border town out in the sticks. House Coburg had a history of distinguished warriors. For their service, many decades ago, the duke gave them a large plot of land- populated by several farms, a small village, and a border fort. Their primary charge was to patrol and defend the border from Vermaigoth invaders. Lady Adelita knew her newborn son would someday become one of the strong men-at-arms defending their homeland.

***

Red and orange leaves fell from dying trees with the fall wind. Squirrels stirred, finding their last meals before the winter. Nearby, in a modest noble manor, the shouts of children playing echoed. There was a sweet scent in the air from the baker's hut in the village, which was just a short walk away from the manor. Five winters have passed since Wolfgang von Coburg's birth. He was a young boy playing soldier with his siblings in the manor courtyard.

"Take that!" Wolfgang's oldest brother and eldest sibling, Uwe, shouted as he swung a wooden sword.

Wolfgang raised a small wooden shield to block. As he did, his other older brother, Johanne, charged at him with a spear. The spear was little more than a small piece of wood shaped like a staff with a small cloth tied to the end.

"I'll get you, fiend!" Johanne yelled.

"We'll see about that!" Wolfgang shouted.

He stepped back onto his right leg to his rear and spun to his right, moving the shield and Uwe with it. That put Uwe right in the path of Johanne's spear, striking him in the side.

"Ha, you're dead Uwe!" Wolfgang smirked.

"Na-uh, that was only a graze! If this were actual combat, I'd still be alive!" Uwe shouted angrily.

"No fair, cheater!" Wolfgang replied as he readied his sword and shield. "Okay, then come at me, just you!"

"Oh, not this again. Come on, Uwe, you don't need to pick on our little brother so much!" Johanne said sympathetically.

"Shut up, weakling! This is between us. Wolfgang, I'm coming!"

Uwe lunged forward, swinging his sword. Wolfgang instinctually threw up his shield in defense. He fumbled as he prepared for the strike, utterly unready for it to hit.

Uwe's wooden blade slashed the rounded edge of the shield, forcing it out of Wolfgang's hand. Before Wolfgang could react, Uwe brought the sword up and smacked Wolfgang in the head. Wolfgang fell to the ground and Uwe looked at him. The strike broke the skin and drops of blood stained Wolfgang's green tunic and yellow hose.

"Look, I told you I was better!" Uwe said with a wide grin on his face.

"Yeah, better at cheating!" Wolfgang replied, sticking his tongue out.

"You should respect me. I'm your older brother, red eyes!"

"Hey, what did I tell you about calling him that?" a thundering voice shouted behind them.

It was Sir Welter, their father. Wolfgang got to his feet and followed his siblings.

"I—sorry, father," Uwe said, his eyes cast toward the ground.

"Look, son, you're the eldest child in the family. It's your responsibility to protect your family," Sir Welter said as he patted Uwe's head affectionately. "And you, Wolfgang. I know you're almost five, but in a few years, you'll head off to House Eiken for squire training. Uwe here is going at the end of this summer. So, I need you to work hard and get stronger."

"Okay," Wolfgang replied timidly.

"Hey, let me see that welt on your head."

Sir Welter approached Wolfgang and pulled his chin up so he could properly inspect the wound on his forehead.

"Looks like a big one. Go see Stefan before dinner."

"Yes, sir."

"As for you two." Sir Welter turned his steely gaze to his other two children. "Go help your mother and sisters prepare for dinner."

"Yes, sir!" they replied excitedly before running inside.

***

Wolfgang sat by an open window in the small manor's library. A few shelves of dusty old books lined the walls, with a table in the center. The door on the opposite side of the room opened and an old gentleman walked in. His kind eyes complimented his gray hair and long mustache. He wore a blue, lamb fur robe with a green cloth lining.

"Stefan!" Wolfgang shouted with excitement as he leaped from the windowsill. "Can we play chess or Alquerque again today? Please?"

"Calm down, young master," the gentle old servant began. "I must tend to your wound first. Then you must go help your siblings prepare for dinner."

Wolfgang hadn't noticed, but Stefan held a bucket of water and a rag in one hand, and a bowl full of ground herbs in the other. He set the bowl on the table and approached Wolfgang. Stefan then washed Wolfgang's forehead with the rag.

"You three always play so rough. You should be more careful, Master Wolfgang."

"It's not my fault! Uwe was cheating again!"

"Oh, maybe so. But in real life, your opponent rarely plays by the rules." Stefan turned to grab the bowl of ground herbs.

"But you always play fair in chess!"

"That's merely a game, young one. You'll understand one day. Now, take this. Swallow it all."

Stefan held the bowl against Wolfgang's mouth and lifted it up. Wolfgang begrudgingly swallowed.

"Now open your mouth. Show me you swallowed it all."

"I did!"

"Young master," Stefan said, folding his arms.

Wolfgang swallowed a second time, then opened his mouth, showing it to be empty.

Stefan smiled. "Perfect. You're a good boy. Now, go to the dining hall. I'm sure they're waiting for you."

Caleb the Writer

"Okay," Wolfgang said, slowly leaving the library.

The dining hall was loud and lively. Sitting at the ends of the table were Sir Welter and Lady Adelita. To the left of Sir Welter were Wolfgang's brothers, Johanne and Uwe. On the other side were his sisters; the eldest and Johanne's twin, Petra; the middle sister, Lea; and the newest child in the Coburg House, Julia. Wolfgang approached the table and sat next to Uwe. His plate was already prepared with a slab of pig meat with buttered bread. A rare delicacy for the average person on the Kontinent, but as lower nobles, they had more wealth than the average peasant. Sir Welter clasped his hands together and the rest of the family followed.

"Our Father out in Heaven," Sir Welter began, "Please bless this—"

Stefan cut him off as he approached from the hallway. "Sorry to bother you, sire, but there is a matter of great Importance."

Stefan stepped aside and beckoned another man forward. The man wore mail armor and a bassinet. He had a red and white cloak around his neck. In his right hand, he held a poleax; a staff weapon with an iron head with one side shaped like an ax, the other a hammer, and at the top, a pike. The man put his arm across his chest and bowed.

"I'm sorry to disturb you during your family's meal, my lord. The Vermagoth sent a rather large raiding party our way. Somehow, they snuck past our scouts."

"Those damn skamelar. The gall of these knaves. How dare they attack us again, and so soon, at this hour!" Sir Welter shouted as he stood up.

At that point, the Vermagoth raiders' attacks were routine. They normally attacked around noon Mondays and Thursdays, but sometimes they'd carry out surprise attacks. They never did much damage and the small fortress on the border always stopped them, so they were more of an annoyance than anything.

"I'll go get my armor on. Captain, go get the men ready. What are their numbers?"

"Around a hundred, sir," the man in armor replied.

"No need to awaken our off-duty troops, then. Those in the fortress will be enough. I'll meet you there." Sir Welter strolled out of the dining hall.

The captain left with more haste, taking the invasion more seriously.

"Wait, father!" Wolfgang shouted as he stood up from his chair and chased Sir Welter into the hallway. "Take me! I want to fight too!"

"What?" Sir Welter turned to face Wolfgang, an annoyed look on his face. "Son, you're far too young to fight. You can't even beat your brothers—Hell, you can't even defeat a soft rabbit. The battlefield isn't a place for children."

"But, Father, I—"

"Enough, sit down and finish your meal. I can't delay anymore."

Sir Welter turned back to the hallway and left. Wolfgang closed his small fist in anger. Lady Adelita stood up, walked over, and slapped Wolfgang across the face. He stumbled back.

"How dare you talk to your father like that!" she shouted. "Sit down, child, and quietly finish your meal."

Wolfgang begrudgingly sat in his chair again. Uwe snickered. His sisters looked at him across the table, and they snickered, too. After a few seconds, their snickers turned to laughter. Lady Adelita slammed her hand on the table.

"Quiet, all of you!" she shouted. "Finish your food and have some respect."

The children quickly quieted down. Wolfgang picked up his plate and shoveled the food into his mouth as fast as he could.

"Wolfgang, that's no way for a noble to eat! I taught you manners many times. How often are you going to ignore our lessons?" Lady Adeltia asked as she put her hand to her head.

Wolfgang ignored her and kept eating. He set the plate on the table and stood up.

"Excuse me, ma'am, I'm done eating and will take my leave," Wolfgang said as he jogged out of the dining hall.

"W-wait, child!" Lady Adelita shouted.

It was too late, for Wolfgang had already made his way to the foyer and ran out the door. Stefan was close behind and stood in the doorway watching Wolfgang run toward the wooden gate of the manor's walls.

"Careful, young master. You know your father will be angry when he gets back," Stefan shouted.

"I don't care!" Wolfgang responded, trying to hold back tears.

He was angry and emotional, but this wasn't uncommon for him. Everyone always treated him differently than others.

"Don't go into town without your hood!" Stefan shouted as Wolfgang ran off into the distance.

Wolfgang ran down a small path leading away from the village to the south. The path wound through a patch of trees. Once he was out of sight of the manor, he stopped to catch his breath. He walked through the forest, listening to the songs of the nightingale perched high in the branches of the tall oak trees. His steps matched the cadence of the bird's song as he continued his trek through the woods.

Eventually, he made his way to an opening in the thick bushes. The trail ended, and the trees gave way to a vast field of yellow daisies. Wolfgang entered the field, admiring his surroundings. The place was special to him. He discovered it while exploring a couple months prior and returned whenever he felt too overwhelmed.

Wolfgang threw his arms up and fell backward into the flowers. They were soft, like a bed of hay. He let out a sigh as he stretched, then put his arms behind his head and used them as a pillow. A breeze caused the petals of a daisy to tickle Wolfgang's face. He stared at the orange evening sky, shifting his gaze to the moon. He stared at the two halves and the debris in between. The moon's shards formed a fine ring around the planet of Nyrene, so one could always see evidence of the Splitting, no matter where they looked up at the sky. The moon's slight green tint contrasted with the darkening sky. Distant stars appeared. He wondered what it may be like to live on the moon. Were there people there? Cities and villages just like on Nyrene? A strange feeling, like he was being watched, interrupted his thoughts. He sat up and looked around. Out by the tree line, near the woods' entrance, was an old man with not a single strand of hair on his head. He wore black priest vestments and a large gold cross around his neck and had tired eyes. He sat underneath a tree, juggling an apple with his right hand. The wind blew dead leaves around the old priest. Wolfgang stood up and walked over to him.

"Hey, old man, what are you doing watching people out here?" Wolfgang asked as he approached.

The oldest priest continued juggling the apple for a moment. He then snatched it out of the air and looked up. His unusually kind eyes met with Wolfgang's.

"I suppose I should ask you that, son. I was here first, after all," he replied in a soft voice.

"What? No way, I was here first!" Wolfgang shouted as he pointed at the priest.

"Just because you didn't notice me doesn't mean I wasn't here. There are often things unseen but still present."

"Huh? What's that supposed to mean?" Wolfgang asked as he sat down next to the priest. "Whatever. What's a priest doing out in a field, anyway?"

"Oh, I'm just wandering," the wandering priest replied. He put his hand to his chin like he was in deep thought. "And what is a boy doing out in a field like this?"

"No reason," Wolfgang said defiantly.

"Looks like there's some blood on your tunic. Were you in a fight?"

The wandering priest pointed at the blood from the sparring match with Uwe. It had faded into the tunic and was barely noticeable.

"No, not exactly. Hm. I wish I was fighting right now," Wolfgang sighed.

"You wish to fight? Whom do you want to fight?"

"The Vermagoth of course! They're our enemy! They need to be killed," Wolfgang shouted.

"And what did they do to be your enemy?"

"Huh?" The wandering priest's question caught him completely off guard. "Well…"

Wolfgang stopped for a moment to think. He looked up at the falling leaves as he prepared a response.

"They attack us, right? Doesn't that make them our enemy?"

"Perhaps. But have you ever thought of another way to resolve this conflict?"

"I don't get what you're saying. If we fight them and win, it's over, right?"

"Things are rarely that simple." The wandering priest set the apple on the ground and stood up. "Put up again thy sword into his place. For all they that take the sword shall perish with the sword. The only enemy that we face is the enemy within. People of the world are our family, even those that have not seen the light."

The Wolf's Song

"I still don't get it, Priest," Wolfgang said as the priest turned toward the woods.

"It's getting dark. You ought to go back home." The priest then walked into the dark forest, presumably wandering to his next stop.

"What a peculiar priest," Wolfgang said to himself.

He looked back at the field, watching the last sliver of light leave the sky. The stars twinkled in the dark. The moon shone through the clear sky, providing just enough light for Wolfgang to see. He stood up and began making his way back home.

He made his way through the woods, back down the now barely illuminated path that took him to the field. As he walked toward the manor walls, something strange caught Wolfgang's attention. The clang of metal hitting metal echoed through the darkness. It came from the blacksmith's workshop was just outside of the manor's front gate.

Wolfgang approached the large wooden gate to the manor. He grasped the handle and pulled, but the gate wouldn't budge. It was locked. He then looked over at the gatehouse to his left. Wolfgang knew a guard should be inside. He walked over and banged on the wooden shutter covering the window.

"Huh? Who's there?" a voice called from inside the room.

The wooden shutter lifted to reveal a young man in mail armor and a bassinet on his head. He had a white and red waffenrock over his armor. He leaned his head out of the window and looked side to side before looking out and seeing Wolfgang.

"Oh, it's you. Your father wanted me to let him know when you got back. Stay here for a moment."

The guard closed the window and Wolfgang heard him fumbling with the door. After a moment, the main gate to the manor opened, and Sir Welter stood with his arms crossed and a mean look in his eyes. He sighed before approaching Wolfgang. Sir

Caleb the Writer

Welter raised his hand and slapped Wolfgang across the face.

"How many times are you going to run off like this, boy?" Sir Welter shouted.

"S-sorry, sir," Wolfgang replied, trying to hold back tears.

"Your mother is about to put your siblings to bed. Go change and join them. Don't forget to clean your teeth." Sir Welter sighed, "Please, stop worrying your mother." He turned and walked back into the manor. Wolfgang did the same.

The bedchamber door opened, and Wolfgang stepped through wearing a white nightgown. Lady Adelita sat in a chair in the center of the children's bed chambers. She had a leather-bound book in her lap. Wolfgang's siblings waited eagerly in their beds for a bedtime story. A few candles lit the room dimly.

"Wolfgang, you're here? I assume your father already scolded you. Go to your bed," Lady Adelita ordered.

Wolfgang went to the empty bed on the far side of the room and laid down. He pulled the wool covers over himself.

"Okay, children. I'll read you a story before you go to sleep."

"Yeah!" Johanne exclaimed.

"What story is it today, Mom?" Uwe asked.

"Is it the one about the girl and the wolf?" Julia asked.

"Calm down, children. Today I will read you..." she trailed off as she opened the book. "Ah, the story of the man on the moon. Settle in children." She looked around at her kids, who eagerly waited for the story. Wolfgang nodded his head multiple times, excited to hear the tale.

***

There was once a man from Nordlicht. He was a gloomy thief and a terrible liar who ate his neighbors' cabbages. Every Sabbath,

The Wolf's Song

when no one was around, he stole his neighbors' kindling to make a fire for himself. He'd boil the stolen cabbage over the stolen kindling every Sabbath eve. One Sabbath morn, he saw a pretty, young maiden churning butter in her home. He saw her while he stole his neighbors' kindling and fell in love with her. She soon caught the man in the act, stealing her own kindling.

"Who are you, sir, and what is that burden on your back?" she asked.

"This is my kindling for a fire. I'll boil cabbages later," he said.

"But why are you working on the day of Sabbath, and why are you stuffing my kindling into your burden?"

"My fair lady, I could ask you the same."

The two spoke long before parting ways as nightfall approached. Every Sabbath, as he passed by her house, he saw her churning butter. They spoke and laughed well into the night, and soon, they fell in love. On one Sabbath morn, as the man paid the pretty maiden a visit, another man in fine clothes approached.

He asked of them, "Now why are there two people working on the day of sabbath? Don't you know today is a day of rest and worship?"

"My good and noble sir," the man began. "Sumaday in Heaven or Mornday on Nyrene, 'tis all just days to me."

"May I ask another question, this time to the young maiden?" the man in fine clothes asked. "Why do you work on the Sabbath?"

"Oh, good sir, this is the only time I can churn butter in peace."

"Not so much peace, if this man and his burden are bothering you. One more question. Do you prefer the moon or the sun?"

"Why the moon, of course. It is far cooler and prettier than the sun," the young maiden said.

The man with the burden nodded and agreed.

"Then," the man in fine clothes raised his hand high and pointed toward the sky, "you can churn butter for eternity on the Sudenhalf of the moon. The man with the burden of kindling sticks who greets you every Sabbath will join you, with a burden made of thorns, on the Nordhalf of the moon." With a snap of his fingers, the two were gone, forever cursed to do their duties on the moon. The man walks aimlessly with a burden of thorns and the woman continues to churn her butter. But even this couldn't separate them. They loved each other so much that every time the moon became full, they'd meet in its center and talk. Then, one day, the moon split in half, and they could never see each other again. Now, they must stare longingly across the Broken Canyon every full moon. They scream and scream across the way, but the distance is so great their voices become silent. Remember this tale, remember it well: never disrespect the Sabbath, by stealing or working, if one doesn't want to share the fate with the man on the moon.

***

Lady Adelita closed the book and sat back in her chair. She looked around the bedchamber at the children. They were all asleep. She went around the room and blew out the candles and stepped out.

"Sleep well, children," she murmured as she left.

***

The following month saw the change in the season. The sun rose over the manor, reflecting on the snow covering the manor's roof and courtyard. As dawn broke, Stefan awoke the children. Wolfgang got out of bed and rubbed his eyes. It was time to start the day. The children had chores to take care of before breakfast. After eating, they'd sit down with Lady Adelita for literacy and mathematics lessons. That was standard for most weekdays. As the afternoon blended into the evening, the children had time to play. Wolfgang and his brothers usually played war in the courtyard.

"Hyah!" Uwe shouted as he swung his wooden sword at Wolfgang.

Wolfgang brought his sword up to defend against the incoming blow.

"Now, Johanne!" Uwe called.

"Take this!" Johanne yelled as he charged with a wooden spear. Even though the spear was nothing more than a blunt stick, it still hurt when it dug into Wolfgang's side. His thick fur coat helped deflect some of the pain, but not all of it. Wolfgang dropped his sword and fell to the ground, making an impression in the snow. Uwe moved in and pressed the edge of his sword into Wolfgang's neck.

"I, the hero general of Prussia, have slain the evil Wolf King!" Uwe shouted.

"I won't give up that easily!" Wolfgang yelled as he grabbed his sword out of the snow and shot at Uwe. It caught Uwe by surprise, and he was unprepared for the strike to the back of his head. As soon as Wolfgang made the strike, Uwe started crying.

"W-why did you hit me like that?" Uwe shouted through a waterfall of tears. "That's not fair, I won!"

"Oh, come on, no one even got a killing blow on me!" Wolfgang said. Just then, Wolfgang felt the wooden spear strike his back hard. He fell to the ground.

"How about that for a killing blow?" Johanne said.

"G-good job!" Uwe congratulated.

"Talk about not fair!" Wolfgang spat. "Why do you guys always team up on me?"

"Because you're always the bad guy, duh!" Uwe said, fully recovered from the strike to his head.

As they argued, their little sister, Julia, approached from inside the manor.

"Are you guys fighting again?" Julia asked.

"We wouldn't be fighting if they played fair!" Wolfgang yelled.

"You're just a sore loser," Uwe replied.

"Now, now, you children shouldn't be fighting like this," Stefan said as he stepped from behind Julia. "You kids should enjoy the time you have together. At the end of spring, Uwe will go to the capital to begin Esquire training. You'll miss these times."

"Well, I hope he doesn't come back," Wolfgang shouted as he stuck his tongue out at Uwe.

"You've done it now!" Uwe shouted back.

He raised his wooden sword, preparing to strike at Wolfgang.

"Stop it, you two," Stefan intervened. "Your mother is calling for you to go back in and help with chores."

"Ah, really?" Johanne complained.

"Wolfgang," Stefan began, "It's the 14th of Lupus. Today is your birthday. Your mother said you can play until dinner."

"Really?" Wolfgang smiled.

"No fair! Why don't we celebrate my birthday?" Uwe muttered as he went inside.

"You get to celebrate your name day, Uwe. Now, it's the middle of the week, so there are many chores to be done," Stefan said as he went back inside.

***

Wolfgang went inside for dinner when he finished playing. He ate pig intestines with barley, argued with his siblings, and went to bed. As the months passed, the seasons changed. The spring finally dawned, and the snow melted. It was a Sutterday, the day before the last day of the week, Somday (or the day of Sabbath). In the old times, Sutterday was the day the Aeternian Imperial festival of Sutternelia began. It had become the day designated for cleaning. The most common practice across Gotheca was to bathe and do one's laundry on Sutterday.

It was early one morning that Wolfgang was told to go with his sisters and wash the family's clothes in the river.

"Why do I have to go with them? Isn't washing clothes a girl's chore, anyway?" Wolfgang protested to his mother.

"A chore is a chore, son. Your sisters need help carrying and washing the clothes, so stop complaining and go," she replied. "Your sisters and three of the watch are waiting for you by the gate. Hurry now."

Wolfgang made his way to the manor gates and picked up one barrel of clothing. He followed his sisters as they walked along a road leading far beyond the manor. They traveled east to a small river, forming the border between them and Vermagoth. The three men from the watch followed close behind. They wore leather armor with checkered red and white cloth waffenrocks and kettle helms on their heads. Each of them carried a bill and had a small dagger on their belt. Their bills were farming tools that could be easily fashioned into a weapon of war. It featured a metal head sharpened to a point with a circular swoop that jutted out toward the wielder. Wolfgang listened intently as they spoke to each other. It seemed like they were trying to whisper, but they were loud enough the entire group could hear.

"Why are we stuck on babysitting detail again?" one of them complained.

"In case we get attacked. After all, Vermaigoth is right there," their sergeant replied.

He spoke in a deep gravelly voice, like a man that had seen a lifetime of violence.

"But, Sergeant Eiken, we watch these kids every Sutterday. Nothing has ever happened," the third watchman said.

"Stop complaining, or I'll put you on latrine duty," Sergeant Eiken snapped.

"Yeah, we don't need you babysitting. If any Vandalgoths show up, I'll kill them myself," Wolfgang muttered.

After walking a couple of hours, they arrived at the river on the border. It was a river of modest size and wasn't deep. Julia took off her shoes and walked into the river. She was the shortest of the children, and the river was only as deep as her knees. The other girls did the same.

"Come on, Wolfgang, take your shoes off and bring in the clothes," Julia shouted.

"I don't want to get my trousers wet! Or ruin my tunic!" Wolfgang replied.

"Oh, come now, brother. We're getting our dresses wet. Your tunic will be fine," Petra scolded.

"Come on, the water isn't even that cold!" Lea shouted as she stepped into the river.

"But it's my favorite green tunic," Wolfgang muttered to himself as he took off his shoes. He picked up the barrel of clothes he carried and stepped into the river. "Why can't we just hire servants to do this?"

"Do you know how much that would cost?" Petra asked.

"But we're nobles, aren't we?" Wolfgang grumbled as he dipped the clothes into the river.

"Not like that, brother. With this!" Julia said she handed him a washboard.

"You don't know much, do you, brother? We're barely nobles. The only reason we—" Lea began before being cut off.

The Wolf's Song

"Well, it's hard to know anything when I'm never allowed in town and can barely leave the manor grounds!" Wolfgang shouted.

"Will everyone please stop fighting? Big brother, it's fine. Let's just wash the clothes and go home," Julia said.

An awkward silence befell the siblings, and they returned to their work. Wolfgang listened to the rushing water of the river intently. Small fish darted by his feet just beneath the water's surface. It was a peaceful moment. Wolfgang even stopped scrubbing his brother's blue tunic so he could enjoy this moment. Yelling and rustling from the other side of the river broke the peace.

"What do we have here?" a man shouted from the river shore.

He wore patchwork leather armor with a kettle helm and carried a bill. Several men appeared from behind him.

"By God, Vandalgoths. What are they doing here?" a watchman asked.

"It's a small group, so it wouldn't be too hard for them to cross the mountains," Sergeant Eiken said.

"There are three watchmen and five of us. We can make quick work of them. Unless you surrender and let us take the girls, they'd fetch a high price for sure," the Vandalgoth who appeared to be their leader, said.

"Children back to the shore!" Sergeant Eiken ordered. "You!" He pointed at a watchman. "Take the kids and run. Tell Sir Welter. Make haste."

"Yes, sir!" the watchman said.

The girls ran toward him and began making their way toward the path. Wolfgang stood defiantly in the river.

"No way am I running!" he shouted, clenching his fists like he was about to fight.

"Run boy! They'll kill you!" Sergeant Eiken yelled as he entered the river.

The other watchman was close behind. The Vandalgoth raiders entered the river, too. They drew closer to each other, preparing to meet. Sergeant Eiken grabbed Wolfgang and picked him up.

"What are you doing?" Wolfgang shouted.

"You need to run!"

The other watchman readied his weapon and engaged one raider. They were both armed with bills.

The watchman waited for the raider to make his move. The raider planted his feet firmly into the river's sediment, with his right foot forward and left foot back. The watchman did the same, mirroring the raider's stance. The raider positioned his bill by his abdomen and thrusted forward. The watchman brought his bill up and hit the raider's weapon's staff, pushing it away, then slashed the sharp point of his bill across the raider's neck. The raider staggered back. The cut wasn't deep enough for him to bleed out. Taking the initiative, the watchman charged forward, thrusting the bill's head into the raider's chest. Blood flowed into the river as the raider collapsed. The other four raiders made their way toward the watchman and surrounded him. He desperately tried to fight, but couldn't. The watchman could only focus on one opponent at a time. The raider's weapons pierced his back and legs, causing him to scream in pain before going limp and falling into the river. His armor stopped his body from floating. Then they turned their attention to Sergeant Eiken, who looked on in horror as he tried to hold Wolfgang back.

"Two of you, go after those girls. One of you, stay with me while we finish these rats," the raider leader ordered.

"Don't you see, boy? You need to run!" Sergeant Eiken yelled as he threw Wolfgang to the shore.

Wolfgang was stunned, too afraid to move, but Sergeant Eiken's orders circulated in his head. Should he run? Should he try

The Wolf's Song

to fight? If he fought, what could he do?

Before he knew it, his feet moved on their own. He ran away, but he didn't want to. Sergeant Eiken was fighting all alone, and Wolfgang was running. His body decided for him, but it was too late. One raider grabbed Wolfgang from behind and threw him to the ground. Wolfgang struggled but couldn't break free.

"Look at this runt. I don't think he'd be worth much. Probably better to just kill him," the raider muttered to himself as he wrapped his left hand around Wolfgang's small neck.

Wolfgang struggled to breathe and beat on the raider's arm.

Wolfgang's body went limp and his arms fell to the ground. His right hand fell on a small rock. That's when he got an idea.

In a desperate bid for survival, Wolfgang grabbed the rock and, with all the force his little arm could muster, he slammed it against the raider's head. The raider let go of Wolfgang's neck and put his hand to his forehead.

"You little bastard!" the raider shouted. "Just give up and die!"

"N-no, I won't give up! I can't give up!" Wolfgang said bravely.

Wolfgang held the rock high and prepared for the raider's attack. He knew he couldn't fight in a proper duel, so he waited for the right opportunity to enact his plan. When the raider charged, Wolfgang threw the rock at the raider's head as hard as he could. Wolfgang turned to run as soon as he let go of the rock, not barely glancing back to see if it hit. The rock slammed into the raider's eye.

The raider fell to the ground in pain as blood poured from his eye socket. Before he could stand, Sergeant Eiken's bill plunged into his neck.

As Wolfgang made his way down the path, he looked back again at the horrific scene. He hadn't realized it, but Sergeant Eiken had defeated both opponents. With four men down, there was only one raider left—the one that left to chase the girls. Wolfgang realized, as he ran down the path, he'd eventually run into the raider. He stopped, panting, barely able to catch his breath. He froze, unsure of what to do. Once again, indecisiveness gripped him. *Should I go back or go forward? Back there are the lifeless bodies of the raiders and the watchman that didn't make it.* He didn't want to see such a bloody sight. Forward was another raider, and his sisters. *Do they need help? If so, what could I do?* He strategized, contemplated, try to decide, but he just couldn't.

Sergeant Eiken ran up behind him.

"What are you doing, boy? Stay here, I'll go for your sisters. We'll send word Sir Welter and he'll come get you," Sergeant Eiken shouted as he sprinted past.

Wolfgang stood in place, completely unable to move. He couldn't even sit down. He wasn't sure how much time had passed. It could've only been a few minutes or a few hours.

As dawn arrived, Sir Welter appeared, walking down the path with a small company of troops. He approached Wolfgang with an evil look in his eyes.

"The guard sergeant told me what happened. Sounds like a watchman died because of you."

Sir Welter's words stung Wolfgang like a poisoned dagger. Did that watchman really die because of him? Sir Welter kneeled and put his hand on Wolfgang's shoulder.

"You're a child, and a terrible fighter, nothing like your brothers." He sighed. "So, you need to learn to run away. You aren't strong. You aren't a warrior. If Vandalgoths come, all you need to do is run."

"R-run?" Wolfgang asked.

"Yes, son. Otherwise, people will die. Including you. I don't want that. No one does. Don't think. Just run." Sir Welter stood up. "We'll have to forgo expensive meats for a while. I'll be hiring maids to take care of our clothes. You head home and get dinner. The guard sergeant will escort you."

"Come on, Master Wolfgang." Sergeant Eiken ushered Wolfgang toward him.

He obliged and followed the guard sergeant down the path.

"I-I can't just run away," Wolfgang muttered to himself.

"Hm?" Sergeant Eiken asked.

Wolfgang kept speaking to himself, ignoring Sergeant Eiken.

"I-I can't give up. I will get stronger. I won't give up!" he shouted.

"With that kind of tenacity, you may become a great warrior someday, kid," Sergeant Eiken laughed.

***

It had been sometime since the incident at the river. Things had mostly returned to normal. Flowers bloomed and leaves grew big as the height of spring arrived. It was the Month of Virgo. Stefan and Wolfgang were playing chess in the manor's modest library just before dinner.

"Checkmate!" Wolfgang shouted.

He threw his hands up in celebration, then leaned back in his chair and folded his arms.

"Looks like you've learned quite a lot, Master Wolfgang," Stefan said.

As they spoke, the library door opened. Sir Welter stepped through. Stefan stood, put his right arm across his chest, and bowed.

"Sir Welter, I trust you're well. Was your time at Starke Castle eventful?"

"Of course not. Sir Starke declined to send a regiment to help us, even though Vandalgoths threatened my daughters a couple of weeks ago. That son of a rat isn't worth the throne he sits on." Sir Welter paused for a moment and sighed. "Stefan, go help the chefs prepare dinner," Sir Welter ordered.

Stefan lifted his head and walked out.

"Wolfgang, I heard you've been learning the art of smithing."

"Oh-uh, y-yes, father," Wolfgang replied, looking at the ground. "I-I just, I think metalworking is really sweet and, well, swords and weapons are sweet, too, so I like to learn about them."

"Hmph. No need to make excuses. I'm not angry with you. Lord knows you're not much of a warrior. Your brothers show far more aptitude for combat than you, and Uwe starts esquire training in a couple of months. Johanne will follow next year."

Sir Welter approached Wolfgang. "Raise your head, boy. You act more like a servant than a nobleman." He looked at Wolfgang as he raised his head. "Well, your mother and I have been talking, and we're fine with you becoming a gentleman. I doubt your aptitude for combat will improve over the next couple of years. So, if you want to train as a blacksmith or scholar, then fine. When the time comes, we'll send you to Schlossnacht University in Eifenhart."

Sir Welter turned to walk away.

"But... I want to be a knight, like you, Father!" Wolfgang blurted out.

"Give it up, boy. You don't have what it takes. You may better serve the land as a scholar or monk. Not everyone needs to fight to contribute."

Sir Welter walked out and shut the library door behind him. Wolfgang cried after hearing his father's words. Some people would be elated to not have to become a warrior, but not Wolfgang. He'd always wanted to fight, just like his father did.

"No, I'll do it. I'm going to do it. I won't give up." Wolfgang wiped away his tears and stood.

He balled his hand into a fist and shouted—to an empty room—that he wouldn't give up.

***

It was evening near the end of spring, in the latter half of Virgo. Once again, Wolfgang played war with his brothers in the manor's courtyard, but Wolfgang was more determined than ever to win. Johanne stood with his wooden spear to Wolfgang's ear, and Uwe, armed with a wooden sword, stood in front. Wolfgang had a wooden shortsword and a round wooden shield. He planted his feet on the ground, ready. Uwe lunged at him; sword held high above his head. At the same time, Johanne charged from behind. Wolfgang maneuvered so he could see them both.

Wolfgang blocked Johanne with his shield and clashed his sword against Uwe's. He pushed his shield up, forcing Johanne back. He then turned to Uwe. Wolfgang pushed his sword to the side, forcing Uwe's sword down. He then used the initiative and stabbed Uwe in the gut, hard. Uwe stumbled back but didn't fall.

Wolfgang smiled, satisfied with the battle's result. Until Johanne plunged his wooden spear hard into Wolfgang's back, causing Wolfgang to fall to the ground, narrowly missing a puddle of mud.

"Ha! You forgot about me, didn't you?" Johanne boasted.

Wolfgang angrily slammed his fist against the ground. Before he could say anything, Stefan approached them.

"Julia is going to the village. She wants to visit the jeweler. Your father gave her a small purse. Do any of you want to escort her?"

"Huh? Why not have a watchman do it?" Uwe asked.

"Sir Welter deployed all the watchmen to the fort-Fort Tyra, just along the border, in front of the large valley. There are only a handful of catchpoles around. He's been a little on edge since the river attack. I suppose it's only natural," Stefan replied.

"Oh, oh, can I go? I want to go!" Wolfgang shouted with excitement.

"Okay, but you need to get your hood," Stefan said.

"Yeah, yeah, I know. Tell Julia to wait for me!" Wolfgang replied as he ran inside the manor to grab his woolen hood.

The hood rested on his shoulders, and with a quick flip, it covered his face. If he kept his eyes down, no one would recognize him.

"Okay, I'm ready!" Wolfgang shouted as he approached Julia standing at the manor gates.

"Let's go, brother!"

"Don't be out for too long. I'm certain it will rain soon!" Stefan yelled as the pair hurried outside.

"His knee is probably sore. It always aches when it rains," Julia said.

The two walked down a path that led from the manor's hill into the small village. There were several houses made of wood with straw roofs supported by large wooden beams. Many people walked around the muddied street, taking care of chores, putting shoes on horses, and laughing with each other. Wolfgang loved going into town and seeing all the cheerful people enjoying their day.

Just past the stone chapel, in the center of town, were several shops. Some had stone foundations, others wood. They were built along a circular street. At the center was a large stage and a pillory. The town used the stage for important announcements at town gatherings led by the village council, the bailiff, or Sir Welter. Wolfgang grinned as he walked past the many shops. The smell of bread and candy from the bakery, the people joking and laughing at the alehouse, the fresh apples at the fruit stand. There was even a small stand where out-of-towners were selling all kinds of unique weapons. Wolfgang wanted a closer look, but his sister beckoned him into the jewelry shop.

Inside the jewelry shop were several displays sitting atop wooden shelves. There were rings, earrings, bracelets, and many other items made from gold, silver, and bronze. Some had diamonds, rubies, and other stones impeded in them. Behind the shop counter was an old man and a young girl around Julia's age. Between a sea of gray, small slivers of brown hair still peppered the old man's head.

"Hello, welcome!" the old shopkeeper said with a friendly smile.

"Are you going to buy something? Please buy something!" the young girl said.

"Now, now, you mustn't be so forward with customers," the old man scolded. "I'm sorry about her. She's my granddaughter, and she started shadowing me this year. She'll be running this shop when she's older."

"Okay, well, I think we're gonna buy something," Wolfgang said. "Right, Julia?" He turned around and saw his sister staring at the bracelets on one of the display shelves. She ogled them like she was in a trance.

"Big brother! Which of these looks better?" she asked as she held up two bracelets. They were both made of silver. One had three rubies impeded in it, and the other had a diamond.

"Well, which one do you like more?" Wolfgang asked. "Wait, can you even afford those? How much did father give you?"

"He gave me enough. Well, I'm asking you, anyway. Which is better?" She held both up to Wolfgang's face.

"Uh... well... I kinda like the one with the rubies more." He pointed toward the bracelet in her left hand.

"Yay! This looks great!" she shouted as she slipped it over her wrist. She set the other one back on the shelf and approached the old man behind the counter. "I want this one!"

"Of course, my lady. Do you have money?" he asked.

"Oh yeah, I have... uh... two!" Julia fumbled around in her small sack before pulling two coins out and setting them on the desk.

"Two guilders?" the old man asked as he inspected the coins. They were about half the size of the old man's hand and made of gold. The front had a stamped eagle and on the back were the words "Pro Deo, Imperio, & Iustitia."

"Is... that enough?" Julia asked in a sad voice.

"Yes, my lady. Uh, do you know how much a guilder is?" the old man asked.

"Well... it's uh... one guilder, I guess," Wolfgang said, desperately trying to come up with an answer.

"A single guilder is one thousand grotschen. Well, I thank you for your business. Enjoy the bracelet and please come again!"

The children left the shop and stepped back into the busy street. Julia spun around, smiling and staring at her new bracelet. She celebrated her new piece of jewelry, completely oblivious to her surroundings, narrowly avoiding village folk going about their day. As she spun around, she knocked into Wolfgang, causing him to fall to the ground.

"Oh no, are you 'kay brother?" Julia stopped dancing to check on Wolfgang.

"I'm fine."

His hood fell off as he sat up. Julia reached her hand out to help him up, but he stood on his own.

"Come on, let's go home."

He brushed the dirt off his green cotton pants. He looked up to see several onlookers staring at him. At first, he was confused, but then he realized his hood was down. More people gathered and whispered.

"Is that Sir Welter's boy?"

"I thought he was a leper."

"Those eyes, they're like a demon."

"Honestly, being a leper would've been better."

"No wonder they were so secretive about him."

"I can't believe it. Are they devil worshippers?"

As the whispering continued, lightning cracked in the distance. Thunder echoed throughout the land and rain fell. Some onlookers in the crowd left to avoid getting soaked, but most stayed to mock and question. A young man who couldn't have been older than twenty approached Wolfgang. He looked at Wolfgang and asked a simple, terrifying question.

"The old legend. I'm sure you've heard of it." He turned to look at the crowd. "I'm sure you've all heard of it!" He looked back at Wolfgang. "When he died, that accursed demon, he said he'd be back. He said he'd destroy the world, didn't he?"

Wolfgang didn't know what to say. He stood silently; his tears hidden by the downpour. He knew the legend too well. His brothers often reminded him of it, but he never actually understood the gravity of the tale. The man that brought Gotheca to its knees, who many believe split the moon, claimed he'd return.

"Well, your eyes—the legend says he had red eyes! So, explain yourself!" the man continued as he bent down to pick up a rock. "Tell us, boy! Does the blood of the Wolf King run through you?" he yelled, throwing the stone at Wolfgang.

A figure appeared, blocking the attack. It was Sergeant Eiken. The stone hit the guard sergeant in the chest, and he stood defiantly against the crowd.

"What's wrong with you?" Sergeant Eiken pointed at the man. "This is a nobleman's son. Do you want Sir Welter to have your head?"

The crowd finally realized exactly what they were doing. They knew if Sir Welter or Lady Adelita found out about the events, they could end up in the pillory, or worse, dead. They scattered and ran off to find cover from the rain.

Sergeant Eiken put his arm on Wolfgang's shoulder and led him down the street toward the manor. Julia followed, still in shock at seeing her brother attacked like that.

"Don't let it get to you, boy. People are naturally distrustful of what they don't know or understand. They'll come around eventually," Sergeant Eiken said.

***

A couple of days had passed since the event in the village. Wolfgang no longer wanted to leave the manor. Sir Welter would likely be furious if he heard about what happened, especially the accusations of their family being devil worshipers, but he hadn't left the fort in nearly a week. The rain persisted throughout the days, seemingly unending.

Wolfgang stood in the rain in the middle of a dark forest. There was nothing around him but dead trees and blackness. Suddenly, flames danced on the horizon and screams echoed in the distance. He couldn't move as the flames and screams drew closer. The roots of the trees wrapped around his legs. Before he knew it, the flames engulfed him, but they were cold, not warm.

Wolfgang shot up in his bed, heart racing. It was a dream. He put his hands on his head, listening to the sound of the rain hitting and rolling off the manor roof. Lady Adelita stepped into the children's bed chambers. She sat on Wolfgang's bed and spoke to him.

"Son, the blacksmith just finished an order of horseshoes. Could you go pick them up?" she asked.

"In the rain? Besides, isn't that Stefan's job?"

Lady Adelita leaned down and hugged Wolfgang.

"I know you went through an ordeal a couple of days ago, and I know your father isn't here to deal with it. But you can't stay inside the manor the rest of your life."

"Why not?" Wolfgang asked as he pulled his wool blanket over his head.

Lady Adelita pulled the blanket back and placed a silver necklace around Wolfgang's neck. He sat up and looked at it. The chain was silver and at the end was a small cross. *Ego semper tecum* was engraved on the horizontal board of the cross.

"It means I'll always be with you. Me, your father, all of us. Even when we fight, we'll be there for you, and so will The Lord. You have nothing to fear, my son," Lady Adelita said as she stroked his hair. "There's a cloak next to the door. It will protect you from the rain. Go on, see the blacksmith. You'll be okay."

She stood and walked out of the bedchamber. Wolfgang stared at the cross. The chain was a little loose around his neck, but he didn't mind. Looking at it, he realized how much his family cared about him, despite the trouble he got into. The realization invigorated him. A huge grin stretched across his face as he got up and marched toward the manor entrance hall.

He threw on a leather coat and boots and headed out into the storm.

There was barely any light outside as dusk was falling, so Wolfgang had little time to get the horseshoes and return.

Caleb the Writer

He made his way through the mud and down the path to the smithy. He waved his hand in the air as he approached the blacksmith.

"God be with you," the blacksmith started. "Though you shouldn't wave your arm like a lunatic, boy."

The blacksmith was an older man with a bald head and a gray mustache.

"Yeah, whatever. I'm here for the horseshoes," Wolfgang said as he stepped under the smithy's roof.

"Hmph. They sent you out in the rain on such a mundane task? The manor must be short staffed."

The blacksmith walked over to a rack full of tools and horseshoes. He grabbed eight of them and placed them in a deerskin leather sack.

"Well, Mother wanted me out of the manor. Look, she gave me a sweet necklace!" Wolfgang held up the cross he wore around his neck. "It's the snake's fang, right?"

"Impressive," the blacksmith said as he handed Wolfgang the sack. "You should head back now, before the rain—" A man covered in blood and mud staggering up the path leading to the manor cut him off.

The blacksmith ran over to him and helped him into the smithy.

"The manor—Sir Welter, he needs to know," the man stuttered.

"Know what?" Wolfgang asked as he approached the bloodied man.

"The village—can't you hear the screams?"

Wolfgang and the blacksmith looked toward the village. The heavy rain had masked the sounds of screaming and pain coming from the villagers. They could barely see a red glow through the fog;

fire. The village was on fire!

"The Vandal—" A fit of coughing broke the man's words.

"Boy, it's them. The Vandalgoths. You need to let Lady Adelita know, and fast!" the blacksmith ordered Wolfgang.

Wolfgang turned and ran into the storm, back up the path as fast as he could.

A moment later, he busted through the manor door and ran into the entrance hall. Stefan walked up to him. Out of breath, Wolfgang struggled to speak.

"Master Wolfgang, what's the matter? Is someone hurt?" Stefan asked.

"No, the village—Viesenville—it's under attack. Where's father?" Wolfgang shouted.

Lady Adelita heard the yelling and rushed into the entrance hall.

"Did I hear you right, son? Did you say Viesenville is under attack?" she asked.

"There was a man covered in blood and fire coming from the town. Where's father?"

"Your father is at the fort. If the enemy is here, then—" She cut herself off as tears formed in her eyes. "No, I'm sure he's fine. He's probably fighting them right now." She turned to Wolfgang. "Stay here. I'll gather your siblings. Stefan, grab the other servants and whatever weapons we have. Ready the horses."

"Right away, my lady."

Stefan and Lady Adelita both left the hall. Wolfgang waited for their return. He grabbed the end of his green tunic and twisted it, wringing the water out before it soaked in. After what felt like a lifetime, Lady Adelita returned with Wolfgang's siblings.

"Hey, what's happening?" Uwe asked.

"We-we're under attack!" Wolfgang stated.

"No way. Father would be here to protect us if we were. Right, mother?" Johane asked.

"Your father is fighting in the village now. Yes, he's fighting so we can escape," Lady Adelita told the children, trying to keep them from realizing the grim reality of the situation.

"No…" Uwe muttered in disbelief.

"Now, we're just waiting for Stefan. He and the other servants are getting the horses ready. Then we'll make our way to Starke Castle."

The children gathered around their mother, terrified and on the brink of tears, waiting quietly for their rescue. If Stefan could get the horses in time, they'd be saved.

The rain continued falling against the manor's roof. Each raindrop filled Wolfgang with more anxiety. It felt like he'd lived through several lifetimes by the time the manor doors swung open.

Lightning cracked and echoed through the lands and Stefan stepped through from the rain. What was supposed to be their rescue became their nightmare. Stefan held a longsword in his right hand, barely able to grip it. Blood streamed from his chest from an open wound near his heart.

"S-sorry, my lady. I'm no warrior. My best—" were Stefan's last words before collapsing to the manor floor.

A pool of blood formed around him as his skin turned pale. Lady Adelita and her children were shocked, so much so they didn't notice the men step into the manor. Six raiders dressed in ragged leather armor and iron helms. Four of the men held bills whilst the others carried longswords. The man in the pack's front had a long brown beard and a nasty scar across his face. He grinned as he approached the terrified children.

"We don't want to hurt you. After all, you'll fetch a higher price without damage," he said in a deep, scratchy voice.

"Come on, we don't need to sell all of them. I'm sure Lord Narrick wouldn't mind taking the boys and turning them into serfs or stable hands," one raider mentioned.

"No, you won't lay a hand on my siblings!" Uwe shouted as he charged forward.

He ran past the raider and picked up Stefan's longsword. Uwe tried to raise it, but it was far too heavy. Before he could do anything, a raider stabbed Uwe through the chest with a bill. Uwe's gray and blue tunic stained with blood. He tried to gargle words through the blood seeping from his mouth. Then he collapsed.

"B-brother?" Wolfgang said in horror.

"Well, now look at that. You didn't have to kill the kid," the raider with the long beard scolded. "We gain nothing if they're dead."

The raiders ran forward and grabbed the children, separating them from Lady Adelita. They screamed, cried, kicked, and fought, but it was all for naught. Lady Adelita desperately tried to hold on to her kids—the raiders having to pry Julia out of her arms.

"No! Don't you touch my babies!" she screamed.

The bearded raider grabbed her by her hair.

"We might not be able to sell this one. Too old. But we can sure have fun with her!" he laughed.

Lady Adelita grabbed the man's wrist and tried to pull his hand away, but it was to no avail. His grip was too strong.

"Mother!" Wolfgang shouted as a raider dragged him away by his arm.

Wolfgang clawed at the ground, kicking as hard as he could, but his fighting was pointless. He was losing all hope of escape. Then a horse busted through the manor doors. It whinnied as its hooves slammed against the floor. It was Sergeant Eiken.

His waffenrock was torn, and there was a hole in his armor. He'd tied a rag around a gaping wound in his abdomen, a hasty attempt to stop bleeding. He assessed the situation whilst the raiders were stunned. Wolfgang was the closest, and the raiders had all the other children firmly pinned down. Sergeant Eiken grasped his bill tightly and threw it as hard as he could at the raider dragging Wolfgang. A metal clang echoed through the entrance hall as the bill connected with the raider's helm. The raider let go of Wolfgang and fell to the ground.

As the raider laid on the floor in pain, Sergeant Eiken rushed to Wolfgang and held his hand out. Wolfgang grabbed it and Sergeant Eiken pulled him onto the horse. As he did, the raiders, armed with bills, dropped the kids and ran at the horse. If they killed the horse, it would be over. Sergeant Eiken spun the horse around and, with a crack of the reins, they were off into the storm.

"Wait, what about my sisters, my brother?" Wolfgang shouted. "We need to go back."

"I can't fight them all. Your father wants someone to live. I can only save you."

"Mother, sisters, Johanne!" Wolfgang shouted as they rode toward the village.

"We need to go through Viesenville to the road that leads to Starke Castle. Close your eyes. Best you don't see the carnage."

Wolfgang clung to Sergeant Eiken and kept his eyes shut as they made their way through the village. The smell of burning flesh and blood filled the air. Villagers desperately cried for help. Wolfgang decided he couldn't keep his eyes closed anymore and opened them.

The first thing he witnessed was a charred body outside of a burning home. As he stared, he realized this was the old jeweler.

Burns covered the man. Cradled in his arms was the lifeless corpse of his granddaughter. He must've tried to protect her.

The rain did nothing to stop the flames of the burning village. In fact, they seemed to burn brighter with every house they rode past. Multiple raiders trudged through the mud ahead of them. They rode right into them, nearly running them over.

"You bastard!" one shouted, drawing back a bowstring.

Wolfgang looked back at him, wide eyed and terrified.

"W-watch out!" he shouted as the raider released the string.

The arrow cut through the rain, seemingly unaffected by the wind. It arced over the dead bodies of the villagers before hitting its target. The sharp arrowhead cut Wolfgang's left cheek and stuck deep into Sergeant Eiken's back. Scared, Wolfgang tried to ask if he was okay, but couldn't muster the words or courage to find out.

"I'm fine, boy. Just... keep your eyes closed a b—a bit longer," he said through gritted teeth.

As hard as he tried to mask the pain, his grunts told Wolfgang the truth.

***

The storm cleared as dawn broke. The blood on Wolfgang's face from the large gash in his cheek had dried. He didn't know how long they'd been riding. His expressionless face turned pale. He was still in disbelief. It all had to be a bad dream.

It was early morning when the pair finally arrived in front of Starke Castle. Farms and homes surrounded the castle. It sat atop a steep hill. A stone bridge connected the castle gates to the village below.

The horse trotted along the bridge, and two guards approached them. They wore a four checkered cloth waffenrock colored white and red over their mail armor. Armed with bills, they both raised their free hand, signaling the horse to stop. As it slowed, Sergeant Eiken fell from the saddle. One guard turned to face the gate.

"Open the gate! Get the barber!" he shouted. "Tell him to get his surgery tools."

Wolfgang hopped down from the horse and kneeled next to Sergeant Eiken. He shook him, trying to get him to move.

"Move. Come on, move. You must be fine, sir," he repeated.

A guard approached Wolfgang as the gate opened and several men ran out.

"Stand back, boy. These men will carry him inside. Is he your father? What happened?" the guard asked.

Wolfgang looked up at him. The man jumped back when he saw his red eyes.

"V-Viesenville... is gone," he told the guard.

"What do you mean 'gone'?"

"They came and killed everyone."

"Do you mean the Vermagoth?" another guard asked. "If that's true, this is an act of war. Are you sure they weren't raiders?"

"Look at the boy."

A man approached from behind. The guards stood firm at attention and placed their hands, palms facing out, at the brim of their kettle helms. The man wore expensive looking plate armor, but was unarmed. He kneeled next to Wolfgang and put his hand on his shoulder.

"I'm the guard captain here. Tell me, what's your name? Is that man your father?"

"W-Wolfgang. My name is Wolfgang von Coburg. That man is one of our town watch."

"Coburg?" the guard captain asked in shock. "You must be Sir Welter's son. This can't be good. Come, you need to see Sir Starke."

The guard captain helped Wolfgang to his feet, and they walked into the castle. He motioned toward the other guards to take care of the horse.

They marched through the large gates and into the safety of the castle's stone walls. Inside were stables and a few wood buildings. A large stone structure with a huge metal portcullis stood in the center. As they got close, men on the inside rotated large wooden winches that pulled chains and forced the gate upward.

"This is the keep. Sir Starke should be in the throne room soon. You'll be his first affair for the day."

They entered a small throne room. The windows were angled to let light could in, but one would have trouble seeing outside—or inside. They weren't normal windows; they were embrasure. A special type of window designed as a battlement for defense. In between the embrasures were solid red banners with House Starke's family symbol, a full body white wolf standing on its hind legs, wearing a crown.

The guard captain instructed Wolfgang to wait in the back of the throne room and approach only when called. A brief explanation of court etiquette was hopefully sufficient to not offend Lord Starke.

After what felt like a couple hours, the castle's lord finally arrived. In that time, many people arrived and lined the walls, awaiting their chance to speak with the man they swore allegiance to about one issue or another.

The large doors of the throne room swung open and an older man in ornate clothing stepped through. He had a long, flowing grey mustache and a silver crown on his head. He wore a purple and red silk robe and a purple cape with the design of a wolf's head. Everyone stopped speaking and bowed their heads as he approached the throne. As soon as he sat down, the guard captain approached.

"My apologies for foregoing pleasantries and ceremony, my lord, but there's an urgent matter that cannot wait," he said with a bowed head and his hand over his heart.

"Well then. If it's so important we must forget to show me respect, then go ahead. Tell me," Lord Starke shouted in a sarcastic tone.

His voice thundered throughout the throne room, echoing off the walls. The guard captain motioned for Wolfgang to step forward.

"This young boy has disturbing news for you, sire."

Wolfgang approached the throne and kneeled on his left knee, his head down and eyes cast toward the ground, just as the guard captain instructed. Lord Starke immediately noticed the dried blood and large gash on his cheek.

"Captain, why have you brought this bloodied boy before me? Who is he, and why is he kneeling?"

Lord Starke's voice went from sarcastic to annoyed, upset over the disrespect of foregoing the ceremony, because of an important matter. Yet the boy kneeled, embracing ceremony.

"L-Lord Starke, I am Wolfgang von Coburg. I hail from-"

"I know where you are from. Where's your father? Did he send you to beg for more troops? Can't he ever just do his duty properly?" Lord Starke sighed.

"Father—Sir Welter is dead," Wolfgang mumbled.

Gasps and shock filled the throne room.

"Viesenville was attacked. My family is gone."

"By God," Lord Starke replied. He made the sign of the cross over his chest before continuing. "Was it Vermagoth? Boy, what were the attackers wearing?"

"Well, they had tattered and patchwork armor on. They looked feral," Wolfgang replied.

"I see." Lord Starke stroked his mustache. "Sounds like raiders. Can't be Vermagoth if they're wearing cheap gear. If they acted feral, they're probably not a battle band either. Most likely wild men."

"Uh, sire, I recommend we send troops to Viesenville immediately. There may be more survivors," the guard captain chimed in.

"Ah, yes. What's an appropriate amount? Maybe, a platoon?" Lord Starke asked his council.

"Well, if we don't want to anger Duke Roemgram, we should probably send at least a company. We can leave the other company here to defend the castle," an old bald man standing on the side of the aisle leading to the throne suggested.

"Ah, good idea, Marshall Grumenstein. Captain, send a company."

"A company?" Wolfgang asked. "If you have a company to spare, why didn't you send them when my father asked?"

"What's that boy?"

Lord Starke's demeanor changed. He looked at Wolfgang with scorn in his eyes.

"Why did you do nothing?" Wolfgang shouted in anger.

He made eye contact with Lord Starke, a gesture that violated court etiquette and showed disrespect. Lord Starke hated being looked in the eyes.

"How dare you? You think you can talk to me like that when you're from such a low house? You're barely nobility, and those eyes! Why do you look like the devil's spawn?"

"Uh, sire, this boy is just in shock," the guard captain explained. "Please forgive his insolence. I think it's best to send him to the capital, along with the man he rode in with. They can go with the supply caravan heading back in a couple of hours."

"Hm, fine. Get this damned demon out of my sight. The duke can deal with it."

"Yes, sire," the guard captain said.

"And call me lord, like everyone else. Stop shortening it."

"Of course, my lord."

The guard captain led Wolfgang away from the throne room and outside of the keep. They walked to the castle gates without speaking a word.

"What will happen now?" Wolfgang asked.

"That depends on you. I'll send you and Sergeant Eiken to Eifenhart, the capital of our country. After that, well, who can say? The supply caravan is getting ready to leave. They're down at the edge of the town. Stay here for a minute. I'll get you a wet rag for that wound on your cheek. Wash it regularly so it doesn't get bloated."

***

After a couple of hours, when the sun was at its highest point in the sky, the caravan left for the capital. Wolfgang sat in the back of a crowded wagon, holding the wet rags on his face. Sergeant Eiken laid on the wagon floor. Wolfgang was happy to know he was still alive.

"You're gonna need some new clothes when we get there. You're covered in blood and mud," Sergeant Elken said.

"Yeah, so will you," Wolfgang responded.

"I'm a soldier. I'm used to it. You should rest, boy. It'll be a long ride there. You need the sleep."

***

After a day on the road, and a brief stop to rest at a small village, the caravan arrived just south of the city. Eifenhart was large, and they built it along the shore of Lake Konstanz. They approached a massive castle, one at least five times larger than Starke Castle. It had five colossal towers extending into the air off the battlements, each topped with a pointed blue roof. An enormous wall surrounded the entire castle. It was so tall Wolfgang couldn't believe people could've built it. The most impressive part of the structure, however, was that they built it into a mesa.

The landform was larger than the castle itself, and they built the castle into the flat edge of the mesa. The other end of the mesa faced the west, so the castle faced the east. The man driving the wagon turned to address his passengers.

"Alright, anyone who doesn't have business in the castle, get off here. These are royal wagons and horses, so we must return them."

All the passengers shuffled their way to the end of the wagon and got off, except Wolfgang and Sergeant Eiken.

"Strange, you two have business here? Well, okay. We're about to go in."

The large portcullis gate opened, and the caravan marched through. Inside the castle was a vast courtyard full of people and buildings. It was large enough to be a small village. In fact, it was only a little smaller than Viesenville.

The caravan made their way through the narrow streets to a stable. The stable was big enough to hold at least a hundred horses. As the caravan came to a halt, several men in armor inspected the wagons and talked to the drivers and remaining passengers. They wore kettle helms and mail armor, with red cloth waffenrocks over them. Each waffenrock had the head of a white wolf sewn into it. One man approached the wagon Wolfgang was in.

"You there, disheveled boy. What business do you have here?" the man asked.

"I-My name is Wolfgang von Coburg. I request an audience with the-the duke!"

The man was taken aback. He stood there for a moment, analyzing Wolfgang. Then he looked at Sergeant Eiken.

"Is he with you?" the man asked. Wolfgang nodded his head. "Hmm... something isn't right. I'll be back. Wait here."

After speaking with several people and waiting for quite some time, they granted Wolfgang an audience with the duke. They took Sergeant Eiken to be looked at by the barber and get further treatment while they took Wolfgang into the keep built inside the mesa.

Several winding staircases and long hallways led to two large wooden doors. On the other side was the throne room. A man in expensive, ornate clothing stood in front of the doors. He wore a white wool collar, a puffed out red and gold tunic, and purple striped hose. He wore his hair short but had a long twirly mustache.

"My name is Lord Richtonstein. I'm the marshal for Duke Roemgram von Ludwig, the most powerful man in the country. Mind your manners. I will greet you. Ah, that means I'll announce your entrance to the throne room. Stay here and wait for the duke to shout enter."

Lord Richtonstein opened a door and stepped through. A moment later, a thundering voice sounded.

"Enter!"

Wolfgang nervously opened a door and entered. The throne room had silver chandeliers, each with at least a hundred burning candles. There were no windows, as they were deep inside the mesa. Banners of each noble house of Wolfkonigsland (referred to as the Reich by its denizens) decorated the walls. Many people gathered on each side of the aisle leading to the duke. Wolfgang walked down the aisle, with people whispering and gossiping as he approached.

They spoke of his dirty clothes, scarred cheek, and red eyes. They were the nobles of the Reich—no—of the holy Aeternian Empire. The ones who allowed his village to be burned and the conflict with the Vandalgoths to stoke like a terrible dancing flame. Duke Richtonstein put up his hand, telling Wolfgang to stop, as he was about eight feet from the duke. Wolfgang remembered what he had to do with the last noble, and kneeled.

"Don't kneel, boy with red eyes. Please, stand and look at me. If what I've been told is true, then a great evil has been committed."

The duke's voice was surprisingly kind. Wolfgang had been looking at the ground when he walked down the aisle, so he hadn't gotten a look at Duke Roemgram. As he turned his head upward, he made eye contact with the duke. He had deep blue eyes and long gray hair. On his chin, he sported a subtle stubble and a long mustache. Atop his head was a golden crown with the image of a wolf's head carved into the front. The duke wore a red surcoat with a white wolf's head sewn onto it, but with a wreathe surrounding it and a sword just above the wolf's ears.

"My-my name is Wolfgang von Coburg, sire."

"Oh, you're Sir Welter's son? Hm, I thought so." The duke paused for a moment. "You wouldn't remember, but I held you not too long after you first breathed life in this world. You were just a small babe back then, but there aren't many that have eyes like yours. In fact, there was only one other..."

He trailed off. Wolfgang took a deep breath, about to speak and interrupt the duke, but Lord Rochtonstein shook his head and Wolfgang settled down.

"Oh, yes, if you appear to me like this, then I fear what's

occurred on the border."

"Y-yes, sire. My-my village is gone."

"Gone? Viesenville?" Lord Richtonstein asked.

Everyone in the throne room gasped and sighed, the same reaction the nobles of Starke Castle had. Wolfgang balled his hands into fists.

"Yes, it's gone. The entire village burned down. My father didn't stop them. My family couldn't fight back. I couldn't stop them. But what about you?" Wolfgang's anger permeated the throne room with every one of his words. "Why? Why did none of you help?"

An uncomfortable silence fell over the court. No one said a word, and Wolfgang stood, panting, staring directly at the duke. Duke Roemgram stood up and stepped down from his throne. He kneeled next to Wolfgang and hugged him.

"Poor boy. You went through so much. I owe Sir Welter my life. I'd be nothing short of a sinner if I didn't repay him." He stood back up and looked at Wolfgang. "My son, Otto—he's always wanted a brother. What say you?"

"W-what do you mean?" Wolfgang couldn't believe what was happening. Members of the court looked on with confusion and frustration.

"You're just a child who's gone through terrible pain," the duke sighed. "I lost everything too, once. It was your father who helped me pick up the pieces. So, this will settle my debt to him. Besides, you came all the way here. You clearly have a fighting spirit. I can sense you'll make a fine squire, maybe even a knight. So, Wolfgang von Coburg, you shall become a Ludwig. My second son, and second in line to the throne. Wait—third, actually. Elise still hasn't been betrothed, so she'd be second..." He trailed off again.

"I-I don't know what relation you have to my father. But I will become a warrior. And unlike him, I'll defend this country. I won't let this happen to anyone again."

"Full of spirit, eh my lord?" Lord Richtonstein stated.

"Shall I take him to get fresh clothes and a bath? Oh, and a room too," another man in the court said.

He stepped into the aisle, his long red cape swirling to a stop over his poofy golden tunic.

"My name is John Cunningham. Eh, pardon my accent, I'm from Angland originally, so my Gostrasprechen may be a little hard to understand. I am the Chamberlin."

"Angland? Where's that?" Wolfgang asked.

"Far from here," the duke laughed. "They even speak a different language. You're probably too young to know this, but Gostrasprechen is what we speak. Ah, these questions are better suited for our vice clerk, a young woman who will handle your scholarly studies. Both her and Sir Cunningham have been invaluable, since the two of them have taken over all of my late wife's roles." He paused for a moment.

"Hold on, my lord," an overweight man with a short mustache began. "Is this a good idea? Not to question your judgment, but he's barely nobility. He's practically a commoner—"

"That's enough, Lord Neudern. I've made my decision." The duke put his hand on Wolfgang's head. "Everyone is born perfect. Do not think you need to hide yourself here. Now boy, go. Sir Cunningham will take care of you. There are other matters for the court to attend to."

***

After getting cleaned up, Wolfgang received a new tunic and a new pair of gray hose. They gave him a room inside the keep, in the same wing as his new siblings. His room was much larger than his bed chambers at the manor, and it was all his. He didn't have to share it with anyone, which was strange to him. After some time, Wolfgang decided he wanted to explore and walk the castle grounds. He left his room and walked to the entrance of the keep. Sir Cunningham was there and stopped him before he left.

"Where are you going, young master?" he asked.

"I-I don't really know. I'm just looking around, I guess."

"Well, you shouldn't wander. Just because the duke adopted you—well, some people may still want to harm you. The adoption also hasn't been announced yet. You would do best to just sit quietly in your room. Alas, children love to play, don't they? If you want to explore, go to the gardens. Just follow that path to the eastern side of the castle walls."

Sir Cunningham pointed toward a small dirt path that led around the far side of the keep. Wolfgang nodded and ran off.

As he made his way down the path, he noticed an archway covered in vines. He'd seen nothing like it before. Wolfgang followed the path further through the cave of vines growing around wooden arches. On the other side of the archway was a large fountain sitting on a small pond surrounded by many colorful flowers and fruits growing from numerous plants. Wolfgang's eyes lit up with excitement as he wandered through the garden.

When he reached the other side of the fountain, he saw an incredible sight. A young girl in a white dress, about the same age as him, was tending to a bed of roses. She had flowing blond hair and soft, silk-like skin. Her eyes, as blue as crystals, focused on the flower bed, but Wolfgang focused on her. Along the left side of her neck was a small darkened spot. He was stuck in a trance, held captive by her radiating beauty. She stood up and looked over at him. He tried to speak but couldn't. He was utterly embarrassed when he realized she knew he was staring.

"Uh-uh," were the only sounds he could muster.

"Oh, hello," she said in a soft voice. "My name is Elise von Ludwig. Who are you?"

"I—uh—" Wolfgang stepped back and began to make his way out of the garden. For some odd reason, he couldn't speak. As he ran off, three other children walked into the gardens. They were girls wearing fancy dresses.

"Oh, look, Elise is tending to the castle garden again." one of them snickered.

"This is a private place. You don't have permission to be here." Elise responded. Her tone was harsh and her denamour had shifted to that of annoyance.

"Whatever, dark spot. Let's go, before she calls her father's guards on us."

Wolfgang made his way back to his room and laid in his bed. The hay beneath the cotton bed sheet was soft and warm. He pulled his thick wool blanket over himself and looked up at the ceiling. He shoved his face deep into his cotton pillow.

***

As evening came, Sir Cunningham arrived at Wolfgang's room to inform him that dinner was ready, and the duke wanted to introduce him to the rest of the family.

Wolfgang found himself in the banquet hall, a part of the keep meant for dinners and parties. There were several tables inside the main banquet hall, but just past that was another room—the private dining room. It housed a single long table.

As Wolfgang entered the room, he saw the table was full of people. The duke sat at the end of the table, and to his left were two girls. One was a few years older than Wolfgang and had blond hair tied in a knot. She had dark blue eyes, just like the duke.

Sitting next to her was Elise—the girl Wolfgang saw earlier that day, still wearing the same white dress. His cheeks turned red when he made eye contact with her, and he quickly turned and looked to the other side of the table. A young boy about the same age as Wolfgang sat there, just to the right of the duke. He had curly blond hair and light blue eyes. He wore a blue tunic that had a gold stripe sewn across the chest.

"Wolfgang, sit here, next to your new brother." The duke pointed at the empty seat next to the young boy.

Wolfgang sat down.

"Hi, new brother. My name is Otto. Hey, can I call you brother? Oh, let's play after dinner!" the boy blurted out.

"Now, now, Otto. Give the boy some space. I know you're excited, but remember what we talked about. He's been through a lot," the duke told Otto, calming him.

"Oh—of course, father."

"Now, girls, do you want to introduce yourselves?"

"I'll go first. My name is Jene von Ludwig. A Frunkish name, given to me by my mother, who was originally from The Frünreich on the other side of The Kontinent," the older girl said.

Upon the mention of her mother, Otto seemed to get a little uncomfortable.

"My name is Elise—but you already knew that," Elise giggled.

"Oh-uh, yeah," Wolfgang responded with embarrassment.

"The food will be out shortly, I'm sure. Please, socialize with Wolfgang," the duke said.

"Oh, brother, what things do you like? What games do you play?" Otto asked.

"Uh, I don't know. Chess, I guess."

"Is that it? There must be more?"

Otto kept hounding Wolfgang with questions. He tried to respond, but it got on his nerves.

"Stop it already!" Wolfgang shouted.

Silence quickly befell the dining room.

"I was just trying to learn more about you," Otto muttered.

"Brother, he's been through a lot. He needs room to breathe," Elise chimed in.

"You're right. I'm sorry, Wolfgang."

"It's fine. Everything is fine," Wolfgang said.

Wolfgang looked at the table, before briefly looking up. His eye met Elise's. She smiled as he looked at her. Wolfgang felt an odd sense of empathy. He felt as if there was some understanding between them, almost like they spoke with their eyes alone. He started to blush and looked back at the table.

***

Later that night, long after dinner, and long after the children went to bed, Wolfgang sat up in his bed chambers unable to sleep. It had only been two days since the fall of Viesenville, and Wolfgang hadn't slept a single wink. How could he sleep? His mind raced with questions and anger. He knew someone was at fault for what happened, but whom could he blame? His father for not defending the village? The nobles for standing by and doing nothing? The duke for not securing the border? The Emperor of the holy Aeternian Empire for allowing his subjects to fight among themselves? What could Wolfgang even do about it? Should he strike them down and take their lives? Should he make peace with them and seek forgiveness? Should he strive to become better than they are? His mind was full of unanswerable questions. But with a single knock, the answer came to his door.

"Who is it at this time of night?" Wolfgang whispered to

himself.

Assuming it was another member of the court coming to explain something to him, he allowed them to enter. "Come in."

He was shocked to see Elise. She stepped into his bed chambers wearing a long white nightgown. Wolfgang shot out of bed and stood up, becoming flustered.

"W-what do-do you need? Uh, Elise?"

She walked up to Wolfgang without saying a word and embraced him. She pulled his head down toward her chest and squeezed him tight.

"I can see the anger and sadness in your eyes. There's no need to hide the pain any longer. It's just you and me here. I... understand your pain."

Wolfgang was stunned. With her kind words, a torrent of emotion hit him. Tears fell from his eyes uncontrollably. He realized he hadn't cried once since the fall of Viesenville. Not once during those two days had he felt anything but anger. Wolfgang felt grief, guilt, and worse-regret. He saw flashes of his family—of Uwe and Johanne, of Julia and Petra. He remembered playing in the courtyard and going to the jeweler with Julia. Wolfgang thought of his father and every time he scolded him, but also the times when he played with him. He saw Lady Adelita and the cross she gave him, that he still wore around his neck. Even the times they fought and argued made him cry. He'd lost everything, and it was only beginning to hit him. Wolfgang buried his head in Elise's embrace and wrapped his arms around her.

"They-they're really gone, aren't they? Why? Why did this happen? Why did I run? Why didn't I fight?"

"Could you have fought? You've lived on this world for just a handful of years. What could you have done? You blame yourself and carry a burden with you, but there's no need." Elise stroked his head. "I can relate to this pain. Otto and I are twins. Our mother died during childbirth. The birthmark on my neck- other children have told me it was a punishment for killing my mother. Both me and my brother bear this pain. I've seen the way they treat you too- the way they talk about you for your eyes and low birth."

"But I can't simply abandon these feelings! I can't allow something like this to happen to anyone else!" tears continued to stream down Wolfgang's face.

"Then I shall help you bear your burden. You don't need to go through this alone. I'm here for you. Otto is, too."

"What shall I do?"

"Protect the realm."

Elise put her hands on Wolfgang's chin and lifted his head, looking directly into his blood-red eyes. The light from the candles on his nightstand reflected in his eyes, making them look like they were glowing.

"Yeah, if I become a soldier, I can stop this from happening, right?"

"Yeah, maybe," she giggled.

Her voice made Wolfgang's heart flutter.

"But will that be enough? Only the highest person in the land can stop this from happening," Elise said.

"The duke? No, the emperor." Wolfgang's eyes widened at the realization. *Does Elise realize this too?* "The selfish nobles, the pointless skirmishes... he could put a stop to it all. But how do I reach someone like that?"

"Don't just reach him, become him." Elise's words were sweet but also painful, like the thorns on a rose.

"That's impossible," Wolfgang protested.

"Nothing is impossible. Not when I'm by your side." She moved her right hand from his chin and placed her index finger on his lips. "We're family now. We can achieve anything together."

"Family… yeah, you're right." Wolfgang straightened his back and wiped away his tears. "Thank you, Elise."

"Of course, anything for you, brother."

Elise smiled and put her hands behind her back. Wolfgang blushed and looked away from her in embarrassment.

"Right. Well, it's getting late, so I should go to bed."

Elise left the bed chambers and Wolfgang fell against the bed. He felt like the weight of his burden had lifted, even if just a bit. It wasn't much, but it was enough for him to fall asleep.

When morning broke, servants informing him it was time to start the day woke him. There was lots to be done if he was to be accustomed to the castle and to royal life. When he stepped out of his room, he encountered Otto, who was leaving his room as well just down the hall.

"Oh, good morning, Wolfgang," Otto said, trying his hardest to be as formal as he could.

"No need to be so formal, brother," Wolfgang said with a smile.

"Brother?" Otto's eyes lit up.

"Yeah, my brother."

***

In the following weeks, they held a funeral in Eifenhart for Sir Welter and the victims of Viesenville. Although the bodies of Sir Welter and many others weren't found, they were all presumed dead. The news traveled across Öustria, and of course the Vermagoth denied involvement, blaming it all on a band of wild men. The funeral was a solemn affair, with many people lining the main street of Eifenhart as priests and monks carried empty caskets to a small monument that was commissioned by the duke.

They buried 250 caskets under a large stone cross that sat just outside the castle portcullis. Most of the victims of Viesenville's sacking were too burned and mutilated to be recognized, or missing entirely. Wolfgang stood under the cross as the caskets were being lowered into a sixteen-foot-deep hole. After an old monk from the nearby Holy Divine Monastery—which sat just outside of the city—gave a eulogy, Wolfgang was called to his side as the sole survivor of the village.

Wolfgang put his hands together like a cup and received a blessing from the monk, before going back to where he stood under the cross. It provided a small comfort for Wolfgang, at least. In the back of his head, he hoped that some of his family had lived, but it was a hope he didn't want to hold on to too dearly. He needed to move on with his new family, the Ludwig's. Winter came, and Wolfgang's life would change once again.

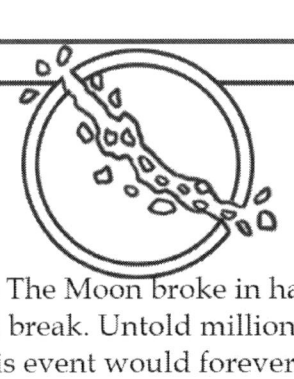

Lore: When The Moon broke in half, so too did the world break. Untold millions were killed, and this event would forever change mankind. The Moon is responsible for the tides, and as the Moon broke, the oceans changed. The tides are now unpredictable, as is the extreme weather that plagues the world- hurricanes and typhoons are common and unpredictable. Becuase of this, oversea trade is handled by large fleets of merchant ships. Between the extreme weather, ever changing tides, and pirates, the men who brave these dangerous seas are reveered across Gotheca. Merchants also make up the bulk of the naval forces. If a King needs to transport troops over seas, he hires the merchants. If a Duke needs pirates killed, he hires the merchants.

Homage: In the year 1178 AD, monks in the town of Canterbury witnessed an astroid strike The Moon. They claimed that the upper horn of The Moon split in two, and that it was writhing in pain. The crater the astroid struck is named after astronomer Giordano Bruno.

Chapter 2

Otto sat at a modest wooden desk in his bedchambers. Before him laid a piece of blank parchment. The quill with fresh ink on the tip nearly dripped onto the paper. He placed the feather against his chin and looked up at the ceiling, deep in thought. He was contemplating many things, mostly how he can rhyme unique words.

"Hm, what can I rhyme with apfelsine? Hm..."

His bedchamber door slammed open, interrupting his thoughts. Wolfgang barged in and pointed at Otto.

"Brother, did you hear? We start the squire regiment soon!" Wolfgang blurted out.

"You-you ran in here to tell me that?" Otto asked, putting his hand to his head.

"Of course! This is so awesome! I can't wait to stab things and ride horses! Oh, and wear armor! You're excited too, right?" Wolfgang threw his hands in the air.

"Why would I be excited? We all have to go through this. I think I'd rather be a gentleman than a squire anyway," Otto sighed.

"What?" Wolfgang pointed at Otto again. "What's that?" he

shouted even louder.

"Can you stop shouting? And—look, never mind. When are we supposed to start the regiment?"

"Oh, late spring, your father said. I mean, our father. By the way, what are you doing?"

"Writing poetry. Or at least I was until you came in."

"Poetry? That's too complicated for me." Wolfgang crossed his arms and laughed.

"Really? And here I thought you were an intellectual," Otto replied sarcastically.

"'Course I am. I can even do addition," Wolfgang said proudly.

"Anyway, since I forgot what I was going to write, we should play in the courtyard."

"We can't."

"Why not?"

"Sir Cunningham told me I'm supposed to join you for scholarly lessons, starting today. Oh, I was supposed to get you and go straight to the lesson. But then I saw the duke, and he told me about our squire regiment, and now I'm here."

"Wait, what!?" Otto shot out of his chair. "What do you mean you were supposed to get me and go straight there? Hold on, what time were you told?"

"Oh, around when the sun was there." Wolfgang pointed toward the east, with his arm at a forty-degree angle. "Now it's there." He pointed straight up.

"You were told in the morning but waited until noon to come get me? What were you doing?"

"Well... I got distracted by a mean dog by the stables. It wouldn't stop barking at me, so I barked at it until the stable master came and shooed me away. Then I chased a colorful butterfly. Oh, and I saw Elise in the garden but ran—I mean, talked to her and had a normal conversation."

"You're absolutely hopeless, you know?" Otto sighed. "Well, come on. The vice clerk has been waiting for a while. Hopefully, she hasn't left."

The two made their way outside the keep to a small, two-story wooden building near the castle courtyard next to a modest chapel and a smithy. Otto opened the heavy oak door and beckoned Wolfgang inside.

Full shelves of books from all over Gotheca lined the library, forming narrow passageways to the building's center. There was a small, open pit lounge area with tables and chairs where one could look up at the second floor. Railings surrounded the pit, and even more bookshelves above.

"I'm up here," a feminine voice called from the second floor.

Otto guided Wolfgang to a set of stairs that led up.

Sitting at a table near the wooden railing of the pit was a woman, roughly in her thirties. She had brown hair that flowed to her chest. Her black surcoat mostly covered her gray dress that fit loosely around her large bosom. Resting on her nose, partially hiding her brown eyes, was a pair of spectacles, the lens held in by a thick wooden frame. Wolfgang ran up to her.

"What are those on your face?" he shouted, pointing at her eyes.

"Um... these are spectacles, to help me see." She paused for a moment. "Wait, you need to introduce yourself. Manners are important!"

"I'm Wolfgang, Wolfgang von Ludwig!"

"I see." She pushed up her glasses and stood up. "My name is Izabel Nowaski, and I hail from the kingdom of Polenia, a country to the north. I am the vice clerk of the royal family, Ludwig."

"Lady Nowaski is impressive! She was the fourth woman ever to graduate of Nordlicht University!" Otto praised.

"Wow! Why is that impressive?" Wolfgang asked.

"What? Nordlicht is the capital of the HAE, where the emperor lives! The university there is one of the oldest and most prestigious in Gotheca!"

"Oh, that does sound impressive!"

"Anyway, let's get started," Otto said as he sat down at the table.

"Well, we should've started hours ago. Being late isn't like you, Otto," Izabel scolded.

"W-well, I didn't know we had lessons today."

"I had someone send for you, though."

"Oh, what are we going to learn about, Izabel?" Wolfgang asked as he sat down.

Izabel's eyes narrowed and her brow furrowed as she looked right at him. She picked up a wooden ruler sitting on the table and slapped Wolfgang across the face with it.

"Since when did I say you could address me by my first name? It's Lady Nowaski to you."

"Ow, that hurt." Wolfgang rubbed his left cheek. "You hit me right on my scar."

"And I'll give you more scars if you don't show me proper respect." Her demeanor changed from a gentle teacher to a sadist in an instant.

"Y-yes, Lady Nowaski!" Wolfgang shouted.

"Okay, let's begin," Izabel's voice flipped to a gentler tone.

The Wolf's Song

"S-scary," Otto muttered.

"Since you showed up late, I'll cut the literary lesson and focus on… history and arithmetic."

"Is it going to be sweet history or lame history, Lady Nowaski?" Wolfgang asked.

"All history is sweet history, Master Wolfgang. Of course, if you think otherwise, you could always spend more quality time with the lady ruler…"

"No, no, you're right. History is great!" Wolfgang shrunk in his seat.

"Okay, do either of you know the history of our country, Wolfsreich?"

"I know a little from fairy tales," Otto answered.

"There was a war or something my father fought in," Wolfgang said.

"Yes, there was. But our nation was founded long before then. The people of Öustria are a mix of cultures. Some were originally from the ancient tribes here, others came from Etalia during the times of the Aeternian Empire, and some came from the East. Many even call Öustria the cultural basket of Gotheca. It was the winter of 1386 D.R., on the 5th of Pictor, that the karl Grunner Kula became the first Kaiser of Wolfsreich. Uh, Wolfgang, you know the months, right?"

"'Course I do! In order from the beginning of the year to the end, is Lupus—the month I was born—Gemini, Aquarius, Virgo, Corvus, Orion, Norma, Leo, Aquila, Taurus, Sagittarius, Pictor, then the year ends!"

"Correct. Otto, do you know what they're named after?"

"Yes, ma'am! Each month corresponds with a constellation!" Otto beamed.

"Correct, specifically the month the constellation corresponds to is when that constellation is visible in the sky." She stopped to adjust her glasses. "Now, before I continue, are there any questions?"

"Yeah, what's a karl?" Wolfgang asked.

"Karls are freemen, men with no allegiance, or those who choose their lord. They're like errant knight's, who are sons of knight's or nobles that don't serve a lord. Now, let's continue. In the following years, the Vandalgoths—descendants of the ancient tribes—formed bands of wild men and attacked the Reich. When they tried to take back what they saw as their ancestral land—"

Wolfgang interrupted her.

"What did—" A ruler smacking him on to the top of his head cut him off.

"Now, now. Boys need to show manners. Especially royals. Now, raise your hand if you have a question. Quietly." She looked at Wolfgang as he slowly raised his hand. "Yes?"

"Well, did we actually take the land from them?"

"Good question. A few decades before, easterners from the Steppe invaded Gotheca. They were called the Khanate but have since split into the Silver Hordes, Ariq Khanate, Qaimish Khanate, and Mangala Khanate. But back then, they united under a single khan.

"They attacked Ostenhalfen and killed many people. Eventually, after nearly a decade of war, they were defeated. But many of them had already settled in these lands, forming the Tribal Councils of Kherzan in the south, and settling in different parts of Ostenhalfen; from Slovana to Wallaxia to Lasvia. This brings us back to the Vandalgoths. The Khanate hordes displaced them.

"After the wars ended, many who settled in this land were scattered and trying to pick up the pieces. That's when Grunner Kula came. He helped the people rebuild their lives. It was under him that this very castle we sit in was constructed. The Wolfsreich would be formed, but the Vandalgoths wanted their land back. The last kaiser, who was demoted to a duke, did nothing to stop them. The Vandalgoths united under a charismatic leader—whose son now rules over the Kingdom of Astragoth—and attacked the Wolfsreich with a force of over 14,000. Our kaiser's incompetent leadership led to the fall of the reich, and our demotion from being a reich to being a simple duchy." She stopped as Wolfgang raised his hand. "Yes?"

"What's the difference between us now and us then?"

"Well, we have less land. A reich is a kingdom formed by conquest and can only be declared by the holy emperor of the HAE. He decides if an HAE state is worthy of the title. A kingdom is also large, like a reich, but forms through politics and trade—normally political marriages or small conflicts. Duchies are too small to be considered kingdom's or reiches, and a grand duchy is a state that isn't deemed worthy enough to be a kingdom by the emperor. As for specific criteria, well, it really depends on what he says."

Wolfgang raised his hand again. "So, what happened next?"

"Yes, Master Wolfgang, eager to learn, I see. Well, your father, Duke Roemgram von Ludwig, led a revolution. In 1463—exactly eighteen years ago—the duke and many nobles overthrew the old kaiser. The duke and his wife, the late Lady Joane, stabilized our nation's economy and secured the border." She looked over at Wolfgang. "Well, mostly secure. My condolences."

"It's hard to believe. That doesn't sound like Father at all," Otto said.

"Things have been hard for him since Lady Joane passed," Izabel said somberly.

Otto looked at the table, an uncomfortable look in his eyes. Izabel clapped her hands together and smiled.

"Time for arithmetic! Let me teach you your multiplication

tables!"

"That sounds boring. I want to learn about more sweet stuff like war," Wolfgang blurted out.

"Boring?" Izabel stood up, grasped her ruler, and tapped it against her palm. "Math isn't boring!"

"Ah, yes, I can't wait to learn, Lady Nowaski!" Wolfgang said in fear.

***

Their lessons continued into the evening. Izabel dismissed the pair, and they left the library to play in the courtyard. Three other children showed up to play as well.

"Hello! Have you guys met my new brother?" Otto asked. He pointed at one child wearing a blue tunic and had short brown hair. "This is Hans Neudern." He then pointed to the boy next to Hans, who was larger in stature and had curly brown hair. "This is Klaus Gunter, and the kid next to him is Emerson Kial."

"We're all nobles sent here for study last year by our families. But why are you here, and what's with those eyes?" Hans asked accusingly.

"What, are you some commoner the duke took pity on?" Emerson laughed.

"Huh? I'm from Viesenville. I'm here to become a warrior! Someday, I'll even be the holy emperor!" Wolfgang said.

"You think you'll be the holy emperor? Really?" Hans replied sarcastically.

The three children busted into laughter.

"'Course I will. Laugh at me all you want, but I know I'll succeed, right Otto?"

"Uh, yeah," Otto replied. "Hey, why don't we play somewhere

else?"

As Wolfgang and Otto turned to leave, Hans grabbed Wolfgang by the arm and pulled him back.

"You're not going anywhere, red eyes. We can't let a demon like you stay in this castle."

"Hey, what's your—"

A punch to the gut cut Wolfgang off. Hans then threw him against the stone wall of a nearby building. Otto moved to step in, but Wolfgang put his hand up.

"I've got this, brother."

Wolfgang put his fists up to fight, but he didn't really know what he was doing. He swung at Hans, but Emerson stuck out his leg, causing Wolfgang to fall. The three children kicked and beat Wolfgang as he covered his head.

"Stop it!" Otto shouted.

"Shut up, Otto. I can't believe the duke's son would defend this devil spawn," Hans told him.

Otto turned and ran off.

"See, he came to his senses. He won't stick around to help you."

Wolfgang tried to get up, but the children kept kicking him down. His cries of pain soon turned to an angry growl, like a ferocious cornered wolf. As Hans's foot came toward Wolfgang's face, Wolfgang grabbed it and threw it in the air, causing Hans to fall on his back. Wolfgang used the opportunity to stand up and raise his fists, ready to fight. Hans got back on his feet and the children surrounded Wolfgang again.

Before they could move, a bill's blade appeared between Wolfgang and the kids. A castle guard stood firm, holding the weapon.

"How dare you? What do you think you're doing?" Hans shouted.

"Following my orders," Otto replied as he approached them. "In case you forgot, Wolfgang and I are sons of Duke Roemgram von Ludwig. What you're doing now is nothing short of sedition."

"Yeah, se-sedi-what he said!" Wolfgang struggled to sound out the word but concurred with his brother.

"That's enough now," a deep, thundering voice sounded across the courtyard.

A man with a thick, black beard and short hair approached the children. He had a nasty scar across his face, right over his right eye, which was covered with a small leather eye patch. The man wore expensive looking plate armor.

"Knight-Captain Eiken!" Otto shouted.

"Eiken? Where have I heard that name?" Wolfgang muttered.

"Look at you kids. What a pitiful sight," he began with a disappointed tone. "Three against one. Only cowards fight that way. Then you ran off to get a guard instead of fighting side by side with your brother. What is this? Kids these days have no honor." He walked up to the guard and motioned for him to go away. "All of you will train under me come spring. If you want to fight, wait until you're older. Once you start fencing, you can challenge each other all you want at the training grounds. Assuming you last that long," he laughed as he turned to walk away.

"Oh, Sergeant Eiken!" Wolfgang blurted out, completely ignoring the knight-captain's reprimand.

"Hm?" Knight-Captain Eiken turned to him. "Ah, you're from Viesenville. You would know him. That slimy bastard is my second younger brother. How in Hades he survives anything is beyond me. Don't concern yourself with him. You should start using honorifics with me, boy. Soon, you'll be in a Hades of my making," he laughed as he left the children.

"Come on, let's go play somewhere else," Hans said to the other children.

"Thanks for helping me, Otto," Wolfgang said to Otto as blood trailed down his face.

"I'll always help you. After all, you're my family." Otto slapped Wolfgang on the back with a big smile on his face. "Now, let's go get you cleaned up, brother."

***

As autumn came and went, Wolfgang and Otto continued their studies with Izabel. They had lessons Mornday through Sutterday, with Sabbathday being their only day off. As winter came, so did the Feast of The Lord, a celebration of the birth of the Messiah in the Divinian religion. During that time, Otto and Wolfgang had an entire week off, although they had to spend much of that time in church. It was finally the 13th of Lupus. As Wolfgang's birthday fell on Sumaday, or the Lord's day, Otto and Elise prepared a celebration in the solar—a room built into a keep for the reigning lord and his family in secret.

"Why are we going to the solar?" Wolfgang asked Otto, who was beckoning him down the halls of the keep.

"You'll see, come on," Otto replied as he opened the doors to the solar.

Wolfgang stepped into the large room. There were several couches, and even a couple of beds. There were many shelves full of board games. At the center of the room were a couple of tables. Sitting at one of them, with a feast prepared, was the duke and his children.

"Happy birthday, my son!" Duke Roemgram shouted as Wolfgang entered the room. "I know you aren't named for a saint like most children are, but I'd still like to celebrate with you."

"Woah, this is awesome! We never had feasts like this back in Viesenville." Wolfgang sat down at the table with excitement. "I thought we couldn't have food in here, though?"

"Normally no, but since today is a special day, it's okay," Sir Cunningham said as he walked into the solar, Izabel just behind him.

"Hello, Master Wolfgang. Having a merry birthday?" she asked as she sat down.

"Oh yeah, this is super sweet!"

"Merry birthday, brother," Eise murmured as she stood from her chair and approached him. "Here, I made this for you." She handed him a set of beads strung together with a rope. "It's a bead bracelet."

"Oh, y-yeah, thank you!" Wolfgang blushed.

He clasped the bracelet around his right wrist.

"Can we eat now, father?" Jene asked.

"Oh, yes. I saved some of the best meat for this occasion! We have duck and pork!"

"Oh, meat is such a rare treat!" Izabel said, her mouth watering.

"Before we eat, let's say a prayer."

Duke Roemgram clasped his hands together, and the others did the same. Once the prayer was over, everyone filled their plates—quickly throwing food onto their dishes with little regard to anyone else at the table. Wolfgang and Otto fought over pieces of duck, whilst Jene sat quietly awaiting her turn.

"Oh, Elise, you didn't get any pork. Here, t-take some from my plate!" Wolfgang offered her a cut of meat from his plate.

"Oh, you offer her some pork, but not me?" Otto asked as he crossed his arms. "We're twins, you know, so you should split the piece between the both of us."

"I'm alright," Elise laughed.

"Oh, come on kids, stop fighting." Izabel's words were barely heard through her stuffed mouth.

"My lady, you do know it's rude to talk with your mouth full?" Sir Cunningham said.

"And you know it's rude to not eat this delicious food," she said as she scarfed down more meat.

"Come on now, you need to act like nobility." Sir Cunningham sighed.

"Hey, I wanna know, how did you get all the way here Cunninger—Sir Cunningham?" Wolfgang asked as he also stuffed his face with food. "After all, I learned in Lady Nowaski's lessons that Angland is on the other side of Gotheca."

"Yes, it is," Sir Cunningham sighed, clearly upset that Wolfgang was also talking with his mouth full. "I was the steward of quite an idiotic merchant. I traveled with him all the way here, and we arrived about eight years ago. He lost all his wealth and titles after being scammed by someone from Slovenia. So, I made my way to Eifenhart. The duke was looking for talent, and he hired me."

"Oh, don't be so modest. Sir Cunningham here saved my life from an angry horse."

Duke Roemgram and Sir Cunningham both laughed at what must have been quite the memory.

"Oh, that's sweet," Wolfgang said as he continued stuffing his face.

"Talking while eating isn't good manners, Master Wolfgang," Sir Cuningham scolded.

"Oh, I'm sure he'll learn plenty of manners when he gets to training under Knight-Captain Eiken. He has trained two generations of noblemen at the military academy," the duke laughed. "Oh, Wolfgang, before I forget—Sergeant Eiken has finally recovered. He'll be working in the Eifenhart Juad Quarter starting this spring."

"Really? I'm glad he's okay! I'll have to go see him when he's back to work. Oh, I wonder if I can have him forge me a sweet sword when I become a soldier!"

Wolfgang's excitement was evident even through the food stuffed in his face.

They spent the rest of the night eating, laughing, and enjoying each other's company.

Becoming a Knight

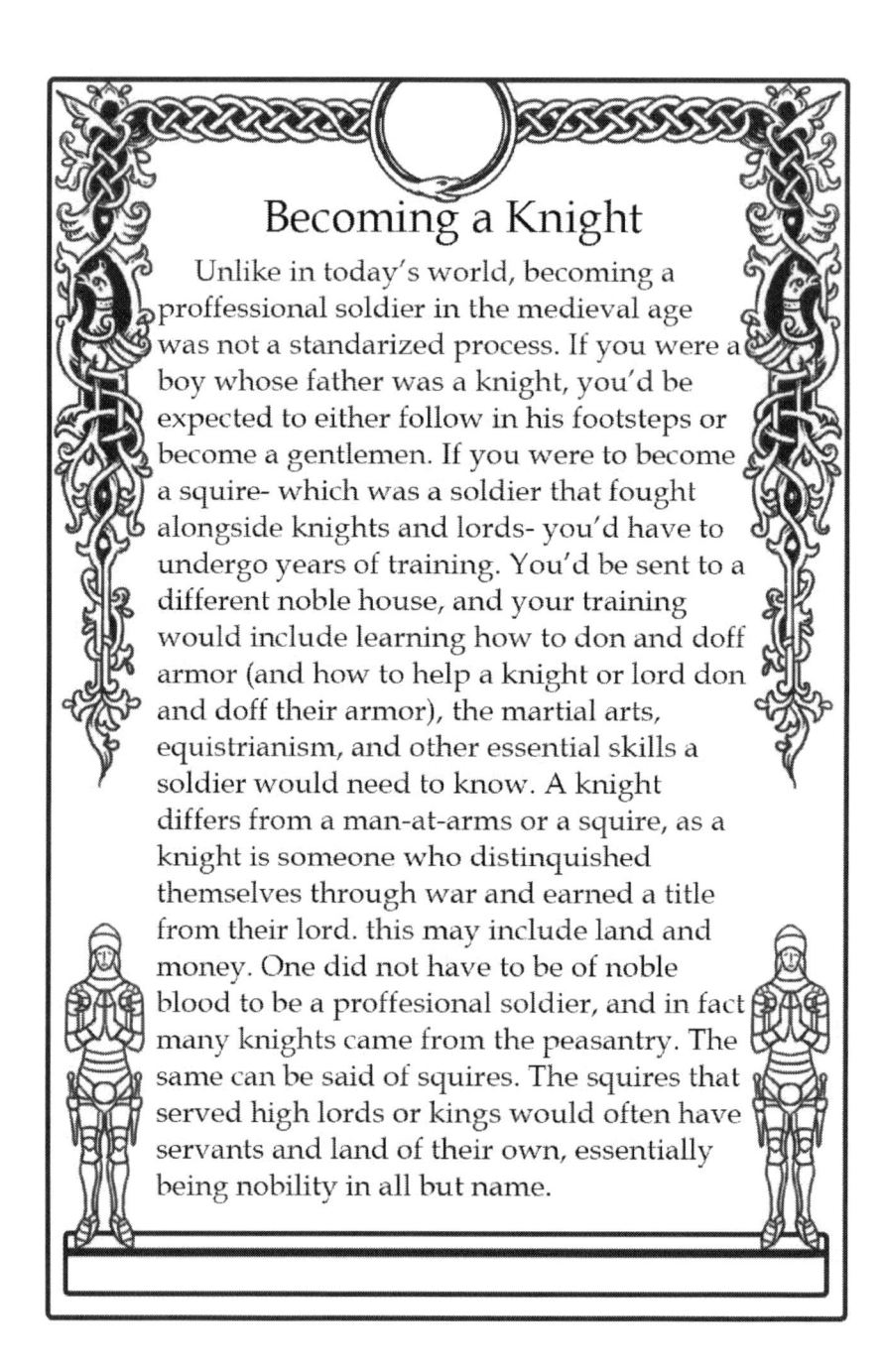

Unlike in today's world, becoming a proffessional soldier in the medieval age was not a standarized process. If you were a boy whose father was a knight, you'd be expected to either follow in his footsteps or become a gentlemen. If you were to become a squire- which was a soldier that fought alongside knights and lords- you'd have to undergo years of training. You'd be sent to a different noble house, and your training would include learning how to don and doff armor (and how to help a knight or lord don and doff their armor), the martial arts, equistrianism, and other essential skills a soldier would need to know. A knight differs from a man-at-arms or a squire, as a knight is someone who distinquished themselves through war and earned a title from their lord. this may include land and money. One did not have to be of noble blood to be a proffesional soldier, and in fact many knights came from the peasantry. The same can be said of squires. The squires that served high lords or kings would often have servants and land of their own, essentially being nobility in all but name.

Chapter 3

The seasons changed, and the months passed. It was the month of Aquarius, and spring reared its head. It was almost time to begin the squire regiment at Eiken manor, just a mile south of Eifenhart. The standard practice in Gotheca was for noble sons to receive their squire training from a different noble house. The Eiken family had been responsible for training soldiers of the reich for generations. They nicknamed it the "Eiken Military Academy."

The manor itself was rather small, but it was built on top of a steep hill. At the bottom were cramped guard barracks, a chapel, stables, an archery range, and a sword training ground. On a cold, wet day, with the ground full of mud from melting snow, the squire regiment began.

Early in the morning, before dawn broke, Wolfgang, Otto, Hans Neudren, Klaus Gunter, Emerson Kial, and another boy Wolfgang didn't recognize all shivered. It was still too dark to see, so they each carried a torch. The unknown boy approached Wolfgang and Otto. He had a square jaw and was oddly muscular for a kid about the same age as Wolfgang and Otto.

"My name is Alphonse von Richtonstein. My dad is the duke's marshal. It's a pleasure to meet you. You must be the Ludwig boys.

The Wolf's Song

I've heard a lot about you from my dad," he laughed.

"Yeah, I'm Wolfgang and this is Otto."

"Well, glad to meet you guys. Hey, since we're gonna be here together, let's be friends!"

"Oh, sure, yeah," Otto responded enthusiastically, trying to match Alphonse's motivation.

"You really want to be friends with me? You're not put off by my eyes like the other kids?" Wolfgang asked.

"Ha! Why would I be?" Alphonse laughed. "You're silly. You shouldn't be ashamed of who you are, no matter what some naysayers claim. Let them be put off. We're here to become warriors of the reich, anyway." He closed his hand into a fist and held it out.

"W-what are you doing?" Wolfgang asked.

"It's called a closed fist salute, a special salute between reich soldiers. Here, hold out your fist out like mine," Alphonse instructed.

Wolfgang followed and did what he asked. Alphonse then bumped his fist against Wolfgang's.

"See, now we're comrades in arms." He grinned.

"Yeah, we are! Hey Otto, you do it too! Then we can all be comrades." Wolfgang smiled.

Otto and Alphonse bumped fists.

"You know, I'm pretty sure you made up this closed fist salute thing," Otto said.

"Nah, I learned it from Dad!" Alphonse laughed.

Thumping footsteps and clanking armor interrupted their conversation. It was Knight-Captain Eiken, with a wide, unsettling grin stretched across his face.

"So, these are the pathetic wretches I have to deal with," he said in a deep, angry voice.

"Hey, you can't talk to me like that. I'm nobility!" Hans said.

Knight-Captain Eiken's eyes narrowed. He approached Hans and slapped him across the face.

"Nobility? Royalty? Ha, do you understand the situation you're in? You're just a slimy maggot. If you can't handle that, maggots, then you don't have what it takes to be a warrior. Now, line up in front of those boulders!" He pointed to a line of rocks next to the fencing and sword training area of the training grounds.

They all walked over there before he yelled again.

"Faster, maggots. Do you think the enemy will wait for you to meander?"

They all dropped their torches and ran. After lining up, he stood in front of them.

"You're sons of the reich's most staunch leaders and defenders. If you too wish to take up the mantle of warrior, of soldier, to defend our nation and lead our troops, you need to be fit, smart, and an expert on all things violent. Over the next six years, I will break and rebuild you. Now you are boys, nothing but useless maggots, but I will make you men!" He paused for a moment. "That requires a response. You will refer to me as 'Captain,' and I expect a 'yes, Captain,' or 'no, Captain!' Do you understand me?"

"Yes, Captain!" the boys shouted back.

"Louder!" Knight-Captain Eiken demanded.

"Yes, Captain!" they shouted again.

"Now, before you, is a rock. This rock will be your best friend over the next couple of weeks. From now until dusk, you will pick it up, hold it over your head, and set it back down again. Do you understand?"

The Wolf's Song

The group exchanged confused glances. He couldn't be serious, right? What could that task possibly help with? It seemed like an utterly pointless thing to do. Then, Knight-Captain Eiken breathed in, and yelled so loud his voice could shatter glass.

"What are you waiting for, maggots? Where is my 'yes, Captain'? Why aren't you picking up your rocks?"

"Yes, Captain!" they all shouted in fear.

Wolfgang bent down and grabbed the rock, but shot back up after he got hit in the back with a small stick.

"Wrong form! Lift with your legs! Squat, then pick it up! Once it's in your hands, lift it over your head, squat, and set it back down! Then return to the standing position before doing it again!"

"Y-yes, Captain!" Wolfgang shouted.

He followed the instructions and lifted the rock with the correct form. The others did the same.

"This'll be easy," Alphonse said, effortlessly picking up and setting down the rock.

After several hours had passed, Knight-Captain Eiken was nowhere to be seen. Otto set his rock down and stopped.

"This is too much. I can't do this anymore," he said, panting.

"Yeah, this is stupid. What does that captain know anyway?" Hans added as he also stopped lifting the rock.

"I think I need water—"

The feeling of a terrifying presence cut Otto off. Just behind him, Knight-Captain Eiken appeared out of nowhere. He got close to Otto's ear, so close Otto could feel his angry breath down his neck.

"I don't remember telling you to stop," the knight-captain whispered. "So why aren't you lifting your rock?" His voice became louder in an instant. "Do you even want to be a soldier? Or are you just a gentleman?"

"Well, actually I—"

Wolfgang, still lifting his rock, cut Otto off. "No, Captain! We won't give up!"

"That's the motivation I like to see! Keep lifting those rocks! I'll make you men yet." He stepped in front of the boys and set a goat skin sack in the mud. "You maggots show up to training wearing expensive noble clothing and dress shoes. Pitiful. In this bag are cloth war jacks and leather hose, along with leather war boots. Each of you will get four pairs of hose and jacks, and two pairs of boots. I expect you to keep them clean and in good condition. You won't be getting more until you grow older. You can collect them after you're done with your rocks."

"How-how much longer, Captain?" Otto asked through a river of sweat.

"I already said until the sun goes down."

"Wait, really?" Alphonse yelled. "Even I'm getting tired."

"Oh, is that so? Is the enemy going to stop and let you have teatime? Are you going to tell the man that's about to run you through with a poleax to take a time out?"

"Uh, no, Captain!" Alphonse replied.

"Good. Now, you'll get three water breaks a day. At your second break, you'll get one loaf of bread. At dinner, you'll get bread and an apple. You will stop at dusk and start again at dawn. Welcome to Hades, boys. If you survive, you can stand tall and call yourself men."

***

When dusk came, the captain took them not to the keep, but to the guard barracks. They ate in the public dining hall and slept on hay with the guards. It was humiliating and painful for the young nobles to be treated like animals, but a necessary step to their development.

"One cannot lead a pack of animals unless they themselves have been led like one," was a phrase Knight-Captain Eiken repeated often to the boys.

For an entire month, they repeated the same process. They picked up rocks and set them down all day, ate and slept in the barracks, and woke to do it again. The only day they had to rest was Sumaday, the day of the Sabbath. Being nobles, they were expected to stay in church for almost the entire day. They were all at their breaking points. Finally, in the month of Virgo, they received a break. As they all stood in front of their rocks, Knight-Captain Eiken walked out in front of them.

"Today... you won't be touching those rocks."

"Really?" Otto asked.

They couldn't believe it—they were finally free from the rocks, at least for a bit. The boys sighed in relief.

"But today is no break! Come, we'll march to the stables. It's time you boys learned the first step in becoming a squire, maintaining your animal." He paused for a moment as he looked them over. "Yes, it's time you learn how to march, too. An army is composed of many units, and as sons of noble houses, you will carry your house banner into battle. Your men-at-arms will gravitate to you and follow your example, as will your levies. As long as your guidon is in the air, you and your men haven't wavered.

"But an army needs organization. You can't fight in a giant chaotic mob. So, you need a cadence to step to. On the battlefield, we use flutes and horns to communicate between companies of troops, as well as keeping men in step whilst moving. Troops may also sing cadence while on the march, although they wouldn't do this when faced with actual battle."

He walked to the center of the line and faced the boys.

"When I say left face, you turn to the left. When I say forward march, you step forward in sync with your left foot. As you march, I will count. With every number, your left foot should strike the ground."

With a left face and a forward march, the boys stepped off and marched toward the stables. It was only a short walk—just on the other side of Eiken Manor's steep hill. When they arrived, Knight-Captain Eiken ordered them to stop and gather around.

"First, I'll show you how to put on a horseshoe. Typically, you'll have a farrier in the camp followers who can take care of this for you, but while you're here, you'll take care of your horse. A horse is an extension of the soldier, just like his arms and armor. It can be your best weapon, best defense, and you best chance of survival if things go wrong. So, you need to take good care of it. You'll be practicing after I show you on wooden hooves until I trust you with an actual horse."

Knight-Captain Eiken led a horse out of the stables and took a knee next to it. In one hand, he had a horseshoe, and in his other, two nails. He set a hammer on the ground by his knee. He picked up the horse's leg and held its hoof so the boys could see it.

He showed them how to attach a horseshoe properly, also showing them which way to point the nails so they don't hurt it. He then showed how to put on a saddle, first the saddle pad, the saddle itself, and then how to tighten the girth; front and back straps.

He then led the boys to an area next to the stables. There were several wooden horses and horse hooves laid out in front of them next to a tool shed. "You can get hammers and shoes from there. There are also some basic saddles in there."

The boys spent the next few weeks practicing. Every morning, they'd wake up, eat, pick up their rocks until noon, eat, then practice saddling a horse and putting on horseshoes. It was grueling, but it drilled the basics of equestrianism into their heads.

***

As autumn came, it was time to learn the basics of riding. Knight-Captain Eiken taught them how to mount a horse and how to control it.

Wolfgang was the first to try riding. He hopped onto the horse and grasped the reins—his pinky and index finger underneath the reins, and his thumb on top.

"Okay, now—"

The horse bucking cut Wolfgang off. He flipped through the air and landed in the mud. He then stood up and tried again.

After several attempts, he was finally got the horse to accept him. Hans, Klaus, and Emerson laughed as Wolfgang struggled.

"Alright, you beast. Hiya!"

The horse charged forward, and Wolfgang snapped the reins. It galloped faster than he could control toward a fence at the edge of the training grounds. It planted its feet into the ground to stop and Wolfgang flew off, flipping through the air and landing in the mud. Whilst the others laughed, Otto and Alphonse ran to see if he was okay.

The other children had no issues riding, but it took Wolfgang some time to get used to it. Knight-Captain Eiken gave them special clothes for practicing riding. Their riding pants were dark leather and riding shirts were cotton with a wide V-neck. As the winter approached, it was time for a break. They'd all go home for three months and return early spring.

Wolfgang and Otto were relieved to sleep in a proper bed and eat actual food. They dreaded having to return to Eiken Manor, but the duke was proud of them for sticking with their first year of training.

Aquarius came once again. Early in the morning, before dawn, the boys met, once more lined up in front of their rocks. But didn't look so green. They knew what to expect and were ready. Knight-Captain Eiken arrived on horseback with a wagon in tow. In the back of the wagon were several deerskin rucksacks.

"Come on, get it. We don't have much time," he ordered.

The boys hopped into the wagon.

They rode east just past Fortress Oberstein—a large stone fortification that protects Eifenhart—and into the hills. They stopped along a road and were instructed to grab a rucksack and get out. Each rucksack was heavy and difficult to lift.

"What's in here?" Hans asked.

"Rocks," Knight-Captain Eiken responded as he detached his horse from the wagon. "You l got weak and fat over the winter. I need to make sure you stay in shape. So, throw on your ruck and follow me up the hill."

With unsatisfied groans, they did as they were ordered. Knight-Captain Eiken remained on his horse and led them to the top of the hill. When they finally made it, the boys sighed in relief.

"Down there is Radwald," Knight-Captain Eiken proclaimed, pointing southwest.

The sun rose over the hills, and the sky turned purple as the light hit the small village. The furrowed fields and towering windmills were all now perfectly visible.

"Wow, what a beautiful sight! Would make for a great poem," Otto said.

"Ha!" Knight-Captain Eiken laughed. "You won't have time to write a poem when you're rucking back to the manor."

The boys all turned to face him, their faces horrified. They couldn't have heard him right.

"That's right. The manor is about nine miles from here, so you'd better get walking. I want to see you by nightfall. Better hurry too, it looks like rain is coming."

He pointed at the rolling clouds, then rode off into the woods back down the hill. The boys exchanged a few confused glances before heading off. Otto stood for a second, taking in the sunrise's moment.

"Come on, Otto!" Alphonse called.

Otto nodded his head and followed. Klaus and Emerson followed Hans down the hill back toward the road. Meanwhile, Wolfgang had another idea. "If we go straight through the hills, it should be faster," he said.

"Seems like it would be more work than using the road, but alright," Otto agreed.

The trio made their way through the woods and over the hills. They walked along dirt paths and through bushes. With the sound of thunder echoing from the sky, rain fell. The terrain became muddy and difficult to walk on. As the three tried to make their way up a steep incline, Otto slipped and fell.

"Ow!" he shouted as he hit the ground.

"Otto!" Wolfgang carefully made his way down the incline as fast as he could. "Are you okay, brother?"

"Uh, yeah, I'm alright."

"Here, I'll help you up," Alphonse offered as he approached. They helped Otto to his feet, but when he stepped on his left foot, he cried out in pain.

"This isn't good," Wolfgang exclaimed.

"I think-I think I twisted my foot."

"Damn, what are we going to do now?" Alphonse asked.

"Sorry, guys," Wolfgang apologized through gritted teeth. "I thought if we took a more direct route, we'd get back faster."

"You have nothing to apologize for. I'm the one that fell after all." Otto leaned against a tree.

"We can still make it back. If we go south and find a path, we can leave the hills and walk on flat land," Wolfgang suggested.

"How will we get Otto out of here?" Alphonse asked.

"Well, I can carry him if we leave our rucksacks," Wolfgang answered.

"Hm, we'll probably get chewed out if we leave them." Alphonse thought for a minute. "Well, I can carry yours if you carry Otto on your back, and then we can leave his here."

The three agreed to the plan.

Wolfgang kneeled so Otto could climb onto his back. Otto's legs sat inside of Wolfgang's arms, and Otto wrapped his arms around Wolfgang's chest for stability. Alphonse picked up Wolfgang's ruck and wore it around his chest. They were all ready, so they headed toward the edge of the hills.

***

As nightfall came, Hans, Klaus, and Emerson arrived at the barracks at Eiken Manor. The knight-captain stood in the barracks doorway to not get soaked as he waited for the other three to return. Darkness fell across the land and the rain let up.

"I wonder where the others are," Klaus said as he and the other two boys laid in their hay pile and prepared for sleep.

"Who cares? We'd probably be better off if they didn't return. Especially red eyes," Hans commented as he closed his eyes and drifted off to sleep.

***

Knight-Captain Eiken lit a torch in front of the doorway and was getting ready to look for them. But, out of the darkness, he saw three figures approach. Wolfgang carried Otto, and Alphonse carried the rucksacks.

"S-sorry we're late, Captain. We had an issue on our way here," Wolfgang said.

"Hm. I see that. Did Otto get hurt?" Knight-Captain Eiken asked.

It was an odd question, considering until that point, he never actually referred to any of the boys by name.

"Yes, Captain," Otto replied.

"Okay, come inside and dry off. I'll get the barber to look at you," Knight-Captain Eiken said in a surprisingly understanding tone. "You three stuck by each other and didn't give up. That's what it means to be a warrior. Stay by your brothers."

***

Otto's twisted ankle healed in a matter of weeks. Throughout the rest of the year, Knight-Captain Eiken taught them matters of battlefield logistics and strategy, how to avoid the spreading of disease among the troops, and where to dig latrines. They learned how the levies muster call worked and the basic weapons of the battlefield. They continued to practice horse riding and doing physical training every morning.

***

The new year came and went, and it was the third year of their training. They'd learn how to don and doff plate armor. It's essential for a squire to understand that, as a lord would expect them to help him into his armor before battle. They learned to start with the shin graves, strapped to the back of the shin. Then the upper leg protection, attached to the thigh and knee guard via a harness called a "cuisse." The top of the thigh plate had a small rivet, called a stop blade, on it to prevent blades from digging into the spine. Next was the maille skirt, then the voiders and breastplate, then the plackart. They tied a rope around their waist, then put the plackart on to help the armor suck in and make it easier to fasten the straps. Then the vambrace and arm protection.

Knight-Captain Eiken made them practice with each other and they spent weeks donning the armor, then doffing it. Whilst wearing full armor, the boys had to climb a twenty-foot-high ladder leaning against bales of hay, pick up their rocks, and run around the manor grounds. It was exhausting but necessary to get them used to maneuvering in heavy armor.

In their fourth year of training, they learned the art of combat. They started with archery; the longbow being an essential weapon on the modern battlefield. Then they learned to grapple and hand to hand fighting techniques before fencing with a variety of weapons—the bill, poleax, short staff, quarterstaff, and longsword. Knight-Captain Eiken showed them various stances, cuts, and defenses. They practiced for hours against dummy's made of hay. Knight-Captain Eiken taught them about the body's four quarters, the upper left, lower left, upper right, and lower right, and how all combat derived from that concept. Near the end of the year, as the trees changed color, the boys finally had the chance to spar with one another. Wolfgang and Hans were the first two to fight.

The breeze blew orange leaves across the small practice field. The two stood opposite of each other, wearing padded gambesons over their shirts to stave off the pain of a blow from their wooden practice longswords. Wolfgang placed his left foot forward and his hilt next to his temple, the point of the sword facing Hans. That was the ox stance. In response, Hans took up the iron gate, which required him to place his left foot forward, place his hilt by the groin, and tip the point of his sword toward the ground.

"Good stances. Now, begin!" Knight-Captain Eiken ordered.

Wolfgang was the first to move, charging forward. He maneuvered his sword to attempt a low cut, a cut below the opponent's left arm. Hans countered by raising his sword and meeting Wolfgang's. The two swords clunked as they clashed, both blades being forced upward.

Hans slid his right foot forward and let his blade rest on his back, his hilt by his right eye. He entered the lady's right-side defense. That position was helpful for both defense and offense. Wolfgang moved the hilt of his blade just above his temple, the blade pointing to his left running just above his eyes. It was a window defensive posture. His footwork was sloppy, however, and both his feet were in line with each other. Wolfgang foolishly tried to swing from his position, but lacking leverage and speed, Hans countered. Hans stepped off his right foot and placed it behind— Wolfgang's blade just passing in front of his face—whilst also moving his left foot forward diagonally. That allowed him to avoid the blow completely and get behind Wolfgang. With a single swing from above, Hans his Wolfgang in the back and he fell to the ground. He lost.

"Ha! I knew I was better," Hans gloated with a grin.

"No way!" Wolfgang shouted as he stood up. "Again, let's go again!"

The two went on for hours, but eventually Knight-Captain Eiken stopped them. Wolfgang never landed a single blow against Hans.

"That's enough, you two. Don't fight until exhaustion. Remember what I told you, in full armor, you can only fight around ten minutes before getting tired and having to go to the rear. So, you need to stop and take breaks when you can. Wolfgang, keep practicing on the dummy's," Knight-Captain Eiken ordered.

"Fine, but mark my words, I'll beat you some day!" Wolfgang shouted at Hans.

***

Wolfgang practiced for hours every day, on practice dummies and with Alphonse. He knew he needed to get better. Just before winter arrived, Knight-Captain Eiken released the boys from the manor to go home. They visited the stables and prepared their horses. Each of them wore their riding clothes, a loose-fitting cotton shirt with a wide V-neck and baggy hose.

"Ah, we can finally go home. I can't wait for this training to be over," Otto complained as he led his horse to a small road across from the stables.

"Oh, come on. It's not that bad," Alphonse replied.

"Yeah, for you, you meathead. You have no problem with the physical training."

"Don't hate me just because I'm strong like an ox!" Alphonse joked.

"And as dumb as a rock," Otto retorted.

They laughed as they climbed onto their horses.

"Hey guys," Wolfgang began as his horse slowly trotted in front of the two. "Wanna race to the castle?"

"Race? You realize the castle is almost two miles away, and we must go through the city, right?" Otto pointed out.

"Sounds like you... are gonna lose!" Alphonse shouted, as he cracked the reins of his horse and set off at full speed.

"Oh, no you don't!" Wolfgang replied as he did the same.

"H-hey! Wait up!" Otto yelled as he tried to catch up.

The boys raced down the road, Alphonse in the lead.

They passed by farmlands and huge windmills, their blades spinning in the air. Wolfgang got beside Alphonse and grinned as he passed.

Since he wasn't looking, he didn't see a man with a handcart walking down the road. Wolfgang quickly pulled his reins and moved his horse to the side, but still knocked over the man's cart, causing fruits to spill all over the road.

"S-sorry!" Wolfgang shouted.

He whipped his reins and tried to regain the lost speed as Otto passed him.

"I swear, you two are a menace!" Otto yelled as he got in the middle.

Wolfgang, not wanting to be outdone, whipped his reins once more and his horse gained speed. The three continued trading first place until they reached the city.

"I see the city ahead, so we should slow down!" Otto suggested.

"Slow down? We're racing to the castle, not the city!" Wolfgang replied.

"You don't mean to race through the market, do you?"

"Sounds like you don't want to lose!" Alphonse shouted as he pushed forward and passed Otto, who was in last place.

Wolfgang took the lead and raced full force right into Eifenhart's main street. People yelled and jumped out of the way as they raced by. As they made their way down main street, they reached the market. On the other side was the prison and bailiff's house, then the road to the castle. People gathering to sell their animals before winter tightly packed the market.

"Hey! Get out of the way!" Wolfgang shouted at the busy crowd.

Stunned, people rushed to get away, some tripping over pigs and other animals. Wolfgang saw a stall selling fruits and grains ahead of him. He didn't have time to move out of the way, so he kicked his horse's side, urging it to jump. It leaped just high enough to avoid destroying the stall. The vendor stood in shock, his jaw agape as he watched the horse barely miss his products. That wasn't the case for Alphonse, who ran right through the stall, sending the poor vendor's products all over the street. The men fell to his knees in disbelief.

"My... produce..." he said to himself.

As the boys continued to race dangerously through the streets, the catchpole appeared, running after them.

"Do they think they can catch us on foot?" Alphonse laughed as he caught up to Wolfgang.

"This is way too far!" Otto shouted from the rear.

The boys finally reached the road that led directly to the castle. Alphonse was in the lead, but Wolfgang was close behind. Alphonse looked back and pointed at Wolfgang, laughing. But Alphonse's horse was exhausted and was slowing down.

Wolfgang passed him, grinning. He motioned for the guards ahead to open the portcullis. He ran through the gate, raising his hand to the sky in victory. The cross around his neck had fallen out of his shirt, and the light reflected off the bead bracelet around his wrist. The other two caught up, and the three stopped to catch their breath.

"You two *really* are a menace," Otto scolded.

"You're just mad you lost!" Wolfgang laughed.

"You're still wearing that necklace and bracelet? I don't think I've ever seen you take those off," Alphonse said.

"'Course I am. I won't ever take these off," Wolfgang said. Just then, the bailiff came running through the gates of the castle.

"You three menaces!" He shouted.

"What do you mean, three?" Otto asked, offended at being lumped in with the other two.

"Do you know the amount of destruction you caused?"

"What have my boys done?" the duke asked, approaching the gate and wearing an expensive tunic.

"They ran their horses through town! They destroyed a vendor's shop, probably injuring countless people. I saw it all! They passed right by me!"

"That sounds serious. I'll pay a fine of, say... ten guilders for any damages occurred. As for you two." The duke turned to face the boys. "I'm glad you're home. I was waiting here to greet you. But there's no dinner for you after this stunt."

"What? No way!" Wolfgang complained.

"Do you want to go to the pillory? You should be happy we got off this light," Otto whispered.

"Oh, my lord, please don't tell my father about this," Alphonse pleaded.

"Of course, I'll tell him," the duke replied. "Oh, get your things ready. I know you just got home, but we are going to Eisenstadt next week."

"The Duchy of Eisenstadt? Why, Father?" Otto asked.

"Well, Otto, you're betrothed to the daughter of Lord Elvald."

"B-betrothed?" Otto blurted out in surprise.

"Oh? Is our little Otto finally going to become a man?" Alphonse joked, as he put his arm around Otto's shoulders.

"Wh-whatever, shut up!" Otto blushed. "Besides, by that logic, you're not a man either!"

"Oh? Well, that's not true at all," Alphonse laughed.

"Wait, you mean to say you've... uh... courted a girl?" Otto asked. Alphonse leaned in.

"A real man doesn't kiss and tell," he whispered.

"Uh, you can be so insufferable," Otto said as Alphonse laughed.

The Edelwiess

The Edelwiess is a white mountain flower found growing on high mountains in Central Europe, like The Alps. The name comes from The German words for "white" and "noble". Named so due to it's white color and persistant noble attitude to grow in rough conditions. During the 19th century the flower would become an important symbol of European culture. It would be used as a symbol of many hiking and ski clubs. It's popularity would soon translate to the military.

Austro-Hungary would use the edelwiess as the logo for their alpine troops. In 1907 Austrian Emporer Franz Joseph I would form The Imperial-Royal Mountain Troops, with the edelwiess as their unit symbol. In the 1930's during the rise of The Nazi Party, an organization was formed to oppose the Hitler Youth program. They were known as The Edelweiss Pirates. Their rebellious movement was largely ignored by members of the party, until the onset of WWII. They would go from being a minor nuisance to a force of resistance. In November of 1944 thirteen members of The EP were executed. Despite this, the group kept fighting for freedom. The Edelwiess was also the symbol used by The Wehrmacht's mountain rangers. They are still part of The German Army today, now known as "Gebirgsjager", and still use the edelwiess as a unit designator. The Edelwiess was adopted by U.S. military units after WWII and the recently formed 10th Mountain Assualt Brigade of Ukraine. The symbol was also used by The Wolf Children. They were German orphans escaping The Red Army in 1945 during a mass evacuation of East Prussia. Thier namesake comes from the fact they wandered the woods in search of food like lost wolves. Many of these children would be adopted by Lithuanians living close to the border.

Chapter 4

A modest castle sat atop a tiny hill. It had wooden walls and a small stone keep overlooking the village at the base of the hill. The village was small, with only a handful of buildings. Surrounding the village were large, furrowed fields and at least three dozen windmills. Behind the castle was a small forest. Sitting to the east of the castle was an enormous statue of a man on a horse standing roughly three stories tall. He wore a bassinet and heavy armor. In his left hand was a bill and he held a cross in his right.

The Ludwig family approached the rustic place in a caravan, along with several retainers. Riding in front was the duke on a muscular stallion. Beside him was Lord Marshall Richtonstein. Behind them were Wolfgang, Otto, and Alphonse. Then, in a wagon, were Jene, Elise, Sir Cunningham, and Izabel. Behind them were a handful of guards on armored horses.

"There it is, Elvald Castle," the duke exclaimed. "Oh, I can't wait for you to meet your betrothed, son. I remember when I met your mother. Although, it was a little different. You see, we…" he trailed off.

Tuning him out, Alphonse turned to Otto. "Yeah, I can't wait either. We're finally gonna see our little Otto all grown up!" he laughed.

"Ah, come on. This is super embarrassing. Why do you gotta tease me?" Otto asked.

"Probably 'cause it's fun, little Otto," Wolfgang added.

"Little Otto, ha!" Alphonse and Wolfgang laughed.

"You guys are the worst, you know."

"What's that?" Wolfgang asked, pointing at the statue overlooking the castle and village.

"That's the statue of Saint Stefan!" Izabel shouted from the wagon.

"H-how can she hear me?" Wolfgang asked.

"You're really loud," Otto replied.

"Am not!"

"It's really sweet," Izabel continued. "Saint Stefan is revered across Öustria. He drove back the Khan's men during the great invasion in the battle of Kohl field. He died atop his horse, carrying his bill and the cross. Saint Stefan received a divine revelation just before the battle. He knew he'd win, but only at the cost of his own life. That happened right around here, where Elvald Castle was built. Pretty sweet, huh?"

"I wonder what she looks like?" Alphonse said, completely ignoring Izabel.

"Hey, are any of you even listening to me?" she shouted at them.

"I'm sure she'll be pretty," Wolfgang added.

"Hey, Otto, what's your type? You like girls with big bosoms—"

"Oh, will you quit it already!" Otto shouted, his cheeks flushing as he cut Alphonse off.

The Wolf's Song

They approached the castle gates and hailed the guards. After a moment, the large wooden gates opened. A slightly overweight man in ornate clothing stood behind the gates, ready to greet them. He sported short gray hair and a long twirly mustache.

"Oh, Lord Elvald! Happy to see you!" Duke Roemgram greeted.

"Of course, sire. This is a joyous occasion, so I wanted to greet you personally, along with my court." Lord Elvald bowed.

"Where's your daughter?" the duke asked.

"Ah, Emilia is currently getting ready for the banquet tonight. She... well, I instructed her to be on good behavior today. As you know, she's a few years older than your son."

"Yes, she's scared off every suitor so far!" the duke laughed. "Oh, but Otto is resolute. Isn't that right, my boy?"

"Um, Father, what do you mean by 'scared off by every suitor'?" Otto asked.

"Oh, this is gonna be fun," Alphonse joked.

The group entered the castle and headed toward the solar. It was much smaller than the one in their castle, and ordinarily, only family members of the reigning Lord could access it, but Lord Elvald was trying hard to impress them.

***

As the evening came, a servant arrived and led them to the banquet hall. The Elvald keep only had three stories and a handful of rooms, so the banquet hall was almost directly across from the solar. They stepped in and took their seats. Lord Elvald then entered, his court retainers behind. Then, entering last, was her—Emilia Elvald. She tied her orange hair in a bun and wore a loose-fitting blue silk dress. Her eyes were as green as pastures during the height of summer, and they complimented the freckles spotted across her face.

"Wow... she looks completely different from Lord Elvald," Wolfgang pointed out.

"She was adopted," the duke began. "I don't know the full story, but she originally came from the Kingdom of Briefle, on the other side of Gotheca."

"Ah, that's close to Angland. The Sea of Damona separates the two islands," Sir Cunningham added.

Lord Elvald and his court sat across from Duke Roemgram and his. Emilia sat next to her father. Servants brought silver chalices to the patrons and poured them wine. Before long, they brought the food out. It was beef with barley, bread, and various fruits. Lord Elvald stood up and held out his chalice.

"Let me formally welcome our guests from Wolfkonig—I mean, the Wolfsreich. They've traveled far, and we shall satisfy their parched throats and hungry bellies at our table. Cheer!"

Lord Elvald raised his chalice high. Duke Roemgram stood and raised his chalice as well. The rest of the court raised theirs whilst remaining seated. Then, they drank and ate.

"Man, she really is a looker, huh Otto?" Alphonse whispered, nudging Otto.

"Y-yeah, she's alright," Otto responded, clearly embarrassed.

"What do you think, Wolfgang?"

"Yeah, she's fine," he began as he stuffed his mouth with meat. "Not as pretty as Elise, though."

He stopped eating as soon as he realized Elise was sitting next to him within earshot. She looked over at him and giggled, his cheeks turning red.

"You're hopeless," Otto said.

As they spoke, Emilia stood from her seat with a pitcher of wine and walked to the other side of the table to Otto.

The Wolf's Song

"Let me refill your glass," she whispered.

Otto's hand shook as he held his chalice up, and she refilled it. She bent over far enough that her loose dress tightened around her bosom. Otto stared directly at her, not realizing how obvious he was being. She stood back up and smiled.

"Ha, you were totally lookin' at me, weren't ya?" she bellowed in a thick Brieflen accent.

Her noble demeanor was immediately gone.

"W-wait, uh, I—" Otto tried to explain himself but couldn't.

"Ah, don't worry, love." She leaned in, so close he could feel her breath on his ear. "I like a man that knows what he wants."

"Eek!" Otto jumped up in embarrassment.

Emilia laughed.

"This, this is why she scares away all her suitors," Lord Elvald muttered.

"This is great!" Alphonse laughed. He wrapped his arm around Otto's shoulder. "She's perfect for you."

"Why is that?" Otto asked, somewhat offended.

"Well, you need a strong woman in your life. Lord knows you'll never take the lead. You're way too scared for that."

"Oh, come on, you're teasing too much!"

"Really, if you don't marry this girl, you'll be alone forever!" Alphonse laughed. "We can't have a lonely person take the throne when-."

"That's enough!" Lord Richtonstien shouted.

"Don't worry about it, love," Emilia began as she leaned in once more. "I love men I can wrap around my finger." She laughed before turning to walk back to the other end of the table.

Otto sat back down.

***

They spent the rest of the evening enjoying food and company. After spending the night, the Ludwig's and their retainers left early in the morning. They met Lord Elvald at the castle gate.

"I... hope you enjoyed the banquet," Lord Elvald said as the group was leaving.

"It certainly was... lively," Duke Roemgram responded.

"No, thanks to my son," Lord Richtonstein said, glaring at Alphonse.

"I... feel like I'm gonna be in danger when we get back," Alphonse muttered. He turned to Otto. "Well, Emilla is an interesting girl. Can't wait to see her around the castle."

"Oh, and their kids too," Wolfgang joined in.

"Ha! That will be a riot. Wonder if they'll take after their father or mother?"

"Come on now, can't you see you two are making Otto uncomfortable? Besides, he can always choose another noblewoman. After all, there are many marriages that may be helpful for the reich," Duke Roemgram weighed in.

"No... I..." Otto began.

"Hm? Speak up, son."

"I... do like her. I wouldn't mind... marriage."

"Ha! I knew she was your type!" Alphonse blurted out.

"That's enough! I can only take you teasing the duke's son for so long," Lord Richtonstein ordered.

"Right, sorry, Father."

Anatomy of a Warrior

Prudence

Upper Right Quarter

Upper Left Quarter

Speed

Boldness

Lower Right Quarter

Lower Left Quarter

Strength

Chapter 5

The new year had come, and it was Lupus. Wolfgang had just turned fifteen and eagerly awaited his return to training as the boys were entering their final year.

Wolfgang sat in the solar, looking out the small window of the room, watching snow floating into the courtyard. Otto, excitedly approaching, broke Wolfgang's trance.

"Brother, are you busy?" he asked.

"Not terribly, no. Why?"

"Well, the constellius for Lupus began yesterday in Eifenhart. It will go until tomorrow. Alphonse wanted to go."

"Constellius? Oh, the festival to celebrate the month. I've never been to one before."

"Perfect! It'll be tons of fun. Go get ready. Dress warm."

"Wait, is uh… well… can Elise come?"

"Hm? Sure, go ask her."

"Well, maybe you should ask, brother."

"Come on, Wolfgang. You're almost a man now. Stop being so nervous around her all the time." Otto laughed as he left the solar.

"I think she's in the garden," he shouted from the hallway.

***

Wolfgang donned a heavy fur cloak and walked into the castle's garden. Elise knelt by a strange flower in full bloom with bright violet petals. It stood vibrantly against the gray colors of the dead, snow covered plants covered surrounding it. A thin layer of snow stuck to Elise's wool coat.

"Oh, uh—hey, Elise." Wolfgang began nervously.

"Oh, Wolfgang. How are you?" Elise asked in a soft voice as she stood up and brushed the snow off her coat.

"What, uh—what is that flower?"

"This? It's called a frostbell. It's a special flower that only grows in the cold. They're native to Norsica. When it's fully bloomed, you can crush the petals and use it as a spice."

"That's nice. Maybe we can use that for dinner sometime."

"Maybe." She smiled. "Did you need something?"

"Oh, uh yes—um, well, Me, Otto, and Alphonse are going into town for the constellius. I wanted to know if you, uh—" Wolfgang was so nervous he could barely get the words out.

"I'd love to join you," she interjected.

"Oh, great. We should head over to the gate to wait for the others."

"Okay." Elise approached Wolfgang and held out her hand. "The streets can be very busy during the celebration. Take my hand so we can stay together."

"Oh, right—okay."

Wolfgang's slightly shaking hand grasped Elise's, and the pair made their way to the castle gate.

Caleb the Writer

***

The four made their way into the city. Hundreds of people filled the large streets. Vendors handed out wolf-themed wares. People played chess on makeshift boards outside shops, banners and flags with a white wolf's head fluttered everywhere. Elise kept a tight grip on Wolfgang's hand as they made their way through the crowd.

"Wow, this is a little overwhelming. Where should we start?" Wolfgang asked.

"Well, normally the first thing people check out is the royal banquet," Alphonse answered.

"Royal banquet?" Wolfgang asked.

"Yeah, Duke Roemgramm should be at the main square. He and the court sit at an enormous table, and people come by and talk to them. They even have a jester cracking jokes at the duke's expense."

"Ah, that got canceled this year," Otto said.

"Really?" Alphonse asked.

"Yes. The Holy Emperor called all the electors to Fesista, the capital city of Wolderan, and the seat of the HAE. He didn't say why they were called, though."

"Will he miss the whole festival?" Wolfgang asked.

"Maybe. He's supposed to be back tomorrow."

"Hey, let's go to the Juad Quarter!" Elise shouted, tugging Wolfgang.

"O-okay! What's over there?" Wolfgang asked.

"I want to visit some jewelers! The cobblers too!" Elise replied excitedly as they walked through a busy alleyway, the others following behind.

"The Juads in Eifenhart are renowned for their skills as cobblers and jewelers. There's also a great furniture shop down Faler Street. Most of the castle's furniture was custom made by the Juad man that runs the shop," Otto added.

"I get it. But what do you mean by Juad?" Wolfgang asked.

"They're a group of people who hail from the Mid-East," Otto answered.

***

The group made their way through the gate in a large stone wall leading to a large street packed with buildings. The street ran uphill in the densest part of the city. Wolfgang noticed large groups of men gathering outside several shops, speaking in hushed tones.

"What's up with them?" he asked.

"Who knows? Festivals bring out the odd ones," Alphonse replied.

"Hey, over here! Let's go to Elijah's Jewelry!" Elise said as she dragged the group to a shop.

The shop was built out of wood with a straw hatch roof. A sign out front proudly proclaimed; "The Best Jeweler this side of the Great Channel!"

The four of them stepped inside. A large man with a twirly mustache stepped from behind a counter with his arms outstretched. He wore an armband with a yellow star sewn into it.

"Welcome, welcome!" he began. "It's always nice to see young people out during the festival! Please browse my wares. I make custom jewelry too."

"Wolfgang, look over here!" Elise exclaimed as she walked over to a shelf full of ornate necklaces.

She picked up a necklace off the shelf and put it around her neck. It was a silver chain necklace with a wolf's head pendant at the end. She looked at Wolfgang and smiled.

"It looks good, right? Kind of reminds me of you."

"Oh, um—yeah, it looks great on you, Elise," Wolfgang complimented. "Ah, I wish I brought money with me," he whispered to himself.

Alphonse tapped him on his shoulder and carefully handed him a small purse.

"You owe me," he whispered.

"Ah, thank you!"

"Hey, what are you two talking about?" Elise asked.

"Oh, nothing! Hey, I can buy that for you!" Wolfgang said.

"Really?" Elise lit up. "Thank you so much, Wolfgang!"

"Sounds like you found something!" The man approached them. "Hey, you aren't Elise von Ludwig, are you?" he asked.

"Yes, I am! I'm surprised you remember me, Elijah."

"How could I forget the daughter of the duke? Last time you were here, you were barely up to my knees!" he laughed. "Well, come over to the counter and I'll check you out."

As Wolfgang set the purse on the counter, people were yelling in the street caught his attention. It differed from the joyful shouts you'd expect from a festival. Instead, it sounded angry, almost violent. Wolfgang finished the transaction, ignoring whatever was going on outside.

"That'll be two guilders." Elijah said.

"I have, uh..." Wolfgang dug through the purse, then dumped it onto the counter. "I have two hundred Grotschen. I think."

"I'll... just take all of it. Have a good day and enjoy your new piece of jewelry!" Elijah smiled.

"Hey, we should get going," Alphonse said.

"Yeah, where should we go next?" Wolfgang asked.

"I wanted to see the chairbler at the furniture shop. He works under the carpenter there. I was thinking of having a new chair made for my room," Otto suggested.

"Hey, something is happening outside," Alphonse said as he peered out the shop's doors. "We should probably leave."

"Hm? Is it something bad?" Wolfgang asked.

"Don't know, but we shouldn't stay to find out." Alphonse replied.

The four of them left the shop. As they stepped into the street, angry crowds yelling at the various shops and vendors greeted them. People brandished swords, clubs, and torches. Wolfgang saw a young boy and his mother trying to walk through the angry crowd—both wearing star arm bands. A large man shoved them to the ground. He raised a club and shouted at them.

"You Juads! You come to our city with your pagan rituals, then ruin our economy. The duke isn't here to protect you! We'll be better off without your kind!"

"Hey, what do you think you're doing?" Wolfgang shouted.

"Brother, wait."

Otto tried to stop him, but Wolfgang ran to the mother and her boy.

"Why are you doing this? These people clearly have no quarrel with you!"

"Who are you?" the man angrily yelled. "Those eyes of yours. I see. You must be some kind of devil, coming to protect these scum!"

The man swung his club and hit Wolfgang in his abdomen.

Wolfgang fell to the ground, holding his side. He looked up at the man, wracking his brain for a strategy to fight back. The man swung again. As the club came down, Alphonse grabbed it and pushed the man back.

"How dare you speak to us like this, you commoner!" Elise shouted. "Do you not recognize royalty?" She stood in front of Wolfgang. "You just attacked Wolfgang von Ludwig, threatened Elise von Ludwig and Otto von Ludwig, and fought with Alphonse von Richtonsetin. That is a capital offense! Shall I call guards to imprison you? Shall we throw you in the pillory?"

"Sister, I think you made your point," Otto whispered as he helped Wolfgang to his feet.

"Royal kids? Hmph. It's your kind that's allowed these scum to dwell in our once great city! You can call for guards, but there are none here," the man shouted.

"Hold on, maybe we shouldn't hurt them. Things can get bad if we do," another man shouted from the crowd.

"Fine. You kids better run. This place won't be safe for you soon."

"We'll go. But we're taking this woman and her child with us," Wolfgang said.

Alphonse helped the mother up, and the group slowly backed away before running down an alleyway. They stopped for a moment to catch their breath.

"Thank you. I need to get home to my other kids," the mother said. "I don't know what is happening. I need to make sure they're safe."

"It'll be okay. We'll get back to the castle and organize the garrison force," Wolfgang promised.

"Brother?"

Wolfgang's statement surprised the group.

"Yeah, if we can get back to the castle, we can deploy the garrison and end this."

As they spoke, they noticed ash falling with the snow. They ran to the other end of the alleyway. Buildings on both sides of the street were ablaze. It was almost dusk, but the fire lit up the sky so bright it could fool one into thinking it was day. People drug Juads from their homes and beat them in the streets. Some Juads tried fighting back. Some tried to run. Bodies of men, women, and children littered the streets. Wolfgang grabbed Elise's hand tightly.

"We need to get out of here. Stay close to me. Alphonse, take up the rear. Otto, do you know the way out of this district?"

"Y-yes, brother. I can lead us out. I think we're on St. Seraphim Street. We shouldn't be far from the north gate."

The group quickly made their way down the street. Blood soaked into the muddy snow. It looked like they darted across a mushy velvet carpet. They turned down several streets and ran through several alleyways covered with bodies and blood. Finally, they reached the north gate. The gate was open, and several catchpoles stood outside, drinking ale and laughing. It was like they couldn't hear the screaming and violence happening right next to them. They approached the gate.

"What are all of you doing?" Wolfgang snarled.

"Huh? Who're these kids?" a drunken catchpole shouted.

"I asked you a question. Why are you drinking when there's a riot going on?"

"Who do you think you are to talk to us?" another catchpole chimed in.

"We are Duke Roemgram's children," Elise stated defiantly. "I am Elise von Ludwig. Now answer Wolfgang's question."

"Oh—uh, wait, really?" the drunken catchpole replied.

"Hey, sorry about my men," a catchpole in heavy plate armor holding a sword said.

He had a messy beard and reeked of alcohol.

"Hey, I recognize you. It's me. You remember me, right?"

"Sergeant Beck?" Wolfgang asked.

"Yeah, the man who saved you in Visenville!" he laughed. "Ah, but they made me captain now. Hey, what are you doing here, anyway?"

"Dang it, now's not the time for this! Why do you smell like alcohol? Can't you see there's a riot going on? People are dying," Otto shouted.

"Oh, right, uh... well, we got orders not to interfere. This came from the bailiff, I think. Oh, I was doing my rounds checking on the men at the gates, I didn't really—"

"Are you daft? Your job is to protect the citizens of this city! That includes The Juads!" Wolfgang added. "You're going to do as I say right now, Captain. By royal decree."

"Uh, can you actually do that?" Captain Beck asked.

"Does it matter? If you don't listen, the duke will have your head. Close this gate right now. Go to the other gates and lock them. This will prevent the riot from spreading outside of the Juad Quarter. We'll go to the castle and mobilize the garrison force to quell the riot."

"Uh, really?" Captain Beck asked.

"Yes, now get moving!"

"Okay, okay."

Captain Beck barked orders at his men. They shut the gate, and he ran off to relay the orders to the other catchpole. The rest of the city carried on like normal, like nothing was happening. People were drinking, celebrating, playing games, and eating cake. Seeing so many people smile and laugh while such violence was occurring only a few streets away horrified Wolfgang.

***

The group made their way back to the castle. Otto went to find the garrison commander, while Alphonse woke the troops in the barracks. Wolfgang took Elise to the castle's solar. As he shut the door to the solar, she fell to her knees and started crying.

"E-Elise, are you okay?" Wolfgang rushed over to her.

"I'm scared," she said through tears. "Wolfgang, I thought Eifenhart was safe. Why did this happen? What if we got hurt?"

"Don't worry, Elise." Wolfgang wrapped his arms around her and consoled her. "I'll be here to protect you." He held the pendant of her necklace in his hand. "This. Let this be a reminder that I will always protect you."

***

The commander of Ludwig Castle's garrison force mobilized his men in just under an hour. With about two hundred and fifty troops, he laid siege to the Juad Quarter. He ordered his men to only enter through the north gate, and they made their way through each street, subduing rioters and killing those that didn't surrender. After six hours of battle, they pacified the rioters. They reduced most of the Juad Quarter to cinders. As the fires died out and the smoke smoldered, Duke Roemgram returned to his city.

In the early hours of the eighteenth of Lupus, 1490 Divine Regnum, Duke Roemgram would sign a royal decree executing those that orchestrated the riot, as well as the bailiff that allowed it to happen. History would forever remember the day as the Great Pogrom of Eifenhart.

Pogrom of 1389

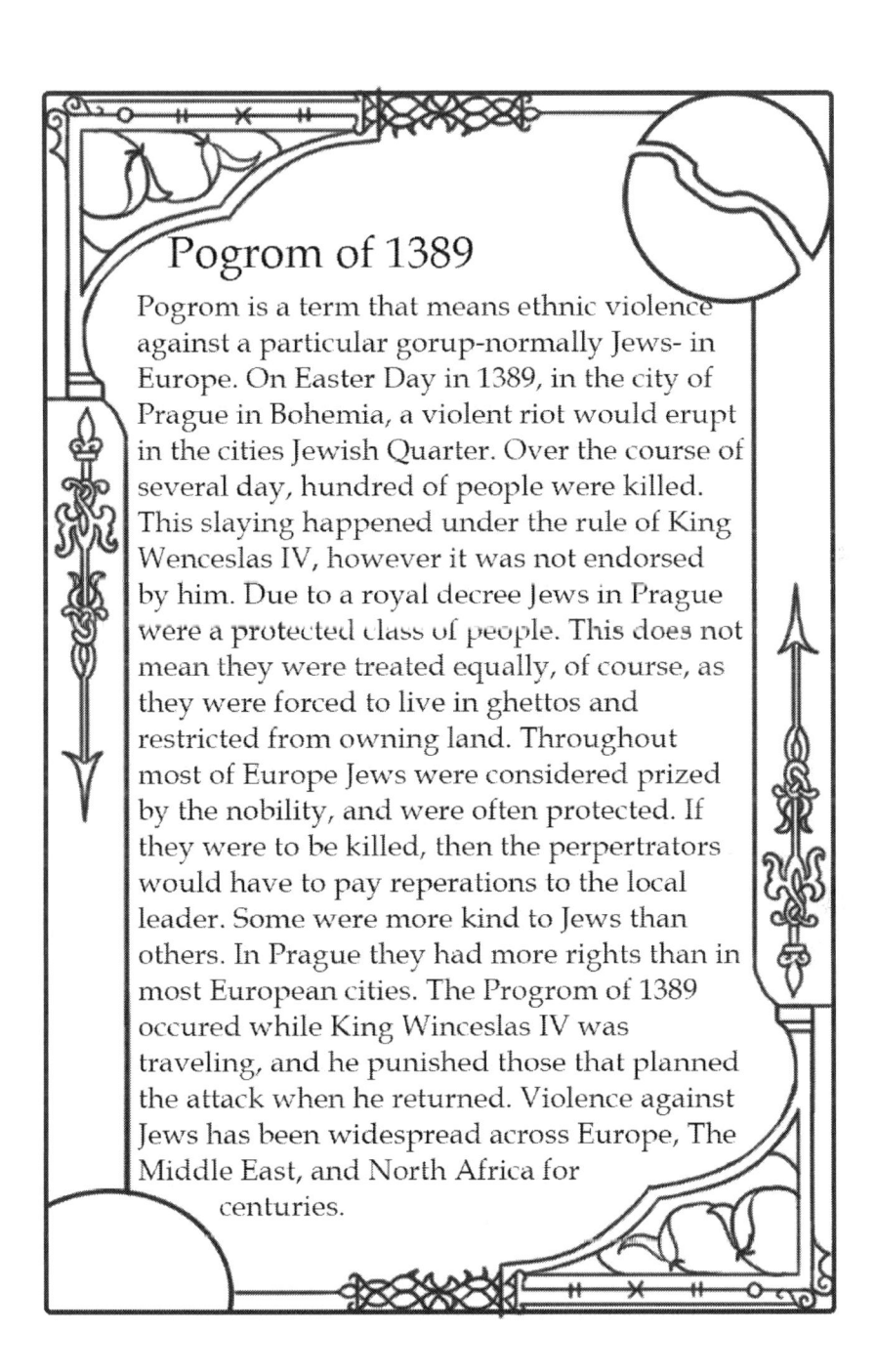

Pogrom is a term that means ethnic violence against a particular gorup-normally Jews- in Europe. On Easter Day in 1389, in the city of Prague in Bohemia, a violent riot would erupt in the cities Jewish Quarter. Over the course of several day, hundred of people were killed. This slaying happened under the rule of King Wenceslas IV, however it was not endorsed by him. Due to a royal decree Jews in Prague were a protected class of people. This does not mean they were treated equally, of course, as they were forced to live in ghettos and restricted from owning land. Throughout most of Europe Jews were considered prized by the nobility, and were often protected. If they were to be killed, then the perpertrators would have to pay reperations to the local leader. Some were more kind to Jews than others. In Prague they had more rights than in most European cities. The Progrom of 1389 occured while King Winceslas IV was traveling, and he punished those that planned the attack when he returned. Violence against Jews has been widespread across Europe, The Middle East, and North Africa for centuries.

Chapter 6

———⚜———

As the seasons changed it was finally spring. The scars of the Pogrom were still in the minds of many, and nobody knew if Eifenhart would ever fully heal. Still, life had to go on, and the boys needed to put that night of violence out of their heads. They had entered their final year of training. After that, they'd be ready to take to the battlefield. The previous years' lessons were reinforced, and Knight-Captain Eiken tested the boys on everything they had learned. As the months passed, they practiced, trained, and had their tests. Near autumn, Wolfgang had a final test. He always struggled with the fighting portion of training, and although he beat Otto occasionally, Hans always bested him. Wolfgang and Hans would square off one last time before the boys would return to their houses.

    Wolfgang and Hans stood apart from each other on the training grounds, like they had done so many times before. The wind blew and clouds shifted, darkening the sky. An autumn storm was coming. Wolfgang stood with his right foot back, left foot forward, and held his sword with his arms stretched out, only slightly bent. He pointed his sword just above Hans's head. The long guard stance. Hans looked on with confusion. That stance, he thought, wouldn't prove advantageous to Wolfgang. And differed from any he'd used before. Hans took up the long-tailed guard, requiring him to place his right foot back and left foot forward with a bend at the knees. He pointed his sword behind him on his right side, angled so he could counter any attacks quickly. He assumed, because of Wolfgang's position, that he'd begin with a thrust.

The two stood for only a moment before Wolfgang made the first move. He charged forward and thrusted his sword at Hans, just as he had expected. Hans moved his sword up, but as he did, Wolfgang suddenly pulled back.

In one movement, he let go of the sword with his right hand—which was by the crossguard—and moved his left hand to the top of the hilt, where his right hand had been. He then reached his right hand underneath his left and grabbed the hilt where his left hand had been. His arms crossed in front of his chest, and his left foot was forward. He transitioned into the Key Guard. Hans's blade was past Wolfgang's head, the hilts almost touching.

With all the strength he could muster, Wolfgang twisted his blade to the right, forcing Hans's sword out of his hand. Wolfgang's arms were no longer crossed, and he transitioned into a reversed iron gate, with his left foot forward, right foot back, and his blade pointed down. He quickly raised his blade in a sweeping low cut, hitting Hans in the chest and chin. He collapsed to the ground, stunned.

"You finally did it. Good job!" Alphonse shouted from the sidelines.

He and Otto clapped, glad to see Wolfgang finally winning.

"Yeah! I'm a warrior now, finally!" Wolfgang exclaimed as rain fell.

"Is that so?" Knight-Captain Eiken asked as he entered the training grounds. "Hans, leave. Hand me your practice sword."

"Hm? What's wrong, Captain? Shouldn't we get out of the rain?" Wolfgang asked.

"You've won a single battle in what, dozens? Hundreds? And you think yourself a warrior. Fine. Prove you're a warrior. Beat me."

"I-I don't understand."

"You heard me. Take up a stance and beat me."

Confused but determined, Wolfgang moved into a position. He turned to his left, his right side facing the knight-captain. He placed his right foot forward, toes pointed to the left, and his left foot back, toes pointed to the rear. His sword was down at an angle, the tip facing the ground. It was the middle boar's tusk. The knight-captain stood without taking up a stance, with only one hand on his long sword.

"Come at me!" he shouted.

"No stance? Okay, fine!" Wolfgang said as he ran at the knight-captain.

He raised his sword, attempting a sweeping low cut, but the knight-captain, in one movement, stepped to the right and grabbed Wolfgang's arms with his left, binding them together. He then hit Wolfgang with the edge of his sword, and Wolfgang fell into the mud.

"See? You're no warrior," Knight-Captain Eiken said as he turned to leave.

Wolfgang stood up, a stream of blood flowing from an open wound on his forehead.

"I won't give up! I will be a warrior!"

"Really?" Knight-Captain Eiken turned to him. "Then take up a stance."

The two continued for hours. No matter what stance, guards, plays, or cuts Wolfgang tried, he got knocked down every time.

Covered in blood and mud, he kept standing and trying to fight, but each time Knight-Captain Eiken knocked him down in a single move.

It had been at least an hour, and it embarrassed the other boys to watch. In their most recent bout, Wolfgang landed face down on the ground. He tried to get up, but slipped in the mud and fell on his back.

"How much longer shall we go?" Knight-Captain Eiken sneered.

"I-I won't give up! I will become a warrior. I will fight and become the holy emperor. I will protect the people of the reich and all Gotheca!"

Wolfgang could barely stand. His body was bruised and bleeding. Before he could even take a stance, the knight-captain hit him on the head with the hilt of his longsword, and Wolfgang fell to the ground on his back. He closed his hands, grabbing a fistful of mud, and tried to stand. The knight-captain placed his boot on Wolfgang's chest.

"You're no warrior. Your aspirations of emperorship? Is this a bad joke? You've barely passed any of the tests I've given, failed to defeat your opponents, and despite your determination, have hardly improved. You'll die on the battlefield and will get other people killed, too. You have no place wielding a sword. You'd be better off as a clerk."

Wolfgang tried to respond, but couldn't. He could barely breathe through the blood pouring from his nose. The rain masked his tears as the knight-captain's words pierced his heart and stung like a thousand angry wasps. Was it all for nothing? Would he never be able to protect anyone?

From the sidelines, Otto moved toward Wolfgang. He wanted to help. But Alphonse put his hand on his shoulder and shook his head. It was best for them to leave Wolfgang alone. They walked away. Wolfgang had no one to come to his aid. Once again, he was just a liability.

"Blessed is the man who remains steadfast under trial, for

The Wolf's Song

when he's stood the test, he'll receive the crown of life God has promised to those who love him," a calming voice called out.

Wolfgang turned his head. A kind looking, bald priest with tired eyes sat on the fence at the edge of the training grounds.

"Shall you just give up?" the priest asked as he folded his arms.

"W-what? Who are you?" Wolfgang could barely get the words out.

"Just a wandering priest," he responded.

"Wait, I know you. I remember you." Wolfgang pushed himself up.

"Really? I don't recall you." The wandering priest put his hand to his chin, like he was trying to pull hidden knowledge from his mind. "No matter. You look hurt. Are you okay?"

"That's an understatement! My body hurts all over."

"Body? Oh, no. I was talking about you, your soul. What's inside."

"What? You're not making any sense." Wolfgang climbed to his feet and stumbled over to the wandering priest.

"You, my son, are broken. Your brokenness is beckoning you to give up. But what of your dreams?"

"What dreams? It's obvious that I don't have what it takes." Wolfgang tightened his fist.

"So, you're knocked down. But you stood back up. If you can pick up your body, you can pick up your spirit."

"Pick up my spirit?" Wolfgang leaned against the fence, the rain soaking him.

"Yes." The wandering priest looked up at the sky as the rain stopped. "Now go. Prove yourself."

"But... how?" Wolfgang paused for a moment, his eyes cast to the ground. "How will I ever prove anything to anyone? I'm no good as a warrior, and people turn away from me as soon as they see my eyes."

"You should not allow others to determine your worth. Their judgements bear no fruit, and should be brushed aside as nonsense. Don't cast your eyes down. Look up towards the heavens, and keep trying. Go and prove yourself."

"I still don't get how I am supposed to prove myself." Wolfgang snapped.

"That's for you to find out." The wandering priest hopped down from the fence. "But I hear there's value in the edelweiss. But, there's also value in peace. What passions you feel are fleeting. You have the freedom to choose, so think hard about your path." He then walked away.

"Where are you going?"

"To wander," he responded with a smile.

***

The boys collected their things and headed back to their houses. Wolfgang arrived at the castle covered in bruises, but still determined to find a path forward. He visited Izabel in the clerks' offices in a small building just outside of the keep.

Izabel sat in a room surrounded by other clerks. There were stacks of books and parchments. At the far end of the room was an empty desk for the head clerk.

"L-Lady Nowaski?" Wolfgang approached her.

She was deep in her work, hardly paying attention to what was around her.

Wolfgang stepped closer. "Lady Nowaski?"

"Hm? What? Yes?" She shot up, her trance-like state broken.

"What does 'there is value in the edelweiss' mean?"

"Huh? I don't understand."

"Well, what's an edelweiss?" Wolfgang looked at her with curious eyes.

"Oh, it's a flower."

"A flower?"

"Yes, the edelweiss grows in the Alpiana Mountains, which lie on the border of Etalia City States and the Kingdom of Schizwizts. In Gothecan tradition, young men climbed to the mountains' peak and pluck it during times of peace to prove their worth as a warrior. Although there have been plenty of wars, so I don't think many still follow this tradition."

"Thank you, Lady Nowaski!" Wolfgang's eyes lit up.

"Oh, do you want me to tell you more about the history of the edelweiss?"

"Nope!"

Wolfgang left.

Later that day, the duke called him for an audience. It wasn't a normal father-son interaction, but an official calling for him to appear before the court.

Wolfgang dressed in a fine silk tunic and waited outside of the throne room to be called. When he entered, he walked down the aisle and bowed his head with his right hand over his heart.

"Wolfgang. Do you know why I have called you here?" the duke began.

"Um... no, sire," Wolfgang nervously replied.

"It's no secret that you wish to court my daughter and your

adoptive sister, Elise. Is this true?"

"Uh… well…" Wolfgang fidgeted slightly.

"Be honest boy."

"Uh… yes, sire. I've been in love with Elise for many years."

"Yet, you fail to understand the basics of the martial arts."

The duke's words surprised Wolfgang. He looked up at him.

"That's right. Knight-Captain Eiken reported your and Otto's progress. I know you failed to best him. You think you can take my daughter's hand in marriage when you can't even become a warrior?"

"But…" Wolfgang's chest tightened. His world was unraveling before him. "I… I can become a warrior!"

"Is that so? How? Because thus far, you've disappointed me. You gave a grand speech when you first came here, do you remember? Now what?"

"The edelweiss, sire. I'll return with one."

"But is that truly enough?" Duke Roemgram sat on his throne contemplating before standing up. "So it shall be. If you want Elise's hand in marriage, you need to return to me with an edelweiss and a dowry of 40,000 guilders."

The court gasped. There was no way Wolfgang could return with such a large sum.

"I shall," He replied.

"Good. This winter you will turn sixteen, you'll be a man. When spring comes, you will leave on your journey. I shall instruct the royal smithy to prepare a set of armor for you and a sword—no, a pole arm weapon will do you better, since you're so inept with a sword."

"Yes, sire. I'll be ready when the time comes. I won't return until I've succeeded."

Wolfgang turned and walked down the aisle, listening to the whispers of the court, just like he had all those years ago. Doubt left the lips of many people, but he had to succeed.

***

Over the next few months, Wolfgang trained his body rigorously. He was in the castle courtyard almost every day, practicing fencing with a wooden longsword or poleax. He'd run and lift heavy rocks, everything he could to prepare for what would likely be an impossible journey. Sometimes Otto would join him, and Elise often watched from her bedchamber window, which gave her a good view of the courtyard. Finally, the time came. The snow melted, the flowers bloomed, spring had arrived.

Highwaymen of Europe

Bandits and highwaymen were a common issue across Europe during The Medieval Age. One of the worst was Christman Genipperteinga. He was born sometime around 1569. In only 13 years of life, he supposedly murdered 964 people. He lived in a complex cave network in rural Germany- the inside of which had an entire house. On May 27th of 1581 30 armed men attacked his compund and finished him off. Another famous German bandit was Peter Niers. Born in 1540, he would be responsible for 544 deaths. Whether or not he actually killed that many people is still debated by historians. Most of what we know comes from ballads. He was supposedly a dark magician who communed with demons. During the 16th century Germany was beset with multiple robber-killer gangs that attacked travelers along the highways and raided small villages. Another famous outlaw was the English Roger Godberd, who some say was the inspiration for Robin Hood. He was active during the reign of King Henry III, and committed similiar crimes to Robin Hood.

Chapter 7

Wolfgang stood at the castle's portcullis with all the gear the duke had made for him. He wore a white padded gambeson with maille voiders on his shoulder, leather gloves, leather hose, and plate metal armor around his legs and knees. A kettle helm hung from a large deerskin rucksack by the straps normally used to fasten it to one's head. The top of the rucksack had a wool and cowskin sleeping bag tied to it. In his right hand, he held a full, darkened metal poleax. Its ax side had three crosses cut out of it, and its hammer side was a forged wolf's head. There was a small dagger in a scabbard fitted to his belt. Elise stood with him.

"Have you seen your brother?" Elise asked.

"No-no, I checked his room earlier too," Wolfgang replied.

He had kicked open Otto's door, but his room was empty. He also looked around for Alphonse, but couldn't find him either.

"Well, it's alright. At least I could see you off," Elise said.

"Y-yeah. Well, I guess I should get going." Wolfgang bent down on one knee and grabbed Elise's hand.

"L-listen, Elise, you-you're the root of my heart. I want to be with you! I will become a warrior, I will marry you, and someday I'll become the holy emperor, I promise!"

He stood up and swung the leather strap fastened to the staff of his poleax around his upper body, securing the poleax to his back. He then put his rucksack on.

As he turned to leave, someone behind him laughed. It was Hans Neudern.

"I was dreading seeing my father, but this just made my trip worth it. Warrior? Holy emperor? You can hardly hold a sword, much less lead the empire." He continued laughing. "You're just a devil spawn. You won't survive out there. You might as well give up and die."

"Hey, listen, you!" Wolfgang pointed at him. "I will achieve my goals! Because I made a promise, I will never give up, no matter what! I will prove myself; I will prove that my life is worth living—"

Elise, grabbing his chin, cut him off. She leaned in and kissed his cheek.

"Don't listen to Hans. I believe in you. Come back safe. I'll be waiting for you," she giggled and stepped back.

"Right, of course, of course I will!" was all the surprised Wolfgang could muster.

"Tsk. Whatever. I'm bored now anyway," Hans grumbled, shoving past them.

Wolfgang waved at Elsie one last time, then walked outside the castle and the portcullis gate closed behind him. Never had the road leading to Eifenhart looked so imposing.

As he stepped forward, a rush of footsteps came from behind. Before Wolfgang could look behind him, something tackled him to the ground. It was Otto and Alphonse. They helped Wolfgang to his feet.

"Thought you could leave without us?" Alphonse asked.

He had on a leather jack with a maille hauberk draped over it and a padded leather hose. Attached to his back was a longsword placed in a fancy scabbard, with a wolf etched into it. Attached to his rucksack was a steel cervelliere, fastened similarly to Wolfgang's.

"Yeah, we're coming with you," Otto chimed in.

He was wearing a blue gamerson with maille voiders, like Wolfgang's. He had steel vambraces fashioned on to his arms and leg armor tied around his leather hose. Fastened to his belt was an open-faced bascinet, with a maille coif resting inside. He, too, had a longsword on his back, but he also carried a bow and a quiver of arrows. All three of them had rucksacks and sleeping bags of similar material.

"Guys, really? Why would you want to come with me?" Wolfgang asked.

"Do we really need a reason?" Otto responded with another question.

"Don't you remember? We're comrades!" Alphonse held his hand out in a fist.

"Yeah, you're right," Wolfgang smiled as he bumped fists with Alphonse.

"But, uh, well—our fathers don't know we're leaving. I mean, Elise is going to tell them tonight, but, well—we should probably get some distance between us and the castle," Otto said.

"A lot of distance," Alphonse agreed.

Just like that, the trio set off on their grand adventure. They marched south through Eisenhart, looking at the people in the markets buying various products. They passed the vendor who's stand they destroyed with their horse race. They continued past Eiken Manor and looked on nostalgically at the training grounds, a place where they'd truly become friends. The group cringed at the rocks, still lined up, awaiting the next generation of victims. They passed furrowed fields of wheat with spinning windmills towering over them.

They stopped for the night in the village of Halsburg, along the river Drün that flowed from Lake Konstanz. The lake, and the three large rivers that flowed from it, were the reich's lifeblood. The logging industry flourished because of them. The boys agreed to stay at Elvald Castle and resupply with provisions before heading out for their actual destination.

They needed money if they wanted to cross the Great Channel into Westlichtenhalfen. The best place to earn money was in Ettelstein, the capital of the Grand Duchy of Wiess. It was Öustria's most prestigious nation, at least since the fall of the Wolfsreich. Its capital was a metropolis and the largest city in Öustria. Thus, that was their destination.

The night fell upon them as they traveled along the road to Elvald Castle. They were still a couple of days away. Not wanting to block the path for other travelers, they made camp a little way in the woodland. They set up a fire and their sleeping bags and sat around the flames as they used a metal pan to cook dry-salted bacon. Yellow lightning bugs lit up the dark forest. As they ate, Wolfgang noticed a blue light in the distance. After a moment, several more appeared. He stood and walked toward it.

"Where are you going?" Alphonse asked.

"You see that?" Wolfgang asked.

After noticing the lights, the other two stood and followed him. As they drew closer, they discovered what the lights were; beautiful beetles. Wolfgang put his hand out and one landed on him. It was almost larger than his palm and had four small wings and eight eyes—four on each side of its head. Its skin was made of reflective scales that changed colors from purple to gold when light passed through them. On its abdomen was a large organ generating the blue light. Hundreds gathered around the boys.

"What are these?" Alphonse asked.

"I read about them. They're forest nymphs. Legend says that they commune with the spirits of the forest to protect it from danger. They travel in swarms but are rare to see in person. In the same familia, is the faerie, which is a larger version found in Angland," Otto answered.

"Wow! This is the snake's fang!" Wolfgang smiled as he held the forest nymph close to his face. "So many of them, too. You sure this is a rare thing?"

The beetle fluttered its wings and flew away, joining the rest of the swarm as they flew deeper into the woods. They watched as the blue lights disappeared into the darkness.

***

After a couple more days of travel, they arrived at Elvald Castle. Though unexpected, Lord Elvald welcomed them with open arms. They ate, Emilia teased Otto, and they spent the night. After they resupplied their provisions, free of charge, they set off. They continued south, to the village of Kyner. There, they planned to pay a ferryman for passage across the Drün.

They arrived at the village around noon. It was of modest size, with only a handful of buildings and roughly fifty residents. Surrounding it were several farms and mills, and of course, the river. The first thing the boys did was find the alehouse. They sat at a table outside, as the inside was reserved for the kitchen, kegs, and storage. There were a few others there, but two men stuck out. There was a man with a large rucksack and a longsword with a golden hilt. He had long blond hair tied into a ponytail and a thin beard and wore a dirty brown tunic and torn leather hose. He sat alone, and behind him another man sat, also alone. The other man was of short stature. Even sitting down, one could tell he didn't stand higher than five foot four. He wore full plate armor and a closed face bascinet. The visor was molded around facial features, but it was simple. Two small slits in the eyes allowed the man to see, and two small holes in the nose piece allowed him to breathe. His lips were formed in the visor, but there was no hole for him to eat or drink. He fastened two short swords to his back and had a menacing aura about him.

"Eh, some... interesting customers in this town, eh?" Alphonse joked.

"Where's an alemaiden? We should get some beer, then head out," Otto said.

As they talked, a man approached the alehouse. He wore heavy chain mail armor and had a white and gold striped waffenrock on. Behind him was a group of men wearing basic tunics, armed with sickles, hoes, and bills. They wore practically no armor, save for a few sporting leather caps.

"You five, all of you, come with me," he ordered.

"Wait, who are you and why are you ordering us around?" Wolfgang asked, pointing at him.

"I'm the town's bailiff. Who are you to point at me? And what's with those weird eyes?" The bailiff pointed back.

"We're the sons of Duke Roemgram von Ludwig," Otto said.

"Never heard of 'im," the bailiff responded.

"House Ludwig is the reigning house of Wolfkonigsland, to the north. That would make them royalty," the man with the blond beard said as he stood up.

His voice was deep and full of sorrow, like a man that had lost much.

"And who are you?" the bailiff asked.

"My name is Jurgen Galhorn. I come from the country to the north, so I know a little about them." Jurgen approached the boys.

The Wolf's Song

"Although I have no authority over the royal class, I recommend we go with him. After all, the bailiff will compensate us, yes?"

"Oh—uh, yes. I'll ensure you all get paid, your—uh, lordship," the bailiff said to Wolfgang and Otto.

"Alright, let's go!" Wolfgang stood up.

"But he hasn't said what we're doing yet," Otto said.

"Yes, there is a gang of highwaymen hiding out in some nearby ruins. They've been a problem for a while, but recently they came and stole the daughters of several farmers at the edge of the village. So, we're going to take care of them finally!"

"Saving maidens in distress? Oh yeah, count me in!" Alphonse stood up, knocking over his chair.

The group followed the bailiff and his loose collection of men. The man in armor also joined without saying a word.

They traveled west, off the road leading to the village of Rosewald, and into the deep woods. There were about twenty men, but the five from the alehouse were the only ones with proper weapons and armor. The group stopped their march to rest after traveling for a couple of hours. Wolfgang sat down to eat bread with Otto and Alphonse. Jurgen also joined them.

"It's nice to see someone else from the reich," Otto said to Jurgen.

"Yeah, well, I'm trying to get away from there." He paused for a moment, not wanting to elaborate. "Anyway, I didn't expect to see the sons of Duke Roemgram." He laughed, then leaned in to whisper. "But really, you shouldn't impersonate royalty."

"Impersonate?" Otto stood up, hands clenched.

"Calm down, Otto." Alphonse waved his hand. "I can understand why he wouldn't believe you. But it's true. I am the son of Lord Richtonstein, and Otto is the duke's son. Wolfgang is his adopted son."

"So, the rumors were true, then." Jurgen fumbled around in his rucksack and pulled out pieces of chain mail and plate armor. "Wolfgang, the one with the devil's eyes, formally of House Coburg."

Upon hearing that, Wolfgang tightened his fist.

"Oh, don't worry, I don't believe every rumor. Word gets around, though."

"Word gets around, huh?" Wolfgang said under his breath.

"Hey, you have squire training, right? Can you help me into my armor? Now would probably be a good time to put it on," Jurgen asked as the man in full armor approached the group from behind.

He stood behind Jurgen for a moment, a terrifying demeanor emanating from him. He looked down at them.

"Can-can we help you?" Otto asked.

The man stepped past them and then kneeled in front of a flower. He reached out his hand to pick it up when a butterfly landed on his finger. He stayed there, admiring it.

"Well, I'm weirded out," Wolfgang said.

"Oh, let me help you with your armor," Alphonse said as he got up.

The three of them helped Jurgen into a set of ornate plate armor. His breastplate had a wolf's head etched into it with a gold finish, and golden crosses on his leg armor. He had a great helm that was forged in the shape of a wolf's head.

"That looks expensive," Wolfgang admired.

"It belonged to my father. It probably was."

After their brief rest, the group headed deeper into the woods. One man called out, noticing broken stone walls in the distance.

The Wolf's Song

They arrived at the old ruins they were looking for. There wasn't much other than a few broken walls that used to make up a keep. They approached the ruins, expecting a gang of enemies, but there was nothing.

"Spread out and look for anything! Reports said they were here. They have to be!" the bailiff ordered.

"Something isn't right," Jurgen muttered to himself.

As they spread out, they heard a loud rustling from nearby bushes. Suddenly, large men with swords and bills, wearing tattered leather armor, ran out from the bushes in all directions, surrounding the group. Several of the villagers were killed, stabbed and slashed at by the highwaymen. Their numbers were quickly reduced to only a handful. One highwayman swung a longsword at Wolfgang. Wolfgang quickly raised his poleax with both hands, blocking the blow. The highwayman kicked him in the chest, and Wolfgang fell to the ground. As the highwayman raised his sword for the finishing blow, another sword pierced his neck. Blood squirted everywhere as he fell to the ground. Jurgen came to Wolfgang's rescue.

"Come on." He helped Wolfgang to his feet.

The situation was in complete chaos and only getting worse. The bailiff ordered everyone to fall back into the ruined keep, hoping the damaged walls could provide defense. Instead, they only helped their demise. The men backed into a wall. The villagers held their weapons and farming tools in front of them, trembling.

Wolfgang and the others stepped forward. Being the only armored people there, they'd be the best defenders. The highwaymen numbered at least eighteen. The short man in the face-full visor pinched three of his fingers together on his right hand, and proceeded to make the Sign of the Cross- a common prayer.

Someone clapped behind the highway men. A man in worn out plate armor and a damaged great helm approached.

"So, this is Kyner's response? I extend mercy, and you attack me? Huh," the man said.

"Hansen?" Jurgen shouted.

"Hm?" The man looked the group over. "Oh, Jurgen Galhorn, I recognize that armor."

"Damn, this is what became of you, huh?"

"What's that supposed to mean? What are you doing here, anyway?" Hansen yelled.

"Well, fighting brigands, I guess," Jurgen replied sarcastically.

"Hey, Jurgen, who is this guy? He sounds like a lowly cottar," Alphonse said loudly, making sure Hansen could hear.

"W-what did you say, boy?" Hansen shouted.

"He was... from an opposing house, one that supported the old Kaiser, back during the Wolfreich's civil war. All the houses except the Neudern that didn't support your fa- the duke, perished," Jurgen replied.

"Oh, so he is a lowly cottar." Wolfgang nodded.

"What? Who the Hades are you to talk to me like that?" Hansen shouted, pointing his longsword at Wolfgang.

"Wolfgang von Ludwig. I'm a warrior and someday—"

"Ludwig?" Hansen replied in shock.

"You've done it now," Jurgen mumbled.

"Ha! By The Lord, what fortune is this? Truly, the spawn of that damned traitor, Roemgram. I guess the rumors of him adopting a devil child were true, too."

Hansen moved closer to Wolfgang, his sword ready. As he did, screams echoed behind them.

"Oh, that must be those girls. Bring them here!"

The highwaymen brought four crying, pretty young girls out from behind the bushes, throwing them to the ground.

"Penelope!" one villager shouted.

"Ha, she must be your daughter. Don't worry, we'll take good care of her. Can't damage the merchandise," Hansen laughed.

"To think, you'd end up as a bush knight. I looked up to you back then, damn it!" Jurgen yelled.

"Tsk, who do you think you are, to call me that? Who cares anyway? I'm gonna send you all to Hades, starting with that one—" He pointed at Otto "You look the weakest. Maybe I can sell off the devil kid, too. Get them."

Two of the highwaymen moved toward Otto.

Otto was terrified, so much so that he couldn't take a proper stance. He charged and swung his sword like a wild madman, but it was to no avail. They easily avoided the attack and hit him in the back of his helmet and he fell to the ground. When Otto fells, a loud growl came from Wolfgang. The highwaymen stopped to look at him.

The sun was high in the sky; the light hitting Wolfgang's eyes, making them glow. His growls got more animalistic, like a cornered angry wolf.

He planted his right foot forward and brought his poleax down; the point facing the highwaymen. He took the serpent's stance.

Wolfgang wasn't thinking about what he was doing when he charged forward, catching the highwaymen off guard. The point of his poleax thrust deep into one of the highwaymen's necks. Wolfgang pulled his poleax out as the man fell to the ground, bubbles of blood forming in the gaping hole in the man's neck as he struggled to breathe. One highwayman charged Wolfgang from behind, but a bill from the side penetrated his abdomen. It was the short man in full armor. He nodded at Wolfgang, and the two stood back-to-back. Two more highwaymen armed with longswords rushed at them from the sides.

In sync, Wolfgang and the armored man stepped into the onset of individual combat. Wolfgang had his hands low on the staff part of his poleax, so he could raise it high into the air. He had far more reach than any longsword, and when the axe side fell on the highwayman's shoulder, he was done. When Wolfgang pulled his poleax out of the man, blood flowed with it, covering parts of his armor. He looked at the rest of his opponents, eyes glowing, covered in blood, snarling like an animal. He appeared not like a man, but a ferocious wolf donned in crimson.

The short man in full armor charged his opponent with his bill. He caught him in the leg. The highwayman fell to the ground, and the short man finished him with a thrust from above, right into his neck.

"Here, get up. We can't let them have all the fun," Alphonse said to Otto as he helped him to his feet.

"Wh-what are you doing?" Hansen yelled to a terrified crowd of highwaymen.

The highwaymen looked on in horror, afraid to attack. They outnumbered the villagers, and yet, the boy with eyes of a demon and the tenacity of a wild animal had them frozen in place.

"Come on, follow me," Otto ordered

Alphonse, Jurgen, and the man in heavy armor all gathered around Otto, and they stood behind Wolfgang.

"Brother, are you okay? Did they hurt you?" Wolfgang asked.

His demeanor changed, like the spirit of war itself possessed him.

"No, I'm fine," Otto said.

"Let's finish this. All five of us. We're outnumbered, but we have them scared. Let's charge together," Jurgen suggested.

"Yeah, let's do this. Take up your stances, and on my command, we charge," Otto ordered.

"What's this? You may have defeated a few of my men, but y-you can't take us all!" Hansen shouted.

"Hansen is mine," Jurgen called out.

The boys took up various stances. Wolfgang was once again in the serpent's guard, Otto in the ox, and so on. The villagers watched, frozen, as the men prepared for a battle that seemed impossible to win.

"Now, attack!"

The boys charged, each picking an opponent to fight. As they engaged their enemies, Jurgen stood before Hansen. Around them, Alphonse and the short man cut down enemy after enemy, while Otto and Wolfgang engaged tougher opponents.

Jurgen placed his right foot forward and left foot back, angling his blade so it was in line with his right thigh. Hansen placed his right foot forward as well, but pointed his sword at his rear. With the hilt in his right hand, he grabbed the tip of the blade with his left. Jurgen rushed forward and raised his blade, thrusting at Hansen.

Hansen bent his knees, keeping his body low, stepped to his left, and thrusted at Jurgen's thrust. Their blades clashed, Jurgen pointed his tip down, and pushed off—giving him some distance to switch to a more advantageous play. Jurgen planted his feet and thrusted hard, but the tip of his sword only ricocheted off Hansen's thick plate armor, despite its damaged and rusted state.

Jurgen pulled his sword up and slashed down in a high cut, catching Hansen's blade. He then carried through with the cut, striking Hansen's elbow so Jurgen could get behind him. He placed his left foot at Hansen's rear, moving diagonally. He wrapped his left arm around Hansen's right and pulled him to the ground. Hansen's helmet fell off, he dropped his sword, and he was completely at Jurgen's mercy. Scars covered Hansen's from ear to ear. It was clear he'd seen his share of war.

"It's over," Jurgen said.

He relaxed his arm a bit, preparing to let Hansen turn him into the bailiff. Hansen tried to leap forward and reached for his sword. Jurgen instinctively tightened his grip and ran his longsword through the gap between Hansen's breastplate and plackart. He drove it through until his hilt pressed against Hansen's gut.

"I-I didn't…" Hansen tried to speak, but couldn't bear the pain.

His blood dripped from the end of Jurgen's blade.

"Damn it, Hansen. Damn it," was all Jurgen could say as he pulled out his sword and laid Hansen down on the cold ground carefully.

The rest of the highwaymen dropped their weapons and surrendered. Wolfgang stood in a pool of blood surrounded by bodies, hunched over, leaning on his poleax, puking. Otto was comforting him. Alphonse untied the captive girls and the short man tended to the wounds of the highwaymen. The girls ran to their fathers, who were among the villagers, raised by the bailiff.

"I guess you aren't that bad of a fighter after all." Alphonse said as he patted Wolfgang on the back.

"He just needed the right weapon, I suppose." Otto added.

The boys gathered around the bailiff. He looked at them, a smile on his face.

"Thank you so much for this. We couldn't have stopped them without you!" the bailiff said. "You should all join us for a banquet! Tonight! I'll get things ready!"

"Thanks, but that won't be—" Jurgen began.

"Yeah, that would be great!" Wolfgang shouted.

"You still have a bit of puke on your chin," Otto said.

Wolfgang quickly wiped his face.

"Oh, you—" Otto turned to the short man in the armor. "What's your name?"

"N-name…" he said in a juvenile voice. "Francis… name is Francis Le Bohema." His broken grammar and thick accent indicated that he may not speak Gostrasprechen.

"Hmm… Êtes-vous peut-être du New Frünreich?" Jurgen asked.

"Oui! Vous parlez Frunken!" Francis replied excitedly.

"Wow! You two speak gibberish! That's so sweet!" Wolfgang shouted.

Otto smacked the back of his head.

"It's Frunken, the man is clearly Frunkish," Otto said.

"Well, it seems like Wolfgang is back to his normal self," Alphonse said.

"'Course, why would I not be me?" Wolfgang replied, unaware of his animal-like state during combat.

"My Grostasprechen not good, but I speak basics," Francis said.

"Je peux t'aider à apprendre," Jurgen said, promising to teach him more Grostasprechen.

"Hey, Jurgen Galhorn, right? Your name sounds familiar," Otto said. "Anyway, thanks for the help."

"Well, I always try to help people when I can. The lord I used to serve is no more, so I use my skills to make the world a little better."

"Ah, so you're a knight's errant, then?" Alphonse said.

"Hey, your skill is impressive. Want to join us?" Wolfgang asked.

"Are you sure about that, Wolfgang?" Otto asked.

"Well, I do need someone to help teach me how to fight."

"Really? You seem to have done well in this fight," Jurgen pointed out.

"Yeah, I think these guys are just bad."

Wolfgang made a good point. However, Jurgen had another idea.

"Do you struggle to fight with a sword? You have a pole arm, and pole arms have more reach and better offense than a sword."

"Can I... come too?" Francis interjected.

"Eh, why not?" Alphonse replied. "Come on, Otto. These two could be helpful."

"Sure, why not," Otto said.

"Oh, what are you guys doing out here, anyway? I mean, you're all from noble houses," Jurgen said.

"Oh, well, right now we're planning on finding work in Weiss. I need money and an edelweiss to marry the girl I love," Wolfgang told him.

"Ha, like something out of a fairytale," Jurgen laughed. "Do you really love her that much?

"Yes, she's the apple of my eye." Wolfgang replied.

"Okay, I'll go with you." Jurgen smiled.

"Me too," Francis joined in.

"You want to join too?" Wolfgang smiled.

"Yes, I... am on a path of my own," Francis replied.

***

The Wolf's Song

With that, the trio became a quintet. The boys enjoyed the banquet thrown for them in the village of Kyner. The villagers set tables up in the street and went to work cooking breads, meats, and preparing fruits. Wolfgang and his group sat at a large table with the villagers gathered around them. The bailiff and the abbot of the local church that oversaw the village stood in front of the boys and addressed the entire village as villagers brought out the food and wine.

"Gather around, gather around," the bailiff began. "We must thank these fine gentlemen for saving our village. They vanquished the brigands that held our daughters captive! Ah, what were your names again?"

"Oh, my name is Otto von Ludwig, this is my brother Wolfgang. Over there is Alphonse von Richtonsetin, and that's Jurgen and Francis." Otto pointed at every member of the quintet.

"Wait, von Ludwig? Richtonstein? Like, nobles?" The bailiff was bewildered.

He hadn't realized they were actual nobles.

"Oh yeah, we come from the reich. Me and Otto are the sons of Duke Roemgram," Wolfgang added.

The villagers went silent as they looked on in horror. They were all so casual with them, they hadn't realized their status. In fear, the bailiff bowed.

"Oh, uh—I didn't realize you were nobility."

"What are you doing?" Wolfgang asked.

"You can stop all that. We are here as warriors, not nobles. Treat us as your own," Otto ordered.

"Right, of course. Uh, Abbot, would you say a prayer before we eat?"

Everyone clasped their hands as the village abbot said a prayer.

Then the festivities began. They ate and drank.

"Hey, Francis, right? How're you gonna eat with that big ole' visor on? You should take it off," Wolfgang said, mouth full of food.

"I... can not take off," he replied. "But I have this." He raised up a small stick, the stalk of a strange looking green plant.

He bent it at the top, stuck it into the tankard of wine, and shoved it underneath his visor after raising it a bit.

"This is called bamboo. It comes from the Far East."

"Huh. I still think it would be easier if you just took it off," Wolfgang said as he downed a tankard of wine.

"Can't. I have... *lépreux*," he said somberly.

"I see. It means he is a leper," Jurgen translated.

"What's that?" Wolfgang asked.

"It's... a disease. It can be fatal, over time," Otto answered.

"Oh, sounds rough. But you fight well, so I'm glad you'll be with us." Wolfgang continued dumping food into his mouth.

"Yes... I too am glad... to have friends," Francis mumbled.

As the night went on, several villagers performed various songs and homemade plays. A few men approached the boys—it was the fathers of the captive girls.

"We'd like to thank you all for what you've done for us," one father said.

"No need for that. Besides, we're getting paid, anyway. Wait, how much were we gonna get paid for this?" Wolfgang asked, still shoveling food into his mouth.

"Did someone say they'd pay us?" Otto asked.

"I don't think so," Alphonse commented.

"Well, I don't really need to be paid," Jurgen commented.

***

Morning came, and the boys paid a ferryman to take them to Zoria, Eisenstadt's capital. The city was smaller than Eifenhart, but just as dense, with winding alleyways and streets packed with people. They tried asking for directions to Ettelstein, but people refused to talk to them. They were getting frustrated when an old man asked for their help, beckoning them into a tight alleyway.

As they made their way down it, armed men appeared from both entrances. There were three men on each side, trapping the boys.

"What is this? Are you going to rob us?" Jurgen asked.

Perhaps it was because he wasn't wearing his armor, or maybe because the others in the quintet were young, but he figured the robbers must have assumed them weak.

"Rob you? Sure, we'll take your stuff, but that kid with you, the one with the demon eyes. Why is he with you?" a man with a raspy voice and a thick mustache asked.

"What are you saying?" Otto shouted.

"It's obvious. Don't you know the legend? We always knew it was real. The Wolf King was the only person with red eyes. So, either that kid is him, or a devil! Either way, he needs to go!"

The man with the raspy voice pointed a hand ax at the quintet. Wolfgang reached for his poleax and relaxed his arms, allowing his rucksack to fall. Jurgen put his hand out, signaling for him to stop.

"Are you serious? How stupid can you be? You barely outnumber us, are armed with practically nothing, then talk of superstitious nonsense." Jurgen said.

"Who-who in Hades do you think you are?"

"Tell you what, how about you fight me? I won't even use my sword."

Jurgen dropped his rucksack and longsword and raised his fists.

"You better take us seriously!" the man shouted as he and his accomplices charged Jurgen.

The man swung his ax and Jurgen side stepped, using his right foot to trip the man. As he fell, Jurgen elbowed him in the back. The other two, each armed with sickles, swung at Jurgen at the same time. Jurgen planted his feet and grabbed both the men's wrist as their weapons came down. He tightened his grip, straining their muscles, causing them to drop their weapons. Jurgen let go and punched them both in the face, causing them to fall. He turned to the old man and the other three men on the other side of the alley. The men turned and ran, and the old man fell to his knees in fear. Jurgen picked up his things and swung them around his back.

"P-please don't hurt me, they made me do it!" the old man pleaded.

"We have no reason to hurt you. Just tell us how to get to Ettelstein," Otto ordered.

"Right! Um, go west to Zitternstadt, then follow the road to Schniel Castle, then to Schaffenstadt, Grossenburg, and after that, the road will take you to Ettelstein."

"Thanks. Let's go." Otto turned, and the others followed.

"Things like this may happen again," Jurgen said as they walked away.

"Well, I'm not worried," Wolfgang replied.

"Really? Why not?" Jurgen wondered.

"Because I have you guys with me. If we stick together, we'll be fine. Well, I know you and Francis just joined us, but I think we can call ourselves comrades." Wolfgang held his fist out to Jurgen.

"What are you doing?" Jurgen asked.

"It's a closed fist salute. A tradition among warriors in the reich. Put your fist out too."

"Uh, I've never heard of this, but okay." Jurgen put his fist out, and they bumped them together.

"See, now we're battle brothers."

"Hold on, you've never heard of the closed fist salute? I knew you made it up," Otto said to Alphonse.

"No, no, it's just a new thing that warriors do, or maybe an ancient thing we forgot about," Alphonse said.

"You're really not helping your case," Otto laughed.

With that, they headed out toward Ettelstein.

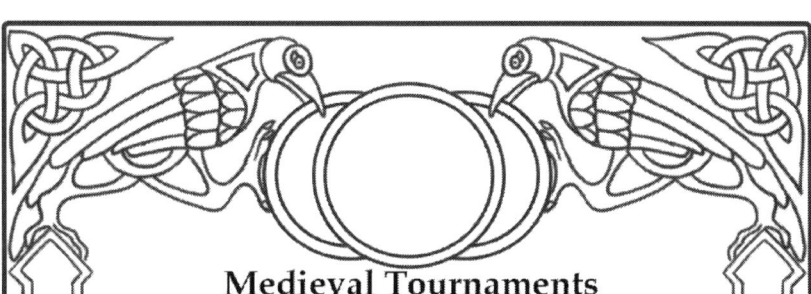

Medieval Tournaments

The tournament, also called a "tourney", was the premiere source of athletic entertainment in Medieval Europe. Armored soldiers would show off their skills by sparring with various weapons- though normally not to the death. Jousting was also a popular sport. In jousting, two horseback athletes would charge each other with lances. You would get points based on where you hit your opponent, or if you knocked him off his horse. There are two types of jousting: Jousts of peace, where participants would use lances with a three pronged tip. This was safer than uses a sharpened tip. The second is Jousts of War, which uses the afformentioned sharp tips. As with any sports, there were many celebrities associated with tourney's. One of the most famous was Ulrich von Lichtenstein, who challenged anyone he could to jousting tournaments all across Germany and Italy. The tradtions of the tourney are still maintained in the modern day by The International Medieval Combat Federation. Modern medieval athletes train for months and travel to Europe from all over the world in order to fight in armored combat tournaments and jousting tournaments. Teams ranging from The U.S., to Japan, to Greece participate in The IMCF.

Chapter 8

The quintet traveled along the prescribed path to Ettelstein. They passed many villages and castles, enjoyed drinks in different alehouses, taverns, and inns, and finally—after about three weeks of travel—arrived in Ettelstein. On their way there, Jurgen trained Wolfgang in the art of longsword fencing and helped Francis improve his Grostasprechen.

Ettelstein, a metropolis larger than any city they'd seen, was quite daunting. People from all over Öustria filled the streets, and the smell of cinnamon mixed with the smell of meat cooking on spigots around various shops. It took them a while to find their way to an alehouse. They sat down inside and ordered beer. As they drank, they asked other patrons and the alemaids where they could find work, especially work that could make them a lot of money. As they spoke, a man wearing a gray silk tunic made of approached them.

"Hello, good men, they call me Martin the Raven," he introduced himself with a light accent. "You five look quite capable. I overhead you're looking for work. Am I correct?"

"Uh, yes, we are. I'm Otto von Ludwig," Otto answered.

Martin's eyes went wide when he heard the name. He then introduced the rest of his compatriots.

"Well, if what I know is true, the Ludwigs are the reigning family in Wolfkonigsland," Martin said.

"Yes, good sir, I and my brother here are the sons of the duke. Also, we still call it the Wolfsreich," Otto said.

"Why ya talking so formal suddenly?" Wolfgang asked. "And what's with that accent?"

"As rude as ever." Otto shook his head.

"I see my accent persists," Martin laughed. "I'm a Normani, although I grew up in the northern part of the Frünreich, in the lands they conquered from the Kingdom of Normania. But that was long before my time." He looked at Francis. "Based on your name, I'd say you, too, are from the Frünreich."

"*Oui—*"

"Remember what we talked about," Jurgen interrupted.

"Yes, right, I am sorry. Ah, the good Jurgen has told me to speak Grostasprechen to help me get used to the language. I come from the central part of the Frünreich."

"Hey, you said you had a job for us?" Alphonse asked.

"Right. I run a modest karlband. We're finalizing a contract with a lord in Oustilüt. There's a war to be fought, and money to be made."

"Oh, so you're a mercenary," Wolfgang said.

"No, no. Battlebands are mercenaries. They're loyal only to coin. Karlbands are freemen that fight for causes they believe in. Although we still get paid, most of the time. But rest assured, I'll pay you handsomely, especially since you're all noble lineage."

"I've never been to war before," Otto said as he mulled over the decision.

"I don't think any of us have," Jurgen added.

The Wolf's Song

"War can't be that bad. We beat those highwaymen just fine!"

As Wolfgang said that Martin's eyes narrowed. Whispers coil be heard by other patrons of the alehouse.

"So, the rumors are true?" One man whispered.

"I can't believe it." Another man said in a hushed tone.

"I say we do it. Are we in agreement?" Alphonse asked.

The others nodded in approval.

"Perfect. But there's one thing. I need to see your skills for myself. There's a tournament going on today and tomorrow. I'd like you to compete. I need to get my money's worth, after all."

"A tournament? Sounds easy!" Wolfgang said.

"Not as easy as it sounds," Jurgen added. "I've only done a couple of tournaments. They can be challenging."

"If it's what we need to do, we should do it. No matter how difficult," Wolfgang said in a surprisingly serious tone. "I need to be a warrior. I must get that dowry. So, we should do it."

"Yeah, right. We'll do it," Otto confirmed.

Martin led the boys to the tournament arena. It was a large building with stone foundations and wooden stands that stretched out in the shape of an oval. They walked through the entrance and a man in a fancy tunic greeted them.

"Sorry, but today's competition is sold out. You can buy tokens for next week's tournament," the man informed them.

"Oh, no—we're here to compete."

"Oh, I see. Well, the team tournaments have already concluded. The single matches will be tomorrow, so you can sign up for them over there." He pointed to a sheet of parchment hanging on a wall. "The tournament features mixed fencing. If you beat your opponent and impress the champions we have, you might go against them and earn more money. You need to pay 50 Groschen each and the prize for winning is 200 Groschen as 2 Guilders."

The boys paid the fee and signed their names. They found an inn to spend the night and returned the following morning.

***

An enormous crowd surrounded the arena, and there were at least a hundred people in the stands watching the spectacle. The crowds cheered as competitors fought one another. As the boys waited in the arena's undercroft, Jurgen explained the rules of the tournament to them.

"So, is this really your first tournament?" Jurgen asked the others.

"Yeah, I'm a little nervous to tell the truth," Otto replied.

"Well, you should've told the arena master. I'll explain things then. The rules are simple: you fight until someone falls to the ground or surrenders."

"Wait, I thought we had to kill our opponent!" Wolfgang chimed in.

"No, we aren't barbarians. Where did you hear that? We're using actual weapons, so injury is possible, of course, but the objective is to knock your enemy down or get them to surrender. There is no honor in killing someone in a tournament."

"Jurgen? Jurgen Galhorn?" the arena master shouted. "You're up. Your opponent is… Uwe the Wolderanian."

A man wearing chain mail with a fancy blue gambeson stood up with Jurgen. He had a noticeably smug aura; it being more apparent by his lack of a helmet. They walked onto the arena field and took opposite sides. Uwe the Wolderanian unsheathed a silver rapier and Jurgen unsheathed his longsword. A man stepped onto the field and waved a yellow flag, indicating the bout had begun.

The Wolf's Song

Jurgen stood firm with his right foot forward and left foot back, pointing his sword to the rear and holding the blade with one hand and the hilt with the other. He was waiting for his opponent to make the first move. Uwe the Wolderanian charged forward, thrusting his rapier. Jurgen brought up his sword and blocked the thrust, then stepped to his right and slammed his hilt against Uwe the Wolderanian's head. He stumbled back and fell to the ground.

"My, what a dishonorable thing to do! Going for the head!" he shouted, holding a small gash on his forehead.

"Your fault for not wearing a helmet," Jurgen laughed.

The others faced their opponents in the following bouts. Alphonse and Otto used the longsword while Francis used his bill. After they beat their opponents, it was finally Wolfgang's turn to enter the field. He'd face off against Yuri the Unbreakable. He was a poleax wielder, just like Wolfgang. Yuri wore a chain mail hauberk and a great helm with a visor. The two stood on the field, awaiting the signal to start.

"You look determined. This will be interesting," Yuri commented in a thick Raskovian accent. "In the Tsardom, I never lost a match."

"Good thing we're in Öustria," Wolfgang replied.

The signal was given, and the bout began. Wolfgang placed his left foot back and bent his knee slightly. He pointed the pike end of his poleax toward the ground at an angle, the hammer side facing the sky. Yuri the Unbreakable placed his left foot forward and right foot back, then swung his poleax over his right shoulder. The ax side faced the sky. From his position, he could swing at Wolfgang with great might.

They stood for a moment, awaiting the other's move. The crowd shouted at them to hurry, so Yuri made the first move.

He swung his poleax from his right side, like Wolfgang figured he would. In response, he raised his weapon straight up and held in firm with both hands, blocking the blow. Yuri stepped offline and reset himself, the same guard as before. Wolfgang placed his right foot forward and mirrored Yuri's guard. He closed the distance as he stepped and waited for Yuri to swing before swinging himself.

Wolfgang stepped forward with his left foot, giving him more power with his swing. The two poleaxes made contact, their metal heads reverberating a loud clang. Wolfgang pushed as hard as he could, forcing the head of Yuri's poleax to the ground. The two of them were now locked together. Before Wolfgang could carry through, Yuri lunged at him, grabbing him by his right arm and trying to get him into a grapple.

Wolfgang stepped offline, trying to avoid the attack, but Yuri was too fast. He had Wolfgang by the arm. His next move would be to swing at Wolfgang with his poleax. Knowing that, Wolfgang quickly pushed forward and grabbed Yuri by his visor. Yuri stepped back, pulling Wolfgang's arm, causing him to drop his weapon. Yuri kicked the poleax away, and Wolfgang was unarmed.

"It's over," Yuri exclaimed.

"No. Not yet. If I'm standing, we fight," Wolfgang demanded as he raised his hands. He kept his arms bent and both hands open, ready to try a grapple. Yuri nodded and swung his poleax hard. As the ax side came down, Wolfgang raised his right arm and grasped the staff below the head, slicing his leather gloved hand to be sliced open. At the same time, he grabbed the bottom of the poleax with his other hand. He stopped the attack, although it hurt him to do so. Wolfgang then twisted the poleax to his left, freeing it from Yuri.

Yuri would undoubtedly try to take it back, so Wolfgang launched at him. He stuck the poleax between Yuri's legs and put his hand over Yuri's visor, blocking his vision. Yuri tried to move behind Wolfgang to get out of the hold, but as he did, he tripped on the poleax and fell to the ground. Yuri lifted his visor, shock in his eyes.

Wolfgang helped Yuri to his feet, then raised his fist in victory.

The Wolf's Song

The crowd cheered. The two grabbed their weapons and headed back to the participants' undercroft.

"That Martin ought to be impressed now," Alphonse said. "We all made quick work of our opponents."

"That is true. But we—" Otto began, but the arena master cut him off.

"You five, good job. But you—" He pointed at Wolfgang. "You had the most impressive bout all day. One champion we have here wants to challenge you."

"Wait, really?" Wolfgang's eyes lit up.

"Yeah, it's Gründal the Undefeated. He's the cousin of Alexandrios Saxan, the son of the holy emperor."

"This doesn't sound good," Jurgen chimed in.

"Ah, don't worry about it. I bet I can beat him easy!"

"So, you accept? Good. Oh, and he only fights against longsword wielders, so leave your poleax here."

"This really doesn't sound good," Jurgen repeated.

"Relax, it'll be fine! You helped train me, after all. Oh, can I use your sword?"

Wolfgang was clearly excited. As they spoke, Martin the Crow approached them.

"Challenged by a champion, huh? You all showed some skill, but honestly, you're a little basic. Nothing I wouldn't find in a typical mercenary. I want the best of the best."

"Wait, are you saying you won't hire us?" Otto asked, looking at his feet.

"Hm, maybe. How about this? If you defeat this so-called undefeated champion, I'll hire you right away."

"I accept your challenge! I'm so going to win!" Wolfgang

shouted.

***

A while later, Wolfgang stepped onto the arena field, wielding Jurgen's longsword. He waited a moment, and another man entered the field. He wore heavy plate armor with a great helm with a liftable visor. Around his waist was a tabard of a black eagle wreathed in flame like a phoenix, with a yellow background. The hilt of his sword was made of gold.

"You are quite interesting," Gründal began in a thundering voice. "You fight like a rabid animal. Your eyes are red like blood. You are the most interesting competitor I've seen in a while."

"Interesting? Is that supposed to be nice or an insult?" Wolfgang shouted.

"What?" Gründal replied, confused.

"Whatever, let's do this!"

Wolfgang placed his right foot forward and bent his knee, holding his sword near his waist at an angle. Gründal placed his left foot forward and placed one hand at the end of his sword, keeping the other on the hilt, and held the sword by his side. The arena master gave the signal to begin the bout. The normally rowdy crowd fell silent, expecting a quick end.

Wolfgang pulled up his sword and swung at Gründal from above. Gründal held his sword and across his chest, blocking the blow. He pushed forward, causing Wolfgang to stumble back. Gründal re-positioned himself with his sword down by his side, still holding it by both the blade and the hilt. He thrusted it into Wolfgang's chest.

Wolfgang stepped back and raised his sword to block, but still felt the blade go through his gambeson. A small tear exposed a fresh cut in his chest. Gründal then grasped his hilt with both hands and swung down in a high cut. Wolfgang held his blade, pointing up parallel to his body.

As their blades clashed, Wolfgang's sword was forced down, but he remained firm and kept it at an angle. Gründal pushed his sword against Wolfgang's until the point of his blade was on the underside of Wolfgang's right arm. He then slid his sword down further until his hilt pressed against Wolfgang's blade, and with a single move, he thrust upward, forcing Wolfgang's arm up, causing him to lose grip of his sword as it went flying.

For a moment, it felt like time slowed down. At this point, the average competitor would have surrendered. In only a short minute, Wolfgang lost. But he couldn't lose. His sword still spun in the air. He knew he had to fight.

Wolfgang stepped back, reached his arms up, and grabbed his sword as it fell. He grasped the blade with both hands. He had no time to change his hand position or take up a guard. The hilt would be his weapon.

Gründal saw what was happening and knew his opponent wouldn't give in easily. He planted his feet, adjusted his sword to point toward Wolfgang—parallel to the ground—and rushed forward in a thrust. If he struck Wolfgang's chest, he could end the bout with one decisive blow.

Wolfgang saw what was coming. He didn't want to give his opponent the chance to take him down. He shuffled his feet and moved to the side, narrowly avoiding the thrust. Wolfgang was behind Gründal. He was about to swing his hilt at Gründal's head, but noticed Gründal re-positioning himself rather quickly for someone in plate armor. But Wolfgang had the advantage, as he was lighter on his feet, and, with the kettle helm, he had peripheral vision.

Gründal knew he was at a disadvantage, and needed to spin around so he was face-to-face with his opponent. He planted his right foot down and used it to pivot himself toward Wolfgang. As he did, he saw a truly unnerving sight.

Wolfgang knew what his opponent was doing. Despite his attempts at being deceptive, ever since the first strike failed, his moves became easy to read. Wolfgang had two options. He could continue moving around his opponent until he got behind him again, or he could move into his opponent and catch him off guard. In a split second, Wolfgang decided on the latter. He stepped offline and right into Gründal. As he did, he swung his sword as hard as he could.

The light from the sun perfectly hit Wolfgang's eyes, reflecting off them so they glowed—streaking as he moved into position. A growl emanated from deep in his gut. Gründal hesitates a moment. He knew a blow was coming; he knew he could block it, but—just for a brief second—fear had struck him.

The hilt of Wolfgang's sword slammed into Gründal's elbow, making a loud metallic clang. He then planted his feet firmly and swung three more times, impacting Gründal's chest and abdomen each time. Although he couldn't penetrate his opponent's heavy armor, he was certainly causing his pain. Gründal tried to move into a guard, but Wolfgang reacted quickly. He moved in and, with his left hand, grasped Gründal's visor, and yanked hard enough to pull him down.

Gründal toppled, the series of events clearly not in his favor. He used his sword as a crutch, planting the point in the dirt to prevent him from collapsing. If he hit the ground, the bout would be over. He grasped the hilt of his sword with both hands and tried to sit up. But it was too late. With no peripheral vision, he didn't know where Wolfgang had gone, and what he feared transpired.

With a loud clunk, Wolfgang hit Gründal in the back of the head with his hilt. Gründal didn't go down with the first hit, so Wolfgang swung again. With the second thunk, Gründal fell to the ground.

The crowd fell silent. No name rookie took down the champion, who traveled and won tournaments all across Gotheca. Wolfgang held his longsword high—still by the blade—in victory. No one cheered. He then turned to the defeated Gründal and showed him an open hand. Gründal grabbed the hand, Wolfgang helped him up, and the two raised their hands high together. The crowd then gave roaring applause. The two nodded at each other, before heading into the undercroft and going their separate ways.

Wolfgang rejoined the others and looked at their stunned faces. They didn't know what to say. They watched the bout from the stands and figured it would be over in an instant. Then, Martin the Crow approached them, clapping.

"A man who fought like a rabid animal, appearing as a ferocious crimson wolf, who with the help of four strangers—one of which was dignified like royalty, another was strong like an ox and quite lecherous, one in armor who helped those he slayed, and another who refused payment. A quintet of odd fellows who defeated a group of brigands and saved a village."

"What are you talking about?" Jurgen asked.

"A rumor from some merchants I was dealing with. See, I didn't come here to recruit new talent. I came here to get supplies for my men up north. But this rumor of an odd quintet that saved some nowhere village in Eisenstadt was the talk of the group. I thought it was all garbage, until I saw you three at that alehouse," Martin answered. "I'm quite impressed with your display, too. Never would've thought you'd use mordhau."

"Wait, does that mean we're famous? Oh, that's super sweet!" Wolfgang said.

"Uh, I think he's saying you're an animal. Pretty sure that's an insult," Otto added.

"Yeah, totally," Alphonse and Jurgen agreed.

"I would not want a name like that," Francis added.

"Whatever, you're all just jealous because I got a sweet name," Wolfgang pouted.

"But you all look more like kids than men," Martin laughed. "Well, except you. You might be older than me!" He pointed toward

Jurgen.

"Hey, I'm only twenty-three. You look like you're at least thirty!" Jurgen responded, offended.

"Well, anyway. I'll higher the five of you." Martin paused for a moment. "Tomorrow at sunrise, meet me at the edge of town heading north. I'll explain everything on the way. We need to meet with the camp followers then link up with the karlband. We call ourselves the Thorns of Roses." He smiled, then walked away.

The boys would then visit an alehouse to celebrate their victory in the tournament. They sat down and ordered their drinks, smiling and laughing.

"I can't believe we did so well!" Wolfgang said with a mouth full of beer.

"I'm not surprised, I was always the skilled fighter." Alphonse sarcastically added.

"Skilled at flailing your arms like a madman, maybe." Otto retorted.

"I am glad I find myself in the company of good fighters." Francis complimented. As they spoke, Wolfgang overheard two loud merchants. They were practically yelling at one another, despite being seated at the same small table.

"Yeah, there were a bunch of slaves for sale, but they were all too young or too frail to till the fields in Lothargia." One of them said.

"Really? Maybe they could be servants in Wolderan!" The other merchant laughed while taking a chug of wine.

"Strange thing is though, most slaves- you'd strip 'em of anything of value. But one of them- a young blonde girl- had a strange bracelet on her."

At this, Wolfgang perked up. He recalled the night Viesenville was attacked. His sister, Julia, has just purchased an odd bracelet with three rubies engraved within it.

"The bracelet has some kind of strange stones in it-" The drunk merchant continued. Wolfgang shot out of his seat, to the surprise of his company.

"That slave girl- you're sure she wore a bracelet?" Wolfgang shouted towards the merchants.

"Uh, yeah- what's it to you?"

"Tell me, where did you see her?"

"Huh? What are you talking about, kid?" The other merchant drunkenly muttered.

"Tell me, right now!" Wolfgang shouted back in anger.

"Okay, okay. Down by the docks. Look for a big ship with a black hull and red trim. It's getting dark, I doubt the sellers are still there."

At this, Wolfgang ran off without saying a word. The others were bewildered. Otto stood up and chased after him.

"What happened to get him in such a spell?" Jurgen asked.

***

Wolfgang made his way to the docks just as the sun began to go down. He ran past workers loading various ships and crowds of people looking at bulk wares. He searched vigorously for the described ship. Eventually he saw it- a black hull and red trim. He ran over to it. A man wearing a large hat and a thin black cloak stood near the pier by the ship. He had a thick beard and a scar below his left eye. Wolfgang approached him.

"I-I heard this ship was selling a girl." Wolfgang was so out of breath he could barely get his words out.

"What of it? You're too young to be buying a slave. But those eyes of yours..." The man replied in a gravely and deep voice. He paused for a moment and analyzed Wolfgang. "You intrigued me. What kind of girl are you looking for?"

"She's close to my age. Blonde hair, a bracelet."

"Oh yes, I know the one. Come with me. I'll show you." He smiled and led Wolfgang up a long wooden gangway and onto the ship's upper deck. The man took a torch out of a small stanchion connected to the main mast. He followed the man down a ship's ladder into the lower decks. The crew were covered in scars and dirty clothing, and a prevailing smell of unwashed clothes and dead fish permeated Wolfgnag's nostrils, making him recoil. It took every bit of will he had to stop himself from puking. He was led five decks down into the lowest deck of the ship. Wolfgang was appalled at what he saw.

At least one hundred people were chained together, all wearing rags. They were malnourished, covered in wounds and sore. They flinched as the light of the torch was cast upon them. Most of these sickly folk were children, some even younger than Wolfgang. He was led to the back, where a little girl sat hunched over. Her long blonde hair covered her face. She was carving something into the deck with her fingernails. Her fingers were bleeding, and yet she continued to carve the picture.

"Look up, and show this man your bracelet." the man commanded.

The girl looked up at them and slowly raised her arm- although she was so skinny it looked as if it took every ounce of her strength to do so. The bracelet she wore was made of copper, and had a small green stone engraved in it. Her face was covered in bruises.

"What's this that you're doing to my deck?" the man asked.

"T-this is my family. See, mother here, father here, and this is me." the girl replied as she pointed to the figures in her drawing.

"I see. Well, your mother and father are dead, dear. They were killed by mercenaries in that raid back in- where was it your form

The Wolf's Song

again? Axonia? No matter."

Wolfgang was no longer able to hold in his bile. He turned to run towards the ship's ladder, tripping over people as he ran. He quickly made his way back to the upper deck, and began to throw up over the side of the ship. Shortly after, the man stepped behind him.

"Wh-what is that?" Wolfgang asked.

"Ha! Never seen a slave ship before, boy? This is the way the world is." the man replied.

"Are you insane? Why would you do that to someone?"

"Hey boys;" the man turned to his crew; "this kid wants to know why we trade in slaves." he faced Wolfgang. "For the fine company." the crew laughed at his cruel joke.

"Dang you, I'll-" Wolfgang tried to threaten the man, but was cut off.

"You'll what? Tell the bailiff? Because slavery is illegal? My boy, our entire world is built on the backs of slaves. Even now, the average scholar and pious altar boy sings the praises of modern progress, whilst sipping on wine whose grapes were plucked off the vine by slaves like the one in this very ship. Yes, it is illegal. But it is only illegal for the commoner. After all, the laws do not apply to those that make them. Fancy that, eh?" his crew erupted in laughter.

"To heck with you, and this whole crew." Wolfgang shouted.

"Ha! Boys, get this child off my ship. You'll learn soon enough how the world is. Servitude is the way of life, and we are merely the profiteers."

Members of the crew surrounded Wolfgang. They grabbed him, and beat him. He struggled but to no avail. One man punched Wolfgang in his gut, and another kicked him in his shin. They carried him down the gangway and threw him down on the pier. Otto ran over to him.

"Brother! What happened? Where did you go?" He asked.

"J-Julia." Wolfgang said, tears streaming down his face.

"Julia?"

"She was one of my siblings. I-I assumed they had all died, but when I heard about a slave- someone that could be her, I was so excited. Brother, why? Why didn't I look for them before? Could they really still be alive?"

"Wolfgang." Otto paused for a moment. "It's okay, brother. I'm sure they're out there, somewhere. We mustn't give up hope. I'll help you search. Everywhere we travel, I'll ask. I'll find slave merchants. I'll help you find them."

"Really?"

"Yeah, we're family, after all. That means the Coburgs are my family, too. Isn't there nothing you wouldn't do for family?"

"Hm. Yes, you're right."

"Now, on your feet. Let's get those tears wiped off and head back. We need to come up with a convincing story for the others."

"Tell them I fought a fierce dragon." Wolfgang smiled.

"I don't think you have enough bite marks for that." Otto laughed, helping his brother to his feet. The two returned to the alehouse.

Before they knew it, morning had come, and it was time to depart. The boys were about to experience war for the first time.

Wolfsreich Coats of Arms

Wolfsreich National House Coburg House Ludwig

House Kial House Neudern

House Starke Wolfsreich Warbanner House Saxe

Chapter 9

The boys walked along a small caravan with wagons full of food, whetstones, weapons, and other supplies. Martin sat atop a horse at the front of the caravan and called for the boys to approach.

"The man we're serving is Lord Alten. He's young, a kid, like you. Well, not all of you." He gestured at Jurgen, who folded his arms and shook his head. "Anyway, his father passed a few months ago. He took over the House, but several other lords have been vying for the land for a long time. The western part of Oustilüt has been volatile for a while. With Lord Furock Alten's death, and the ascension of his son, this is the perfect opportunity to stir up trouble. The big man is Lord Klein, who rules a fief in the southwestern part of Oustilüt in the grünrein mountains. He's allied himself with Lord Fenton of Taltenburg and Lord Oppenstein, who sits closest to Lord Alten's fiefdom. These three, along with several barons and merchants, formed the Owl Alliance. They call themselves this because of Lord Klien's family coat of arms, which features an owl. The Alliance uses a white owl with a blue background as their emblem."

"Why are they fighting him, though?" Otto asked. "Is it just a land grab?"

"Not really. See, Lord Alten's father didn't have an heir for a long time, so he signed an agreement with several barons and lords to leave the iron mines north of his castle with them. Those mines generate most of his family's wealth. Lord Alten is claiming they're his by birthright and refuses to honor the decades old agreement, which was never nullified."

"Hold on, you said this is in the western part of Oustilüt, right? So why doesn't the duke of Oustilüt do something?" Wolfgang asked.

"What would you expect him to do?" Martin laughed. "He—like most dukes, kaisers, and kings—is too busy sipping wine with his concubines to worry about his subjects' quarreling. He'd rather stay locked in his castle in Zurick than intervene. Most nobles don't care what their neighbors or subjects do if it doesn't affect them."

"But, but what about the holy emperor? Couldn't he stop this?" Wolfgang continued.

"The holy emperor probably doesn't even know this backwater duchy even exists. You really are naïve, aren't you?" Martin sighed. "Well, it's a long ride there. It'll take us about a week, so get settled in. I recommend you five get horses when you can afford it. Walking everywhere gets real tiring."

***

After being on the road for some time, they arrived in the Duchy of Oustilüt. They met up with the camp followers just outside of Alten Castle. Martin took the boys to a small tent. Inside was an older man with a thin beard and violent eyes. He was of large stature and had several scars on his face. He wore a chain mail hauberk over a brown gambeson.

"This is my second in command, Aksel Sorenson," Martin introduced.

"Looks like you found a few strays. Always collecting new

talent," Aksel laughed in a deep voice. "What's with that one and his weird eyes?" He pointed at Wolfgang.

"What's wrong with my eyes?" Wolfgang asked, clenching his fist.

"This one's full of fire, huh? He's a little lambkin, huh?" Aksel laughed as he patted Wolfgang's head.

"What's the status of our contract?" Martin interrupted.

"Right. Lord Alten is offering one hundred guilders per settlement or castle taken. He's also offering sixty groschen a day. However, he's having trouble raising his levy. Only around one hundred men have answered the muster call. He's hired two other karlband's and has his men-at-arms, all heading to Oppenstein Castle. We have a force of around seven hundred down there."

"Well, It wouldn't be the first impossible war we've fought."

"It gets worse. He's denied us the right to small wars. We need to rely on supplies from Alten Castle, of which he has few."

"What are small wars?" Wolfgang asked.

"During a siege, to supply our army and harass the enemy, we raid villages and burn farmland. Essentially, we wage a bunch of small wars building up to the big one," Martin answered.

"He wants the support of the people after he has beat the alliance," Aksel added.

"Damn, what a naïve kid. Fine, but that means this siege must end quickly, which isn't ideal. We'll know more when we get to the siege camp, I guess." Martin turned to walk out of the tent. "Get this quintet acquainted and prepare to move out. Should take us about four days of travel."

***

After some time, they arrived at the siege camp, followers in

The Wolf's Song

tow. Wooden palisades surrounded the camp and trebuchets were being constructed nearby. Inside the camp, many men had sleeping bags next to fires, and there were several merchants and smiths in small tents selling their wares and services. Only the commanders and captain could afford tents, and even then, their tents were small. The largest tent, at the center of the camp, belonged to Lord Alten's marshal.

"It's almost dusk," Martin said to the boys. "I'm sure the patrols need to be relieved. You three—Wolfgang, Alphonse, and Otto—you guys have patrol duty. Jurgen and Francis, guard duty on the north gate. You'll be relieved in a few hours."

"Patrol duty? That sounds so lame," Wolfgang complained.

"I could put you on latrine duty instead."

"Uh, no, we're fine patrolling!" Otto said.

"Good. Drop off your gear with the rest of our men and don your armor, then get to it," Martin ordered.

As night came, the boys fulfilled their patrol and guard duties. They joked and talked to break up the monotony. After some hours, Aksel fetched them and brought them to the command tent. Martin and a man with long blond hair and heavy armor stood around a map sitting on a table. The map depicted Oppenstein Castle and the siege camp. It was hastily drawn, but Wolfgang could easily make out its thick wooden walls and the stone keep at the center.

"This is Sir Suruck, Lord Alten's marshal," Martin explained.

"Why did you ask these men here?" Sir Suruck asked, throwing his hands in the air.

"These young men are new to my retinue, and—they're nobles. This is their first war, so they need to learn why and how we fight. Someday they may lead armies, too," Martin answered.

"Fine, fine. Just get on with it."

"We'll attack tomorrow night, after midnight has come, when they are at their most tired and vulnerable. First, we'll move the siege towers into position. Our engineers have gone out already and set up the ropes."

"Ropes?" Wolfgang asked.

"Ah, we move siege towers on ropes. We have small iron rings at each end—two near their walls and two at the camp. Men pull the ropes to move the siege towers closer to the walls." Martin looked back at the map.

"It's a slow process, but if we move under the darkness of night and extinguish our torches, it will be a bit before they see us. Our men with ladders and the battering ram will advance as well. The remaining force will move with mantlets and stay close behind. Once the enemy has spotted us, one of our signaleers in the siege towers will blow their horn, and we'll open with strikes from the trebuchets. We'll focus our efforts on their keep and the garrison inside the walls. Our goal is to both assault the walls and breach their gate."

"What do we need the towers for? Also, why not use the trebuchets to destroy the walls? They're only wood," Wolfgang asked.

"They may be wood, but they're sturdy. If we wanted to destroy the walls, we'd use miners to dig underneath, and we have neither the time nor manpower for that. Ordinarily, a siege would last months at least, and we'd send out several waves of assaults. But we don't have the food for it. Lord Alten's men have already been here for two months.

"As for the towers, we placed the two siege towers on the opposite sides of the battlefield at the edge of our advance. We'll place crossbowmen and longbowmen inside, along with our signaleers. They act as both a means to cover the assault and as a scouting vehicle. They'll also suppress the cannons on their wall. Unfortunately, Lord Oppenstein has two cannons. We built our towers out of their range, so hopefully they can keep them pinned down long enough they won't harass the assaulting wave."

"Why are we attacking at night?" Otto asked. "It will be hard to fight in the dark."

"Part of it is to catch them off guard. The other part is to help prevent the cannons from seeing our ram and ladder-bearers." Martin looked at the boys. "Any other questions? No? Good. Wolfgang, you'll be with Aksel on a mantlet behind the ladders. Otto and Alphonse, you two will be on ladders in the 5th Royal Levy Regiment, led by Baron Sir Tyran, attacking the south-western wall. Jurgen, you'll be on the battering ram. Francis, you'll be on a mantlet with the Stone Knights, a regiment of men-at-arms led by Sir Gunther, Lord Alten's cousin. You'll be in the back with the billmen, since the front ranks are poleax wielders. Everyone clear on what we're doing?"

"Yes!" the boys replied enthusiastically.

"Good. I recommend you take advantage of the services provided in the camp. Get some new equipment, your weapons sharpened, armor repaired. Oh, and if you need to relieve stress before the battle, something to calm your nerves, there's plenty of wine and whores."

"There's—what?" Otto blurted out.

The others seemed surprised as well.

"Welcome to the army, kids," Aksel laughed.

"So, uh—where can I find the—" Alphonse began, before getting cut off.

"No, you lecher, you're not going to an army camp brothel. At least act with some dignity," Otto chastised.

"Oh, come on. We can make you a man." Alphonse grinned, nudging Otto.

"Will you guys stop? We should all get some rest and leave the commanders alone," Jurgen added, being the voice of reason.

***

The night of the siege had finally come. Wolfgang nervously gripped his poleax as he waited behind a wicker and wood mantlet for the sign to advance. Sweat dripped from his chin onto his voiders. Aksel put his hand on Wolfgang's shoulder.

"Nervous, lambkin?" Aksel smiled. "I was too my first battle." He took a swig of a tankard.

"But you're not now?" Wolfgang asked in a soft voice.

"Of course I am. That's why I'm drinking!" He laughed. "Here, drink the rest."

He handed Wolfgang the tankard. Wolfgang downed all of it, coughing.

"Uh, what's in that?" he asked.

"Beer. Or at least, that's what the merchant told me!"

A distant horn interrupted Aksel's laugh. Several trumpets blasted through the army. The enemy spotted the siege towers; it was time to begin the assault.

Five men protected each mantlet, with five in the front pushing it and five behind. Wolfgang was next to Aksel in the front rank. They were the furthest to the right. They pushed the mantlet, its wheels squeaking as they ushered forward. Wolfgang noticed the mantlet in front of them had some levies present for the siege. They wore the Alten colors on their waffenrock—red and yellow, arranged in four vertical stripes. Many of the men-at-arms wore those colors as tabards around their waists or cloth strips around their arms.

As they approached the castle, Wolfgang saw torches lighting up on the walls, with Alliance men shouting insults at the attackers.

Insulting their mothers, insulting their wives—claiming they were unfaithful while away fighting, telling them to give up. Although demoralizing for some, those insults didn't bother Wolfgang.

Rocks from the trebuchet fired into the keep over his head. The attack seemed to progress well; the enemy certainly wasn't prepared. But as they drew closer to the walls—at least one hundred feet away—the defenders opened with an arrow storm. They lit each arrow to illuminate the field and help both the crossbows and cannons find their targets. Hundreds of arrows rained down on them. Thud after thud echoed on the mantlet as arrows impacted the thin wicker and wood, protecting them from an untimely and painful death. One karl behind Wolfgang, wearing modest chain mail armor and an open-faced helm, took an arrow to his neck. With a whimper, he fell to the ground. Wolfgang looked back at him, eyes wide. Any of those arrows could hit his neck next.

"Look ahead, lambkin! Focus on the fight ahead, not the fallen behind!" Aksel shouted.

The battlefield grew louder with shouts and screams of pain. Even more so when Wolfgang heard the most dreaded sound—a cannon firing.

As Wolfgang looked through a small hole in the wicker, he saw the mantlet in front of him—the one with the levies—get blown to shreds. The fire from the arrows overhead gave just enough light for him to see the horrific scene—men's appendages and insides flying, along with pieces of wood and wicker. In a perfect shot, ten men were dead in an instant. The smell of blood filled the air. Fear gripped Wolfgang like a vice, his knees buckled, his cheeks were moist with sweat. He had seen killing before—when Uwe died, when he lost his family. He'd fought before, in the tournament. But it was nothing like that. War was something he never could've truly imagined or prepared for.

"Keep it together," Aksel commanded as he put a hand on Wolfgang's shoulder. "Just keep pushing. Don't stop, don't think. You push, you kill, or they kill you. Don't think. Don't give up."

"Y-yes," was all Wolfgang could muster as he pushed onward.

They made it to a patch of long dry grass, nearly seventy feet from the walls. The cannon blasts had fallen silent as the bowmen in the siege towers moved within range. Another arrow storm rained on the battlefield. As the enemy bowmen fired several volleys a minute, each one came with a sense of terror.

Multiple arrows planted in the front of the mantlet, one breaking through the wicker, the point of the arrowhead only an inch away from Wolfgang's eye. They passed corpses and wounded men, many screaming for help as arrows stuck out of their legs and arms.

Wolfgang's eyes felt irritated, and the air became heavy, restricting his breath. Then he realized the grass field was on fire. It hadn't rained in some time, and the flaming arrows lit the grass on fire. They kept pushing onward, through the fire and flame. Wounded men burning alive in the inferno cried for help, but there was nothing they could do. Wolfgang tried his best to ignore the screams and focus on moving forward.

***

Meanwhile, Otto and Alphonse jogged next to each other, holding a large ladder above their heads. Otto gripped the ladder tight as they ran forward across the battlefield and through the arrow storms. Men holding the ladders fell to the arrows, and others ran from the ranks behind to replace them. An arrow bounced off Otto's bascinet, sending chills down his spine.

They moved quickly and covered the entire length of the battlefield in no time. Otto was tired by the time they reached the walls, but a rush of adrenaline kept him going as they rested the ladders against the wooden bailey. As levies and karls climbed the ladders, the defenders shot crossbows, threw rocks, and dropped cauldrons of hot sand on them. As Otto took his position on the ladder, a man fell from the top with a bolt stuck in his neck. Another fell, burning alive from the sand going in between his armor and

The Wolf's Song

filling his pores. Otto looked at Alphonse on the ladder team next to him. As their eyes met, the clear terror they both felt was clear. No longer was Alphonse the cocky lecher, nor Otto the intelligent scholar. In war, they were nothing but terrified boys.

Otto gripped the ladder rungs and climbed, more sweat pouring down his face with every rung. The ladder next to Alphonse fell over as the defenders pushed it down. Men fell from the battlements while others clashed their swords with the alliance bowmen. Otto was almost at the top. All he could do was pray.

***

Elsewhere, Jurgen pushed the battering ram with several levies. The battering ram was merely a large tree stump with a point carved into the end, suspended by ropes. Above them was a roof and a small mantlet in front that protected them from the hail of falling arrows. They had fastened leather to the roof to prevent the wood from setting fire. Had it not been for the siege tower keeping the cannons pinned, they likely wouldn't have made it that far.

They were finally at the gate of the castle. Jurgen was already exhausted from pushing this heavy vehicle whilst in full plate armor. Crossbows and longbows fired from above, and men threw rocks at them. The roof was being battered hard as the defenders desperately tried to stop them from breaking through the wooden gate.

"Heave!" the men shouted in unison, signaling to pull back the ram. "Ram!" They shouted as they forced it forward.

It slammed against the gate. They repeated the process two, three, four times. It seemed like they'd never get through. Finally, a crack formed in the gate.

"We're almost through!" Jurgen shouted.

Two more hits of the ram and the door fell in, leaving only splinters left on the hinges. At the same time, the enemy dropped a large boulder on the battering ram, caving in the roof. The man in front of Jurgen had his head caved in as the rock and debris fell on top of him. The man just in front of him, at the very front of the ram, became trapped under the broken supports. Jurgen was shocked. He was only a couple of inches away from being trapped as well. The billmen and poleax wielders behind the battering ram—whose plate armor protected them from the arrows—charged into the castle. As Francis stepped by, Jurgen placed his hand on his shoulder.

"Godspeed. Come back to us," he muttered.

Francis nodded, made The Sign of the Cross and kept moving.

***

Wolfgang had just broken through the flaming grass field and was close to the walls. He approached from the northwestern side of the wall. The bailey finally came into view. The ladder-bearers had just begun climbing.

"Come on, lambkin! Climb a ladder, get up there quick! Don't want to miss your heroic moment!" Aksel laughed.

Wolfgang followed, leaving the protection of the mantlet behind. He ran into the ranks of troops filing in, waiting to climb. Rocks and arrows showered them. Before long, it was his turn.

Wolfgang grasped the rungs of the ladder, his heart racing. He panted as he ascended the ladder. He kept his eyes forward as he climbed, but near the top, he looked up. There were two men above him, still climbing. A storm of flaming arrows fired above them. The dancing flames reflected in Wolfgang's eyes.

He stared up at the broken moon, taking in what may be his last moments. It was in its first quarter, although the dark half could still be barely made out. He tried counting the broken pieces forming the always visible ring around Nyrene—anything to keep him from climbing the rest of the way. There were so many moonshards, counting them all may be impossible. The man below him tugged at his leather hose and shouted to keep going. Yes, climbing up the ladder almost meant certain death. But staying there also meant death. No path led to life. He did as he must and kept climbing.

As Wolfgang reached the top, he stepped onto the bailey. The bodies of his allies covered it. Levies and karls laid side by side, their blood pooling on the soft wooden planks of the wall. He stepped over the bodies and got behind the mob of fighting men. He took his poleax off his back and gripped it tight as he waited for an opening.

A bill stabbed the levy in front of him in the eye. The blade went deep into his skull. His body went limp and fell to the ground. Wolfgang made eye contact with the alliance soldier in front of him. Quickly, he pointed his poleax at his foe. He pushed off with his left foot and thrusted his poleax into his adversary.

Wolfgang tried to close the distance, but lost his footing, and ended up thrusting lower than he planned. The alliance soldier thrust his bill forward as well. It ground against Wolfgang's kettle helm, leaving a small mark along the top. Wolfgang's poleax penetrated the man's leg.

The man fell to the ground, writhing in pain. Without thinking, Wolfgang pulled out his poleax and swung the hammer side down at the man. He looked up in shock as Wolfgang's weapon slammed against his face, causing his jaw to tear from his skull. His tongue flopped out and blood rushed from the open hole in his face.

Another alliance soldier stabbed Wolfgang with his bill, penetrating his gambeson and going into his side. Wolfgang grabbed the bill's staff to prevent the soldier from gaining control of his weapon, and with his other hand, lifted his poleax high, bringing the ax side down on his shoulder. The soldier screamed in pain, falling limp, and Wolfgang pulled the bill out of his side, his labored breath getting faster with every second, and prepared to keep fighting.

Francis charged behind the plate-armored men-at-arms into the courtyard of the castle. The Owl Alliance troops hid behind makeshift palisades, arranged around the gate, completely blocking off access to the courtyard. They had two ranks of men with readied crossbows, with billmen just behind. As the men-at-arms charged, the crossbows unleashed. The bolts had no problem cutting through the heavy plate armor, which protected them from the longbow arrows just before. The first rank of men-at-arms fell to the ground, and their allies stepped over their fresh corpses to continue the attack.

The first rank of Owl Alliance crossbow men stepped back to reload, and a second rank moved forward. When a sergeant gave them the order, they fired, littering their enemies with bolts. Another rank of men-at-arms fell. They knew they couldn't reload fast enough to hit the third rank, so they fell back and allowed their billmen to enter the fray.

Men-at-arms at the front rank slammed into the palisades, the force of the men behind them pushing them forward. The alliance billmen stabbed and thrusted at the troops, but it was tough to get through their armor. The billmen's primary goal was to keep the plate armored soldiers at bay whilst others readied their crossbows. Still, they only killed a few men by stabbing between the armor's weak points, like the armpits. One man-at-arms swung his poleax high, right into the head of an alliance billman. The ax split the kettle helm and was stuck in his brain matter. As the man-at-arms tried to pull it out, another alliance soldier stuck a bill through the gap between his great helm and his cuirass.

Once the crossbows were ready, they'd stick through the ranks of billmen and fire over the palisades into the attacking troops. They'd then fall back to reload, and billmen would fill the gaps in the formation.

Scores of dead soldiers laid at the foot of the palisades. Ordinarily, that many losses would warrant a retreat, but the men loyal to their lord knew the siege was too important to lose.

Francis climbed over the growing wall of dead men. Standing at the top, he reached the front rank, just above the Owl Alliance soldiers—even with his small stature. As a crossbowman entered behind a billman and aimed his bolt right at Francis, who brought his bill down into the man's neck.

Blood spurted from the man's mouth. The blood flowing from his neck bubbled as he struggled to breathe. Francis tugged hard to free his bill from the enemy troop's neck, then turned to the man in front.

He leapt down, closing the distance quickly, with his bill pointed to an enemy. Francis caught an alliance soldier in the chest, then stood up and pulled the bill out as he did. His comrades hopped down as well. Finally, on the other slide of the palisades, all they had to do was push through and break the enemy ranks.

The Owl Alliance billmen stepped back, their line breaking into a disorganized mob. The crossbowmen fell into the courtyard, trying to get some distance to fire another shot. Francis pushed forward with his comrades. The alliance troops' bills couldn't penetrate his thick armor, and there were few obvious weak points because of his armor hiding his condition. Behind them, allied levies disassembled the palisades and moved their allies' bodies so the rest of the army could approach.

Wolfgang fought through several ranks of enemy troops on the walls. The remaining enemies laid down their weapons and surrendered. Aksel beckoned to climb down the bailey and move into the courtyard. They needed to push through the rest of the defenders and besiege the keep.

The courtyard was littered with bodies. In front of the keep were several ranks of Owl Alliance troops. As Wolfgang made his way to the battle, a group of alliance troops came from the other side of the courtyard to attack. Strangely, they had almost no armor, but wore blue capes to signify which side they were on. One man, wielding a sickle, ran up to Wolfgang and swung it. Wolfgang easily countered the attack and thrust his poleax into the man's chest. The others were just as easily dispatched.

"Why don't they have armor or proper weapons?" Wolfgang asked.

"They aren't soldiers. The enemy lord is desperate. He's sending his stable hands and cooks out to battle," Aksel replied.

Another alliance troop ran up to Wolfgang, armed with nothing but a pitchfork. Wolfgang responded instinctively, avoiding the strike by ducking low, then rising with his poleax to catch the soldier's neck. Only then did he realize it was just a young boy, a couple of years younger than he was. He was likely a stable hand or cook's assistant, maybe a blacksmith's son. A young boy forced to fight for his losing lord. The thought was revolting. Wolfgang couldn't hold it in anymore, and puked.

"Alright, lambkin," Aksel said as he put his hand on Wolfgang's shoulder. "That's enough. The others will take the keep."

As the battle wound down, Lord Oppenstein announced his surrender. Wolfgang ran from the castle to a nearby stream. Meanwhile, Jurgen searched the castle courtyard for his friends. He carefully and nervously checked bodies. He found Francis near the keep, then Alphonse and Otto. They sat against the castle wall. Alphonse had his hand on Otto's shoulder. Otto stared at this right hand, which was shaking uncontrollably. The two approached them.

"Wolfgang... have you seen Wolfgang?" Jurgen asked.

"I just... why won't it stop?" Otto whispered, unaware of Jurgen's presence.

Jurgen looked around frantically.

"Hey, Aksel is that way. We should ask him," Francis suggested.

Jurgen did just that and discovered Wolfgang had gone to the nearby stream. He ushered the others to follow him, having to physically shake Otto from his trance.

They found Wolfgang, washing his hands in the stream. The boys approached him, watching as he frantically tried to clean the dried blood off.

"I keep scrubbing, but the blood just won't come off," he muttered.

Jurgen kneeled next to him. "I don't see any blood," he mumbled.

"But it's everywhere."

"Wolfgang," Alphonse began. "It's over." He lifted his hand, balled into a fist. "Come on, we're comrades, remember? We can do anything if we're together. All of us."

Wolfgang's eyes widened. Suddenly, the blood was washed from his hands. He looked over at Alphonse, smiled, and they bumped fists.

"Yeah, yeah. We'll be okay."

"We should find Martin and regroup with the karls," Francis suggested.

"Yes, we should," Jurgen agreed. He walked over to Otto and grasped his shaking hand. "Everything will be okay. Let's go."

"Oh, yeah—right. We should regroup, like Francis said," Otto agreed.

The boys set back out to the castle. They regrouped with the karls and received new orders. They helped clean up and bury the bodies. The castle's priest, along with Lord Oppenstein, assembled both armies outside of the castle at the mass gravesite for a eulogy, sending the troops to their judgment. The battle was over. But the war remained.

The Postal Service

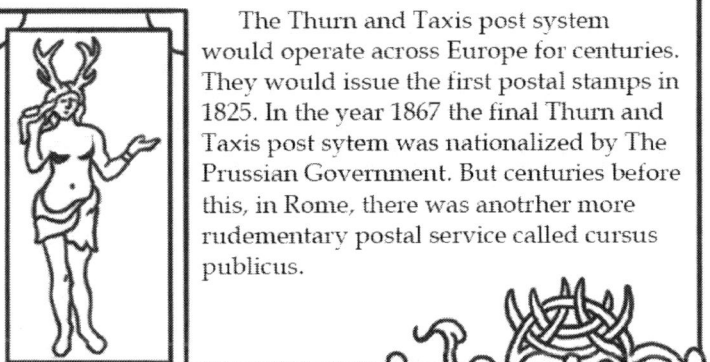

Lore: In the year 1479, the very first postal service was founded by Richtor Von Taxis. It was a guild of couriers known as The Taxis Post. Other couriers who didn't want to join this courier's guild were losing out on profit, so many of them came together to form The Eagle Post in 1483 and The Free Courier's in 1486. The postal offices are represented by horns on the maps.

Homage: If you wanted to send a letter or package in Medieval Europe, you'd have to send it via a servant, freind, or treveling caravan. There was no standardization or postal services, so you would need to trust the person you hired and hope your package was delivered. The noble houses of Taxis and Thurn owned private courier services. In 1489 Franz Von Taxis would become the postal master to Holy Emporer Maximilian I and later to Philip I of Spain in 1504. Von Taxis would carry government and private mail in both countries, forming the first ever publicly funded mail service.

The Thurn and Taxis post system would operate across Europe for centuries. They would issue the first postal stamps in 1825. In the year 1867 the final Thurn and Taxis post sytem was nationalized by The Prussian Government. But centuries before this, in Rome, there was anotrher more rudementary postal service called cursus publicus.

Chapter 10

Wolfgang stood alone, surrounded by fire and smoke. At his feet were the decaying bodies of hundreds of men. He looked around frantically, trying to find anyone alive. Yet, there was nothing. From the dark, he heard a menacing growl—like an enormous wolf's. Its growl grew ever closer, sounding like it came from every direction. Wolfgang swung his head in every direction, desperately looking for the noise's source.

Wolfgang awoke covered in sweat and panting. It was a dream. He was still in his sleeping bag next to a campfire. He was in the karl's camp, just outside of Oppenstein Castle. Wolfgang looked at his right wrist and stared at the bead bracelet Elise gave him. He fiddled with the beads before Aksel's loud voice walked up and down the camp.

"Wake up, get ready to move! We have orders! Gather your things, load up the wagons!" he repeated.

The karlband prepared their things, as did the camp followers, and they headed south. The boys walked at the front of the formation, with Marin and Aksel, who both rode horses.

"You five have had two weeks of rest since the battle ended. Feeling ready?" Martin asked.

"Not sure I'd call burying bodies and disassembling the camp, rest," Otto muttered.

"Was that complaining I heard? Does someone want latrine duty?" Martin asked.

"Uh, no, sir!" Otto responded nervously.

"Where are we going?" Jurgen asked.

"After word spread of the victory at Oppenstein, Lord Alten has had little trouble mustering his levy. Several karls have joined him as well. They were moving to assault Taltenburg, but the Owl Alliance sent a force to intercept them. As far as I'm aware, neither side has engaged the other yet, but they're stuck in a standoff over some valley. This means he can't advance on Taltenburg."

"Wait, are we going to siege Taltenburg?" Wolfgang asked.

"With fifty men?" Martin laughed. "It would take at least a thousand to breach those walls. No, we're going to relieve pressure on Lord Alten's army. We're going to cut the enemy's supply lines. Food and raw materials travel from the village of Suzereck to Taltenburg, and from there it's sent to the alliance army standings in the way of Lord Alten. There's only one highway and a handful of small roads that lead to the valley, so we're going to head south on the most traveled highway and ambush their supply caravan. Without food, we will force the alliance army to retreat, and then we can besiege Taltenburg."

"Oh wow, that's a smart plan!" Wolfgang said.

"It's basic tactics. An army fights on its stomach."

"We gotta ambush them in a heavily wooded area too, to make it easier to conceal our force," Aksel added.

"Hm... I wonder if we'll see any more of those nymphs we saw before," Wolfgang said.

"Doubtful. They don't like large numbers of people. If they do show up, they'll probably attack us," Otto added.

"Woah, you guys saw forest nymphs? Those are rare," Jurgen commented.

"Nymphs aren't the only animals you have to worry about in the woods," Aksel began. "There are wolves, too. Big ones. Wolves so big they stand as tall as a man. They're called dire wolves. And you know,"—he looked over at Wolfgang—"they love to eat little lambs just like you!"

He put his hands up and made a growling face, trying to scare Wolfgang. The group stared at him for a moment before bursting out in laughter.

"Huh, I don't get it?" Wolfgang said, the only one not laughing.

***

They marched south for several days before reaching a large wooden statue. The statue was at least two stories tall, rising above the forest, and was carved to look like a bald man holding a cross.

"It's the monument to St. Iotodois. We'll stage our ambush just a little further south of here," Martin said. "Aksel, let's get ready. Have the camp followers stay up the road and out of sight. We need to be fast since we don't know when the next caravan will arrive."

The karls dug trenches and set up traps on the side of the highway. They dug small holes and covered them with leaves so men could hide inside and be at the front of the attack. On the highway itself, they dug out a trench and covered it with dirt, supported by loose wood, so if a horse walked over it, it would collapse. The others would hide in the woods on both sides of the road, as the ground seeped into slight hills on each side. Thus, they set the trap.

Wolfgang was one of the men in the holes, as he wielded a polearm, which made him a perfect shock troop. Between each polearm fighter was a crossbowman, and together they'd surprise the caravan before the rest of the karls overwhelmed them. Wolfgang smeared his face with dirt and used a hemp net wrapped around his kettle helm to conceal the metal with leaves and sticks. None of the men would be visible from the road.

The attack wouldn't happen for some time. They waited endlessly in position, not wanting to sing songs or talk too loudly as anyone approaching may hear them. So, they sat silently for hours. Wolfgang counted the rocks in his hole, and when he finally counted them all, he looked up at the sky through a small opening in his leaf roof to count the moonshards stretching across the heavens. The moon was no longer visible during the cycle, but the ever-present ring was a constant reminder of the moon's split.

***

Three long, boring days passed by before the caravan finally arrived. The sound of wagons, horses, and marching songs signaled it was the time.

Everyone fell into position and waited anxiously, happy that something was finally going to happen. Wolfgang only had a small slit in between the branches concealing him to see the caravan passing by. A horse neighed, and its hooves stepped just in front of him. It was the pointman for the caravan guards. Following him were many men, mostly walking, wearing Owl Alliance colors. Several wagons were also present, although tarps obscured their contents. There were at least forty men and seven wagons.

Deeper in the woods, Jurgen—who was in the rear and at the highest vantage point with the other bowmen—drew back his longbow and slowed his breathing. Everyone was prepared to fight, all donned in mud and leaves to help conceal them.

One man, armed with a bill and wearing simple armor with a kettle helm, cast his eyes down as he walked. Suddenly, he stopped. The man noticed something odd about the ditch next to the road. He looked closer, and he saw the unnerving sight of glowing red eyes. He was looking directly at Wolfgang, who gripped his poleax tightly. Before the alliance man could do or say anything, the horse at the front of the caravan stepped into their trap, falling into the deep trench, and taking its rider with it.

The crossbowman in the hole next to Wolfgang fired his bolt, piercing the chest of one of the alliance troops. At that moment, Aksel sounded a horn, and the karls leaped into action. Wolfgang jumped out of his hole, through the thin mesh of sticks and leaves that previously concealed him, with the point of his poleax aimed right at the alliance troop.

He penetrated the neck of the alliance guard; the man falling with a stunned look forever locked on his face. Wolfgang yanked his weapon out of the enemy's neck and swung it from above, ax side down, at another terrified guard. The ax tore through his leather jack and owl waffenrock, cutting deep into his chest.

Another alliance guard charged Wolfgang from behind with a bill. In response, Wolfgang turned and attacked using the point at the bottom end of his poleax staff. He crossed blades with the alliance billman and forced the bill down, giving him the opportunity to sidestep and stab the billman in the leg.

The man fell to the ground, bleeding profusely from his thigh. Wolfgang had severed an artery, and the man would be dead in mere moments. One of the caravan drivers, who wore only a tunic and no alliance colors, grabbed a loaded crossbow from behind the seat of his wagon and aimed it at Wolfgang. Jurgen, who was carefully picking off enemies with his bow from afar, noticed and launched an arrow at the driver.

The arrow hit the driver in the throat, and he fell to the ground. Jurgen then drew back his bowstring and fired at another alliance troop. Although firing so close to his comrades was dangerous, Martin explicitly ordered the bowmen to do so to whittle down the enemy's numbers.

A man in thick plate armor and an Owl Alliance tabard draped around his torso stepped out of the back of one wagon and approached Wolfgang. He wore a great helm with a flip up visor and was armed with a poleax.

"You with the demon eyes. Is this attack your doing?" he asked.

"Tsk, as if. I'm just a fighter. Also, what's with this 'demon eyes' stuff?" Wolfgang asked.

"I'm the guard captain for this caravan. Well, fighter, your men have caused a lot of trouble. They call me Killian the Red Bearded, a warrior from Briefle. I will defeat you, demon warrior."

"You're a strange one, Red Beard. But alright."

"It looks like my men already gave you a run through, too. This should be easy!" He pointed at the bloodstain on Wolfgang's abdomen.

"That was from a while ago."

Wolfgang placed his right foot forward and bent his knee, then placed his poleax down near his thigh, ax side up. Red Beard bent his right knee and stretched his left foot behind him, holding his poleax near his temple, hammer side up.

Wolfgang swung first, but Red Beard was prepared. He sidestepped, then planted his foot down on top of Wolfgang's poleax, holding it to the ground. Red Beard then swung his right at Wolfgang's head.

Wolfgang jumped back and pulled his poleax from underneath Red Beard's foot. His opponent's poleax came down, hit his kettle helm, and left a small gash in it, but didn't penetrate it. Wolfgang jumped forward, thrusting the point of his poleax at Red Beard. He got a powerful hit on his breastplate, although it only caused Red Beard to stagger back, and didn't penetrate the thick armor.

Wolfgang seized the initiative and moved in close before Red Beard could take up another guard. He used his body weight to push Red Beard back, then grabbed the man's visor, and pulled him to the ground. He then stepped on his chest so he couldn't get up and pulled his dagger from its scabbard.

"Wait, you scoundrel!" Red Beard shouted.

But Wolfgang was in a battle trance. He lifted his opponent's visor and stabbed him in the eye, ensuring the blade went deep into the skull. As he did, a nearby horse screamed.

Wolfgang stood up to see the surrounding battle ended. Nausea swelled inside him. He leaned on his poleax and puked. Jurgen emerged from the woods and walked up to him, placing his hand on his back.

"You alright? You've done this every battle," he said. The boys soon found them, covered in blood and mud.

"W-well, glad that's over," Otto stated.

"I am glad everyone is okay," Francis added.

"Come on, ladies, help clean up the bodies," Aksel shouted. "Once we've repaired the road, some camp followers will take the supplies to Lord Alten's army."

***

In the following weeks, the karlband ambushed many supply caravans leaving Taltenburg. They even ambushed caravans coming from the village of Suzereck. The Owl Alliance tried to bolster their guards, but it didn't help. Their men became afraid of the karls stalking the woodlands and many refused to even attempt resupplying the army. After three months, in the month of Leo, the alliance finally retreated—only after many deserted due to lack of provisions.

The time to assault Taltenburg had dawned. The karlband returned to Oppenstein for supplies and rest. Whilst they were resting, Lord Alten's men under Sir Suruck constructed the siege camp and preparing for the upcoming battle. In the month of Aquila, the month signifying the eagle, the karlband would have their toughest battle yet.

Traveling in The Medieval Age

Traveling in the 15th century was not as easy as it would be today. Without any paved or maintained roads, most people in Europe would travel alond ancient highways built by The Romans. Smaller roads may be maintained by local villages. Horses were expensive and hard to maintain, so people would commonly travel by foot. This means a journey that today may only take a few hours could take days back then. It would have been uncommon to carry any kind of map. To find your way you'd ask locals how to get to your destination. The most common journey was that of the pilramage, which everyone- regardless of class- was expected to partake in once in their life.

Chapter 11

Rain poured on a dark night as the boys entered the command tent in green wool cloaks. In a show of kindness to his men, Lord Alten issued the cloaks to the army to shield them from the rain. Martin, Sir Suruck, Aksel, and several other commanders from the army stood around a table discussing their plan of attack.

"You five are here. Good," Martin said. "I need a volunteer."

"Oh, I'll do it—whatever it is!" Wolfgang responded.

"Good, you're going out with the men for a hasty assault." Martin folded his arms. "This is the plan. A large stone wall surrounds Taltenburg. But we can't worry about that until we take the outworks. Outside of the city walls are several homes and shops that make up a smaller village. They have turned these buildings into defenses and dug a large trench around the entire city, except for one area, our only point of attack. Here they've built trenches for their crossbowmen and musketeers, and have bunkers for the five canons they've placed on the outworks. Fortunately, the rain makes gunpowder wet, so the muskets won't be an issue. However, the cannons in the bunkers will be. If we can get past that, then we need to navigate through the village and clear out alliance troops. If we can take the outworks, then we can begin plans to take the wall."

"When are we going to attack? Wolfgang asked.

"Right now. The sooner the better with a hasty assault. The levies and karls are already gathering. Calvary would be of little use, since they built the trenches and bunkers into the side of a hill—the entire city is actually elevated. Anyway, go get your armor on. You'll fight with the Chor Village Levies."

Wolfgang donned his armor, throwing the wool cloak over himself to stay dry, and met with the rest of the men. After a couple of hours of preparation, they headed out through the rain toward the outworks. A wooden mantlet protected Wolfgang, and he pushed it with four other men through the mud. Once they got closer to the enemy's fortifications, they heard a loud boom. Then another and another. Was it thunder from the storm? No, it was a different storm. It was cannon fire, followed by crossbows.

The ground shook as plumes of dirt exploded around him as he pushed the mantlet forward. It was dark, and the cannons had trouble aiming, but they still hit a mantlet or two, killing several men. A huge bolt of lightning shot across the sky, illuminating the battlefield for a moment. Then a cannon fired, and its ball flew directly at Wolfgang.

The cannonball easily tore through the mantlet and hit the ground just behind them. Wolfgang fell in the mud, his ears ringing. He rolled onto his stomach and looked at the men with him, seeing only death.

Guts and arms were strewn across the ground, and one man, barely clinging to life, grasped the stub of his leg, like he couldn't believe the rest of it was gone. To Wolfgang's right, another mantlet pushed forward. The man on the leftmost end peered out to see what was in front, only to catch a crossbow bolt through the cheek. He fell, writhing in pain, bleeding into the mud.

Wolfgang tried to stand. As he did, he felt a sharp pain in his side. A piece of wood had penetrated his gambeson and protruded from his torso. He grabbed the wood and tried to pull it out, but it was far too painful. Wolfgang growled, fighting through the pain as he stood. He rushed over to the passing mantlet that was one man down and joined them.

Bolts covered the mantlet as they finally got close to the first trench. Several others were near the trench as well.

"Push it all the way to the trench, then we kill those bastards up close!" a levy instructed.

They pushed the mantlet into the trench. It fell on top of a couple of alliance troops. The others dropped their crossbows and unsheathed daggers, preparing for melee combat. At that point, several others reached the trench as well. Wolfgang pulled his poleax off his back and leaped into the trench. He thrust the point of his poleax into an alliance soldier's chest, while the other charged him with a dagger.

He stepped back and swung his poleax from above, hammer side down, and destroyed the alliance crossbowman's face. The levies reaching the trench stabbed and thrust their bills, as did the karls with their bills and longswords. Before long, they cleared the trench out of enemy troops. Despite that, they endured heavy losses just getting there. Since their options were to fight up the hill through the trenches or climb directly up a steep incline to the next trench, they didn't have the numbers to keep going and they knew that, so a desperate attack would be all that would work. Despite that, many of Wolfgang's comrades spoke of retreat. He hoisted himself onto the trench wall and looked at everyone.

"Hey, we need to keep moving! We can't go back now!" Wolfgang shouted.

"Who in Hades are you to tell us what to do?" a levy shouted.

"Listen, we lost too many of our comrades to fall back now. The way I see it, we need to climb that hill and take their battlements. Are we not warriors?" he shouted.

Many of the men looked at each other, questioning what to do next.

"I said, are we not warriors?"

"Why should we follow you into battle?" a karl asked.

"Because-because I'm the Crimson Wolf!"

Lightning flashed in the sky, and Wolfgang looked onward with determination.

"Follow me, or die cowards, unworthy of your lord!"

Wolfgang grabbed the piece of wood protruding from his torso and growled through the pain as he yanked it out. The rain washed away his blood, but it still left another stain on his gambeson. He then turned and walked up to the steep incline. Alliance men looked down at him, preparing crossbows.

"They don't intend to climb, do they?" one Alliance troop asked.

"If they do, we just need to shoot them down," another replied.

"I will win, no matter what. I have a promise to keep," Wolfgang growled as he lifted his poleax and stuck the point at the bottom of the staff into the mud.

Then he hoisted himself up the incline.

Other men followed suit, using their bills, swords, daggers—anything sharp enough to help them climb the hill.

As they climbed, dumbfounded alliance troops opened fire at them. They hit one levy with a bolt in the leg and tumbled down the hill, rolling into several other men, causing them to fall. A karl received a bolt right to the head and fell into the mud. More men were killed and wounded, but they were determined to make it to the trench. There was no going back.

Wolfgang stopped on a rock and used it to hold himself in place. He was almost at the trench. He looked up at an alliance soldier just above, pointing his crossbow right at Wolfgang. Lightning flashed across the dark sky, illuminating Wolfgang and making his eyes glow. The sight sent chills down the alliance troop's spine, his hands shaking as he pulled the trigger. The bolt skidded off Wolfgang's kettle helm, leaving a small gash.

Wolfgang hoisted himself up the rest of the way and was the first in the trench. He swung his poleax as he landed in the trench, killing the terrified alliance troop. Other alliance soldiers looked on in horror and disbelief. One unsheathed his dagger and charged at Wolfgang. Wolfgang responded by thrusting the staff point at the bottom of his poleax into the troop's jaw.

Several levies stabbed their bills into the alliance soldiers as they descended into the trench. After a few moments of heavy fighting, they finished dispatching the alliance soldiers. Their bodies lay in mud, the rain washing away their blood. Wolfgang stood on the trench wall and addressed the men.

"Which one of you is a levy sergeant?" Wolfgang asked.

"I am!" a man replied.

"Take some men and capture the cannon emplacements. The rest of you will come with me. We need to clear out the rest of the outworks," Wolfgang ordered.

The men nodded and followed suit.

Wolfgang led the pack of forty men toward the small village that had turned into a war zone. Several Owl Alliance billmen all arranged in a loose square formation in the village street met them. Wolfgang and the others rushed the billmen, lightning cracking in the sky.

Wolfgang swung his poleax down at an angle, catching a billman in the neck. The other men fought the alliance troops, thrusting their bills and fighting as hard as they could. Many comrades fell, but as one man died, another would step up to replace him.

Wolfgang killed man after man, his body covered in so much blood and mud even the heavy rain couldn't wash it all away. One billman stabbed Wolfgang in the shoulder, barely penetrating his voiders. The chain mail broke enough for the point of his blade to stick into his arm, but not enough for it to cause major damage. Wolfgang cried out in pain, but his pained yell turned to a ferocious growl. He looked at the billman's terrified face. The billman was young, probably around the same age as Wolfgang. But he was his opponent. Wolfgang brought his poleax up and thrusted the point into the billman's chest, penetrating the leathers jack and waffenrock.

After fighting for a few minutes more, the remaining alliance billmen fell back in a hasty retreat. Wolfgang raised his poleax to the air and shouted at his comrades to keep pushing into the village. They did just that, cutting down the fleeing billmen and attacking any lingering troops.

As Wolfgang made his way through the street, a man in plate armor wielding a poleax ran at him from the darkness of an alleyway. Wolfgang raised his poleax, holding it horizontally across his chest to defend the incoming blow. The plate armored man ran into Wolfgang and pushed him into the closed door of a nearby house. Their weight was enough to break the thin door, and he pinned Wolfgang against the ground.

He wrapped his arms around the armored soldier's arms, holding him in place. Wolfgang knew if the man could get to his dagger, it would be over.

Wolfgang kicked and rolled, but the weight of the enemy was too great. A comrade levy passed the house and stopped to investigate, presumably planning on taking the armor of a dead soldier to sell it.

As he got close, he Wolfgang pinned and leaped into action. The levy placed the staff of his bill around the armored man's neck and pulled, giving Wolfgang enough room to roll over. The armored soldier broke free of his loose bind, but as he tried to stand,

Wolfgang kicked him down and got on top of him. He then opened the man's visor, unsheathed his dagger, and stabbed him deep in the left eye. The man cried out in pain, but his cries lasted for only a moment, his life not taking to leave. As Wolfgang stood, he heard shuffling in the dark.

On the other side of the room was the silhouette of a figure, moving around, presumably preparing to attack. Wolfgang lifted his poleax, lighting illuminating him and his glowing eyes, as he swung at the figure. He heard screaming as he swung. Blood pooled on the wooden floor of the small house, and, with another crack of lightning, the figure's identity was revealed.

It was a young woman, likely in her late twenties. She wore a modest villager dress and held no weapons. Then he noticed an even worse sight—two children hiding under a table.

"M-mom?" one child, a girl, whispered.

Wolfgang stepped back in shock. He thought it was an enemy. No, he was sure of it. Who else would crawl around in the dark? He put his hand to his head, trying to justify what he'd done. But it was no simple mistake. The children ran over to their mother, trying to shake her awake.

"This is your fault!" the other child, a boy, shouted at Wolfgang. "You demon!"

The boy ran over to a hoe leaning against the wall and tried to pick it up. It was too heavy for him to lift, but he held on to it all the same. "I'll kill you!"

"I-I, but—" was all Wolfgang could say.

"Hey, we need to keep running them down. We must thin their numbers before they reach the wall," the levy shouted.

"R-right," Wolfgang replied.

He stepped back out into the rain, and tried to follow the others, but collapsed. A sharp pain permeated his side as blood pooled. Only then did he realize he'd been bleeding the entire time. The wound from the shrapnel must've been deeper than he thought.

Suddenly the autumn rain felt cold, and his skin turned pale. He puked, before falling into his blood and bile. A nearby karl saw him writhing in pain and called a few men over to help pick him up and carry him back to camp. The attack was a success.

Chapter 12

Wolfgang stood alone atop piles of bodies. It was dark, and flame and smoke surrounded him. He called out, but no one answered except for the sound of a growling wolf. He frantically looked around for its source but saw nothing. Then, as the growling got closer, he froze with fear. Wolfgang looked forward, waiting for something to attack. It soon became clear that the sound came from behind. He twisted his head to see the jaws of a giant white wolf appear out of the darkness. It engulfed him completely and chomped down, grinding his body between its teeth.

Wolfgang awoke in a cold sweat, coughing. As he coughed, he felt the pain in his side again. He was shirtless, with bandages around his side. He was in a sleeping bag, next to many other injured men. A man, roughly in his late twenties, wearing a white and green tunic, walked up to Wolfgang.

"You've been out for a couple of days," he started.

Wolfgang put his hand over his wound.

"Don't worry, I cleaned it out with maggots when they brought you in and have been using honey to prevent infections. I'll need to change your bandage and clean the wound with honey every night, but I sewed it close, so as long as it doesn't reopen, you should be fine. I also cleaned up that wound on your shoulder. It's going to leave a scar."

"Who are you?" Wolfgang asked before falling into a coughing fit.

"I'm the camp surgeon. Usually there'd be several, but Lord Alten is a little shorthanded, I guess. I used to be the head surgeon at Oppenstein Castle, but after Lord Oppenstein saw me tending to both his men and Lord Alten's men, well, he exiled me.

"Oh, about that cough. I think you got sick during the rain. I'll come back with some coriander powder for that. Just rest up. It'll be clear weather for a while, but it's going to get cold. Meditate in the sun, relax, and you'll heal in no time."

The surgeon turned to walk away

"Wait, what's your name?" Wolfgang asked.

"Huh, no one's asked me my name. It's Uwe Tuferan," the surgeon replied.

Wolfgang sat back down, staring at the clouds passing by. Behind them was the ever-present ring of moonshards. He laid there with his only thoughts and wept when he remembered what he'd done. Not just the weight of the woman he killed, but of all the souls he'd taken, collapsed on his shoulders.

In the command tent, Martin and Sir Suruck argued over their next plan. The hasty assault had worked, but they still needed to assault the city's thick stone walls.

"I'm telling you, that won't work!" Sir Suruck shouted.

"It's our best option! You and I both know the only way we're going to get through those walls is to collapse them from underneath. We have the manpower, we can do it!" Martin shouted back.

"But can we do it in time? When winter comes, the ground will freeze, mining will slow, and we may have to abandon it all together."

"Look, we have enough resources for more than one avenue of approach. We can build your trebuchets, siege towers, and battering rams. But let's also have miners dig a tunnel underneath the walls. It will take until the end of autumn to prepare the assault, anyway. If we can get a breach, then we can attack from there, and assault the walls at the same time. We have nearly two thousand men now. We can do it."

"Fine," Sir Suruck sighed. "Since you want to do it so badly, your karlband will be in charge of the mining. I'll see about getting you some miners to help, and an engineer to help keep it from falling in on you."

"Thank you, my lord. I'll inform the men," Martin responded happily as he left the command tent.

The army's men moved the former alliance cannons and their ammo to a new location to be used as artillery. Meanwhile, soldiers constructed siege engines, and the Thorns of Roses would help the miners. The boys, wearing light tunics—except Francis, who opted to wear a thicker tunic with a head covering to hide his condition—were in the mine, using pickaxes to chip away at stone, and shovels to move loose gravel.

"I wonder how he's doing—Wolfgang," Alphonse said.

"We should check on him when we get the chance," Jurgen added.

"It's been a couple of weeks. He has to be close to recovering by now," Otto said. "Ugh, this is more exhausting than combat."

"This work is hard. Back in the Frünreich, I had to work in the castle stables. Bailing hay all day was almost as tiring," Francis complained.

"It's not all bad. A good workout at least!" Alphonse said,

chipping away at the rock with a pickaxe.

"You'd say that. You're nothing but muscle," Otto joked.

"You're just jealous because all the ladies walk past you and come to me," Alphonse joked back.

"Yeah right, you lecher. If I wasn't betrothed, I'd get tons of girls."

"Hey, what are you ladies even talking about?" Aksel shouted as he walked down the shaft. "Seriously, are you having teatime or something? What's with you nobles?"

"Come on, you don't have to be that hard on us," Jurgen said.

"As your superior, I do. Now back to work or I'll have ten lashes for the lot of ya."

The cold autumn wind sent a chill through Wolfgang as he sat on a small hill beneath a tree with browning leaves. The hill was tall enough for him to look over the siege camp and watch everyone go about their day. He looked up at the sky, staring at the broken moon. He reached his right arm toward it and looked at Elise's bracelet, still fixed around his wrist. Wolfgang wondered what would happen next. His wounds were almost healed. He didn't want to go back. The boys approached him, Otto bearing gifts.

"There you are," Otto began. "Take this. You'll get sick." He handed a thick fur coat to Wolfgang.

"Thanks, but I'm already sick," he replied.

"You look fine to me," Alphonse added.

"Maybe he isn't sick physically, but spiritually," Francis said.

"What do you mean?" Otto asked.

"It's true, he hasn't been acting right ever since the assault," Jurgen said as he kneeled next to Wolfgang.

"His soul is hurt, I can tell," Francis commented.

The Wolf's Song

"You don't have to talk like I'm not here," Wolfgang mumbled.

"Sorry, Wolfgang," Jurgen said.

"Something is clearly bothering you, bro," Alphonse said.

"Nothing is bothering me. I just... can't go back out there."

"Why's that?" a voice echoed from the bottom of the small hill.

It was Martin and Aksel.

"The surgeon said you can go back to duty. We need help digging out that mine."

"Come on, lambkin, let's get going. It's been weeks," Aksel added.

"I just... can't." Wolfgang tightened his hand into a fist.

"Oh, I know what's going on here. I've seen it plenty of times," Aksel began. "You're getting cold feet because of your wound, right? Afraid you're gonna die out there?"

"It's not that!"

"Well, it's something, and we don't have time for it," Martin shouted.

"Come on, brother. What's wrong?" Otto urged.

"I... I don't... I killed someone—she was just a mother. I thought she was an enemy, but she was just hiding. Then I thought of all the men we fought, the men we've killed... are they any different from us?"

"No, they aren't," Martin replied.

Wolfgang looked at him, shocked.

"The price of war is blood. To win, you must pay the price, in both the death of men and the death of your soul. This is the path of being a warrior."

"Even innocent people?" Wolfgang asked.

"I'm sure we killed plenty of bystanders with our trebuchet back in Oppenstein, or what about the caravan drivers we killed during the ambushes? Besides, every man here has a family, friends, desires, and a life. You just have to get used to it," Aksel said. "This is war. This is what we do. If you don't fight, you don't get paid. Aren't you always going on about that promise you made to some girl?" Aksel kneeled down and put his hand on Wolfgang's shoulder. "You gonna give up now, or fight on to keep that promise? It's up to you, lambkin. But if you won't fight, then I suggest you take the rest of your wage and go home."

"But—I..."

Wolfgang didn't know what to say. He knew if he wanted to keep his promise, he'd have to fight again, but was he able to kill his soul to do so?

"Come on, we have work to do. We'll give him some time to think," Martin said, beckoning the group to follow.

***

Morning dew collected on grass and stone around the city walls. A young levy serving the Owl Alliance, brought into service by a Teltenburg baron, was asleep on the walls. He cuddled a bill and was leaning against the battlements. A punch to the gut woke him.

"What in Hades do you think you're doing?" the soldier that punched him shouted.

The levy stood up and snapped to attention.

"S-sorry! It's cold out, and I've been doing so many shifts lately!"

"Sop it with your excuses. How old are you, boy?"

"Fifteen, sir."

"I don't know why they send us boys when we need men on these walls. Go get some food and proper rest. I'll wait until the relief comes."

"T-thank you, sir!"

The young levy turned to leave, and the ground beneath him shook. Every man on the wall looked at each other with confusion, then horror, when they realized what was happening. The wall was collapsing. Bricks fell, and the ground caved in. The men wanted to run, but they didn't have enough time. They fell, entangled in the tumbling brick, and the wall completely collapsed. The soldiers had covered the tunnel dug beneath the city wall in oil and lit it on fire, causing the supports to fall and the tunnel to cave in. They breached the wall.

In the command tent, men discussed what to do next. Martin, Sir Suruck, and several other army commanders were present.

"The time to attack is now!" Sir Suruck commanded.

"No one disputes that," Martin said. "The question is the method of attack."

"We have a breach. That should be our primary focus," another commander said.

"Getting men to go through a breach will be difficult. Few will volunteer for that. We'll need an incentive. If we can pay one guilder per man that survives the assault on the breach, I think that may be enough," Martin added.

"One guilder? That much?" Sir Suruck paused for a moment. "Ah, but you're right. Fine, I'll dig into the lord's coffers. But we mustn't focus only on the breach. We should do an all-out assault. Advance with siege engines and assault the portcullis, walls, and breach all at once."

"I agree," Martin confirmed. "Now to find volunteers for the breach assault."

"I'll do it," Wolfgang said as he stepped into the command tent. "I'll join the breach attack."

"I see you've made your choice, then."

"I know that someday, I'll keep my promise, and when I do, I can stop things like this from ever happening again. So, I'm going to achieve my goal no matter what—I'll do anything I have to," Wolfgang muttered.

"You sound determined, boy. Although to us, your ramblings make no sense. I say we assault tomorrow," Sir Suruck said.

The other commanders agreed and began preparations.

***

There was a soft snowfall overnight, leaving a thin layer of melting snow over the battlefield. The sky was mostly clear, and at high noon, the signaleer gave the signal to attack. The other boys volunteered to join Wolfgang in the breach, as did several karls. Martin would lead them. They stared at the rubble, twisted bodies entangled in the debris, afraid to move. Martin stood in front of the group.

"You didn't hear the horn? Come on, let's go!" he shouted.

Still, no one moved.

"You don't get the money if you don't fight!"

Wolfgang was the first to step forward, then Otto and the others raced after him. They ran at the breach, and soon the rest of the group followed suit. There was no doubt about the enemy's strong defense on the other side. Assaulting a breach was normally suicide, but it was what they had to do. As Wolfgang stepped onto the pile of rubble, Owl Alliance soldiers charged from the other side. They'd meet atop the pile.

Bills and poleaxes clashed as the two sides saw fierce resistance in each other. Most alliance troops were billmen, but a few plate armored troops were mixed in. It was likely that the Taltenburg defenders were stretched thin. Everyone was tightly packed together, and the breach itself was relatively small. Wolfgang had no room to swing his poleax, so he used it as a pike and thrusted it into his foes. He got one alliance soldier in the neck, and another in the chest. No matter how many he killed, more seemed to pop up from the ranks behind.

Francis's armor was great for deflecting blows from his opponents' bills. An alliance billman aimed low and used the hook to pull his feet, causing Francis to fall to the ground. The alliance soldier tried to stab him through the neck, but he couldn't penetrate the chain mail around his visor. Then, Alphonse attacked with a bill and stabbed the levy in the chest, giving Francis some time to get to his feet. Still, the close quarters fights were hard to move around in, and they were stuck in place, so standing back up was rather difficult. Francis was pushed between multiple men and ended up falling back to the rear, although not intentionally.

The fighting continued for some time, more violent and difficult than ever.

Exhaustion set in for the front ranks. Alphonse took a bill to his face, dislocating his jaw. A billman tried to hook Otto's leg but missed and ended up stabbing him in the foot. Wolfgang engaged in a brutal stand off. The staff of his poleax locked with the staff of a bill, and he and the alliance soldier were desperately trying to overpower the other.

Then, from the distance, a horn sounded. Then it sounded again. It wasn't clear at first what it was, but as a man on a horse rode up behind the alliance formation, they knew what it was. A surrender signal.

"Lord Fenton has surrendered! Lay down your arms!" the horse rider shouted.

It took a moment for the fighting to cease, as many men were battle frenzied, but the back ranks did as they were told. Once the front ranks realized what was happening, they too put down their arms.

"Did you hear that? You need to surrender," Wolfgang told the alliance soldier was locked in battle with.

"If I do, will you kill me?" he asked. "How can I trust you?"

"I'll put mine down first," Wolfgang replied as he let up on his grip and set his poleax down. "See?"

"Alright, alright." The alliance man put down his bill and stepped away.

The surrender was finalized on the agreement that the city would not be sacked or harmed. Lord Fenton would also remain in charge of the city, and the barons would keep their lands. Lord Alten and his men would honor the agreement.

In the coming days, the destruction from the siege would be repaired and life would start returning to normal for the residents of Taltenburg. Winter was coming, and the war was nearing its end.

Oustilut Coats of Arms

House Alten   House Fenton   House Klien

House Oppenstein   Oustilut National

Owl Alliance

Chapter 13

It was late in the month of Sagittarius. Snowfall became more common as winter approached. While the commanders planned their next move, the karls took some much needed time off. Aksel found a nice alehouse, one with seating large enough to fit most of the karlband. The boys sat down, waiting for their drinks.

"Ah, finally we get to rest and take off our armor. I forgot what it felt like to wear normal clothes. Feels like we've been working a year straight," Otto complained.

"We basically have," Alphonse laughed. "At least you got some muscle on your skinny bones now, eh, bro?" He slapped Otto's back.

"I'm just happy we made it through all of that," Francis said.

"Yeah, there were quite a few close calls," Jurgen added.

"Here's your beer," an alemaiden said as she brushed the snow off their table and set several tankards of alcohol down. At another table, one karl slapped an alemaiden on the bottom and she bent over to place the drinks down. Alphonse, clearly getting an idea, reached his hand out before Otto slapped it down.

"Act like nobility, won't you, you lecher," he scolded.

"What, I didn't do anything," Alphonse said.

"You were going to."

"Yeah, he was definitely going to do something bad," Jurgen agreed.

"No doubt. Probably something that would make us all look bad," Wolfgang added, beer dribbling down his chin.

"Come on, I'm not that bad," Alphonse said.

At a nearby table, several men looked at the karls with visible disgust. They drank and discussed the men and their behavior.

"Look at these barbarians," one man said.

"Why did Lord Fenton surrender? We should've kept fighting. He should've finished them," another man said.

"I'm sick of this!" a third man shouted as he stood up. He pointed at the karls who were flirting with the alemaidens. "You kill our friends, and now take our women? Is nothing sacred to you barbarians and your illegal war?"

"Who do you think you are?" a karl shouted.

"Illegal war? It's his lord that started this," Otto muttered.

"What was that, kid?" The man pointed at Otto. "Who are you? And what about that plate armored freak?" He pointed at Francis. "And that devil with the red eyes." He then pointed at Wolfgang.

"What did you say about Francis?" Wolfgang slammed his hands on the table and stood up.

"What did you say about my brother?" Otto also stood.

"Looks like these boys want a fight," another man said.

"You fight them, you fight us all," Aksel shouted, standing.

The other karls stood as well, and many other men at the alehouse also stood.

"Hold on, all of you," Martin shouted. "If you're going to fight, do it in the street. No need to ruin this fine establishment."

"He makes a good point. Alliance men, what say you? Shall we go to the street and settle this?" Aksel asked.

The men and the karls, except for Martin, who opted to stay at his table sipping his ale, walked into the street and faced one another. They were little more than a drunk, disorganized mob, but they were angry and rearing for a fight. The boys stood at the front, preparing themselves for the street brawl.

"What are you waiting for? Scared little karls?" an alliance men, shouted.

"Shouldn't you attack first then, if you're so brave!" Otto replied.

"Forget it, I'll go first!" Wolfgang shouted as he ran forward and sucker punched the man who insulted Francis.

The man fell to the ground, unconscious. Everyone looked on with shocked at first, then the two mobs charged each other and the fight began.

Alphonse picked up a small alliance man and flung him around like a weapon, knocking several other men down. Francis stood still as one man tried to punch him, only to break his fist on Francis's visor. Otto was in a brawling match with a man of the same build as him. They punched each other, both receiving blows, but neither went down. Otto took a punch to the nose, causing it to bleed. He responded by punching the brawler in the gut and kneeing him in the jaw.

Karls and alliance men exchanged fists for a few moments, some men falling to the ground, others taking hit after hit and not going down. Then, one of the alliance men shouted.

"It's the catchpole! The catchpole is here!" That was the signal to run.

"If you get caught you don't get paid!" Aksel shouted, laughing.

"Wait, what's happening?" Wolfgang asked, clueless as ever.

"Just follow me!" Jurgen shouted.

The catchpole, wearing green and blue waffenrocks—the colors of Taltenburg—ran into the mob and grabbed men. They hit others with quarter staffs and short staffs.

Although they were trying to break up the fight, they ended up making the situation even more chaotic. The boys followed Jurgen and dispersed, running into a nearby alleyway.

"Get back here!" a catchpole shouted.

He ran after the boys, along with two others.

"We're being chased! There's three of them!" Otto shouted.

They ran into an adjacent street, knocking over hand carts and pushing people out of their way as they ran. Jurgen pointed at a narrow alleyway. It was only big enough to fit one person at a time, but they dashed into it, anyway.

Wolfgang was in the rear, and before he could make it into the alley, a catchpole grabbed his arm and yanked him back. Wolfgang looked at the man, then, without warning, punched him square in the jaw. The catchpole fell to the ground, and the other two were stunned. Wolfgang ran through the alley to catch up with the others.

"Did you really just do that?" Alphonse laughed.

The boys reached the other side of the narrow passage and stampeded through people minding their own business to get to another alley and another street. They kept running through the town until they reached the city walls. The catchpole was far behind; they were safe.

They leaned against the wall, catching their breath. Then Jurgen started laughing. Soon, all five of them cackled like hyenas. Alphonse put his hand on Wolfgang's shoulder.

"I can't believe you really punched a catchpole!" Alphonse could barely talk through his laughing fit.

"Well-well, what else was I supposed to do? Aksel said we don't get paid if we get caught."

"Yeah, that's true," Otto said as he wiped away tears. "Oh, speaking of which, we still haven't actually got paid."

"Wait, you're right. I didn't even think about that," Jurgen said.

"We've been working for free this whole time, haven't we?" Wolfgang asked.

The five laughed again.

"Oh, that cheap cotter. We need to demand our payment from him as soon as we see him again," Alphonse added.

"Thank you, guys," Francis said. "That was the most fun I have ever had."

"Don't worry about it. We're brothers, right?" Wolfgang walked over and slapped Francis's shoulder.

"Yeah." He started crying.

"Are you alright?" Jurgen asked.

"I am okay. I just... was never treated well because of my condition. My parents were of a high noble house. They tried to hide me from the world, lest I be sent to a monastery or left to die. I could never have friends. Then we lost a war with our rival house. They executed my parents and siblings. They spared me because they thought I was too pitiful to be put to the sword. So, they made me a stable boy and their servant." He pulled a small wooden cross out of a pouch on his armor. "My sister carved this. It's all I have left of them. That and my name, I suppose."

"I never knew," Wolfgang said.

"It is alright. When I inherited the last of my family's wealth, I purchased this armor, my bill and swords, and left for... well, wherever I could go."

"You have nothing to worry about now, bro," Alphonse said. "You may have lost your old family, but we're your new one."

"Yes, you are correct, friend. What about you, Wolfgang? Are you feeling better?" Francis asked, changing the subject.

"Yeah, I'm fine. I don't know if I'll ever get used to what we do. But if I want to keep my promise to Elise." He pulled back his tunic's sleeve to look at Elise's bracelet. "I need to go further. I need to fight harder. I'll do whatever I need to." He paused for a moment. "Hold on, why are we getting all serious? I wanna have more fun!"

"Oh no, he's all riled up now." Otto smiled.

"More fun? We can go find some girls—" Otto quickly cut off Alphonse's suggestion.

"Not that kind of fun, you lecherous dolt."

The boys spent the rest of the night hopping from alehouse to alehouse, getting into fights, running from the catchpole, and causing general mischief.

In the morning, Aksel fetched them. As punishment for being a menace, the five—along with many other karls—helped clear out the rubble from the broken wall. They were hung over, tired, and exhausted as they moved the collapsed wall rock by rock.

"Keep moving! Hard labor is the best way to work off a hangover!" Aksel occasionally shouted at them, laughing.

The year came to a close. The karlband celebrated the Feast of the Lord together, and as the new year dawned, they prepared for what would surely be the war's last battle.

Raising a Medieval Army

Due to the large time scale and many different cultures, there were many different ways across many different eras of Medieval Europe to raise an Army. Unlike the standing armies of today's world, in the middle ages an army would typically surround a noble house or local leader. It would be common for peasents to be recruited for wars due to obligation to the levy, or as a militia for local defense. The true professional soldiers of the times were the men-at-arms, who served specific noble houses, and mercenaries. It could take several years to prepare for war, as war in Medieval Europe was not as straight forwad as today and required lots of political debate and logistics. Once war was declared, the next step was the call to arms. Couriers would set out with letters from the authority declaring the war (or raising armies for a defensive war) to all of his/her vassals. The vassals would then send letter to their vassals, and this would continue until the call was recived at the local villages. This proccess could take weeks or even months. After this, orders would be sent with a time and place for mustering. Levies (or freemen) would arrive at a muster roll with their own armor and equipment. Levies were typically used for local defense and peace keeping, and rarely sent on offensive campaigns.

Auxillary forces like mercenary companies would make up the final pieces of the army. There was no way of knowing how many troops would show up, so a leader would need to plan for any outcome. After the muster roll was complete, the army would sit at an encampent and wait for orders to advance. Movement of armies at the time was also a major logistical feat.

Chapter 14

Klein Castle was built into the side of an enormous cliff, flanked on both sides by steep cliffs and hills. The only option for attack was a large, open valley. It was the worst place to attack. Lord Alten's army amassed outside of the castle in the valley. It was impossible to hide their numbers, which were just over two thousand. The men of Klein Castle could presumably watch their every move. But things were about to get worse.

"Are you serious?" Martin shouted from inside the command tent.

"It's true. If he goes through with it, we'll surely lose this war. Lord Alten was on his way here, but now he'll have to go to Zurick," Sir Suruck confirmed.

"What's going on?" Aksel asked as he entered the tent, the boys in tow.

"Somethin' bad happen?" Wolfgang asked.

"Yes, something terrible," Martin began. "Lord Klein is calling a mediation council with the duke."

"What's a med-ia-tion council?" Wolfgang asked, trying to sound out the word.

"It's when two or more nobles have a dispute, so they call the highest ranking noble above them to settle it. Two barons would call a lord, and a lord their duke," Martin responded. "This is bad for us. Legally, the Owl Alliance had rights to the iron mines. This means, in all likelihood, the duke will sign in favor of them."

"It seems like they could've done this from the beginning. Why now?" Otto asked.

"Mediation councils are rare, and typically seen as dishonorable. If a lord can't handle his affairs, then he's not worth the house he rules," Martin replied. "But, if your house is on the verge of losing, honor matters little. It would take some time to plan out the council, go over the facts, and for the duke to reach a decision. We have a couple of months at most."

"It will take us a month at least to finish setting up a siege camp, let alone construct siege engines and plan an attack. Mining is impossible because of the castle being built into rock," Sir Suruck added. "This will be bad. We need to figure something out."

"This valley is pretty open, so the enemy can see our camp, right?" Wolfgang added, hatching an idea.

"Yes, and it means hiding our numbers is impossible," Sir Suruck responded.

"What if we don't want to hide our numbers?"

"What are you getting at, lambkin?" Aksel asked.

"If they think we have fewer than we do, and we sally forth to attack in what will clearly be a failed attack, they'll likely open the gates to chase us down. But if we have men placed around the side of the cliff, out of view, they can charge in and attack. Then our men being chased can turn around, run inside, and we can close the gates, cutting off any enemy reinforcements. Hm… they'd have to be on horseback for speed and power, and we'd need to make it believable. We need a reason to thin our numbers." Wolfgang stopped for a moment, holding his chin in his hand.

"How about a lie? To complete our deception, we can feed them false information," Otto suggested. "Maybe we can convince them Lord Fenton didn't truly surrender and Taltenburg is rebelling."

"Yeah, that could work. They'd receive the information, then see over half our army leaving shortly after. If they think the tides of war are turning and the fight is no longer in our favor, they'll get arrogant. They'll ride out to meet our cavalry charge, and we can enact our plan." Wolfgang grinned as his plan came together.

"Wow," Aksel began. "I honestly thought you were slow, lambkin. I didn't know you could come up with something like that."

"Looks like he used up all of his brain power too," Alphonse laughed.

"Hey, it's a good plan! Otto helped too!" Wolfgang replied, crossing his arms.

"It is a good plan," Martin said. "I'm proud of you. You're finally acting like nobles."

"That's a good plan, but there are too many unknown variables. How will we trick them?" Sir Suruck asked.

"I can take care of that," Jurgen said. "They must have a system for receiving messages from spies. I'll head back to Taltenburg and have Lord Fenton write a letter, and he'll tell me how to deliver it."

"Are you sure he won't just lie and get you killed?" Sir Suruck asked.

"Well, if he doesn't, we can always sack his city. I'll make sure it works out, somehow," Jurgen said.

"Not very reassuring."

"It's settled. This is our plan of action. We only have one chance to make this work," Martin said.

***

Jurgen traveled alone to the city, being welcomed in—begrudgingly—to Lord Fenton's estate. His manor was large and surrounded by a stone wall, like a castle's keep. After waiting a short time, a servant led him into a modestly sized great hall to speak with Lord Fenton.

"What do you barbarians want from me?" Lord Fenton asked as Jurgen entered.

Lord Fenton wore a silk tunic with a purple cape and sported short hair with a long mustache. He was large, looking like he was only one steak wavy from contracting gout.

"An end to this war," Jurgen began.

"Why would I want to end this? I enjoy hearing about Lord Alten's men getting butchered. Besides, I hear this will end soon anyway, because of the duke."

"Then I suppose we'll have to sack your city. We need resources to keep this war going, and this city is plentiful in food and raw resources."

Jurgen approached Lord Fenton and leaned on the table he sat at.

"You're bluffing."

"Am I?"

"You barbarians signed an agreement!" Lord Fenton's shouts echoed through the hall.

"But we're barbarians, aren't we? Why should we honor any agreement?" Jurgen grinned as he walked away.

"Wait! Fine, what do you want me to do?" Lord Fenton asked.

"I just need a letter. I'll tell you what to write, and you tell me how to get it to Klein Castle."

***

The following night, Jurgen rode out to the castle. He climbed a hidden narrow passage leading to a hidden side gate in the castle. Jurgen lit a torch, put it out, then lit it again. That was the signal to the guards that a spy arrived. They unlocked the small gate, and Jurgen passed along the letter. He then left and returned to the siege camp.

***

They sealed the letter with Lord Fenton's house coat of arms, so a soldier took it to Sir Yugor, Lord Klien's marshal in charge of the castle's garrison in his stead directly.

Sir Yugor woke from a deep slumber by a banging on his door.

"What is it? Is the enemy attacking?" He shouted angrily as he opened the door. One of his soldiers handed him the letter. He opened it and read:

To the honorable Lord Klein and his retinue,

I've heard of the call to a mediation council. Learning this news, I've decided now is the time to fight back. I surrendered only in a ruse, and now my people are rebelling. The detestable Lord Alten will soon fall. We must crush his army, then his spirit.

Be with God,

Lord Stefan, Fenton of Taltenburg.

The news was surprising to Sir Yugor but very welcomed. Still, he had to be sure it was true. When the morning came, he donned his armor and went to the castle walls to observe the enemy force. After only a couple of hours, he watched as hundreds of troops packed up and left for Taltenburg.

"Looks like the information was correct, my lord," a soldier told him.

"Yes. If their army is only numbered in the hundreds, we can crush them outright without having to wait any longer. Then we can regroup and help the fight in Tellenburg."

**

In the siege camp, Martin, Sir Suruck, Aksel, the boys, and the remaining commanders all prepared the next phase of the plan in the command tent.

"Did it work?" Otto asked.

"We won't know until we attack," Martin said.

"My men will gather outside of the enemy gates, along the cliff face in their blind spot. You karls will lead the cavalry charge," Sir Suruck said.

"So, we get the most dangerous job, huh?" Jurgen laughed.

"That's what you're here for," Sir Suruck replied.

"But we don't have any horses," Wolfgang said.

"That's right, boy. You'll be borrowing horses from my men. If any of these animals come back harmed, it'll be your head. Take care of them." Sir Suruck folded his arms and looked over at the men. "Alright, we're short on time. Let's get to it."

**

It was cloudy and gray. The air was icy and the ground was frozen. The karls, numbering only forty men, sat atop horses, in a three rank deep square formation, waiting for the order to charge. Aksel looked through an eyeglass for Sir Suruck's men—as soon as they were in position, the attack would begin.

"This sounded like a good idea. But now that we're about to do it, I'm not so sure," Otto said.

"There was something like this that happened once," Martin began. "It was the Battle of Sephameeny, during the Third Crusade for the Holy Land. Crusaders rode to the city gates on horseback, and their enemies opened the gates to meet them."

"What happened? Were they successful?" Otto asked.

"They rode right past their enemies, into the city, and won. Well, they slaughtered everyone inside."

"Looks like they're in position," Aksel said.

"Forty men on horseback, sixty infantry, and an entire castle to storm. This will be interesting," Jurgen added.

"Okay." Martin unsheathed his sword and pointed it at the castle. "Blow the horn. We ride!"

Aksel blew a horn, sounding the signal. The karls kicked their horses, snapped their reins, and rode toward certain doom. Wolfgang gripped his reins tightly with his left hand and held his poleax in his right. Most karls had poleaxes, though some used bills—especially those that normally fought with swords. Fighting with a polearm would give them the best advantage on horseback, so they kept their swords in their scabbards.

As they approached the castle—only a few hundred feet away—the portcullis opened, and Sir Yugor led the charge. The plan worked. Martin raised his sword high, preparing to give the next order. The two sides drew closer, about to meet in the field, when Martin brought his sword down and pointed it at the ground. That was the signal for the karls to break formation and split up, as evenly as they could, and go around the hostile formation.

"What are they doing?" Sir Yugor shouted as the karls regrouped on the other side of his formation. "Wait... the gate! The portcullis is still open! Turn around!"

What he didn't know was that the infantry had already made their way inside and were fighting for control of the gate. Swords and bills clashed inside the narrow castle walls. Men stepped over their comrades' bodies and walked past walls stained with their blood.

The karls had finally reached the gates. They rode in and up the small incline leading to the courtyard and keep. The courtyard itself was impressively large, like a small village. There were several buildings and a large stable. Most castles had small villages surrounding them, but in the case of defense, most lords placed the castle workers and maintainers inside the walls.

The gates closed behind them, although Sir Yugor and a small group of soldiers made it in. The karls rode through the courtyard, surprising everyone inside.

"Men, take the keep! Aksel and the five noble brats, with me! We have a marshal to kill," Martin ordered.

Wolfgang and the others followed their commands, and alongside Aksel and Martin, rode directly toward Sir Yugor and his men. In total, Sir Yugor's numbers were only two men more, so it was nine against seven.

Wolfgang rode directly for Sir Yugor, who was armed with a spear and shield. He went just past Sir Yugor, trying to get to his rear, and swung his poleax with both hands as hard as he could. Sir Yugor put up his white and blue painted shield just in time to block the blow. Metal clanked and air shifted as the ax blade and shield made contact.

Sir Yugor kept riding before turning around to face his opponent. Wolfgang did the same. The two looked at each other before charging. Wolfgang was certainly at a disadvantage, as he lacked the full plate armor of Sir Yugor, and he lacked a shield. But what he lacked in defense, he made up for in attack and raw power.

Wolfgang aimed the point of his poleax at Sir Yugor as he charged. Sir Yugor responded by placing his sword by his left arm. He was ready to deflect Wolfgang's poleax when he stabbed at him.

As Wolfgang got closer, he lowered his poleax to the horse instead. He stabbed the horse's chest and tore a large hole open, causing its guts to spill onto the cold ground. Sir Yugor landed hard, but quickly recovered.

The Wolf's Song

"Is that all? You have to take out my horse? Come on, I'll finish you yet!" he shouted at Wolfgang.

He held his shield up with his sword held at his side but pointing at his opponent. He planted his left foot forward and prepared to strike.

Wolfgang snapped his reins, and the horse charged forward. He intended to stab Sir Yugor with the point of his poleax, and while he was on the ground, finish him off. As he drew closer, he thrusted forward, hitting Sir Yugor's shield dead on. Sir Yugor shifted diagonally as the poleax connected with his shield to offset the blow, then threw his shield up and rammed his sword into Wolfgang's abdomen.

Wolfgang stopped riding, as blood leaked from his wound and stained his gambeson. He fell off the saddle and spit up blood and mucus. He used his poleax as support as he stood up.

"You think that'll stop me?" Wolfgang growled, wiping blood from his lips.

Martin and Otto had defeated their opponents and turned their attention to Wolfgang's battle.

"Brother, let me help you!" Otto shouted.

"No! I need to do this." His voice was little more than animalistic screeching.

Wolfgang placed his right foot forward and planted himself. He held his poleax over his right shoulder, ax side up. He focused on his opponent. Wolfgang needed to win before he bled out. Sir Yugor took a defensive stance. Wolfgang charged forward, leaving a small trail of blood behind. He swung at his enemy, his ax blade impacting the shield.

Sir Yugor lifted his sword, preparing to thrust it into Wolfgang's neck. Wolfgang dropped, squatting as low as he could, to avoid the thrust. He dropped his poleax as he squatted, then used his legs to jump and tackle Sir Yugor, grappling him with both arms.

As the two fell to the ground, Wolfgang sat on top of his opponent. He used his left leg to hold Sir Yugor's sword arm down, unsheathed his dagger, and prepared the final strike. Martin shouted at Wolfgang to wait, as Lord Klien's marshal would be more valuable alive, but Wolfgang was in a battle frenzy. Aksel ran to prevent the strike, but it was too late. Wolfgang lifted his opponent's visor, and stabbed him through the nose, deep into his skull. He then stood up, stepped back, and collapsed.

"Damn it, lambkin. Must be from blood loss," Aksel yelled as he ran over to catch Wolfgang before he hit the ground.

"Alphonse, get the surgeon!" Otto ordered.

"Right!" Alphonse obliged.

The siege of Klien Castle was over. The gamble had paid off, and the remaining men garrisoned inside put down their arms in surrender.

When the news reached the mediation council, the duke of Oustilüt would rule indecisively, changing his original decision to rule in favor of Lord Klien. He left the decision to the lords and told Lord Klien if he was worth those iron mines, he'd muster up men in the countryside and take his castle back.

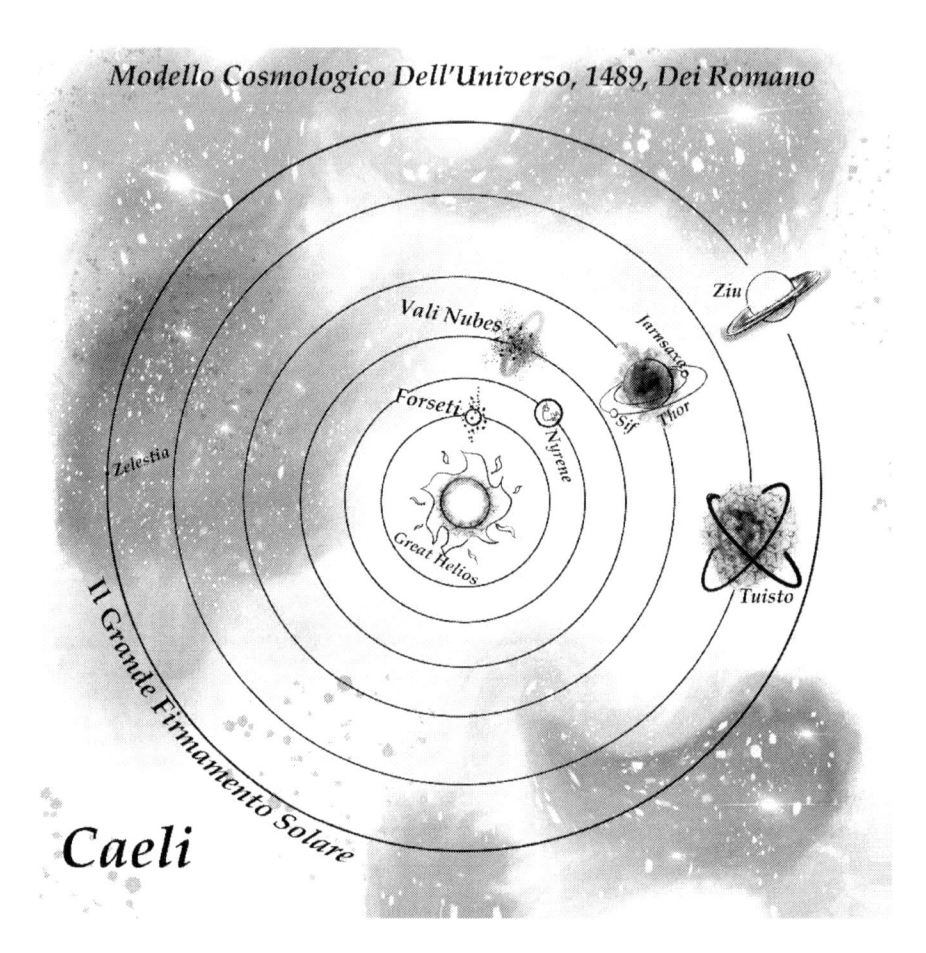

Modello Cosmologico Dell'Universo, 1489, Dei Romano

Caeli

Chapter 15

Wolfgang woke to the sound of a heavy wooden door slamming shut. He was in a small room inside the keep of Castle Klien. He felt a burning pain in his side as he sat up. They placed bandages around his abdomen, covering where his wound.

"You just love getting hurt, don't you?" Tuferan, the surgeon, said as he approached the bed.

"Maybe I just enjoy your happy bedside demeanor," Wolfgang replied sarcastically.

"Oh, I guess I should be flattered. Well, I need to change your bandages and put more honey on the wound."

"How long was I out?"

"Almost a week this time. Count yourself lucky. You got to sleep while everyone else had to clean up the mess from the battle."

"I sure don't feel lucky. My side is hurting a lot." Wolfgang lifted his arms as the surgeon untied the bandage. "So, is the war over now?"

"Probably. Lord Alten arrived a couple of days ago. There will be a big banquet to honor everyone that fought for him tomorrow. Hm, you really did wake up just in time. Got to avoid work, get to eat at the banquet..."

"Hey, what's that supposed to mean?" Wolfgang pointed at him.

"Nothing, nothing. I'm sure you'll be feeling hungry about now, right?"

"Hungry?" Then, loud rumble came from Wolfgang's stomach.

"That's what I thought. I'll have someone bring you food. They have plenty of meat here. Maybe you'll feel better with some chicken soup."

As the surgeon left, Wolfgang got out of bed and approached the small glass window on the other side of the room. *Lord Klien must've been quite rich to afford glass,* he thought as he placed his hand against the smooth texture of the window. The room overlooked the courtyard. It was snowing outside, and many people scurried around, undoubtedly getting ready for the banquet.

***

Sometime later, Alphonse and Otto entered the room, chicken soup in hand. Otto set the bowl on a small nightstand next to the bed.

"You really need to stop getting hurt like this, you know?" Otto said.

"Yeah man, everyone was worried about you. Even Martin," Alphonse agreed.

"Hey, it's not like I wanted to get stabbed!" Wolfgang said.

"So what? I mean, what would happen to Elise if you died? Did you think of that?" Otto asked.

"Well..." Wolfgang paused. "I won't die. It'll be fine, okay?"

"Alright little bro!" Alphonse laughed. "But everyone is talking about your battle with Lord Klien's marshal. You've gained quite the renown."

"Really?" Wolfgang smiled.

"I'm sure you'll hear all about it at the banquet. We still have work to do, so we'll see you tomorrow night."

***

Wolfgang and the rest of the karls entered a large banquet hall deep in the keep. It was large enough to seat almost one hundred and fifty people and hold at least fifty more people standing along the sides. Everyone sat at large tables full of meat and fruit, waiting for Lord Alten to arrive and sit at a large throne in the back of the room.

Wolfgang reached for a chicken leg off a plate full of chicken, but Otto slapped his hand. Just then, Lord Alten arrived.

The doors to the hall opened and a young man with short blond hair and brown eyes stepped in. He wore a purple silk tunic and a blue cape. He looked to be around fourteen years of age. Behind him was a bishop, holding a scepter and dressed in ornate religious garbs.

Lord Alten took the throne, and the bishop turned to address the entire hall. He led a prayer to bless the food, then gave the floor to Lord Alten.

"On this day, in the year of our Lord's kingdom 1492, on the 3rd of Gemini, all the lands and territories owned by Lord Klien are officially abdicated and transferred to House Alten. All those who supported House Klien in the so-called Owl Alliance come forward to swear fealty to me, or my armies shall seize your lands as well."

Despite being so young, he was very well spoken. After that, starting with Lord Fenton and Lord Oppenstein, several people came up to kiss Lord Alten's hand and swear fealty to him. Then, everyone received permission to eat.

As Wolfgang shoveled food and wine down his throat, Lord Alten spoke again. That time he asked for a very specific person.

"Excuse me, everyone. I'd like to thank all of you for your support, and you'll receive rewards after the feast. However, I'd like to see the red-eyed karl that defeated Sir Yugor. I've heard much about him and would like to speak to him."

"That's you, lambkin," Aksel said to Wolfgang, who had nearly half a chicken in his mouth.

"Wait, what?" Wolfgang mumbled.

"No one can understand you with your mouth full. Swallow your food, then talk," Otto said.

"Is the red-eyed karl here?" Lord Alten repeated.

"Yes, he's one of my men, your lordship."

Martin stood and shouted over everyone. He motioned for Wolfgang to stand.

"Don't forget to show courtesy," Martin whispered to him.

Wolfgang, who was drunk and full of food, stumbled over to the throne. He kneeled and placed his hand over his heart.

"Uh, yes, your lordship. I, uh, am the one you want." He burped half the words he said.

"That idiot." Otto put his hand over his face, anticipating a sharp rebuke from Lord Alten.

"Lift your head. I wish to see your eyes," Lord Alten commanded.

Wolfgang obliged.

"Wow, they really are red, just like they say! I've heard them call you the Crimson Wolf, but what's your true name, karl?"

"Wolfgang von Ludwig, and I hall from the Wolfsreich."

"Ludwig? From the Wolfsreich? You wouldn't be in the same family as Duke Ludwig, would you?" he asked cautiously.

"Oh, I'm his adopted son. My brother Otto is with me, too." Wolfgang pointed at Otto, who was trying to hide his face from embarrassment.

"Oh no, don't bring me into this," Otto muttered.

"R-really?" Lord Alten began, standing up from his throne. "You-you're royalty. Then why art thou bowing to me? You realize you're of higher status than me?"

"Oh, uh, really?" Wolfgang stood up. "Politics is still a confusing topic for me. Ah, my brother understands this stuff better. Otto, come over here!"

"I don't think you can hide anymore!" Alphonse laughed.

Otto stood, walked over to Wolfgang, and addressed Lord Alten.

"I apologize for my brother's rudeness. He's not as refined as others."

"Oh, 'tis no bother to me!"

Lord Alten paused. At that point, the entire hall had gone quiet. Everyone was now invested in this strange development of events. "So, why would a couple of royals be fighting with karls?"

"It's sort of a long story—" Otto began, but Wolfgang cut him off.

"We set off on this journey to fulfill a promise. There is a woman I wish to marry, and I must fulfill her father's request to get his blessing."

"Oh, I see. Who are your friends?"

"I'm glad you asked!" Wolfgang shouted. "First there is

Alphonse, he is strong like an ox. A bit of a lecher, though."

"Did you have to add that last part?" Alphonse muttered.

"Francis is the man in the armor. He hails from The Frünreich. He is a little shy and kind of awkward to talk to. Oh, and then there is Jurgen. He speaks all kinds of languages and is skilled with a sword, but he's kind of old."

"I'm twenty three, Wolfgang." Jurgen shouted. The karls in the hall laughed.

"Aksel is the second in command of our Karlband, The Thorns of Roses. He's tough and uh-" Wolfgang went down to a quiet whisper; "A little scary sometimes."

"Oh, I see. And who is the leader of your group?" Lord Alten asked.

"Oh, that would be Martin The Crow. He is a great tactician, and an honest man- although he still hasn't paid us our wages."

"Shut it, you dolt," Otto yelled as he kicked Wolfgang in the shin.

"Ow, that hurt! I'm still injured, ya know?"

"So am I! I kicked you with my stabbed foot!"

"Um... you lot are quite rambunctious, aren't you?" Lord Alten interjected awkwardly.

"Someone needs to teach that kid tact." Aksel commented.

"Hey, I have an idea!" Lord Alten grabbed both Wolfgang and Otto's hands and held them up. "How about an alliance between House Alten and House Ludwig?"

"Oh, uh, sure, why not?" Wolfgang replied.

"Hold on, I don't think we have the authority for something like that," Otto said.

"Come on, an alliance is a good thing, right? When has something like that ever been bad?"

"You have no idea," Otto said, recalling almost the entirety of human history.

"It would benefit us both. I mean, after all you've done for me, this is the best way I can repay you! If House Ludwig is ever in need, my house shall come to your aid!"

"Well, I think we need to clear this with Father first... but... well, I suppose," Otto agreed.

"Perfect! I shall have my clerk's draft up an agreement post haste! What a momentous occasion!"

The entire hall erupted in cheers, and the drinking and partying continued. Servants brought out seemingly endless amounts of food, wine, and beer. A young woman in a servant dress approached the table and poured wine into Jurgen's cup. She then walked away, smiling at him.

"Look at that, she likes you!" Alphonse laughed.

"W-what are you talking about?" Jurgen asked.

"Don't you know what it means when a girl pours you wine like that? She's totally into you."

"Yeah, right, there's no way."

"Jurgen's got a point." Wolfgang began, mouth once again full of food. "She'd have to be into really old men."

"I told you I'm only twenty-three!" Jurgen shouted.

"Come on, go for it! Live a little!" Alphonse urged.

"I'm fine right here," Jurgen responded, his cheeks flushing.

"Alright, but if you don't, I will." Alphonse stood and approached the servant girls.

"That lecher," Otto muttered.

"Hey, what're we doing now that the war's done?" Wolfgang asked Martin.

"We'll pack up and go fight somewhere else, of course. I've heard rumors of conflicts brewing in Cleovet, Axonia, and the Kingdom of Polenia. So, one of those three places will likely be our next destination. You should get your armor and weapons repaired or replaced in the meantime. There are merchants and smiths in the castle."

"Before we head out to the next battle, I think I'll enjoy some rest," Francis said.

"Yeah, you've all earned some time to rest. I'll let everyone know when we leave."

***

The festivities lasted well into the morning, and by dawn, most of the karls were drunk, passed out, and spread around the castle. Wolfgang had fallen asleep in the banquet hall and only woke when a bag banged on the table. He looked up at Martin.

"Here, this is the pay you're owed. Use this to improve your gear." Martin grinned and walked away, and Wolfgang fell back asleep, too hungover to go anywhere.

***

Sometime later, Wolfgang stumbled into the castle courtyard, looking for the smiths. An armorsmith, blacksmith, and swordsmith had a combined store and workshop, which made his mission a little easier. As he approached the door to the smithy shop, he saw several people in rags chained together, marching through the courtyard. Most of them were girls, some were still children. He stopped what he was doing and walked over to the guard escorting them.

"Why are these people in chains?" Wolfgang asked.

"Spoils of war, boy. They supported the Owl Alliance, and now they can be sold to pay loyalty to their new lord."

"You can't do that! Slavery is illegal in the HAE!" Wolfgang pointed at the guard, getting angrier with every shout.

"So what? Are you that naïve, kid?"

"Does Lord Alten know about this?"

"The order came from his retainers. Make of that what you will. Now, get out of my way! You're making a scene!"

The guard tried to push past him, but Wolfgang planted his feet in the ground.

"You'll let those people go right now! Some of them are children!"

"I know, children fetch a higher price."

Out of sheer disgust, Wolfgang readied his fist to swing, but a hand grabbed him and pulled him back. It was Aksel.

"You're making a terrible fuss, lambkin," he said.

"Do you not see this? These people are in chains!"

"So? This is simply the aftermath."

"Aftermath?" Wolfgang scratched his head.

"The price of war is paid in the blood of soldiers and the blood of the innocent. Even after it ends, the scars it leaves may never heal. This is just the way things are in our broken world."

"Are you saying I should do nothing?"

"Well, I won't stop you from trying to fight, but if those guards don't strike you down, then you'll end up ruining the alliance you just formed."

The Wolf's Song

"Tsk," Wolfgang scoffed and balled up his fist. Then he turned to the guard, who was preparing for a fight. "How much?"

"Excuse me?"

"How much for those people?" Wolfgang asked again through gritted teeth.

"Ha! You intend to buy them? They won't be cheap, you know," the guard laughed.

"I said how much?"

"Fine, two guilders and sixty hundred grotschen."

"Alright." Wolfgang dug through the sack of coins that Martin left him.

He had just enough to pay the guard.

"Here."

"Really? Well, I'll be. Fine, you do what you want with 'em. Here." He handed Wolfgang the key to the chains binding them and walked off.

Wolfgang began unshackling the would-be slaves. As he unshackled a little girl, he looked at her, studying her bruised and sad expression.

"Where are you from?" he asked her.

"A-a village just north of Taltenburg."

"Where's your family?"

"T-they died in a raid." She paused for a moment. "A-are you my new master?"

"No." Wolfgang stood and addressed the group. "You're free now. Stay here, return to your villages, do what you want."

He walked away, leaving the freed people alone. He was honestly unsure of what to do with them, but at least they were free.

"Lambkin." Aksel stopped Wolfgang. "You really are a fool. You can't expect to rescue every slave and save every villager in Gotheca."

"Why not?"

"This world is too broken for one man to fix. It may be too broken to fix at all."

"Maybe to you. But I won't ever give up. I have a promise to keep."

"This world will humble you someday. But now I must ask, how will you get new armor? You have neigh a groschen left."

"I'll just keep using what I have, I suppose."

"No. Take this." Aksel dug 114 grotschen out of his pocket. "You can at least buy some chain mail and a new gambeson. Maybe get a color that won't stain this time." He turned to walk away. "Oh, and lambkin, I won't do this for you again, so don't waste your earnings next time."

Whilst the others in the quintet upgraded to plate armor or new, better made weapons, Wolfgang could only purchase a green gambeson, an orange wool skirt, a chain mail hauberk, and a whetstone to sharpen his poleax.

Jurgen and Alphonse bought new swords. Alphonse also bought a set of plate armor. Otto spent his earnings on plate armbraces, shin protectors, and a new chain mail hauberk. The rest of his earnings went toward the new books he found.

***

As the snow thawed, spring arrived, and with their new set of armor, it was time for the boys and the karlband to leave Oustilüt. The camp surgeon, Tuferan, would join them after Martin hired him with a large sum of money. They marched out of the castle gates-

The Wolf's Song

their next destination was Cleovet, to settle a conflict that had been brewing for some months. Wolfgang walked beside Martin who sat atop a newly purchased saddle for his gray stallion. He peered over to Wolfgang, who was marching with his eyes cast down and a furrowed brow.

"What's wrong?" Martin asked.

"Nothing. Wolfgang lied. In truth, he was feeling a mixture of anxiety and guilt. He began to wonder why he was fighting to begin with.

"You can't lie to me. I have seen that look on many men. It's the look of doubt."

"Huh? How did you-" Wolfgang was caught off guard by Martin's keen observation, but he quickly gathered himself. "Why are we going to Cleovet?"

"To fight and get paid." Martin laughed.

"Is that all we do? Travel from one war to the next, fighting for coin?"

"That's all there is to do." Aksel said as he approached them from behind.

"What is that supposed to mean?" Wolfgang asked.

"This is what soldiers do. We go from one battle to the next, make our coin, and move on."

"Soldiers fight for their countries. Karls are different." Wolfgang snarky replied.

"Yeah right!" Aksel laughed. "Do soldiers get paid? Only a fool would fight for free- karls and common soldiers aren't too different- we just travel more!"

"If you want to leave, then go." Martin added.

"Leave?"

"Why not? If you're too much of a soft bellied noble for this life, then go back to your comfortable bed and hot meals."

"It's not a bad life, lambkin;" Aksel began; "We get paid well and we get to see the world. It could be worse. Although no one is forcing you to stay."

"No, I'm not going anywhere." Wolfgang retorted. "I have a promise to keep. I'll do what I have to."

"That's the spirit!" Aksel laughed as he padded Wolfgang on the back.

***

The karlband had to pass through the Duchy of Kapfalz, and it would take them several weeks to get there. As they traveled, Martin recruited more karls, and increased their numbers to just over one hundred. In the month of Virgo, they'd arrive at their destination, and the next adventure would begin.

Love Can Never Be Destroyed

Infante Peter, heir to the throne of Portugal and son of King Afonso IV, was married to a woman he didn't love for political reasons- a woman named Constance. Peter fell in love with her lady-in-waiting, Ines de Castro. Peter and Ines started a secret relationship. When Constance passed on, the two would officially be married. This angered not only his father but the entire royal court. Peter and Ines lived hapily with their three children in Coimbra. But due to the strong disapproval from the court and asristocrats, King Afonso decided to have Ines killed. In January of 1355, several men would ambush her and take her life. Peter would lead and uprising against his father, vowing to find justice for his wife. When he took the throne in 1357, he ordered the arrest of the conspirators and murders of Ines. They were execueted by having their hearts ripped out, as they had "ripped out" his. Now the King of Portugal, Peter wished for his late wife to be recognized as Queen. He had her body exhumed and dressed in royal robes, and had all of the nobles and aristocrats that hated her come and kiss her hand as an act of veneration. King Peter and Ines are buried together in the Monastery of Alcobaca, their tombs built facing each other, so when the two rise upon final judgement, the first person King Peter will see is Ines.

Chapter 16

Hundreds of karls and mercenaries gathered outside of Uto Castle, near the border of Frienburg and Cleovet. They made a large camp to accommodate them all, whilst the leaders of each karlband and battleband met with the lord of Uto Castle. The boys sat around a campfire, waiting for orders.

"I wonder what we'll be doing," Wolfgang said, throwing rocks at the pot of beans over the fire.

"Who knows? I'm enjoying this peace," Otto added.

"I just hope whatever it is, we can get it over with quickly," Jurgen said.

"Hey, Cleovet borders the Great Channel, right? I hope we get to go to the beach. I've never seen the sea before," Otto said.

"Oh yeah, seeing the sea would be so sweet!" Wolfgang agreed.

"Yeah, and there might even be girls bathing in the sea—" Alphonse began before Otto cut him off.

"Anyway, we need to keep our wits, and be ready for anything," Otto said as he poured beans into a small bowl.

"Hey, listen up!" Aksel shouted as he walked through the camp. "We're moving out soon! Heading west!"

"There's a rebellion to be quelled!" Martin added.

"Alright, looks like we have some work to do." Alphonse stood up.

"Let us be careful, friends," Francis said.

The men packed their things and began their march. At the front of the train were Martin, Aksel, and the boys, who inquired about their task.

"So, we're fighting a rebellion?" Otto asked.

"Yes," Martin began. "The lady of Uto Castle, married to Lord Uto, hired us to crush a rebellion. A few months ago, Lord Uto seized lands that once belonged to the church. The nearby villagers protested, and they've mobilized into an army."

"Why would Lord Uto seize land from the church?" Wolfgang asked.

"That's complicated. Nobles seize lands for all kinds of reasons, and of course, the barons purchase land. In this case, the Hazsburgs requested it."

"Who're they?"

"They're the most powerful family in Gotheca. How have you not heard of them?" Otto asked.

"Lady Uto is a Hazsburg, and her third cousin, the patriarch of the family and the King of Kaspia, is requesting money and food to help his war to unite the Iburnika Peninsula. Particularly, he wishes to drive out the Ishlahamic Mooraniens of the south. Anyway, to help pay what he asks, she's repurposed church land for new farms. She's already given the Fief to another lord, and he's gone about gathering serfs to till the lands."

"How come nobles can just take land like that?" Wolfgang

asked.

"Well, it's their kingdom. But things are more complicated than that," Martin said.

"Nobles own the land, brother," Otto explained. "So, the nobility has a right to the land the people live on, and that land makes up the kingdom."

"That isn't quite the case," Martin said. "The people always makeup the nation. That's what this is about. See, the clergy seek to save their souls, the bourgeois seek to buy their souls, and the nobility seek to control their souls. Lady Uto was likely looking to seize the land for some time, and her cousin's request was just the excuse she needed. It's a constant battle between those three. The nobility doesn't want the church or bourgeois to have too much power, and vice versa."

"But why fight at all? Wouldn't it be easier if everyone just left each other alone?" Wolfgang asked.

"It's about opportunity. Evil whispers in the wind, and those that seek power have keen ears," Aksel said. "Now enough about politics. We need to focus on our job."

"Why are we fighting for the nobility and not the rebels? Seems like the kind of cause karls would support," Jurgen asked.

"A karlband needs to make money, too. Sometimes you need to take on jobs you don't like. Neither Lord Uto nor Lady Uto want to raise levies or their men-at-arms for this fight, so there's plenty of money to be made."

"Violence like this just seems pointless." Wolfgang replied.

"Hm. All violence is pointless. But violence is the way of life, and we are merely its profiteers. It's the way the world is. Now, like Aksel said, we should focus."

***

The Wolf's Song

After a couple of hours more of traveling, a young man wearing a leather jack and a round painted shield stopped the army led by Lord Uto's marshal. The boy approached the marshal and informed him that he was a rebel, and the rebels wished to end the fight quickly. The marshal agreed and marched on a little further to a large field. On the other side of the open field was the rebel army, already camped out and waiting. The marshal gave the order to settle, as the fighting wouldn't come for another couple of days at least. They established the army camp, and the men took shifts resting and pulling guard. After a couple of uneasy days, they finally received the order to get into formation and prepare for the fight.

The karls split into three regiments, each with four ranks. The regiments stood behind one another, with the first regiment being armored poleax wielders, the second being more lightly armored bill users, with swords in the rearmost rank, and bowmen and crossbowmen made up the final regiment. Behind the regiments were the leaders of the karls, all on horseback, gathered around the marshal. The rebels were arranged similarly, although they were only armed with bills, swords, and bows.

Wolfgang was in the first regiment, at the second rank, awaiting the order to march. The marshal, with Martin and several other leaders in tow, rode to the front to give a speech.

"Listen men. You're all here for coin, this I know. But realize this, Lady Uto and her husband appreciate your service. You're helping forge the future of Cleovet and put these peasants in their place. So, sally forth, and win the day!"

The marshal rode down the line, giving the speech a couple of times to ensure everyone heard. Then, the leaders rode to the rear, and with the sound of a flute, they marched. The captain leading the regiment led the men in a cadence to keep them in step and motivated for the fight. The rebels also began their march as well.

Jurgen was in the third regiment with the bowmen. At the beginning of the march, they fired an arrow storm. Arrows showered the rebels, cutting through their light armor. The rebels also fired arrows, but most of them bounced off the heavier and more expensive armor the karls wore. After a few more volleys, they were ordered to stop. The bowmen dropped their bows, unsheathed daggers and swords, and left to flank the enemy in a light infantry role.

The two sides met in the middle of the grassy field. The men in front of Wolfgang fought hard, cutting down rebel after rebel. After a few minutes, many men in the first rank grew tired, and Wolfgang moved with others to the front to keep on fighting. With a swing of his poleax, Wolfgang sliced open the neck of a terrified but determined rebel troop. He lifted his poleax, and killed another rebel, then another. It was strange how easy it was to fight them, compared to the men he fought in Oustilüt. They were more than just untrained villagers. It was like they'd never fought in their lives.

Jurgen and the other bowmen made their way around the battlefield and reached the rebels' western flank. The rebel bowmen, who remained in place since the battle began, seemed to lack an understanding of the role of bowmen on a battlefield. The rebellion was little more than an unorganized mob. The karls charged the rebels from the flank, using their swords and daggers to disrupt their formation. At that point, there was little the rebels could do to prevent a breakthrough. Many of them turned and ran in fear.

As the rebels turned to run, many of the karls ran them down. Wolfgang opted instead to go to the rear, as it was clear this battle was over. The entire fight lasted less than thirty minutes. It was more of a butchering than an actual battle.

Wolfgang, as did many others, questioned what the rebellion's point was. Why would they meet a superior force on a field they had no clear advantages on? Could it have been a grave oversight, or was there another plan in motion?

The karls gathered in the camp and awaited their next instructions. After discussing things with the marshal, Martin approached his men to give the next set of orders.

"We didn't suffer a single casualty. Looks like this campaign will be easier than we thought," Martin began as the men cheered. "The man in charge of the rebellion is in the village of Freena. We're to march there, and if the village doesn't give him up, then we attack. The quickest way there is through some ruins. Get your things ready. We set out in the morning."

***

When the morning came, the army began their march. Beyond the large field was a lush forest.

After a few hours, they arrived in front of a large set of ruins. The forest stopped at the ruins' edge, like nature itself couldn't enter the corrupt place. The ruins comprised what appeared to be hundreds of abandoned towers, many made of a strange obsidian-like material that extended high in the sky. The towers' designs were even more bizarre than the materials they were made from. They were sculpted into unrecognizable geometric shapes, some with huge spikes protruding from the sides, others were completely smooth. At the base of the towers were marble pillars that held open massive entrances. As they stepped into the ruins, they saw the inside of the towers were huge, much larger than what regular people required.

"This place is creepy," Wolfgang said.

"Something about it feels wrong," Francis added.

"I'm amazed the Aeternians could've built something like this," Otto said in awe.

"It wasn't built by them," Martin corrected.

"That's impossible. They built all the ancient ruins in Gotheca. If they didn't build this, who could've?" Otto asked.

"According to the locals, this place is called the City of Ash, and legend states it was built over five thousand years ago—long before the Aeternian Empire formed."

"But there were no civilizations before them. No people were around yet to build anything," Otto said.

"Who says this was built by people?" Aksel asked.

Even though he was joking, the implications of his comment were quite terrifying.

"I've heard about this place. Historians have poured over it, and no one knows who built it. Kind of spooky," Jurgen said.

"Who cares who built it? Let's focus on the job," Aksel said.

"At the center of town is a large palace. We're going to camp out there for the night and finish the march in the morning. So—"

Screams from the front of the formation cut Martin off. Suddenly, they were showered with arrows and crossbow bolts. It was an ambush.

The rebels lured the karls into the ruins so they could launch an attack, and a vicious attack it was. Arrows rained down on the men at the front of the formation. The marshal, despite his plate armor, was unfortunate enough to take a crossbow bolt in the eye—right through the small slit on his visor. He fell from his horse, as did many other army commanders. Left and right, karls died, with only a few hunkering down under their shields. Since they were at the formation's rear, the Thorns of Roses were fortunate enough to have time to seek cover.

"Into the tower on the right! Take cover!" Martin ordered.

"The tower on the right! Move to the tower on the right!" Aksel repeated.

The men took shelter in the tower, preparing for their next move. Many karls were still in the street, taking cover behind fallen marble pillars and large cracks in the stone foundations of the towers. Wolfgang looked at their surroundings, analyzing the buildings and the street. He noticed that there was no break in the buildings- that is, the outside facade was a continuous wall.

"Most of these buildings are connected, I think," Wolfgang told Martin.

"Yeah? What are you getting at?" Martin asked.

"The rebels have the others pinned down from the upper levels of these strange towers. If we can get up there and flank them, then we can relieve the pressure from our comrades, and they can get to cover, or fight back."

"I was thinking the same thing. Hm. You really have learned a lot, haven't you?"

Martin was proud of Wolfgang's progress as a warrior.

Aksel led the karls through several massive chambers until they found a way up. Inside a large hallway was an odd statue of a person with four arms in strange armor holding a spear. The statue stood nearly twelve feet tall. The size of the halls and entrances seemed like they were made for someone around that size. But that would be impossible.

Beyond the statue was a hallway and a large staircase. The stairs were spaced in such a way that climbing them would be impossible, but there was a smaller set of stairs next to them, leading the group to believe the large stairs were simply decorative.

As they made their way up the winding, awkward staircase, they arrived at the tower's third floor. They only needed to find a means to get to where the rebels were, and quickly. Aksel poked around several chambers before finding a large, covered stone bridge leading to the other tower. They crossed, then waited by the wall of another chamber.

"The rebels are on the other side of his hallway. We'll move in to attack," Aksel ordered.

"Well, I guess I'll just stay here. Try not to get hurt. If you do, I'll be waiting," Tuferan said from the back.

"I didn't even know you were here, surgeon," Alphonse said.

"Oh, is the surgeon here? You should fight with us!" Wolfgang said.

"No, no, I'm just a healer," Tuferan replied.

"Sounds more like a coward to me," Alphonse said.

"Yeah, definitely," Wolfgang agreed.

"Come on guys, don't be so hard on him. If he's too scared to fight, just leave him be," Otto said.

"Could you guys stop, please?" Tuferan asked, shuffling his feet.

"The surgeon will stay behind. If he dies, who will tend to the wounded?" Aksel asked.

"Yeah, exactly!"

"Alright men. The enemy is just on the other side of the hallway. Stack up against the wall, and when I charge, you follow," Martin ordered as he took the lead.

The chamber the rebels were in was massive, large enough to fit at least two hundred men. Most of the rebels were armed with bows and crossbows, firing from the large windows at the edge of the chamber. Several others had bills, presumably to defend the bowmen. However, most of them rested on the ground, unaware and unprepared for what was to come.

The karls charged in, catching the rebels completely by surprise. Martin slashed a rebel, who was asleep with his sword. Wolfgang smashed one who was eating with the hammer side of his poleax. The other karls slaughtered several of the resting rebels before the rest realized what was going on and ran forward, bills ready. A rebel ordered the bowmen to continue firing, as he and the other billmen rushed to their defense.

Surprisingly, the rebels formed a cohesive line in front of the bowmen. The rebels and the karls locked in a desperate fight. If the karls broke through, it would be the end of the fight.

Francis narrowly evaded a thrust from an enemy bill, and countered with a thrust of his own, stabbing the man in the neck. The rebel in the rank behind him stepped up and swung his bill down. Francis held his bill horizontally above his head to block the blow. The billman then forced both bills to chest level, and the two locked like that, pushing against one another. It was a clever tactic to keep his opponent engaged and allow the bowmen to get more kills below.

Jurgen engaged the rebels with his longsword, putting him at a disadvantage against their polearms. A billman thrust at him, and he held his sword vertically by his side, blocking the blow and directing the bill outward. He then brought his sword up and thrust forward, stabbing the rebel in the chest.

Wolfgang was the first to break through the rebel line. He emerged on the other side, the enemy bowmen in sight. He charged at them. A few rebels left formation to deal with him, but that caused their line to collapse, and the karls broke through.

Wolfgang swung his poleax down at a bowman scrambling to unsheathe his dagger. He was too slow and took the ax side to the jaw. Wolfgang made a somewhat clean cut from one side of the man's jaw to the other, and his jaw completely fell off, his tongue flopped out, and he bled everywhere as he fell from the window into the street below.

Over the next few minutes, the karls successfully slaughtered the rebels, whilst taking only a handful of casualties. With three dead and seven wounded, the battle was beyond successful—for them, at least. The men on the ground suffered extreme casualties. Martin ordered his bowmen and crossbowmen to the windows, including Jurgen and Otto, and told them to open fire at the rebels on the other side of the street.

The karls opened fire and hit several of the rebels, but only killed a couple. Still, the attack was enough for the rebels to call a retreat and vacate the battlefield. They achieved their goal, and the army was completely smashed. Tuferan tended to the many wounded men, and Martin planned the next stage of the war.

"Looks like all the commanders were killed, including the marshal," Aksel said.

"Yes..." Martin smiled. "This is a great opportunity."

"How so?" Aksel asked.

"Well, we can leave the wounded here with the camp followers. Then, we can take all the abled bodied men—who are desperate for revenge—into our service. The Thorns of Roses could expand to three hundred men, at least."

"Can we afford that?"

"We'll be able to after we single-handedly and heroically smash the rebels. They come from the village of Freena, right? We can be there by midnight. They surprised us, so we'll surprise them. They won't expect a raid so quickly."

"Alright. I'll get the men ready."

After assembling the survivors and sharing the plan, the karls set out for the village of Freena, leaving the care of the dead and wounded to the camp followers staying in the City of Ash.

***

Dusk came as they marched across the wetlands, opting not to take the road, as they didn't want to alert the village of their presence. They passed a massive statue, one that stood almost as tall as the oddly shaped towers of the ruins. It was a woman carved in stone holding a Bible. Vines wrapped around the statue. Her expression made it look like she was standing guard, like she was trying to contain the unnatural city. Wolfgang and the others were ready to fight, although they questioned the plan.

"Why would rebels take refuge in an innocent village?"

Wolfgang asked.

"Maybe it's easily defensible, or perhaps they think we won't attack them," Otto said.

"I'm just not too sure about this. But if we take out the rebels, the village will be fine, right?"

"Hey, quiet. We're too close to the village. The rebels may have scouts," Aksel said.

***

It was close to midnight when they arrived outside of the village. There were a few watchmen patrolling the streets, but other than that, the whole place was quiet. It didn't look like a rebellion's stronghold, but Wolfgang knew looks could be deceiving.

They waited in the woods and brush as Martin and Aksel prepared the troops. The bowmen were to fire several barrages of flaming arrows at the village, then the rest would charge forward and attack. Everyone was in position, and the arrows were lit.

"Why do we have to set the village on fire?" Wolfgang asked Aksel.

"To get the rebels out of hiding."

"But what about the villagers?"

"Everyone in this village is a rebel, lambkin."

"Huh?"

The order to attack interrupted Wolfgang's questions. Arrows flew through the sky like comets streaking across the night, landing on the hatch roofs and wooden walls of houses and shops. Then another volley, and another. Then, everyone attacked.

Wolfgang looked around, confused, as the karls charged into the village. He followed them, trying to stay with Aksel, but lost him in the smoke and flames. He looked around at people running from their homes only to be slaughtered by axes and spears, children crying for their parents only to be swept away by those who wished to sell them into a life of servitude, and through it all, Wolfgang stood helpless.

He saw flashes of Visenville in this burning village. He started yelling to drown out the sounds of screaming. It wasn't an attack on rebels, it was a village raid—a massacre. He tried to close his eyes, the smoke mixing with his tears caused his pupils to hurt. No matter what he tried, he couldn't get the images of Viesenville out of his head. He fell to his knees, crying, and dropped his poleax. The violent images of Visenville began to mix with the images of bodies filling the streets of the Juad Quarter in Eifenhart. Blood, suffering, death- these things Wolfgang knew too well.

Wolfgang looked up, and through the smoke, seeing a little girl and her mother on the ground, begging for their lives. For a moment, they looked like his mother and his sister Julia. Then, Aksel cut the mother down with his ax, and picked up the girl. Wolfgang reached out to save them, but there was nothing he could do. Aksel looked at Wolfgang, gazing at him with monstrous and empty eyes, before the smoke obscured him again. Wolfgang didn't know what to do. A hand rested on his shoulder, and a calming voice spoke to him.

"Hey, kid, are you alright?" It was Tuferan, the camp surgeon.

He must've followed to treat the wounded after the battle. "This... this isn't what I thought I'd be paid for."

"Wolfgang?" another voice sounded from the dark.

It was Alphonse, along with the others.

"This is..." Wolfgang reached under his armor and pulled out the cross his mother gave him, and gripped it tight. "This price is too high."

He stood up, picking up his poleax, and turned away from the village, walking into the woods. The boys and Tuferan followed him into the dark, all unable to rationalize the horrors they witnessed.

***

When the morning came, there was nothing left but the charred remains of homes and rotting bodies. The crows and vultures had already begun plucking out the eyes and lips of the dead. Soon, the flies and ants would come to finish cleaning them to the bone. Many of the villagers, especially the children, were taken to be sold.

"Where are the ones we're missing?" Martin asked Aksel.

"Who knows? I bet they ran off," Aksel replied.

"Why would they do that? They haven't even been paid."

"I saw the look in the lambkin's eyes. It wasn't the look of a warrior, but that of a terrified child."

"Nobles are all the same, eh? They never have the stomach for war. They hire us and raise their levies to fight, and turn a blind eye to things like this. They pretend it doesn't happen."

"It's just easier for them. They come from a different world than us, after all," Aksel laughed. "The elite will always send someone else's son to fight their wars. Just how it is."

"Well, I hope those five return home. The battlefield is no place for nobles like them."

***

Wolfgang and the others regrouped in the wilderness. They returned to the City of Ash to gather their things from the camp and set out to the north. They were unsure of what the future held, but they were determined to pluck an edelweiss from the mountain peaks in Etalia.

"I won't be like that, I can't," Wolfgang told the others while they marched.

"You're right, brother. We mustn't allow ourselves to become that low," Otto agreed.

"But you can't blame them. They are, after all, completely different from us," Alphonse stated.

"But one can't excuse such barbarism and atrocity," Francis said.

"He's right, there's no excuse for that," Wolfgang added.

"Well, if you five intend on being moral karls, then I'll lend my services to you. Not like I have anywhere else to go, since I was banished from Oppenstein anyway," Tuferan said.

So, the party of five became a party of six. They crossed the border into Yuunsburg, then went further north into the Duchy of Nammelund—a country renowned for its seafarers. They arrived at the height of summer in the town of Bad Ruckburg, ready for their next adventure.

The Mary Rose

The Regent is based on the author's favorite tall ship, The Mary Rose.

The Mary Rose was comissioned in 1510 and launched in 1511. During Medieval Europe, nations did not maintain large navies. Instead, navies would be made up of merchant ships that were commandeered or purchased. Some noble houses or bourgouise that had ties to merchants would have their own small naval force used for trade.

This would began to change around the time of the Tudor Era, in the late medieval period. Henry the 8th would commission two ships to be built as part of his "army at sea" military doctorine. The Peter Pomegranate would be the other ship. The Mary Rose was likely named after The Virgin Mary, with the rose being the symbol of the King. In 1513 the Mary Rose would win in a fleet race, finishing half a mile ahead of another ship. The Mary Rose would be the flag ship of England's fleet for many years. Cutting edge at the time, by the year of its sinking in 1545 it was begining to fall behind larger and faster carracks and galley's. During an engagement with The French on the Isle of Wight, the Mary Rose would arrive to participate in The Battle of the Solent. King Henry would watch from a southsea castle, as the winds began to blow in the favor of the English, and the fleet was deployed to meet the French. As the Mary Rose sortied, she would fire her starboard cannons. She would then come about and fire her portside cannons. The wind blew too strong, and the ship began to list. The gubports, for some reason, were left open, causing the ship to flood and sink. Only about 35 of her 500 man crew would survive. One man, believed to be a longbowmen due to his shoulder blades being fused together, was found in at the lowest point of the ship in the storage room near the kitchen. The Mary rose was the only ship lost in the battle. One reason why she sank may have been to communication. It was common practice to have various sailors from around the world on board. The Mary Rose had men fron Africa, Italy, France, and Flanders. It's possible that they were unable to understand the orders to close the gunports, or were too slow, cauing the sinking.

Chapter 17

"Wolves," Otto told the group standing outside a small farm on the outskirts of Bad Ruckburg. A light rain shower fell as they spoke.

"Not just any wolves, enormous ones!" Wolfgang added.

"Well, is this farmer hiring us to hunt them?" Alphonse asked.

"Hiring? Like I have the coin for that," the farmer said as he approached the boys. "Go see the bailiff in the village. He can pay yuh. Now, outta me way, I need to get inside. It's raining out!"

They heeded the farmer's advice and find the bailiff. Bad Ruckburg was small, but there was lots of construction going on around the outskirts. The bailiff's office was in the town square. It was a small two-story wooden structure. As they stepped inside, they spoke to a watchman standing guard. The first floor served as both an armory for the watch and a jail. The watchman led them upstairs to the bailiff's office.

"Hey, who's bothering me now?" the bailiff asked, not standing up from his desk.

He was writing on parchment and placing the scribed parchment in an enormous pile.

"Uh, hello, sir. We're karls from the south. We heard you had a problem with wolves and could pay a modest fee for extermination," Otto told him.

"Ah, yes—the wolves. They've been quite the pain. Ever since we began logging the nearby woods to expand to a new district, they've been attacking cattle. That's one thing, but we recently found a girl—the daughter of one farmer—dead. Looked like she was eaten and left out in the wilds. Only a dire wolf could've done that."

"A dire wolf?" Wolfgang asked. "I've heard of those. Are they real?"

"Yes, they're ruthless things. Some are as big as a house. Normal wolves gather around them. See, the giant wolves act as a leader or something." The bailiff set down his quill and looked at the boys. "I'll pay ten groschen for every wolf's pelt you bring me, and fifty for the dire wolf."

"That's a good deal," Alphonse whispered.

"Yeah, and this job should be easy," Wolfgang said.

"Well, at least we're not killing people," Tuferan said.

"Okay." Otto turned to the bailiff. "We agree to your terms. We'll be back with the pelts."

"Oh, before you leave, while you're out there, keep an eye out for a young man about your age. The abbot's son went missing a few months ago. I doubt he's alive, so pay attention to the forest floor."

With that, the boys set off to the local alehouse for drink, food, and to formulate a plan. As they drank beer and ate chicken and bread, they talked about their strategy.

"So, do we just wander the woods and attack every wolf we see?" Wolfgang asked.

"No way. They'd know we're coming. It won't work," Alphonse stated.

"He's right, we'll have to use bows, so that means Wolfgang is out," Otto said.

"I can buy a bow," Wolfgang said.

"Brother, even if you did, your aim is so abysmal, you'd probably hit one of us by accident," Otto joked.

"Hey!" Wolfgang shouted with a mouth full of bread.

"I also lack a bow," Francis said. "If the good Wolfgang and I put out bait, you three could shoot the wolves down."

"That's a good plan," Jurgen said. "Then Tuferan here could standby in case one of us gets bit."

"Works for me," Tuferan confirmed.

"Alright. What can we use to bait wolves?" Otto asked.

"Meat would probably be our best bet," Alphonse answered. "There's gotta be a trapper somewhere in town. I'm sure they sell cheap meat for bait."

"Then it's a plan. We'll buy bait, arrows, and set up a spot in the woods to hunt," Otto confirmed.

***

The boys stayed the night in an inn, and upon morning, went to find the local trapper. A small house with a straw thatched roof sat near the outskirts of town, and according to the alemaidens, it was where the trapper ran his business. Otto led the group and knocked on the building's warped wooden door. A friendly looking old man with a thick beard and a thicker coat opened the door and smiled at them.

"Lookin' for a trappa'?" the man asked in a gentle voice.

The Wolf's Song

"Uh, yeah. We need some bait. We're hunting wolves," Otto answered.

"Ah, I see! I'll give ya some bait, but also, you need some wolf essence to hide yer scent!"

"Wolf essence?" Otto asked.

"Yes, yes! Stay here." The man closed the door and returned with a sack and a couple of nets full of dead rabbits after a moment. "Here, I just slaughtered 'em. Should attract all kinds of wolves. In this sack are vials of wolf essence. Douse it in yer skin and it'll hide ya scent." He handed the things to the boys. "When ye done, bring the bodies back to me. I'll skin 'em for ya, won't even charge ya if you let me keep the meat!"

"Uh... okay, I shall," Otto replied awkwardly.

After that strange exchange, the boys set out for the wilderness. They stepped through thick bushes and trees beyond the local logging site and stopped at a small clearing.

"This looks like as good a place as any," Jurgen said.

"Yeah, we can hide in those bushes over there," Otto added.

"Wolfgang, Francis, put the bait in the middle of the clearing," Alphonse ordered.

Wolfgang and Francis carried nets full of freshly killed rabbits on their backs. They set them down, along with their sacks.

"Alright, let's take out those vials of wolf's essence and douse ourselves to hide the scent, just like the trapper told us to," Otto said.

Everyone except for Tuferan did as Otto said and began rubbing the strange liquid all over their skins.

"Hey, Tuferan, why aren't you covering yourself in essence?" Wolfgang asked.

"Do... do you guys know what's in those vials?" Tuferan asked.

"Well, yeah, wolf essence," Wolfgang replied in a condescending tone.

"It's wolf piss."

"What?" Otto asked, eyes widening.

"That's how hunters hide their scent."

Everyone stared at Tuferan, shocked at what they heard. They were all covered in the wolf piss, and suddenly felt dirty.

"Um... how do they collect it, then?" Wolfgang asked.

"I... I don't care. I just want a bath," Jurgen said.

"We'll need to find a river and wash... everything after this," Otto added.

"I'll wait outside the woods. Come find me if you need me," Tuferan laughed.

The boys clearly weren't hunters. Although they all had experience hunting rabbits and other small game, wolf hunting was a new experience for them. They persisted onward, getting ready to kill whatever came for the bait. Jurgen, Alphonse, and Otto all took up opposing positions in the trees, like a triangle around the clearing. Wolfgang and Francis stayed just beyond the clearing, waiting to help carry the wolf carcasses back to be skinned by the trapper.

Several hours passed, and they were getting frustrated from sitting in the heat for so long. Then, just as Otto was thinking of calling it off, a wolf appeared. Then another, and another. Several of them approached the rabbits and ate them.

The three stood up slowly, drew back their bows, and prepared to fire. They planned on firing in unison. Otto would fire first, then the other two just after. There were five wolves present, so they'd bag at least three.

Otto released his string, his arrow flying. Alphonse and Jurgen did the same. In just a second, three wolves were down. Otto's arrow hit a wolf in the stomach, Alphonse hit one's head, and Jurgen hit one in the neck. The other two ran toward Wolfgang and Francis.

"Brother, two are heading your way!" Otto shouted.

Wolfgang drew his dagger and stood, preparing to attack a wolf. As the wolf drew near, it tried to avoid him by running to the left. Wolfgang jumped at it, tackled it to the ground, and slit its throat. It let out a whine as life faded from its eyes.

Back at the clearing, Otto approached his game, still alive and whimpering. He drew his dagger to finish it, but a strange sadness came over him.

"What's wrong?" Alphonse asked.

"I don't know, this feels wrong," Otto replied.

"You must finish it now. It's the right thing to do," Jurgen said. "Besides, they're attacking people, right?"

"I suppose." Otto drove his dagger into its neck to finish it.

***

They brought the carcasses to the trapper, and he skinned them and kept the meat. Then they brought the pelts to the bailiff and received payment. The boys repeated that process several times over the next few days, bathing every night before returning to the inn.

After a week, one rainy night, they sat in the dining hall of the inn—drinking beer and eating rabbit stew. They were discussing their plans to find the dire wolf and finish the miserable job when a strange man approached them.

"Hey! Did I hear you right? Are you killing wolves?" he shouted at them.

He was bald and looked to be in his late forties, with a pencil-thin pointy mustache and crows feet around his eyes. He wore a dirty tunic and carried a large rucksack on his back.

"Um... yes? Can we help you, sir?" Otto asked politely.

"I knew it! Why are you killing those poor, innocent animals?"

"Hold on, who are you?" Otto asked.

"I'm a traveler! I follow the Code of the Road, like all travelers are supposed to do. Clearly you don't! Answer me!" he shouted.

"I mean, we're getting paid to. Also, you call them innocent, but there's been reports of attacks," Alphonse answered.

"Has anyone seen those attacks?" the odd traveler asked.

"Huh, I guess not? But there's been half eaten bodies found," Wolfgang said.

"That doesn't mean the wolves killed them!" the odd traveler shouted. "Do none of you know the code?"

"What are you prattling on about?" Otto asked, annoyed.

Suddenly, the man started singing completely out of tune.

I live by the code of the road,

Adventure calling me!

"Oh, I know this song! We used to sing it while we marched with the karlband," Wolfgang said.

He then sang with the man. Although Wolfgang had a decent singing voice, he tried to match the out of tune rhythm of the traveler, which resulted in the both of them sounding like broken organ pipes.

"Will you two stop!" Otto shouted as he stood up and slammed his hands on the table. "What are you talking about, good sir? You aren't making any sense!"

"Ah, listen up!" the odd traveler began.

"Yeah, listen!" Wolfgang also shouted, deciding to support the traveler.

"Wolves don't attack people, and they only go after cattle when it's exposed and their food sources dwindle. The people here have been demolishing the wolves' homes and driving away their food. So, they've turned to eating cattle."

"Well, maybe that's true, but what about the dire wolf sightings? And the dead bodies?" Jurgen asked.

"It's said when the forest is in danger, the forest nymphs set out to find a wolf worthy of protecting their pack and turn them into a great dire wolf!"

"That's a nice story, but it doesn't answer my question," Jurgen repeated.

"Fine. The dire wolf is just protecting its folk. As for the bodies, have you ever considered it may be people murdering other people?"

"Well, no, why would we?" Otto asked.

"Also, how do we know what you're saying is even true? I mean, wolves attack people all the time," Jurgen added.

"Not so. Wolves—and this is true for all nature—are meant to have a peaceful coexistence with mankind! It's man who's broken his relationship with nature, causing harmless wolves to turn to great beasts! They fight purely out of desperation, I tell you!" The odd traveler then sat at their table, grabbed Otto's beer, and took a long drink.

"H-hey, I paid for that!" Otto protested.

"Listen, I saw them. Wildmen—out in the woods, I tell ya. I've seen many wildmen in my travels. They must be behind this."

"Wildmen? It's been long since I've seen such creatures,"

Francis began. "They're men twisted by evil, and have taken to the wilderness to attack others and do unspeakable things to them."

"That's an apt description," the odd traveler responded. "Now, I must ask, why do you hunt these wolves? Are you simply trying to help the people of Bad Ruckburg?"

"Well, that's part of it," Wolfgang started. "We also need money to travel to Westlichtenhalfen. We heard ferries are expensive."

"Hmm... I know of a place where you can get a cheap passage across the sea, or at least how to find a cheap passage," the odd traveler said.

"Really?" Wolfgang's eyes lit up.

"Yes, and I'll tell you." He leaned in close. "If you help me!" He smiled.

"With what?" Otto asked.

"Catching the real culprits, of course. Look at this!" The man took off his rucksack, dug in it, then pulled out a rusted dagger with a jagged blade. "See how this blade is jagged? It's wildmen! I found this out by the road. I also saw several men stalking the outskirts of town with no torches two nights ago."

"I think we should help him!" Wolfgang said.

"No way! He's insane," Otto argued.

"But he knows of cheap passage across the Great Channel," Jurgen added.

"The jagged blade is a sign of wildmen. They often modify their weapons in strange ways. I see no harm in helping him, at least until we conclude the truth," Francis said.

"Fine, we can look into the wildmen," Otto agreed.

"Perfect! Meet me here tomorrow morning, and we'll set off

together!" the odd traveler shouted as he stood up.

"Together?" Tuferan asked after being silent during the entire exchange.

"Yes, together!"

"Hm, I just attract all kinds of weirdos, don't I?" Tuferan muttered.

"Did you say something, Surgeon?" Otto asked.

"Oh, uh, no. Also, you do know my name."

"Actually, I don't think we do," Alphonse stated.

"Oh, I do!" Wolfgang began. "It's Taffyon!"

"Taffyon? Like taffy, the candy?" Jurgen asked.

"No, no, it's Tuferan," he corrected.

"What was that? Speak up, Taffyon," Wolfgang said.

"Nevermind, Surgeon is just fine," Tuferan replied, annoyed.

***

When morning arrived, the boys met with the odd traveler in the inn's dining hall. He smiled as they approached.

"Okay, let's get going!" the odd traveler shouted.

"Hold on, we should eat first," Alphonse said.

"I have salted meat we can eat on the way!" the odd traveler replied.

"Hold on, why do you still have your rucksack on? Why not leave it in your room?" Otto asked.

"My room? Oh, I slept outside. I don't have enough money to stay here. 'Tis the life of an adventure!"

"Or someone who's just bad with their money," Otto muttered.

"Come on, the early sparrow catches the flying arrow!" The odd traveler turned and left.

With a sigh, the boys followed.

They ate salted bacon as they made their way to the forest beyond the logging site. They weren't sure what they were looking for, but the odd traveler seemed to know where he was going. After walking into the woods for a few minutes, he stopped.

"Beyond this underbrush is where I found the jagged dagger, which is around a four- or five-minute walk from where one of those girls was found."

"Well, I suppose this is as good a place as any to look," Alphonse said.

"But what exactly are we looking for?" Otto asked.

"If we're searching for wildmen, then we need to look for signs," Francis began. "Campfires, bones and weapons, arrows. They also leave strange symbols painted on trees and rocks, normally with animal blood, and they sometimes make odd sigils to pray to."

"You know a lot about these folk," Jurgen said.

"I had to deal with them in Lothargia when I was traveling east. Wildmen, as far as I'm aware, don't have any shared beliefs or culture. They're simple men corrupted by evil, who take to the wilds, where they can be free to do as they please."

"That's impressive!" Wolfgang said. "I don't know much about these wildmen, but the duke blamed the attack on my village years ago on a bunch of them. So, they must be bad people."

"Indeed, they can be. But they weren't always that way. I remember reading about Duke Edward the Insane, who led the Duchy of the Midlands in Angland. By all accounts, he was a good, honorable man. Until he disappeared in 1283, only to be found years later worshiping a strange sigil made of animal bones, covered in self-inflicted scars, and attacking the folk that found him," Otto said.

"No one knows exactly how somebody becomes a wildman," the odd traveler said in a suddenly somber tone. "I lost a friend to the wilds, once. He was a good man until he took to gambling and heavy drinking. I don't know, the change was fast. Before I knew it, he'd completely lost it."

"If these attacks really are wildmen, we need to stop it quickly," Jurgen added. "Animal attacks are one thing. But wildmen are unpredictable, and beyond dangerous."

"Alright, let's get searching. Everyone spread out, but stay within shouting distance," Otto said.

With renewed vigor, the boys spread out, looking for any clues they could. The woods were thick and stretched for miles, so it would take some time to find any evidence of wildmen. They combed the woods for several hours. Wolfgang saw something on a tree. He peered closer to see a strange symbol painted in animal blood. It looked like a circle, with intersecting lines inside, and something like horns coming out of the top. As he stared at it, he heard a yell from deeper in the woods. It was Alphonse.

"Hey, everyone, come here! I found something!" he shouted.

They all assembled at his position.

What he found was a campsite, roughly a few hours old. There were several arrows with odd sigils carved into their heads and animal bones scattered throughout the camp, almost like whoever there left in a hurry. The boys drew their weapons, just in case the camp's owner returned.

"Look, the kindling from the fire is still smoking. They must've just been here!" the odd traveler said. "This must be wildmen. Look at that!" He pointed at what looked like a makeshift altar with a half-constructed sigil on top.

"Yes, the signs certainly seem like wildmen. This camp looks like it was abandoned in haste," Francis said.

"Could we have scared them off?" Wolfgang asked.

An intense growl sounded from brambles and bushes. Appearing from the thick underbrush was a massive wolf, nearly the size of a small house. Its fur was white, and its eyes almost glowed blue. It slowly walked toward them. The boys pointed their weapons at it.

"No, don't kill it! This is the dire wolf, the protector of the pack! I swear it's harmless!" the odd traveler shouted.

"Look at it, it's going to attack!" Otto shouted back.

"Do you always judge a creature by how it looks?" the odd traveler asked.

"Fine, but you didn't say not to fight it!" Alphonse yelled as he threw down his longsword and raised his fists.

"He... doesn't intend to fist fight it, does he?"

The odd traveler was concerned, as were the others.

The dire wolf rushed forward, its long legs kicking up dirt as it ran. Alphonse moved his right arm up, charging his fist for an attack. As the dire wolf approached, its terrifying jaws just within range, Alphonse's fist connected with the creature's snout. He punched upward, exposing the beast's belly. He then ran beneath it, planted his feet, lifted the dire wolf completely off the ground with a loud grunt, and slammed it into the dirt on its back. With a whimper, it rolled over. It looked at Alphonse and the boys, then turned and walked back into the woods.

"Huh... I thought it was going to attack again." Alphonse stood, confused.

"I told you it was harmless!" the odd traveler shouted.

The Wolf's Song

"Wow, you're strong—like an ox," Tuferan told Alphonse. "Honestly, I've seen nothing like that before."

"I'm feeling rather fatigued, and night is approaching. Shall we head back?" Francis suggested.

"Yeah, and we should warn the bailiff of the wildmen," Otto said.

The group began their march back to Bad Ruckburg. As dusk arrived, they reached the logging site, where several townsfolk being led into the woods by the bailiff greeted them. They were armed with bills, longbows, and torches.

"Oh, it's the karls I hired," the bailiff said.

"What's going on?" Otto asked.

"You karls have done well with extermination, but it's not enough. They found two more girls dead today, and the abbot's daughter was missing. We're going to finish them."

"Finish them?" The odd traveler was shocked.

"You can't kill the wolves!" Wolfgang shouted.

"Why not?" the bailiff asked.

"It's not wolves killing people, it's wildmen!"

Wolfgang's words shocked the villagers.

"Im-impossible. There are no wildmen in Bad Ruckburg!" the bailiff said.

"We found their campsite deeper in the woods. A strange altar made of bones and weird sigils. No doubt about it, they aren't looters or brigands, they're wildmen," Otto said.

"By God, are you serious?" The bailiff stopped for a moment. "But the wolves are still a problem."

"But recklessly killing them won't solve this problem," Jurgen said. "Let's look for the girl and fight the wildmen. We're experienced soldiers, and it would be dangerous for you to stalk the woods alone."

"We also don't know how many wildmen there may be. Could be a dozen or more, or less," Alphonse added.

"Tsk. Wildmen. If what you say is true, then we have little time. Fine. We'll follow your lead," the bailiff responded.

"Listen, if we spread out, we'll increase our chance of finding them. But we need to stay close enough to still see each other," Wolfgang said.

"Yeah, brother is right," Otto began. "Let's spread out about arm's length. With all of us, this should be easy."

The posse headed into the woods, desperately searching for their quarry. They treaded through bushes and brambles; their legs getting cut up by thorns and sticks. None of the villagers had proper armor, and their thin cotton hose tore easy. But it didn't stop them.

After some time, Wolfgang spotted a faint light in the dark. He peered closer to see what looked like a campfire. He then heard laughing.

"Over here!" he shouted. "Hurry, before they get away!" He ran toward the fire and drew his poleax.

When he arrived at the campsite, there were about fifteen men. They wore fur coats and pants, but no shirts or armor. Many of them wore goat and wolf skulls on their heads, and scaring—strange symbols carved into their skin—covered their bodies. The men gathered in a circle around a young man in tattered, expensive clothing, who stood holding a jagged dagger over a young girl tied to a makeshift altar.

"Ah, our guests are here," the man said.

He turned to face Wolfgang. His eyes were blue and devilish, and his curly mustache was unkempt and full of split ends. Wolfgang took up a guard and prepared to attack as the rest of the posse arrived.

"Wait, that's—" the bailiff, who'd just emerged from the woods, began.

"The bailiff, my father's wretched lap dog," the man replied.

"It's the abbot's son," the bailiff finished.

"What? This monster is his son?" Otto was just as surprised as everyone else.

"Monster? You call me a monster? How am I a monster when I am so free? Free to do as I please!"

"You are not free. You are merely a slave to your desires," Francis said.

"Let that girl go!" Wolfgang shouted.

"No." The abbot's son paused for a moment. "I was hoping my father would be with you, but this will do. We're going to kill you all, skin you, and gut you. But first, we need to gut her."

He turned toward the girl and placed his dagger's blade against her stomach. Wolfgang leaped forwards, pushing him to the ground.

"You monster. How dare you do that to your own sister?" he growled.

The other wildmen grabbed various weapons and surrounded Wolfgang.

"Brother!" Otto shouted.

"Don't worry about me!" Wolfgang responded. "Bailiff, have the posse surround the campsite! We can overpower them if we flank them!"

"R-right, do as he says, everyone!" the bailiff ordered.

The villagers did as they were told, and the wildmen turned their attention from Wolfgang to the others.

"Wildmen are dangerous, but they are too far gone to fight properly. As a group, we can win!" Francis shouted.

"Right, everyone! Attack!" Otto said.

The posse ran forward, weapons ready.

Wolfgang looked at the abbot's son, who stared at him with angry, hateful eyes. He stood up and prepared the jagged dagger he had for a fight. The villagers fought viciously with the wildmen, stabbing and slashing at them with their pitchforks, bills, and sickles. The wildmen fought back, but because of their frail and malnourished frames, they couldn't do much damage.

The abbot's son charged forward, thrusting his dagger at Wolfgang. Wolfgang responded quickly, swinging the hammer end of his poleax down. His opponent ducked low, narrowly avoiding the swing. He then leaped at Wolfgang and grabbed a hold of his poleax, taking it out of his hands, and throwing it to the ground. Wolfgang had to fight unarmed. His opponent rushed forward, and Wolfgang put his hands up in front of his chest. As his opponent thrust his dagger at Wolfgang's chest, he stepped to his left and reached his left arm around his opponent's right arm—the hand holding the dagger. Wolfgang bent his elbow and pulled his opponent into a lower bind. He then brought his right hand around, grasped his left, and pulled up. That trapped his opponent in an upper bind. With a quick twist, he dislocated his enemy's arm, then threw him to the ground. Wolfgang picked up the dropped dagger and approached the abbot's son. His eyes were full of fear and his face pain. Wolfgang growled as he placed the point of the dagger on his enemy's neck.

"Do it. Come on, kill a defenseless foe. Be like one of us. Give into your desire to kill!" the abbot's son ordered.

"Brother! Show him mercy!" Otto yelled.

That snapped Wolfgang out of his trance. He threw the dagger aside and stood up. "I'll turn you over to the village."

He then walked over to untie the girl. She was unconscious, so he called Tuferan over to look at her.

"She's breathing, at least," he reported. "We should get her back to the village."

"Y-yes, yes! Hey, someone, take her back to the church!" the bailiff ordered.

"We should bury them, the wildmen," Francis suggested.

"Why? These monsters should have their bodies burned, just like their souls burn in Hades," the bailiff retorted.

"That is not for us to decide. We should do the right thing," Francis replied.

"Well, we can't just leave the bodies out for scavengers. It's dark, but I agree with Francis," Jurgen agreed.

"Fine, I'll have the executioner come and bury them. You can help, but I won't be sullying myself by touching bodies."

***

They spent the next couple of hours digging shallow graves with the local executioner and set the bodies to rest. Francis led the group in a prayer for the departed, and they headed back to the village. On their way, Wolfgang spotted something odd in a clearing. It was dark, and there were branches and bushes in the way. But he thought he saw an old man. Perhaps, perhaps the wandering priest petting the giant dire wolf that attacked them earlier.

Wolfgang broke off from the group and walked toward them, closing his eyes as he pushed through brambles and branches. As he stepped into the clearing, he opened his eyes, but it was empty. No one was there. Could he have simply hallucinated? He looked up at the sky, admiring the stars and broken moon, before heading back into the woods to join the others.

The boys were exhausted, and it was nearly morning, so they slept until afternoon. When they got up, they found the odd traveler waiting for them in the dining hall of the inn. He smiled as they approached him.

"Hey, it's you! The traveler guy!" Wolfgang said.

"Yes, that is me," the odd traveler responded. "Thank you for all your help. I believe I owe you something."

"Oh yeah, you said you know where we can get cheap travel to Westlichtenhalfen," Alphonse remembered.

"Yes! The city of Großhenburg! The capital of Nammelund!" he said.

"Hm, I suppose ferries will be there. But ferries should also be in most towns on the coast," Otto retorted.

"But I know of a special place for real cheap travel! Near the harbor, there's a tavern named the *Dead Sailor's Drink*! The tavern is huge—it's where most of the captains of merchant and pirate hunting vessels drink! Rather than hiring an expensive ferry, find a merchant vessel sailing to your destination, and join them as an unpaid deckhand! Help on the ship, and you'll get free passage across the Great Channel!"

"Really?" Wolfgang's eyes lit up. "Did you hear that, brothers? We can sail for free!"

"Well, it isn't exactly free, since we have to work," Jurgen added.

"Yes, we would. But then we can save money. This journey has been quite expensive and I don't want to be out of coin when we need it most," Otto said.

"I do not mind working on a ship. The ferry I took to get to Ostenhalfen was very expensive," Francis said.

"Then it's settled! To Großhenburg we go!" Wolfgang shouted.

"Well, we need to get the rest of our bounty from the bailiff first," Tuferan said.

"Be careful out there!" the odd traveler said as the boys left. "Don't get too drunk at the tavern! And don't trust anyone who wants to give you free drinks!" he shouted as they walked out. "I really hope they heard me."

The boys received their final pay, gathered their things, and left for Großhenburg. On their way, they found a small merchant caravan also heading in the same direction and were hired on as guards. Little did they know, their adventure was about to take quite a turn...

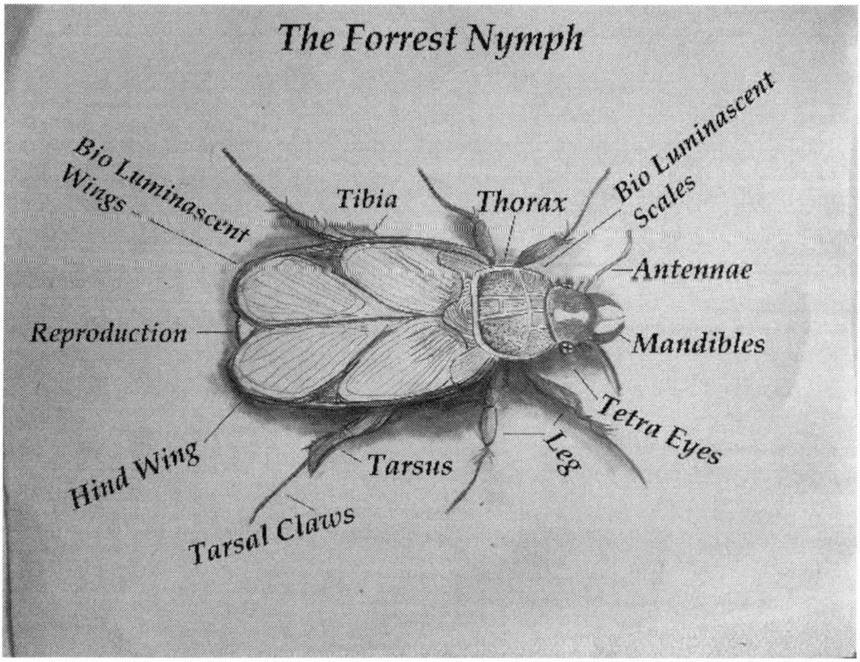
The Forrest Nymph
Bio Luminascent Wings
Tibia
Thorax
Bio Luminascent Scales
Antennae
Reproduction
Mandibles
Tetra Eyes
Leg
Hind Wing
Tarsus
Tarsal Claws

Chapter 18

As the boys made their way westward, they encountered a caravan on a well-traveled highway. They stuck with the caravan as they traveled and shared tales of their adventures with the caravan master and the guards. As they neared their destination, they found a large monument. It was a stone statue, roughly four-stories high, of a woman in a robe, with her left arm outstretched toward the sea, and a sword in her right hand.

"That's the monument to St. Basilia," the caravan master began, talking to Wolfgang and the others. "They call her the Lady of the Water. It's said that a Berberia's pirate ship wrecked near here during a storm. Their ship was full of treasure after attacking a fleet of Kaspian ships returning from trade in northern Ofrika. The pirates sailed north to outrun the vessels chasing them, and got caught up in the storm. Apparently, St. Basilia was a nun at a nearby monastery, and she leaped into the water and saved every pirate. Those pirates all repented and became monks."

"Wow, did that really happen?" Wolfgang asked.

"Of course it did," the caravan master replied, offended. "She's a legend in Nammelund."

"That's really incredible," Otto added.

"Who built the monument? It's massive." Alphonse asked.

"Those monks did." the caravan master replied.

"No, it was some locals that built it. No way monks could build that." a traveler in the caravan chimed in.

"I heard it just appeared here overnight, the day after St. Basilia fell asleep with The Lord." another traveler added.

"No way that could have happened." Otto doubted.

"In any case, it's there, and it's a sign we're near Großhenburg." the caravan master said.

***

They arrived in the city after a couple more hours of travel. Farms and small hamlets filled the outskirts. The massive city hugged the coastline and bled into a huge harbor. Every part of the city smelled of fish and ocean salt. The boys left the caravan behind and set off to find the *Dead Sailor's Drink*.

"It was somewhere near the port, right?" Otto asked.

"We should look around there, then," Alphonse agreed.

"But this port is so big! How are we gonna find it?" Wolfgang asked.

"We can ask the denizens," Francis said.

"I agree. We should ask around and keep an eye out," Jurgen said.

They walked along the docks, checking every tavern and shop they saw. They asked several people, but most seemed reluctant to share the tavern's location. Eventually, they found an old man kind enough to show them the way. The *Dead Sailor's Drink* was in an alley, tucked behind some homes and shops. It was a large building, but its small sign helped it blend in with the surrounding buildings. The sun had just set when they found it, and a group of sailors entered just before they did.

As the boys stepped inside, loud music, shouting merchants, and the smell of meat, puke, and ale accosted their senses.

"This... certainly looks like the place," Otto said sarcastically.

The boys found a table and sat down, ordering mead from an alemaiden.

"So, now we need to find that cheap passage," Alphonse said.

"Is someone lookin' for cheap passage across the sea?" a man with a guitar asked as he approached them.

He was young, roughly in his early twenties. He had short blond hair and green eyes. He wore what looked like an expensive green and red tunic and red leather hose. He had a large white collar wrapped around his neck.

"Uh, yes, we are. I take it you overheard us?" Otto asked.

"Ah, how rude of me—I haven't introduced myself yet! They call me Arthur the Sea Bard!" He put his leg on a stool and leaned into the group. "How about a song?"

"H-hold on, good sir. You said you know of how we can get a cheap passage across the sea?" Otto asked.

"Oh, yes, I do! But first, let's do a drunken sing song! Come on, I'll even provide the ale!"

"Well, I won't say no to free alcohol!" Alphonse smiled.

"We've been working so hard. Let's have some fun!" Wolfgang shouted.

"I have a bad feeling about this, but I won't say no to free drink," Tuferan added.

"Yes, let us have fun," Francis said as he pulled a bamboo straw out of his bag.

"Perfect!" An enormous grin stretched across Arthur's face as he turned away from the boys and grabbed a chair from another table. He jumped up on the chair and looked over at the tavern's patrons. "This song is old, and a beloved one! This goes out to our friendly travelers there!"

The room went quiet as Arthur tapped on the side of his guitar. Then he strummed an upbeat tune. Everyone knew the tune. When he started singing, so did the whole tavern.

Well, me lads, I've been a travelin', almost all my life

I faced my fear, got out of here, into this world of strife

See, I, here, seek no fortune, no glory, gold, or fame

The way I tread far up ahead, the road, it calls my name

Hey! I live by the code of the road, adventure calling me

Yet wine so grand, in this old land, it's where I'm meant to be

Well, I've been far up north, where ale flows like the sea

Nivaby-folk as hard as oak, but not half drunk as me

Then I walked up on across the Great Wolderan

They dress well but bore me to hell, so packed my things and ran. Hey!

I live by the code of the road, adventure calling me, yet wine so grand

In this old land, it's where I'm meant to be

I was up in Berbia. Those pirates, like their knives, got in my way. I could not stay

Got frisky with their wives, so onward to Londonium, behind a hill and ridge

I miss the river Tamesis, helped build the bloody bridge. Hey!

I live by the code of the road, adventure calling me

Yet wine so grand, in this old land, it's where I'm meant to be

Made a mate down in Lothargia, but friendships there are sparse,

Upon my journey on a tourny I kicked the bastard's arse,

I climbed the Alpiana, logged the trees of Flanderan

Then onto fine Kaspian wine, and olives Cyprigulean. Hey!

I live by the code of the road, adventure calling me

Yet wine so grand, in this old land, it's where I'm meant to be. Hey!

***

They drank and sang all night long. Every time the boys emptied their tankards, someone filled them right back up free of charge. Before they knew it, they were close to passing out. A group of men approached them as they drifted in and out of consciousness.

"Hey, we heard you wanted to travel the sea," one man said.

"Uh… y-yeah, we need-we need to go to sea—" Wolfgang drunkenly answered.

"Sorry, lads. But we'll be singing again real soon," Arthur laughed.

"W-what?" Otto asked as the world around him became more and more blurry.

"Hey, grab their stuff. It looks expensive. We can fence it when we reach port in Uotgaurd," one man ordered.

The other men picked up the boys as they all fell into a drunken sleep.

***

Caleb the Writer

Wolfgang awoke the next morning to a bucket of cold water splashing his face. He stood up quickly, only for a large man to push him back down. Wolfgang sat on a wooden deck, surrounded by the others, as well as several people he didn't recognize. He was inside somewhere, and it felt like the entire world rock back and forth. A man with a silver whistle around his neck approached them.

"Wake up, you scallywags!" the man shouted. "You're at sea now. The shipmaster and captain want to see ya, so get up and follow me to the upper deck."

"Hold on, who do you think—" Otto began, but a stick hitting his head cut him off.

"Shut up! Follow me," the man with the whistle shouted.

They headed topside to the upper deck, climbing up several decks.

The ship had four decks total, and two decks at its sterncastle and three at the forecastle. There were blue and white stripes painted along the trim of the decks, with large blue streamers tied to each mast. The mainmast topsail was blue with a white anchor sewn into it. Hemp rope protected the upper deck attached to the forecastle and sterncastle, creating a net that could catch debris in case of a battle. Each side of the deck had portholes for cannons and larger ones for bowmen. Wolfgang spotted Arthur the Bard walking up and down the deck, guitar in hand, leading the crew in a song while they worked. Beside him was a man with a violin and another with a flute. It seemed as if their jobs on the ship were to sing and be jolly.

They weighed the anchor and the ropes we've all set

Bold Riley O, boom-a-lay

Them Großhenburg Mary's. We'll never forget

Bold Riley O, gone away

Rise up, me boys, up from the bay

The Wolf's Song

The captain told us we cannot stay

Our ship may be rotten

But never forget

Oh, homeward bound we're away

Arthur winked at the boys as they walked past and headed to the sterncastle's upper deck. A bald man with an eyepatch stood at the helm—which looked like a spool with a wheel on both sides, and rope in the middle that controlled the rutter. Next to him was a young man—roughly the same age as Wolfgang—with short blond hair and brown eyes. He sported a thin mustache and wore a green tunic with a golden trim and a blue cape.

"So, these are the ones you pressed into service?" the blond hair man laughed. "Well lads, welcome to the *Regent of the Sea*! The most advanced carrack in the world! This is her maiden voyage—I'm Captain Otto von Lindermann, and this, too, is my maiden voyage! The man at the helm is the shipmaster, Orion."

"Hold on, what do you mean, 'this is your maiden voyage'?" Otto asked.

"Oh, I've never actually been to sea before," Captain Lindermann replied.

"Wh-what? How can you be a captain if you've never sailed a ship?" Otto asked.

"Well, that's not how things work. The shipmaster—me—is the one who sails the ship. The captain is our strategist and commander. Typically, a captain could be an army commander and is the son of a noble or aristocrat," Orion corrected.

"Yes! And my father is a master shipwright, so when this ship was finished, it was obviously going to be mine!" Lindermann yelled.

"This is ridiculous, you can't—" An officer swinging a wooden stick at Otto cut him off. Alphonse grabbed the stick before it connected with Otto's head.

"If you hurt him, I hurt you," he warned.

Other sailors surrounded them, ready for a fight.

"Hey, I don't think you realize the situation you're in!" an officer shouted.

"I don't think you realize the situation you're in!" Otto retorted. "When my father finds out about this, there will be war!"

"Why's that?" Orion asked cautiously.

"I'm the son of Duke Roemgram von Ludwig!" Otto shouted.

"Yeah, and so am I!" Wolfgang added.

"We're nobles from the reich, also with us is a surgeon, and a noble from the Frünreich! Are you sure you want to treat us this way?"

Otto sounded confident, but truthfully, he was quite worried. Although he spoke the truth, he had no way of proving what he said.

"Wait, you guys are nobility?" Lindermann asked.

"That's right!" Wolfgang answered. "Well, except Tuferan, he's a surgeon. Also, Jurgen isn't."

"What? I am a noble," Jurgen replied.

"Huh? What house are you from?" Wolfgang asked.

"It's in my name."

"Oh! I know where I heard your name! You're from—" Orion cut Otto off.

"Listen here, kids. You may be nobility, but on this ship. You're part of the crew. Until we make landfall, you'll do as those above you tell you to."

"When will that be?" Otto asked.

The Wolf's Song

"Well, we'll need to stop at Larvenstad for supplies... But not for a while. The purser assured me we had enough supplies to complete our mission," Linderman replied.

"What's our mission? Something sweet?" Wolfgang asked.

"Very sweet! Nammelund's merchant navy is famous for pirate hunting, ever since 1396. It's a tradition for the duke to authorize hunting wars every few years. We'll track down and scuttle pirates, and later we'll be meeting with my older brother and a few others to attack a pirate hideout in the north."

As he spoke, another man pressed into service—a man with a dark complexion—spoke up.

"Ahaduhum yukhbiruni limadha 'ana huna? kan min almuftarad 'an 'adhhab 'iilaa almanzili," he said.

"Huh? What language is that? What did he say?" Lindermann asked.

"He's asking why he's here and not on a voyage home," Jurgen answered.

"You speak his language?" Orion asked, surprised.

"Not just his. I can speak all the world's major languages, including a couple Ofrikan ones," Jurgen replied.

"Get that man a silver whistle!" Lindermann shouted, pointing at Jurgen.

"Captain, you intend to make him an officer?" Orion asked, worried.

"Well, he'd be perfect for relaying orders on the lower decks. After all, several men on this crew do not speak Grostasprechen."

"Wait, how many people don't speak the same language on this ship?" Otto asked.

"We have a crew of about 411, so I'd say maybe two-thirds

speak Grostasprechen," Lindermann answered.

"That's a lot of people who can't understand orders," Otto muttered.

"Hold on, doesn't that provide a tactical challenge?" Wolfgang asked. "How do you fight if you can't understand each other?"

"He makes a good point. I know little about sailing. However, I do know orders require precision. If, for example, the ship listed to its left-uh, port side, and the gun ports were open, would you not take on water?" Francis pointed out.

"Well, yes—" Orion began, but Wolfgang cut him off.

"Yeah, that's a good point. I've never sailed before, but I'm pretty sure the ship would sink if it filled with water."

"That's why the linguist back there will be an officer! I'll have him on the lower decks with the non-Grostasprechen speakers. Now for the rest. You said you had a surgeon, right?"

"That would be me," Tuferan grumbled.

"Perfect! You'll assist our barber-surgeon. The Frunkish man. Your small frame would make you perfect for helping the carpenter. Maybe we can employ you with the master caulker?" Lindermann said. He looked over at the others and thought for a moment. "Alright, you with the blond hair, you with the muscles, and the one with the creepy red eyes will all be gunner's mates."

"Hey! My eyes aren't creepy!" Wolfgang's comment on his looks was ignored.

"We have a shortage of gunners, but I doubt any of you have ever used a cannon before. So, you'll help the gunners on the upper deck. As for the rest, send two to help the master cook, and the rest to help man the guns on the lower decks."

Lindermann turned toward the stern, looking out at the water. He picked up a tankard full of wine and downed it. Wine dripped from the tankard's edges and got on his clothes, although he seemed unphased. He then turned back to everyone.

"The open sea is so beautiful, isn't it? What are you standing around for, me lads? Go get some new clothes from the purser—those tunics and heavy armor will do you no good here. Get to your stations and start learning your new trade."

***

The boys received leather jerkins with cloth hose and loose-fitting white cotton shirts. They all left for their various stations to learn their new duties. Wolfgang, Otto, and Alphonse went to the upper deck for the master gunner to teach them.

"You three will be stationed on the port side guns, here on the top deck," the master gunner, an older man with a thick curly mustache and short hair, began.

"First, you need to check the quality of the powder. Your powder can't be too wet or too thin. When you load the gun—which is what you'll be doing as gunner's mates—you'll need to put the powder in first, then pack it in tightly with rags. Then the ball goes in. We use iron balls on this ship, so they're of higher quality than what you may be used to."

He walked over to a cannon and showed them where everything was. "Maintenance is important. You need to ensure the gun is bored and fast breeched—that means secured to the deck. As for the gunner himself—we don't use quadrants to aim at sea, but things like windage, speed, our ship's direction, and the speed and direction of the target are all things we must consider.

"This is a linstock." He held up a wooden stick notched to fit a match at the end. "We place a match on the end and put the match into the touchhole on the top, which ignites the powder. It's very important to keep the hole and the breach clean and dry. Finally, you need to help the gunner check for accuracy. Measure the length and dispart."

"What's a dispart?" Wolfgang asked.

"That's the difference between the diameter of the breech and muzzle."

"This sounds so confusing!" Wolfgang complained. Thunder rumbled distantly in the north.

"Is that a storm?" Otto asked.

"Don't worry, I'm sure we'll steer clear of it," the master gunner commented.

"Pirates! Pirates off the port bow, sailing toward the storm!" a man in the main mast crow's nest shouted below.

Men below him relayed his report. Lindermann grabbed a handheld telescope and looked out at the sea. Orion did the same, leaving the helm to the ship's pilot.

"Look at that, Captain. Looks like they're around six minutes of latitude away," Orion stated.

"Two galleasses, one galley. They have the firepower to overtake us, no doubt about that. So why are they ignoring us?"

"My guess would be they're trying to get back home. They're probably from the pirate's den up north, the one we're going to."

"They're sailing into the storm. Perhaps they think we aren't worth the fight?"

"Most likely, Captain."

"Let's show them we are." Lindermann walked to the edge of the sterncastle deck and looked down at the men on the upper deck. "Full sail, unfurl the bonnets, unfurl the mizzen, and brace for the storm! We're chasing those pirates, and we're going to wreck them!" He laughed.

"Ch-chasing them? Like, into that storm?" Otto asked.

"That's right, it'll be just like the Derby Run! I bet my

The Wolf's Song

grandfather is looking down on me with glee!" Lindermann kept laughing.

"The Derby Run? I don't know what that was, but it doesn't sound good," Alphonse said.

"It was back in 1398. Berberia pirates made a mockery of Gotheca, attacking every vessel they saw—from the Golden Gulf to the Great Channel, all the way to Albion. To support their raiding in the north, they'd turned the Anglish port city of Derby into their hideout. Merchants from all over Öustria had enough. They gathered in Nammelund, using every vessel they could.

"Our duke, at the time authorized the merchants to fly under Nammelund's banner. They set off to Derby, 116 ships in tow. But a storm had blown in from the north. They could've turned back, but they persisted! Only thirteen ships survived, and my grandfather was a shipmaster at the time! They caught the pirates of fguard, and laid waste to the entire port! Not one of the three hundred ships berthed there survived!"

"That's great, but I'm not really a sailor, so could we just ignore the pirates?" Alphonse asked sarcastically.

"Don't be so cowardly!" Lindermann said.

"We're not cowardly! We're brave and super sweet! Isn't that right, guys?" Wolfgang shouted.

He turned to face the others, but Alphonse and Otto both wore terrified looks on their faces. "Come on, we can fight some pirates!"

"That's the spirit! Now, let's ride into the storm like my grandfather did!" Lindermann laughed maniacally.

"Alright, prep for combat! Make sure we tie everything down!" Orion ordered.

"Hey, help us secure the deck. We need to make sure we tie everything down," the master gunner ordered. "Afterward, we'll grab anything useless—silverware, plates, stuff like that—and secure it to nets outside the hull. This will provide a little extra armor. Oh, and grab your weapons from below in case we get boarded. Keep them secured to your bodies tightly, else they be washed away in the storm."

"Arthur, where are you?" Lindermann shouted over the chaos of the crew preparing.

Arthur appeared from the forecastle. "Here, Captain!"

"Sing us a song, lead us to our heroic deed!"

"Aye, I know just the one!" Arthur responded with excitement. He began to kick his feet against the deck to begin the beat, then he strummed his guitar, and started singing.

The year was 1398

Written was our fate

Berbian pirates did lay waste

The Empire only ever braced

In Derby there the bastards lie

Nammelund folk would not comply

Young I was, but tall and mean

Joined the ships hundred sixteen

Raise the sails up high me boys

The wind is growing strong

We go to war with cannon roar

The journey it is long

The merchants gathered up their guns

Elders fare-thee-welled their sons

Moonsoon season coming down

But they would bring those pirates down

The North Channel we did cross

The captain he was at a loss

A mighty storm came way too soon

Sailed right into a typhoon

Raise the sails up high me boys

The wind is growing strong

We go to war with cannon roar

The journey it is long

In the lower decks, Jurgen desperately tried to keep order by relaying commands in several languages. Meanwhile, Francis, the carpenter, caulker, and their assistants prepared wood, nails, and other items for on-the-spot maintenance in case of a breach in the hull or other damage to the ship. Tuferan helped the master surgeon prepare tools and medicines to treat the wounded.

"Did I hear that right? Are we sailing into a storm to fight pirates?" Tuferan asked.

"Seems that way," the surgeon replied.

"Oh man, everything just keeps getting worse. I should've been a blacksmith or something."

Rain fell softly against the hull as the tides got bigger and bigger. They were entering the storm. Whether the decision was brave, foolish, or both no longer mattered. All they could do was fight and pray.

Öustria, East Central Gotheca

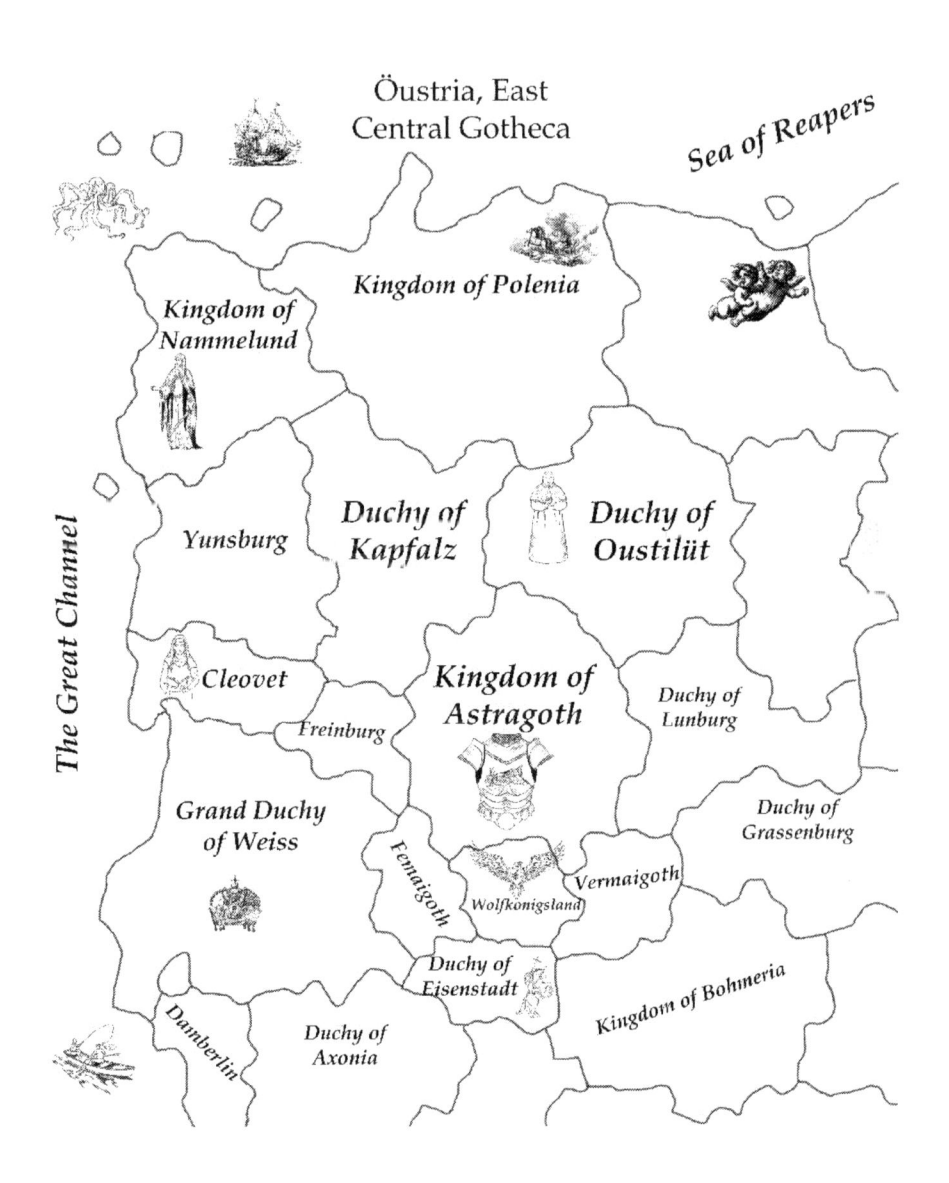

- Kingdom of Nammelund
- Kingdom of Polenia
- Sea of Reapers
- The Great Channel
- Yunsburg
- Duchy of Kapfalz
- Duchy of Oustilüt
- Cleovet
- Freinburg
- Kingdom of Astragoth
- Duchy of Lunburg
- Grand Duchy of Weiss
- Fernaigoth
- Wolfkönigsland
- Vermaigoth
- Duchy of Grassenburg
- Damberlin
- Duchy of Axonia
- Duchy of Eisenstadt
- Kingdom of Bohmeria

Chapter 19

Lightning flashed across the darkened sky as the ship tossed and turned with the high waves. Otto and Alphonse worked on smaller iron breech loaded guns, while they placed Wolfgang on a large bronze muzzle loaded gun. They held onto ropes tied around the edge of the deck for stability as the storm threw the crew about. Wolfgang could barely hold back the puke as he got seasick.

"There! A galleass, off the port quarter!" Lindermann shouted. "Shipmaster, get us close! I want to hear those cannons sing and crossbows scream!"

"Aye, Captain! Everyone, get ready to fight! But, don't use crossbows- they are useless in this weather." Orion ordered. "Pilot, let me take the helm. She needs an experienced touch!"

Orion grabbed the wheel and turned the ship's port side. Then the man in the crow's nest shouted.

"Rogue wave!"

"Aye, everyone brace!" Orion said.

Wolfgang squatted and held onto a rope as tightly as he could. The ship angled into the wave.

As they rode the massive wave, it felt like the entire world was being lifted. Wolfgang watched the edge of the bowsprit through the hemp rope net stretched over the upper deck. Lightning struck as they reached the wave's apex, the bow briefly leaving the water. In only a moment, they slammed against the sea. Water rushed over the forecastle and onto the upper deck. Wolfgang looked through a porthole and saw the ship they were chasing as lightning illuminated it in the dark sea.

"Roughly four hundred meters off the port! Get us in nice and close!" Lindermann ordered.

"Aye, we won't lose her!" Orion said.

The northerly winds whipped the sails and pushed the ship forward, racing at over twelve knots toward their enemy, keeping their broadside facing them and not exposing their flank.

As they drew closer, the ship was perfectly within sight—only about forty meters away. The cannons were already loaded and ready to fire, the gunners lining up their shots and getting ready to ignite their guns.

"Open the port gun ports!" Orion ordered.

Officers blew their whistles and relayed the order to other decks. On the second deck, Jurgen shouted at the gunners in multiple languages. They responded to the command slowly. Despite that, they'd surely know to fire their cannons once everyone else fired.

"Wait for it, men, wait for the perfect opportunity!" Lindermann ordered, a huge grin across his face.

"On my command, ready..." Orion paused as the storm-tossed the ship about, waiting until they reached the perfect alignment to shoot.

Once the *Regent's* broadside lined up almost parallel to the pirate ship, he gave the order.

"Fire!" Whistles blew, and they relayed the order.

"Get out of the porthole!" the bronze cannon gunner yelled at Wolfgang, watching the other ship.

He moved to the side so he wouldn't get blown back by the cannon fire. With a light of his match and a stick to the touchhole, the muzzle lit in a ball of flames. The sound it made was like a roaring thunder ripping through Wolfgang's ears. For a moment, all he heard was ringing. He didn't even notice the gunner shouting at him to load the next round.

The cannons fired, their iron balls tearing through the storm, barrelling toward the pirate ship. They impacted her hull on the starboard side, sending small chunks of debris into the sea. The cannons couldn't fully penetrate the hull. However, it was clear the enemy wasn't prepared for the fight. The *Regent's* crew loaded more rounds and prepared for the next fire order. Meanwhile, the pirates desperately prepped their guns to return fire.

Wolfgang grabbed powder wrapped in paper cartridges out of a small ammo box and shoved them deep into the cannon's breech. He then grabbed several rags from another box and stuffed them inside. He packed them down with a stick, then struggled to load the heavy cast iron ball. He loaded slower than the experienced men—and the storm's tossing certainly didn't help.

After a couple of minutes, the next volley fired. The galleass was sleeker and faster than the large carrack that was the *Regent*, so she'd fallen slightly behind the pirate ship. Still, they struck at the enemy. The rounds fell short of her upper decks but tore through the large ores on the ship's side—which were stowed in their upright position for the storm.

As they loaded their next rounds, the pirate ship returned fire. The rounds hit the port side hull of the *Regent*, impacting the pots, pans, and silverware tied in nets over the hull for extra protection. None of the rounds damaged the hull, save for some minor splintering of a few planks.

"Ha! They've finally woken up, those slothful knaves!" Lindermann laughed.

He seemed to have fun, despite the clear peril they were in.

With the order to fire, the third volley launched from the *Regent*. They hit deep in the pirate's hull, breaking the middle ribbands and putting a small but noticeable crack in her keel.

"Shipmaster, we've cracked her keel!" Lindermann celebrated.

"Aye, another volley may do her in," Orion responded.

"She's getting away from us. We can't keep up. I have an idea." Lindermann pointed past the bow. "I see another rogue wave coming fast. Turn into the pirate ship, force them to take the wave at the wrong angle, and the keel should break on its own!"

"You're insane, Captain. Let's try it!" Orion laughed. "I haven't felt this young in ages!"

He turned the ship toward the pirates, forcing them to turn to avoid a collision. After a minute, the enormous wave struck. The *Regent* was roughly at a forty-five-degree angle, perfect for taking the wave and minimizing damage. The ship lifted along the massive wave before slamming against the sea again. The pirate ship also lifted, but as it fell against the sea, it couldn't take the stress of gravity. Its keel broke in half, and the ship sunk under by the tides. Pirates were pulled into the sea and drowned, while the sails from the ship floated on the water's surface.

"We did it! They've been scuttled!" Lindermann celebrated.

He looked through the telescope, searching for the next target. He spotted a pirate galley off the port bow.

"I see our next target! Off the port bow!"

"Aye! I see her, Captain!" Orion shouted as he steered the helm, shifting their direction toward the pirate ship.

Waves crashed against the *Regent's* hull as they were tossed

The Wolf's Song

with the sea. As they drew closer to the galley, they observed the pirates for combat. They readied their cannons, but because of the storm, couldn't put out nets for extra armor. It appeared very chaotic and unorganized—likely because they weren't expecting a fight in the middle of the vicious storm. Just as the two ships aligned their broadsides—whilst also trying to battle against the force of the waves. Lightning shot through the cloud and tore through the pirates' galley's main mast. The sail caught fire, and the ship went up in flames.

"Look at that, lads! God must be on our side!" Lindermann laughed.

The pirates stopped trying to put out the fire and grabbed long ropes with hooks attached to their storage. They threw six ropes across the way, all of them attached to the *Regent*.

The hooks stuck in the upper deck's portholes and the stern castle. They tightened as the two ships drifted from each other, pulling them close. The pirates yanked on the ropes, battling against the force of the storm.

"They're going to board us! Their ship is doomed. They want ours!" Orion stated.

"Men, cut their ropes!" Lindermann ordered.

The crew used daggers and swords to cut through the thick ropes. After a moment, they cut all the ropes. As the *Regent* moved away, she was pulled toward the pirate ship. They'd missed one. A hook stuck in the net deployed on the hull. They couldn't get away, and the two ships would surely perish in the storm.

"Someone needs to cut that line, lest we're all pulled into the deep!" Orion shouted.

"I got it!" Wolfgang shouted back.

He tightened his poleax's strap to ensure it wouldn't slip from his back and stopped in the middle of the deck—lining himself up with a bowman's porthole.

"Wh-what are you doing?" the gunner shouted.

"Just watch!" Wolfgang replied confidently.

The entire deck focused on him, awaiting whatever heroic or stupid thing he was about to do.

Wolfgang ran forward as fast as he could, rushing at the small five-foot-tall porthole opening. He jumped and ducked, narrowly avoiding hitting his head on the deck rail. He placed his lead foot on the bottom of the porthole and pushed off. Everyone—especially Otto and Alphonse—were shocked.

"Hope he gauged the jump," Alphonse muttered to himself.

Wolfgang slammed against the galley's deck railing. This ship differed from their carrack, with the upper deck being open rather than having a hemp rope net above it. Wolfgang barely held on and pulled himself over the railing before he lost his grip. He breathed a sigh of relief, then looked up to see several confused pirates. Just then, something thudded against the hull. Wolfgang turned to see Otto clinging to the ship's side. Wolfgang rushed over to help him aboard, and as he did, Alphonse slammed his feet against the deck. The pirates scrambled to draw daggers and swords, and the boys also drew their weapons.

"This was a stupid idea!" Otto complained as he gripped his longsword tightly.

"Well, we're here now—so what do we do next?" Alphonse asked.

"I didn't really think that far through," Wolfgang admitted.

"What do you mean you didn't—" Otto turned to face the approaching pirates. "Ah, we better think of something quick."

"We must cut the rope. Otto, you cut it while Alphonse and I defend you," Wolfgang said.

The Wolf's Song

Otto nodded and ran down the deck to where they tied the rope. Alphonse and Wolfgang followed him and took up guarding his back. Otto used his longsword to cut the hefty rope, while the pirates charged at them. Alphonse ran forward, slashing a pirate's neck. Another swung a sword down at him, and he responded by swinging his from below. He parried the attack and thrusted his sword down into the pirate's chest.

Wolfgang moved forward, taking advantage of his superior range against the pirates armed only with swords and daggers. He held his poleax with the point facing forward and thrust it into a pirate's chest. As the two tried to gang up on him, he quickly jumped back, and use the bottom point of his poleax's staff to stab the one attacking from the left, and swung the ax side into the pirate attacking on the right. He stood firm as more pirate's approached. They were being surrounded quickly.

"This isn't good!" Alphonse said. "How's the rope coming along?"

"It's—I'm almost—"

Otto tried to answer, but as he cut the ship rocked with the large tides and he dropped his longsword into the deep.

"Ah, blast it all!"

"What's wrong?" Alphonse asked.

"I dropped my sword!" Otto responded.

"What? We can't fight them off and cut the rope."

"Alphonse, give him your sword. I have an idea. Trust me," Wolfgang said as he prepared to lung at the surrounding pirates.

"I'm not sure I like your ideas, brother!" Otto said.

With a scream like a ravenous animal, Wolfgang lunged forward—holding his poleax parallel to his chest—and pushed the pirates into the growing fire under the galley's main mast. As he did, flaming wood fell behind him, trapping him into a flaming arena with the enemy. Alphonse quickly dispatched the few remaining pirates and helped Otto finish cutting the rope.

One pirate thrusted his longsword at Wolfgang. He held his poleax with the point facing up at an angle and met the longsword blade with his staff. He pushed back against the blade and forced the longsword down, then used his staff's bottom point to stab the pirate in the leg. The pirate fell in pain. Another pirate threw a dagger at Wolfgang, which cut through his hose and deep into his leg—narrowly missing vital arteries. He collapsed in pain, and more flames fell from above. Several pirates were trapped under the collapsing lifts and braces. Pieces of hot wood landed on Wolfgang's back, burning through his jerkin and cotton shirt, scarring his shoulder blades.

"Brother! Brother, we need to go!" Otto shouted as Alphonse cut the last strands of the rope.

Things only got worse as the galley listed to its port side, causing it to drift away from the *Regent*. Wolfgang grabbed a chunk of wood and put it in his mouth. He bit down as he pulled the dagger from his leg. The pain was immense, worse than anything he'd ever felt. As he growled through the pain, he fell to his knees. The pain was so immense it was almost unbearable. After a moment, he finally tore the blade from his flesh, and much of his blood along with it.

"Brother!" Otto cried.

Wolfgang looked at the flames dancing around him and stood. He turned, wrapped his poleax around his back, and with all the bravery he could muster, jumped through the flames.

He appeared on the other side of the fire, clothes burnt and body bleeding. The other two looked at him to ask if he was okay, but he put his hand up to stop them. They drifted further from the *Regent*, and it wouldn't be long before the pirate's galley became their grave.

"We-we need to jump, now! Get a running start, and jump!" Wolfgang coughed.

The others nodded.

The trio stepped back, as close to the fire as they could get, and ran toward the deck railing together. They launched off the galley, using all the strength their legs could muster. Lightning flashed behind them as they flew. For a moment, it felt like time slowed—Wolfgang could see the individual raindrops as they fell around him. But the moment was fleeting.

They were quite short of the portholes in the upper deck and had to grab onto the nets put out around the hull instead. Wolfgang slammed against the netting and couldn't get a grip. He tumbled until his foot caught in the lower part of the net.

"Brother!" Otto shouted.

"I'm fine, climb up!" Wolfgang replied as blood dripped from his leg onto his face.

"A rogue wave!" Orion shouted.

"Hey, get those three abroad now! They'll be washed away!" Lindermann ordered.

Sailors rushed over to the deck's edge to help them through the portholes. Otto and Alphonse climbed. Wolfgang rocked back and forth, building the momentum and abdomen strength needed to hoist his body up to grab the net.

Finally, with a loud grunt, he swung and grabbed a hold of the net. He climbed up, but his left foot was stuck between a pot and some silverware. He tugged on it but couldn't get it free. With the ship rocking, it felt like he was about to fall into the sea. They closed in on the rogue wave—he didn't have much time. He reached down with his left hand and pulled the pot away from the net, wiggling out his foot.

After freeing his foot, he climbed the net once more. The ship continued rocking, making it rather difficult for him to keep his grip. He grew weaker as he climbed from blood loss. Members of the crew gathered by the portholes, helping Alphonse and Otto aboard. Wolfgang still had at least a deck to climb, and not a lot of time.

"Don't slow down, bro! Come on!" Alphonse shouted.

"I... I don't think I can... make it," Wolfgang responded with exhausted gasps.

"Brother!" Otto shouted. Jurgen and Francis emerged from below deck. They rushed over to the porthole.

"We heard what was happening. Is he stuck?" Jurgen asked.

"Hey! Are the gun ports below shut?" Orion asked Jurgen.

"Yes, the guns are stowed, and we shut the ports!" Jurgen responded. "Hey, let's lower Francis down. He should be light enough—"

"Not with all my armor on. It makes me quite heavy," Francis said.

"Right. Alphonse, you and me will lower Otto. He'll grab Wolfgang before he falls!"

"Right! We need to be quick," Alphonse agreed.

Otto leaned out the porthole as the other two grasped his ankles. It was hard to hold on to him in the storm, and they worried they'd lose their grip any moment. Wolfgang stopped climbing and rested on the net. Otto stretched his hand out to him.

"Brother! Brother, wake up!" He shouted.

Wolfgang couldn't hear his cries. He'd passed out and was in a deep trance.

Wolfgang stood in front of the gates of the old manor in Viesenville. He didn't know how or why he was there. Wolfgang carefully opened the doors and stepped through. He saw his father

The Wolf's Song

and mother playing with his siblings. Uwe, Petra, they were all there. Julia was the only one that was missing. He cried as he stepped toward them. Sir Welter put his hand up and shook his head. Wolfgang stopped in his tracks.

"But… father!" Wolfgang shouted.

Sir Welter simply shook his head again. Suddenly, Wolfgang heard shouting from the manor gates. It was Otto.

He rushed toward the gates and left the manor. His eyes opened and shot up. He was awake.

"Brother! Grab my hand!" Otto shouted.

Wolfgang had tangled his arms in the net so he wouldn't fall. He pulled them out and grabbed on Otto. As they were pulled up, the rogue wave struck the ship's side. Alphonse and Jurgen held on as tightly as they could. Several other crew members rushed over to help.

As Otto and Wolfgang were pulled onto the deck, the *Regent* sailed into the wave's apex, and crashed into the sea. The shock sent Wolfgang and the others flying toward the stern castle. They slammed against the wooden walls.

"Everyone alive?" Orio asked.

"You three are insane!" Lindermann said.

"Tuferan! We need to get Wolfgang to the surgeon, now!" Otto shouted as he held his unconscious brother.

A couple of their crewmates helped pick him up and carry Wolfgang below deck.

"Back to your stations!" Orion commanded.

The crew scrambled to their stations and began fulfilling their duties. Meanwhile, Wolfgang was taken to the barber-surgeon's quarters. Arthur the Bard was also below deck and approached to learn what was happening.

"Tuferan! He needs help!" Otto shouted desperately.

"Ah, this damn kid. Set him down on this bed here." Tuferan pointed toward a straw bed. "I need to cauterize his leg to stop the bleeding first, then treat the burn with honey and aloe. This will take a while, so clear the room."

"What happened?" Arthur asked as Otto left the quarters.

"He did something stupid again," Otto grumbled.

Otto went topside to help with various tasks as they continued sailing through the storm. After another hour, the rain stopped, and the storm passed. Dusk arrived and Otto looked at the setting sun. He watched as the orange and yellow light refracted through the darkened clouds.

"It's a shame we only got two of the three," Lindermann sighed.

"Not a bad haul, Captain. Especially for your first time at sea," Orion comforted.

"Soon, we'll be fighting them at their hideout, and the northern seas will be safe again. How far did the storm take us, anyway?"

"We seem to be on the eastern side of the Four Island Alliance."

"Ironic name, considering it's actually six islands," Lindermann laughed.

"We'll pass through the island straits, and onto the Sea of Banshees. We still have some time before we meet up with your brother."

"Right! Then I'll really earn a name for myself fighting at the Dead Man's Cove!" Lindermann clenched his fist as his face lit up.

"But for now, Captain, I think you should get some rest. I'll handle taking down the nets and bringing the ship to a passive state."

"Aye. Thank you, shipmaster." Lindermann nodded and walked

down into the stern castle.

    The crew survived a terrible storm and a difficult battle. They still had a long voyage ahead of them, and an even more difficult battle would rear its head.

Saint Olga of Kiev

In the year 945 AD Igor I of Kievan Rus was assasinated by his subjects. Ascending the throne after him was his wife, the first female ruler of Russia, Olga. He was killed by members of several slavic tribes that were vassalized under Kievan Rus, chiefly among them the Drevlians. After Igor I was killed, the Drevlians assumed that Olga would be easy to coerce and control- after all, she was a nomblewoman, and the men of the time had deeply held beliefs regarding the place of women in society. The Drevlians arranged for her to marry their own Prince, a man named Mal. She agreed, but only if the highest chieftans of the Drevlians would come to the capital of Kievan Rus for a feast and to collect her. When they arrived, she directed them to the bathhouse, where she locked the doors and burned it down with them inside. With most of the Drevlian ruling class gone, she hatched a plan to finish off the rest. She announced that she wished to travel to the Drevlians captial for a feast. After the Drevlian aristocrats were drunk and full of food, Olga had 5,000 of her soldeirs execute them. Following this, she would set fire to the city and burn her remaining enemies- almost completely wiping out the tribe. She was cruel, violent, and barbarous- but as we know, God is merciful and forgives those that seek him. She would visit the Holy city of Constantinople, and be inspired by the great Christians she met. She would be baptized by the Emporer himself. Repenting of what she had done, she returned to her home country- a land ruled by pagans who for generations killed Christians (even invading Byzantium), and begin to convert her people. Using the wealth she gained through conquest, she would start missionary trips. This included the establishment of hospitals, welfare for the poor, and churches. She would use her position to teach about the Word of God and heal the nation so beset by violence. One lesson from Saint Olga is that one does not need to be perfect to ascend- they only need to get back up when they fall.

Chapter 20

It had been several days since the battle with the pirates. Wolfgang was healing, although the wounds he suffered left terrible scarring on his back and leg. He couldn't handle too much heavy lifting, but performed his job as a gunner's mate. Alphonse, Otto, and Wolfgang were all on the upper deck early in the morning, cleaning out the cannons. Wolfgang shoved a wet rag deep into the muzzle of his assigned large bronze cannon.

"Hey, make sure you get all the way back there, right in the breech," the gunner said. "It needs to be perfectly smooth. Any left over residue can mess up my shot."

"Ah, this sucks! Why can't the back open like theirs?" Wolfgang complained.

He pointed at Otto and Alphonse cleaning their assigned breech loaded guns.

"That's a completely different cannon. Now stop complaining and clean! Don't forget to get the gunk out of the touchhole, too."

"One minute a hero, the next a maid," Arthur laughed as he walked by.

"Hey, keep talking like that and you'll be the next maid," Orion shouted from the top of the stern castle.

"Uh, hey lads, how about a song!" Arthur shouted, trying to change the subject.

His assistants, the violinist Toby and flute player, James, rushed over to him.

"How about one just for our friends from the reich?" Lindermann requested as he looked down on the crew from the forecastle.

"Ah! I know just the one!" Arthur faced the crew and began singing.

Oh, out from the city and out from the slums, I beckon for distant lands. Destiny comes, so I find me a ship, lacking good crew. Greatest mistake that I ever did.

Mary await my call. Back to Eifenhart soon. We'll haul, Mary, my dear oh, soon I'll be here. My Mary awaits my call.

Well, when I come back I'll have many tales. I've seen southern winds blow hard in our sails, from the White Gulf to the Middle Sea to travel. The endless blue is to be free.

Mary await my call. Back to Eifenhart soon we'll haul, Mary my dear oh, soon I'll be here. My Mary awaits my call. Well then, we went round

The Berbian coast, dodging the pirates, harder than most, braving through storms On the Sea of Ice. To cheat Davy Jones, my dear, we did it twice

Mary, await my call. Back to Eifenhart soon we'll haul, Marry my dear oh, soon I'll be here. My Mary await my call

Our journey took us to Ofrikan sands, Oasis Aegyptian. Beautiful lands or weeks there we've seen, no drop of rain, dreaming of seeing our

Mary again, Mary await my call. Back to Eifenhart soon. We'll haul

Mary, my dear oh, soon I'll be here. Oh, Mary await my call, oh Mary await my call.

They sang the song multiple times so Wolfgang and the others could learn it. Meanwhile, Francis and a carpenter's apprentice were lowered to the hull's side via ropes attached to a plank they sat on. They repaired the ship's damage from the storm and battle. They carefully removed the nails holding the board in place, then handed the damaged board up to the carpenter. Then they received a new board, hammered it in, then used caulk around the edges to water seal it. They repeated the process multiple times and replaced several planks on each deck as well.

***

After a long day of work, they went to the lowest deck for dinner. Orion stood near the cooks as the entire first shift sat at a small table waiting for their food. The room had no portholes being deep within the hull, so candles lit the room.

"Well lads, looks like we're having hardtack tonight. Sorry, but we can't dine on meat all the time," Orion informed them.

"Uh, what's hardtack?" Otto asked.

"It's the last thing you'll ever need to eat," a sailor replied.

"Are you sure it's that good?" Otto asked skeptically.

"No lad, he means it's the last thing you'll ever eat—this stuff is so dry it'll choke weak men," Orion laughed.

The cooks passed small pieces of hardened bread to each sailor.

"Oh, these look like the biscuits we ate when we were in the Thorns of Roses," Wolfgang said.

"Yeah, but... these have bugs on them," Otto said.

"Just eat 'em away from the candlelight. If it's dark, ya can't see 'em, and the bugs got no taste," a solider told him.

"Wow, he's right, you can't taste the bugs at all!" Wolfgang said as he chewed through the cracker.

"I think I'd rather just go hungry," Otto said.

"If you don't eat, I'll throw you overboard!" Lindermann laughed as he walked toward the kitchen.

"Ah, Captain!" Orion jumped.

The crew stood, but Lindermann motioned for them to sit back down.

"Because the purser didn't get all the supplies I wished, we're going to have to save our heavy food for special occasions."

The crew sighed.

Lindermann grinned. "Like right now! We survived our first battle together, so I'll have the cooks make us rabbit stew and open bottles of wine and ale for grog!"

The crew cheered and celebrated.

"But there's one thing. Someone spilled a bunch of fish guts on the upper deck. I need a volunteer to help clean that up."

"I'll do it!" Wolfgang shouted. "I just ate anyway."

"I'll go up there, too. Make sure it gets done right," Orion stated.

Wolfgang and Orion went topside to help clean up the mess. Meanwhile, the crew drank and celebrated while waiting on the cooks. They sang songs and shared stories. Alphonse arm wrestled members of the crew. None could match his strength. At another table, Otto bored his crewmates with stories of Gotheca's history and cultures. After a time, the cooks brought out the stew.

"Hey, I'll go get Wolfgang," Otto said. "Save me a bowl."

The Wolf's Song

He ran over to the ladder and climbed onto the upper decks. As he stuck his head up, he saw Wolfgang looking over the sea with a mop in his hand. Otto was about to call out to him but heard him singing under his breath.

"Elise, await my call. Back to Eifenhart soon. We'll haul. Soon I'll be there. Elise await my call," he crooned.

Otto had never seen that side of Wolfgang before. Could it be he felt saddened the entire time? Perhaps the brave and innocent face he put on was just for show. A mask he wore to hide his true feelings. Before Otto could ask him, Orion approached Wolfgang.

"Missing ya girl, boy?" he asked.

"Eek! Uh, you heard that?" Wolfgang replied.

Otto, not wanting to intrude, headed back down.

"Didn't mean to startle you. But we are done with the cleaning—have been for a minute. What's bothering you?"

"It's just... yes, I miss someone. A girl I care for deeply. I went on this journey for her," Wolfgang replied.

"Hm... interesting," Orion said, intrigued. "Are you worried about her?"

"Of course I am. I just." He turned to face Orion, then looked up at the sky through the netting strewn above the upper deck. "When I was a boy, my mother... she told me this story. About a man and woman on the moon. They loved each other, but then the moon split in half. Now they're separated by a great chasm, unable to embrace each other."

He looked up at the broken moon and reached his right arm toward it. His sleeve slipped away, exposing Elise's bracelet. The moon was in its Waning Gibbous phase, as such darkness obscured much of it.

"You're worried about losing her?" Orion asked.

"I just hope she's still waiting for me. But what if she found someone else? What if I never come back?"

Tears formed in Wolfgang's eyes. The emotions of everything he'd been through over the last year welled inside him. We was sure he could handle the violence and adventure of war, but now he stood in the middle of the sea, farther from home than he ever imagined he'd be. At any moment the ship could be lost, his body sunk to the bottom of the sea, never to be found. His fate could be that of an unknown soldier, dying in mud, as his allies tread over his lifeless corpse.

"These are normal things for us sailors and soldiers to worry about, lad. We all have a reason for partaking in our journey to sea or to war. Sometimes we have no choice. But in the end, we do it for them—those we love, those we leave behind." He paused for a moment. "You look up at that broken moon, and I'm sure your girl is looking at the same moon right now, waiting for your return."

Orion didn't know it, but what he said was true. Back in Eifenhart, Elise stood in the castle courtyard almost every night, looking up at the moon, or its shards, worrying about the young naïve boy sent into a dangerous and unforgiving world. She believed in him, but she couldn't stop herself from worrying. A part of her hated her father for sending him away, but another part knew why he did it. It was customary for noble boys to head out into the world and return as men. But she wished he could've stayed by her side. Back on the ship, Orion put his hand on Wolfgang's shoulders and smiled.

"Come on now, lad. Wipe away those tears. Let's head below deck and get some stew."

"R-right! Thank you, ship master!" Wolfgang's eyes lit up as he dried his face and headed down. His mind was slightly more at ease, but his heart was full of anguish. Sooner than he knew, his anguish would consume him.

Gotheca, broke down by region

- Briefly
- Angland
- Iburnika
- Lower Fruncia
- Fruncia
- Rhianlund
- Occitania
- Lothargia
- Usrenta
- Alpiana
- Etalia
- Hollesh
- Denlund
- Central Gothic
- High Gothic
- Norsica, land of Stormjarl's
- Belkans
- Illanica
- Öustria
- Scippia
- Rumyia
- Easern Flanks
- Lower Steppes
- Raskovi

Chapter 21

"This looks so good!" Wolfgang said, as he sat down to eat his stew.

"Don't eat too fast," Orion said as he also sat down.

"Hey, shipmaster, how about a competition? Who can hold more booze?" a drunken sailor asked. "You too, you crazy red eyed kid."

"What did you call me?" Wolfgang perked up. "You think you can out drink me? You're on! You're so on!" he shouted as he pointed at the sailor.

"This won't be good," Otto muttered to himself.

"In fact, I can out-drink anyone here!" Wolfgang assured. The crew went silent.

"Well, you heard him, lads. Fifty groschen to anyone who can beat him!" Orion wagered.

The crew gathered around the table and, one-by-one they challenged him. They drank tankard after tankard of ale, and one after another, the sailors collapsed. Wolfgang stayed in the fight the whole time.

"I knew it. He has a bottomless stomach," Otto laughed.

The Wolf's Song

"I don't know, he might not survive this," Alphonse said.

After about a dozen sailors fell ill, Orion sat in front of Wolfgang.

"Okay, boy, you have gumption. Now, let me humble you," he laughed as he set his tankard full of wine on the table.

They locked eyes, and the entire room went silent again. They grasped their tankards tightly and drank. It only took a few seconds for them to down their ale before their tankards were filled again. They went three tankards in, then five, then seven. Before anyone knew it, they were at ten.

"Can... can they even be human?" Otto asked.

"I am unsure. I have never seen anyone drink this much," Francis added.

After fifteen tankards, they both swayed. It was anyone's guess who'd fall over. Orion lifted his tankard to his lips, then... he fell over. The entire crew gasped. No one had ever defeated Orion in a drinking match before.

"Hey... shipmaster... hey... does this mean... does this mean I get the coin?" Wolfgang could barely burp out the sentence.

As he celebrated, Francis sat down. He set his tankard on the table, took out a bamboo straw, and stuck it inside. He began drinking down his ale. Wolfgang looked at him, confused.

"Well, shall we drink? As I recall, no one has beaten you yet," Francis said.

"Oh... yeah... I'll beat everyone!"

Wolfgang scarfed down the ale. Before he could finish his tankard, he fell over and passed out.

"On a technical level, this means I won," Francis celebrated.

"Not quite." Alphonse sat down in front of him. "You're small.

There's no way you could beat me."

"We will see," Francis accepted the challenge.

"You won't beat me," Alphonse said as he downed his tankard.

Francis drank from his straw until the tankard was completely empty. Then, sailors refilled their tankards, and they did it again, and again. By the time they reached their tenth tankard, most of the crew was already passed out drunk.

"This… is impossible. How are you drinking this much?" Alphonse asked, as his eyes got heavy.

"Well, I do not feel it. So, I can keep drinking," Francis said as he sipped his sixteenth tankard.

Before Alphonse could say anything, he fell over unconscious.

"Hm… I suppose that fifty groschen is mine now," Francis celebrated as he laid down on the deck and fell asleep.

***

The crew woke with cold water splashing on their faces. Wolfgang shot up and immediately put his hand to his head. They were all severely hungover.

"Ah, my head is killing me. Can I go back to sleep?" Wolfgang asked.

Orion, the one waking everyone up, threw a raw eel at Wolfgang's face.

"Here, kid. If you feel you can't stand up, get an eel. Eat it raw, and down it with some almonds. That should cure your hangover. Hurry now, all of you. The captain wants to speak to the entire crew topside."

After helping each other up and scrambling to their feet, the crew shambled to the upper deck. They all stood facing the stern castle, awaiting Lindermann. Multiple crew members threw up over the portholes, including Wolfgang and Otto.

"I think eel made things worse," Otto said.

"Brother... Brother, I don't think I'm going to make it," Wolfgang said as he puked into sea.

"At least that storm is gone. I hope never to see something like that again," Otto complained once more.

"I'm sure you will!" Orion laughed as he walked by.

"Don't tell me... are storms like that common?" Otto asked, trying not to puke while he spoke.

"There was a time when the seas were calm. Alas, lad, that was many years ago. Long before any of us walked the world. Now the seas are broken."

"All of you, gather around!" Lindermann shouted as he stood above the crew. "Listen up! You've all done well. The ship's and this crew's maiden voyage has proven we have mettle! But our hardest fight is yet to come! We have fifteen hundred leagues to go! In just over a month, we'll be in the Scandal Wastes, besieging the Dead Man's Cove! This place is the newest hideout for these barbarous pirates! We'll have my brother's support and the merchants fleet. After our battle, we'll resupply in the frigid snowlands of Uotgaurd!"

He raised a tankard high in the air to salute his crew. "So, steel yourselves for the journey ahead! Arthur!"

"Aye, Captain?" Arthur emerged from the crowd, guitar in hand.

"Sing us a sea song! Something to motivate the crew!"

"Aye, Captain!" Arthur shouted enthusiastically.

He strummed his guitar. Toby and James prepared their instruments and joined in. In a matter of seconds, the entire crew danced and sang to the upbeat tune. It was like the music cured their hangovers. Everyone except Otto, who was still puking by the porthole.

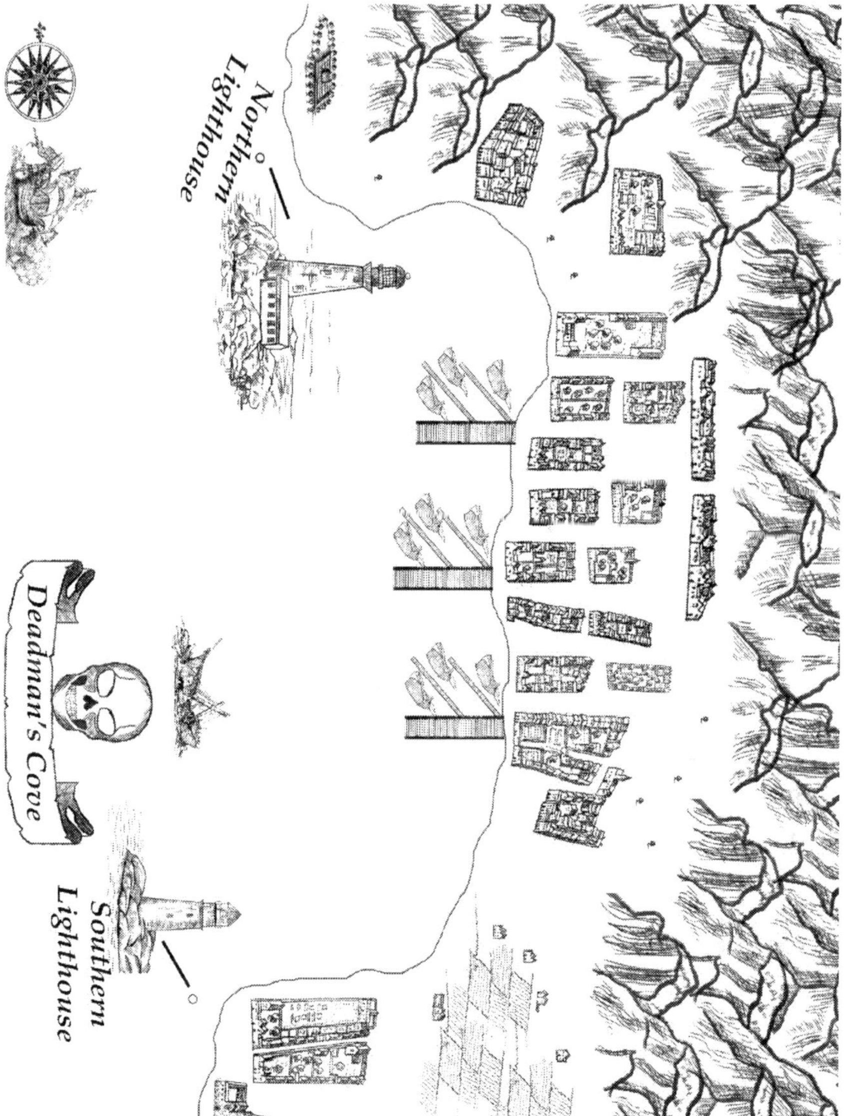
Northern Lighthouse
Deadman's Cove
Southern Lighthouse

Chapter 22

Elise stood on a balcony overlooking Ludwig Castle's courtyard. She watched children chasing each other, smiling and playing. A young boy approached a young girl with flowers in his hand. They stopped playing and watched as he nervously handed them to her. Elise smiled at the blossoming young love. Behind her, the door to the balcony opened. Her father walked through.

"My daughter, it is time. We must go to Astragoth post haste," Duke Roemgramm ordered somberly.

"Yes, father." Elise replied as tears formed around her eyes.

"Now, now. Don't be like that." he said as he wiped the tear from her cheek. "This has to happen, for the good of our nation."

"Yes, father," she replied with her eyes cast down.

She grasped the wolf pendant around her neck.

"Wolfgang, why aren't you here to protect me now? Where could you be?"

***

Waves crashed against the *Regent's* hull as wind whipped the sails, beckoning the ship north. The crew went about their various tasks, singing and telling jokes as they did. On the lower decks, Francis carved new planks for the ship, Jurgen barked orders at his charges, and Otto sat in the barber-surgeon's quarters as Tuferan mixed up medicine in a bowl.

"Wine and wormwood 'oughta make the sickness go away," Tuferan said as he handed Otto the bowl. "Drink it up. All of it."

"Okay," Otto said as he downed the mixture. He coughed and gagged, but did his best to keep it down. "Will this really work?"

"Yeah, it should. Really, though, how are you still getting seasick? We've been on this tub for what, almost three months now? Should be used to it."

"It's not like I want to feel sick or anything," Otto snapped.

"Okay, okay," Tuferan laughed.

"It is true, however, that I'm getting used to life at sea. That being said, not a day goes by that I don't miss my time on land."

"I can agree to that." Tuferan grabbed the bottle of wine he used to make the mixture and started drinking it.

"Shouldn't you save that to treat seasickness?"

"Well, I'm feeling a little seasick right now!" he laughed and continued to drink.

On the upper deck, Alphonse scrubbed the inside of the breech-loaded cannon they assigned him to. His gunner shouted at him to make sure it was perfectly clean with no defects. Alphonse stood up and wiped the sweat off his forehead.

"I didn't think cleaning could be this exhausting." he complained.

"Tell me about it!" Wolfgang said as he walked by with two buckets of dirty water.

"Stop complaining and start scrubbin'!" Orion shouted from

the sterncastle.

Wolfgang got down on all fours and scrubbed the deck with a rag. He occasionally wrung it out into the bucket, just to scrub again.

"Ships ahoy! Off the port quarter!" the lookout in the crow's nest shouted.

The men below him repeated the report until it reached Orion and Lindermann, who were observing the crew from the sterncastle.

"That looks like our fleet," Lindermann said as he observed them through a telescope.

"Yes, that right there is my brother's ship! A galley called the *Hammer and Iron*."

Lindermann paused for a moment. He watched the man in the crow's nest of his brother's ship signal to them. He held two flags—a blue flag pointing toward the sky, and a green flag held out at his side, making the shape of an L.

"He wants us to join his formation," Orion said.

"Yes, he does. He'll probably want to come aboard and speak to us, too." Lindermann put down the telescope and turned to Orion. "Okay, shipmaster. Signal that we've received the order. We'll join the formation and await further instructions."

The *Regent* dropped to half sail to slow themselves and steered into formation just behind the *Hammer and Iron*. Wolfgang stood and looked across the sea at the large floating heaps of wood.

"There's so many of them," he said. "They look like huge floating cities of wood."

"There must be at least one hundred," Alphonse added, also marveling at the size of the fleet.

Several other crew members joined them, gawking at the ships.

"Hey, what are you sorry sacks of potatoes doing?" Orion shouted. "Get back to work, the lot of you! Unless you want to be on barnacle scraping duty!"

Wolfgang ran back to his buckets and the other crew rushed to their duties.

"How about a tune to get everyone moving?" Arthur yelled as he strummed on his guitar. Soon, the entire crew was singing along.

Well, come now boys, say your goodbyes

Stow the hoses hoist the sails

Look ol' Mary in the eye

Brace for taking on the gales

Well, soon we're setting back for home

Stow the hoses hoist the sails

Find a Mary of our own

Brace for taking on the gales

Fare well you ladies of the eve

Stow the hoses hoist the sails

Kaspia. We had well received

Brace for taking on the gales

***

A small rowboat launched from the *Hammer and Iron*, the men on board rowing ferociously toward the *Regent*. As it approached the ship, they threw ropes down and a man climbed up to the sterncastle. He wore a large leather cloak with golden silk clothing underneath. His puffy shoulders were decorated with gray and purple patterns, like rich pauldrons. He had a tall hat with a large brim and two green feathers attached to the top. His curly mustache

The Wolf's Song

complemented his large beard.

"Hello, brother! It's so good to see you!" the man shouted as he approached Lindermann.

"Ah, good to see you too, brother," Lindermann replied. "Oh, shipmaster, this is my brother, Herbert Prien von Lindermann."

"But you can call me Captain Prien!" he laughed.

"Pleasure to meet you, Captain. I am the *Regent's* shipmaster," Orion said.

"Ah, hello shipmaster. So, it's you who keeps my brother in line!" Prien laughed. "I hope you don't keep him on too short of a leash!"

"Hold on. What? I'm on no one's leash!" Lindermann shouted back.

"Calm down brother, I only jest. Now, down to business." Prien pinched the end of his mustache between his fingers and stroked it as he spoke. "We've found Deadman's Cove. That much I'm sure you're aware of. This merchant's war fleet has been assembled to crush it, wiping out the largest hideout of pirates north of the Great Channel."

"It's hard to believe you've actually found it," Orion said. "I'd heard stories of it even way back when I was but a green deckhand. The only place outside of the Berbian Islands ruled entirely by pirates."

"Honestly, it's hard to believe it's any more than a legend," Lindermann said.

"Aye, but most legends turn out to be true, don't they?" Prien laughed. "Let's head down to your map room."

They went below the sterncastle's upper deck to a cramped room full of cabinets stuffed to the brim with various charts and maps. At the center of the room was a table covered in compasses, sextons, barometers, and various other tools. Prien approached the table and brushed all the clutter aside before pulling a map out of his cloak and placing it down. The map displayed the country of Svenland and a jagged coast extending north.

"Our flotilla is here, about thirty miles from Svenland. Our prize is to the north, right here."

He pointed to the map, then moved his finger to a small cove in the Scandal Wasteland. He pulled another map out of his cloak and laid it on top of the other one. It had *Deadman's Cove* written at the bottom. The map had the west at the top. It displayed a town and several docks, along with two lighthouses, one in the north and one in the south.

"Is this it?" Orion asked, his eyes lighting up.

"Aye. It cost me a fortune to get a hold of this map. But this gives us a detailed look of the cove, and even the streets of the town. Roughly six thousand people live here—all of them pirate scum," Pren said.

"So, brother, how are we going to do this? They must have a vast fleet there and defenses," Lindermann asked.

"Aye. Our merchant's war fleet has three groups: wine runners from Kaspia and the Ibernika Peninsula, arms dealers from Angland, and those from the Nammelund's United Sailors Guild. Our fleet numbers nearly two hundred ships."

"Two-two hundred?" Lindermann shouted in shock.

"Aye, little brother!" Prien laughed. "Even larger than the Derby Run. Us merchants really hate those pirates. It didn't take much for our duke to gather the support needed for this expedition. But this is our one chance. If we fail, the pirates will move elsewhere and go into hiding. We won't have the resources to mount another strike or find their new hideout. This is our only opportunity to end this menace in the north."

"If that's true, I trust you have a detailed plan of attack, Captain Prien?" Orion asked.

The Wolf's Song

"Aye," Prien began. "We'll split into two attack groups. Upon nightfall, the first group—which the *Regent* will be in—is going to attack via the northern lighthouse. The *Anglish* will accompany you. The carrack, *Peter Pomegranate*, will lead the charge. Once you strike and probe their defense, the second attack group—led by me—will charge into battle via the southern lighthouse. These lighthouses will give us a tremendous advantage when fighting at night, since they won't be able to guide ships into the bay. It will hide us from the shoals."

As he spoke, there was a knock at the door to the map room. A sailor stepped in.

"Sorry to bother you, captains. The captain of an Anglish ship is here," the sailor reported.

A man brushed past him and entered. He was large, with a square jaw and mean eyes. His leather cloak was full of patches, desperately trying to cover various holes.

"Ah, Captain Smith." Prien greeted.

"Greetings to you, fleet leader," Captain Smith began. "I am captain of the *Peter Pomegranate*. My Grostasprechen is not best, my sorries."

"He can hardly speak," Lindermann complained.

"Eh, not much different from most of our crew," Orion joked.

"I have plan. Our attack group will split into two forces, one led by you and one by me. I will take mine on—"

He stopped for a moment, trying to find the right words to use. Grostasprechen was not his first language- or his second.

"North! On north side of lighthouse, through narrow passageway. You take southern side. We catch enemy by surprise."

"Just like the Derby Run!" Lindermann shouted, his eyes glowing with excitement.

"My ears, brother. I am standing right next to you." Prien

looked back at the map. "So, are you both ready?"

"Indeed, brother! Let us lay waste to these fiends!"

"Uh, yes. This will surely be a historic battle," Orion added.

With that, the two departed the *Regent* and returned to their own ships. It would still be two weeks of sailing before they reached their destination. In that time, the crews of each ship grew excited and anxious. It would likely be the biggest battle most of the sailors had taken part in—and they prayed it wouldn't be their last.

***

On the fifth of Norma, the month of the carpenter, the flotilla reached its destination. It was nearly dusk as the various crews prepared their ships for combat. They readied their weapons, cleaned their cannons, and set up nets full of pottery and silverware on the hull of their ships. Orion observed the cove through a telescope. They were just over a mile away, and a thick fog had descended upon the shore, making it impossible to see anything. The light from the twin lighthouses peeked through the fog.

"Well, I can't see a thing. This is a double-edged sword, Captain," Orion stated.

"What do you mean, shipmaster?" Lindermann asked.

"Well, they can't see us, but we can't see them. Two hundred ships passing would be hard to hide, so they would've seen us coming. But now we have the advantage of surprise. However, this applies to us, too. Since we can't see their defenses, we could be walking into a trap."

"A trap? Do you honestly think they know we're coming?"

"I can't say. A fleet this size is hard to hide. It doesn't take much for word to get out. They may have already abandoned the hideout."

"For the first time on this journey, I hope you're wrong."

"Met too, Captain." Orion paused and put down the telescope. "Well, let's prepare for the attack."

Wolfgang, Otto, and Alphonse carried ammo and gunpowder to the upper deck. The entire crew was busy with combat preparations. Hatches buttoned down, items secured with ropes, weapons drawn, and armor donned. Francis joined the armored marines preparing to repel boarders and counterattack enemy ships by boarding them.

They assigned Jurgen to the lower gun deck, since he could quickly translate orders in multiple languages. Wolfgang, Otto, and Alphonse all remained as gunners' mates on the upper deck. Several bowmen stood by, anxiously looking out portholes on the upper deck, armed with powerful crossbows.

***

Night fell as the two attack groups entered their respective positions. The *Regent* would split off from the *Peter Pomegranate*, with twelve ships of wine runners behind them. They'd remain in a tight formation until they breached the first battle line, which was on the other side of the lighthouse. At that point, they'd break into an echelon formation, heavy on the starboard side with a wide distance between ships.

Lightning cracked across the sea, startling much of the nervous crew. Wolfgang, who was observing the fleet from the cannon's gun port, jumped and fell onto his back.

"Calm down, men! It looks like a squall is coming. The wind is at our backs!" Orion shouted.

Within moments the storm was upon them, and as they crossed to the other side of a steep cliff and into the cove, as the northern lighthouse, and a terrible surprise, became visible.

Formation of the Holy Roman Empire

The HRE lasted for almost one thousands years, being dissolved in the year 1806. At times the Empire was a powerful force to be reckoned with, but most of it's history was full of petty squabbles and division. King Charlemagne conqured much of central Europe throughout the 8th century. On Christmas Day in the year 800 he was crowned Emporer in the city of Rome. Upon his death, his grandsons quickly fought for control of the empire. Ultimately it was split up into three major parts: Lotharingia (Middle Francia), West Francia, and East Francia. It was agreed that the head of Lotharingia would be the Emperor, however the Carolingian Dynasty has died out, and Lotharingia fell into civil war. In the 10th century, the ruler of the Kingdom of Germany (formally East Froncia) Otto I invaded norhtern Italy and married an Italian princess named Adelaide. He was now both King of Germany and Italy. The Pope would crown him Emporer and restore the old empire, and thus, The Holy Roman Empire was born.

Lore: The Holy Aeternian Empire is based on the real world HRE, although it encompasses far more territory than it's real world counterpart. The politics of the HAE are complex, but it's basic structure acts as this: The Holy Emporer is elected by the heads of the imperial States (the dutchies, rikedoms, kingdoms, crowns, and reichs) and is confirmed by The Pope. He rules from the capital of Wolderan, and his wife the Queen rules Wolderan whilst he rules the HAE. He does not rule it in the sense of a normal nation, as each imperial state acts mostly independantly. As long as they pay taxes and follow a few royal decrees, they are mostly left to their own devices. This lack of true governance has allowed violence and political scheming to flourish, although some strong and respected emperors have been able to keep control of the imperial states, in rare instances.

Chapter 23

Rain fell like rocks onto the *Regent's* deck. The lighthouse stoop and cannons firing in the distance illuminated the rain. The *Peter Pomegranate* entered combat. But it was far too soon, as they hadn't even crossed the first battle line. That's when a terrifying realization hit the crew. It was a sortie. The pirates knew they were coming.

"Stand fast, men!" Orion shouted from the sterncastle. "Pilot, keep her steady. We need to break through!" Orion then turned his attention to the crew. "The wind is strong! Give me quarter sail on the mainmast and half sail on the mizzen!"

"Ships ahead! We have three carracks coming on our starboard side!" the lookout shouted from the crow's nest.

Several men echoed the report to Orion.

"Pilot, steer us to port! Let the wine runners take the carracks," Orion ordered.

Then he spotted a large galley in front of them. It was barely a hundred feet away. The ship was painted black with red trim and had obsidian black sails. It blended in perfectly with the darkness of night.

"Galley ahead! The bastard snuck up on us!"

"Crap!" Lindermann exclaimed. "Quick, get ready to fire!"

"Wait, brace yourselves! It's going to ram—" The entire ship violently shaking cut Orion off.

The shaking threw Wolfgang back, and he slammed his head against the deck hard enough to bruise.

"Ow!" he shouted as he rubbed the back of his head.

"On your feet, boy!" his gunner shouted.

The galley scraped against the hull of the *Regent*, stripping off the protective nets. Once it finished, it opened fire on the wine runner's ships closely following them. The cannon fire from the massive galley tore several of them apart.

"One more! A galley straight ahead!" the lookout shouted. "About four hundred feet from the lighthouse! Be careful!"

"Pirate galley on our port side! Prepare for combat!" Orion ordered.

The galley was longer than the *Regent*, but it had the same number of guns. The storm raged on as the two closed the distance. Before long, they were broadside to broadside. They were just close enough that Wolfgang spotted a boy about his age bracing for combat on the deck of the pirate's ship. He watched him through the gun port before the gunner pulled him back. As he did, Orion gave the order to fire.

Their cannons sung like a deadly chorus as cannon balls cut through the rain. The pirate's responded quickly, firing at almost the same time. Balls impacted each ship's hull. The pirate's galley was mostly unscathed, but the *Regent's* hull was torn through on the lower decks.

Jurgen relayed commands to the gunners and other crew. A cannonball broke through the hull and deck, flying so close to Jurgen that the force knocked him down. The ball struck a man carrying a box of gunpowder, turning him into little more than a red paste on the deck planks.

"Report, shipmaster! Two hull breaches!" an officer shouted from the upper deck.

"Bowmen, fire at will! Gunners, prepare for another volley and quick!" Orion ordered.

The pirates had bowmen at the ready, firing first. Their bolts struck several crewmen. Wolfgang stuffed charges down the cannon's breech, preparing for the next shot, as a crossbow bolt flew through the gun port and narrowly missed him. His gunner wasn't as fortunate.

The bolt penetrated his chest, and he slumped to the ground, his blood soaking into the deck. Wolfgang leaned against the rail, unsure what to do. The *Regent's* bowmen fired back, and the ship's cannons sounded. Wolfgang quickly stood and grabbed his gunner's matchlok. He lit the match and placed it into the touchhole, firing the cannon. The ball landed in the sea. He didn't realize it, but the pirate ship passed them.

The pirate's galley quickly turned—so fast that it listed slightly to its port side. As they came around, their sails—which were at full—caught the wind, giving them just enough of a boost to be broadsided with the *Regent's* starboard side. The ships shot a cannon volley at each other, but neither did much damage. The pirate ship's crew grabbed ropes with hooks attached.

"They intend to board us?" Lindermann shouted, shocked.

"This isn't good," Orion said. "Get ready for boarding action!"

Wolfgang ran over to a hatch leading to the lower decks. He was planning on getting his poleax to help repel the borders. Meanwhile, Francis stood with his bill in hand, and several men beside him, ready to fight.

The pirates threw their ropes, most of which successfully hooked onto the *Regent*. Unexpectedly, the tides shifted, causing the pirates to lose control of their ship. They slammed into the *Regent*. Both crews stumbled and fell as their ships shook. With the carrack and the galley deck-to-deck, the pirates quickly made their way over. Some hopped through the portholes on the upper deck, while others climbed above and cut the protective netting. Others climbed the sterncastle.

Lindermann drew his sword and charged at a large pirate armed with a bill. The pirate thrust his weapon forward. In response, Lindermann swung his sword up from his lower left quarter, parrying the attack. He then leaped forward and stabbed the pirate in the neck.

Meanwhile, Francis stuck his bill through a porthole, stabbing a pirate trying to reach the upper deck. Several pirates jumped down from the top of the upper deck after cutting through the netting, catching the crew by surprise. They killed and wounded several crew members before Francis turned his attention to them.

The pirates were armed mostly with longswords and wearing little more than leather jacks. One pirate pushed an unarmed gunner's mate to the ground. As he raised his sword to finish him, Francis charged, thrusting his bill into the pirate's side.

"Are you okay?" Francis asked, trying to check on the crew member.

Another pirate swinging a sword at him cut him off. Francis quickly raised his bill above his head, parallel with the ground, to block the blow. He kicked the pirate's abdomen, causing him to reel in pain. Francis then stabbed the man's chest, finishing him.

As the battle continued, Wolfgang emerged from the depths of the ship, poleax in hand. He was ready to fight. It was dark and chaotic, and he was having trouble differentiating the pirates from the crew.

"We can't control the ship like this!" the pilot shouted. "If something isn't done, they'll run us into the shore!"

"We need to free ourselves of those damned ropes!" Orion confirmed.

"Then we shall counterattack!" Lindermann yelled as he ran to the edge of the sterncastle. "Men, charge the enemy ship! Get on their galley and do as much damage as you can! Everyone else, repel the boarders and cut the ropes!"

As everything was happening, Otto picked up a longsword from a felled pirate. He saw Wolfgang standing on the deck, unsure of what to do.

"Brother, is it about time we joined the fray?"

"Y-yeah. Let's attack their ship!" he replied.

Otto nodded, and the two ran over to a porthole and squeezed through. The galley was so close they only needed to step across a small gap. Several other crew members joined in the attack. The battle for both ships became more chaotic.

A group of four pirates, two with bills and two with longswords, approached the brothers. Wolfgang placed his left foot back and lowered his poleax so the point faced outward. Otto placed his right foot forward and held his longsword close to his chest, point facing up.

"I'll take the ones on the left with the bills," Wolfgang said.

"How perfect. I'll leave them to you brother, the swordsmen are mine," Otto confirmed.

Wolfgang recklessly charged forward, swinging his poleax from his upper right quarter at one billman. The pirate thrust his bill upward, meeting Wolfgang's poleax and locking them in a stalemate. The other pirate ran to his back, prepared to stab him from behind. Wolfgang pushed one pirate back, then spun around to counter the second.

He placed his left foot back and held his poleax low, with the point facing the pirate. He waited for his opponent to make the first move. The pirate lunged forward, thrusting his bill at Wolfgang's neck. Wolfgang sidestepped at the last moment to avoid the blow. He then pivoted on his left foot and swung his poleax as he did. He caught the pirate in the lower back, just deep enough to stun him. As he fell to his knees, Wolfgang finished him with a blow to the head, using the hammer side of the poleax.

The other pirate ran forward, swinging his bill from above. Wolfgang quickly raised his poleax above his head, holding the staff with both hands. He held it parallel with his shoulders. The bill connected with the poleax's staff, the force of the blow vibrating through Wolfgang's arms. He twisted his poleax to the left, forcing the bill to the deck and pinning it. He then thrust the bottom point of his poleax backward, stabbing the pirate in the temple. The pirate fell back and collapsed.

Meanwhile, Otto dueled the sword wielding pirates. He placed his sword on his right side, pointing toward his back. He bent his left knee and braced for an attack. One pirate charged, swinging his sword from his upper right quarter. Otto responded by swinging his. The two blades clashed. Otto pushed up on his hilt, thrusting the point of his blade into the temple of the pirate. The pirate fell onto the deck, covered in blood. Otto turned to face his next quarry. The other pirate appeared more cautious, taking up a guard, but not acting.

Otto taunted his opponent by raising his left arm, putting his thumb on his front teeth, then flicking it at the pirate. The gesture was an insult-it was called "flicking someone off"- and it was just enough to get the pirate to swing at him. Otto swung as well. The blades crossed and Otto pushed forward so the two were hilt to hilt. He then grabbed his opponent's blade—lacerating his hand—and yanked it back. At the same time, he kicked the pirate in the knee. He executed the move as a single motion and the pirate was on the ground, disarmed.

While the battle raged onwards, Orion coordinated the crew. He shouted orders like an experienced general, doing anything to keep the ship running whilst repelling the boarders. Through the rain and chaos of war, the lookout relayed a report once more.

"The lighthouse! We're headed straight for the lighthouse!"

"What?" Orion shouted.

Lindermann picked up the telescope and observed the path in front of them. There it was, only a few hundred feet away.

"We-we're heading straight for land! We need to detach from the pirates at once!" Lindermann ordered.

"Yes, Captain. Men, focus on cutting the ropes! Quickly!"

***

Alphonse and Francis fought back-to-back, eliminating any approaching pirates. Upon hearing the order, they knew what to do. They both nodded, which was all the communication they needed. Pirates surrounded them. Their only option to get to the ropes was to break through and fight later. They pivoted on their heels to face the starboard side of the ship, then charged forward with all their might. They pushed past the surprised pirates, knocking them to the ground as they ran to the deck rails. Alphonse grabbed a rope and cut it with his longsword, and Francis did the same with the end of his bill. Other members of the crew rushed over to help them.

"The last rope is cut!" Alphonse shouted.

"Quickly, pilot, get us away from the lighthouse!" Orion ordered.

The situation was hectic, and no one was sure of anything. The crew of the *Regent* were completely unaware that Otto and Wolfgang were still fighting on the pirate's galley.

***

Wolfgang and Otto were completely oblivious to what the rest of the crew were doing. They fought viciously on the pirate's galley.

The two of them stood next to each other, several dead opponents around them, slowly being surrounded by pirates.

"B-brother, our ship! It's drifting away!" Otto noticed.

The two were facing the stern of the pirate's ship, unaware of the lighthouse quickly approaching.

The entire ship shook violently as it crashed into the rocks under the lighthouse. Wolfgang flung backward. Wood splintered in every direction and gunpowder lit, causing a fiery explosion. The galley split in two. Otto and Wolfgang ended up on the opposite sides of the ship as a large pit opened between them. Otto slipped into the crevice, falling several decks into the darkness. Wolfgang tried to reach his hand out to grab him, but another explosion rocked the boat. A plank of wood hit him in the chest, throwing him back.

Wolfgang tumbled along the deck, falling from the galley and landing in the cold dark water. He desperately swam upward, following the dim light from the lighthouse. Bodies, cannons, pieces of rope, and wood sunk into the surrounding depths. His lungs ached for air. The guiding light dimmed. He was feeling weaker with every passing moment. He kept swimming as hard as he could, refusing to give in to the sea.

Wolfgang emerged from the depths, breaking through the water and into the storm. He took several large breaths as he struggled to stay afloat. Water filled his mouth every time he tried to take a breath. He'd spit it out and try again, struggling against the waves. Eventually, the tides pinned him against the rocky shore. Land was only a couple feet above him but trying to reach up and grab it while waves crashed against his body was exceedingly difficult. The water would drag him under and he'd swim back to the surface to grab the slippery rocks, only to get dragged under again.

After struggling for several minutes, he could get a firm hold on a sharp rock. As he gripped it tight, his hand sliced open, but he ignored the pain as he pulled himself onto the shore. He rolled onto the rocky beach and looked up. Just above him, sitting atop a cliff, was the lighthouse. He was on a small island that wasn't connected to the mainland, but at least he wasn't in the water anymore.

Wolfgang coughed violently. Water spilled from his lungs onto sharp obsidian rocks.

Wolfgang stood up, surveying his surroundings. The rain was letting up, no longer the intense storm it was a moment ago, but a light sprinkle. Flaming debris and dead pirates surrounded him. He didn't see Otto anywhere.

"Brother! Otto! Can you hear me?" Wolfgang began shouted frantically. "Brother!"

He walked around the island, sifting through debris, hoping Otto was okay.

As he made his way to the other side of the island, he saw a wounded pirate standing in a curtain of rain. It was the boy Wolfgang saw on the galley earlier. He was bleeding from his arm, and he held a longsword in the same arm. Wolfgang approached him, but the boy raised his weapon.

"Wait! Hold on, we don't need to fight. The ship is gone. We should—" Wolfgang tried to console the boy, but he was cut off.

"Quiet, you devil! You did this! You killed my friends!" the boy shouted.

He charged Wolfgang, swinging the sword wildly.

Wolfgang dodged the boy's blow by ducking. He then grabbed a sharp rock and stood up. The boy turned, ready to swing again, but before he did Wolfgang threw the rock. It hit the boy's temple, stunning him. He was in a daze, holding his head in pain. Wolfgang tackled him to the ground and wrestled the sword out of his hands. The boy punched Wolfgang multiple times as hard as he could. Wolfgang struggled to restrain him. He tried to hold the boy's arms down, but the boy kept breaking free. He tried to grab the sword, and Wolfgang pulled away from him as hard as he could. When he did, he accidentally sliced the boy's neck.

Wolfgang dropped the sword and put his hands over the boy's neck. He pressed the wound to stop the bleeding, but the blood continued gushing out. The boy looked at Wolfgang with hatred in his eyes, which soon turned to fear, then nothing. His eyes went blank and his body was limp. It was over.

Wolfgang sat back, looking at the boy's lifeless corpse.

"S-sorry... I—"

Wolfgang was unsure of what to say or do. He didn't mean to hurt the boy. Not even the rain could wash away the blood covering his hands and clothes. Someone then cried for help nearby.

He stood up and listened intently. Then he heard it again. Could it be Otto? He ran toward the shouts from the shore on the other side of the island.

"Brother?" Wolfgang shouted as he approached a mass of flaming debris.

He peered inside to see a pirate pinned beneath a large wooden bulkheads.

"H-help me! Quick!" the pirate shouted.

"O-okay, hold on," Wolfgang replied.

He moved chunks of debris out of the way, but as he did, the wood inside the mass shifted. A crate fell and spilled open just in front of the fire. He stopped for a moment to look. It was a crate of gunpowder. He realized what he'd done in an instant, and instinctively turned to run, but it was too late.

The fire set off the gunpowder, causing a tremendous explosion that threw him into the water. His ears rang as the cold water enveloped him once again. The waves took him further from the island.

Wolfgang struggled for air, trying desperately to get to the surface. His back slammed against a hard rock. He cried out in pain, but all that could be heard under the water was a whimper.

The waves took him into the shoals, his head crashed into a rock. Blood tinted water surrounded him as the darkness took him. He lost his energy and his will. Before he knew it, there was nothing but blackness.

Hygiene in Medieval Europe

Despite popular belief, Medieval Europeans were not unwashed or unclean people. During these times, it was believed that disease was spread by miasma or bad smells. Because of this people wanted to smell good, as smelling good meant you were clean and healthy.

Traditional tooth brushes did exist, but they were most commonly used by the elite. The commoner would brush their teeth with a hazel twig. By chewing the end to expose the soft insides, it was easy to use it as a brush. One could also use spices to help freshen their breath. A common combination was salt and a clove. First you would put the two spices in a bowl and grind them up, then dip your hazel twig in after getting it wet, and brush your teeth. These spices freshened up your breathe and acted as a form of medieval tooth paste. Medieval Europeans actually had better teeth than we have today. Due to their diets not consisting of sugars, preservatives, chemicals, and other things that are bad for our teeth, they rearely had cavities. When they did the tooth would simply be pulled out.

Washing ones hands is the easiest way to prevent disease. Medieval Europeans understood that dirty hands could lead to disease as well. Remember, smelling bad meant one could be carrying a disease, so you would want ot stay as clean as you could. The first step would likely be simply rubbing your hands on grass or a bush- but never on your clothes. Then you would wash your hands in a puddle, stream, or a pot of water if you brought one with you. If that doesn't work, you could use soap. Despite popular belief, soap is actually one of the first inventions in Human history. A clay tablet from ancient Sumeria (about 2800 BC) displays a recipe for an olive oil soap. The medieval elite would likely use a similiar olive oil soap developed in Castille. This white powdery soap was very expensive and out of the price range of a commoner. Black soap was the cheapest soap avaliable, but was still rather expensive. For the average person, they would have made their own soap. Ash was widely avaliable and easy to make. One could visit the local charcoal burners or burn wood themselves. Adding water to ash makes lye, a common ingredient in soap. Combine that with animal fats and you have soap.

Medieval Europeans would also bathe and wash their clothes quite regularly. Typically you would bathe once a week at a public bathhouse, or in a river/lake. It would be common to wash daily with soap and water, to clean mud/dirt off of your skin. But a full fledged bath was seen as a liesurely activity and, since private bathes were essentially non existent, it was a social activity as well.

So, were medieval people clean? Yes. In fact, in some ways, they were cleaner and healthier than people today. So the modern view of them all being covered in dirt and living in rags is completely false.

Chapter 24

Wolfgang didn't know where he was or how he got there. A dim light hung above him. He took a couple of steps, only to hit a wall. Wolfgang put his hands on it, feeling the cold moist rock. He followed it back to where he started. He was inside a dark pit. It couldn't have been larger than a few feet in diameter. The dim red light above must be the sky. As Wolfgang stared up at it, something tugged at his pant leg. He looked down to see a rotting corpse rising from the ground, trying to drag him under the swampy miasma that formed around the pit. He pulled back and fell against the wall. Several more corpses rose from the miasma, their bony hands reaching toward him. A corpse, coming out of the wall just behind him, viciously grabbed him, wrapping its hand around his forehead.

***

Wolfgang shot up, panting. He looked around to find himself in a well-furnished room, one that belonged in a manor. A red patterned rug covered the floor, and someone had draped a thick wool blanket over him. His clothes were gone, replaced with a nightgown. Sitting next to the bed was an old woman he didn't recognize.

"Sorry, honey. As soon as I put my hand on your forehead to

check your temperature, you shot up. You must've had a bad dream, weren't you?" she asked in a kind voice.

"Uh, uh... hold on, where am I? Who are you?" Wolfgang asked.

His body writhed in pain and he realized bandages covered his body; wrapped around his head, chest, and left leg.

"Ah, I am Lady Orwin. I own this manor." She paused for a moment. "I thought you were just another body that washed ashore. I was going to have my servants bury you with the others, but as they picked you up, you coughed."

"I washed ashore? Wait, did anyone else survive?" Wolfgang asked.

"Hm? No, you were the only one. The rest had already passed."

"I-I need to check the bodies. I need to know—" Wolfgang tried to stand, but the pain kept him from moving.

"Hold on dear, you need to rest."

"I am sick of resting in beds like this. Why must I be so weak?" he shouted.

"Weak?" Lady Orwin laughed. "Dear, I've seen the scars covering your body. I bandaged it myself. I don't think a weakling could survive all of that. Even as you laid on the beach, your body still fought for life."

"But I need to make sure none of those bodies are my brother."

"You can check when you're better. For now, just rest. I'll bring you some soup."

Lady Orwin stood up and walked to the other side of the room. She pulled back the curtains, revealing a glass window which she propped open. Sea salt perfumed the air. The window overlooked the sea, and the top of the lighthouse peeked over the edge of a steep cliff.

"A glass window?" Wolfgang asked.

He was surprised at how clear the glass was. Even the few glass windows at Castle Ludwig weren't like this. "Is there even glass there? I feel like I could stick my hand right through it."

"It's very high quality. The sun is good for you. It will help you heal." She smiled and left the room.

Wolfgang laid back in the bed, the plush pillows sucking him in. He stared at the wooden roses carved into the ceiling, then turned his attention to the blue and green striped walls.

"Where are you, brother?" he whispered. "Elise... are you still waiting for me?"

***

Sometime later, Lady Orwin entered the room with a bowl of soup and handed it to Wolfgang. He scarfed it down like a ravenous rat.

"Oh dear, you were starving, weren't you?" Lady Orwin laughed, sitting in the chair near the bed. "Well, eat up. It's only noon, so there'll be more food later."

"Did you make this?" Wolfgang asked, mouth dribbling down his chin.

"Swallow your food first, dear," Lady Orwin ordered.

Wolfgang swallowed everything, then asked again. "Did you make this?"

"Yes, with help, of course. I enjoy cooking, but at my age it's hard to move around, so my servants, Julian and Niva, help me when I need it."

Wolfgang set the now empty bowl on the nightstand that stood next to the bed. He then threw the blanket off and pulled himself to his feet. He grunted in pain as he did. Lady Orwin put her arm around his to help him up.

"Thank you. Do you have my clothes?" Wolfgang asked.

"Uh, no dear. Your clothes were torn up and soaked. I can get you fresh ones, although I don't know if they'll fit. But you really shouldn't be up right now."

"It's fine. I need to check those bodies."

"I can see you're determined." Lady Orwin paused for a moment. "Okay, I'll fetch you some clothes. Julian will show you to the graves." She stood and left the room.

A few moments later, a woman opened the door and entered the room. She was middle-aged with short brown hair and green eyes. She wore a maid outfit and held neatly folded clothes with a pair of boots on top. The woman sat them on the bed.

"Hello, master. I am Niva, Julian's sister, and servant to Lady Orwin. You can wear these," Niva said in a soft voice.

She bowed, then left the room before Wolfgang could say anything. He stared at the white cotton shirt with green hose, leather boots, and a black leather belt with a large bronze buckle.

After changing, Wolfgang opened the door and stepped out of the room into a huge hallway. Standing opposite of the door was a middle-aged man wearing an apron and a purple tunic.

"Hello, master. I am Julian, Niva's brother and servant to Lady Orwin," the man said in a stern voice.

"Yeah, I gathered that," Wolfgang said. "Where're the graves?"

"Come with me."

Wolfgang followed Julian through the manor's halls. The building was enormous, with what seemed like endless rooms. They entered a large foyer with a golden chandelier hanging from the domed marble ceiling.

The Wolf's Song

They left the manor and walked down a granite path lined with rose bushes. Plants from all over Gotheca decorated the manor's front, some Wolfgang hadn't seen before. They made their way down a winding path to a large patch of disturbed dirt about a hundred feet from the edge of the shore, flanked by steep cliffs. Debris still covered the beach. Several ships' hulls poked out of the water on the horizon. Wolfgang noticed one ship with a red and white checkered pattern flag hanging from the bow—the remains of the *Peter Pomegranate*. Above the disturbed dirt was a small shovel.

"We buried fourteen people. The tides may bring in more," Julian said.

"Right. I'll get to work," Wolfgang said as he grabbed the shovel.

He gritted his teeth and grunted through the pain as he dug up the graves. Julian stood by and watched as the hours went by.

***

Dusk had come, and Wolfgang wiped the sweat and dirt from his face. He set the shovel in the dirt and inspected the bodies. He could tell none of them were Otto.

"Are you satisfied, master?" Julian asked.

"Satisfied? No," Wolfgang sighed.

"What did you expect to find?"

"I don't know. None of these are my brother, so he may still be alive. But what happens if I don't find him?"

As they spoke, Lady Orwin approached. She had a short, dignified stride like a noblewoman.

"Niva is preparing dinner. Julian, why don't you rebury the bodies. I will take the young man back to the manor," she ordered.

"Of course, madam," Julian said.

Wolfgang crawled out of the shallow graves, grunting as he walked. He held his side as he approached Lady Orwin.

"I told you not to come here until you were better," she scolded.

"I'll-I'll be fine," Wolfgang replied.

***

Wolfgang entered a large banquet hall. The table was huge, even though only he and Lady Orwin ate at it. Three ornate chandeliers hung from the ceiling. Several oil lamps sat on small tables around the room's edge. Behind Wolfgang's chair was a set of plate armor, and on hooks above was a poleax. The pitch black poleax had a golden sheen and two red jewels forged into its staff. Wolfgang stared at it, enthralled by the intricate design.

"It was my husband's," Lady Orwin said. "It's made with Damascus steel, although I'm not sure what that means. He was proud of it, though."

"Oh, yeah, it looks well made. Was your husband a soldier?" Wolfgang asked as Niva brought plates of pork and bread to the table.

"Something like that. In his youth he was a karl, like you."

"Hm? How did you know I was a karl?" Wolfgang asked as he ate.

"Oh, I just assumed because of your scars. That's more than any regular sailor." She paused and took a sip of wine from a chalice Niva brought. "Eventually, he became a pirate."

"A pirate?" Wolfgang stopped eating.

"Yes. I met him here, in Deadman's Cove. He was a great man, even became a captain of his own ship. You remind me of him." She sighed. "It seems I've lost my appetite. Eat, dear. Tomorrow I'll head into town to buy some lavender. You shall accompany me."

Lady Orwin stood and left the room. Wolfgang continued eating, thinking about his circumstances. He was in a former pirate's home, but he was there to hunt pirates. It would be impossible for Lady Orwin to know that, however. Still, he felt uneasy.

Castle von
Aufgehenden Sonne
(Castle Ludwig)

Chapter 25

When the morning came, Wolfgang got dressed and Niva led him to a set of stables. There he met Lady Orwin wearing a white dress. Julian stood next to her and smiled when Wolfgang approached. Behind them was a wooden carriage with two horses hitched to it.

"Good morning, dear," Lady Orwin said.

"G-good morning. Where are we going today?" Wolfgang asked.

"Into the town. Climb inside the carriage. It's only a few minutes away."

***

Wolfgang stared out the small carriage window as they headed into the town. Several farms surrounded the village outskirts, people tilling the fields and wiping sweat from their brows. The village itself was densely packed, although it seemed quite small compared to Eifenhart. Only a couple thousand likely lived there. People visited stores, bought wares, and ate food; it hardly seemed like a pirate's hideout.

The carriage stopped in front of a modest store with wooden

walls and roof. Julian opened the carriage doors and helped Lady Orwin down. Wolfgang followed. As he exited the carriage, he noticed a group of kids playing a game with a stick and a ball just outside of the shop.

"Lady Orwin!" a young woman, only a few years older than Wolfgang, said as they entered the shop.

Shelves and cabinets covered in various types of flowers and plants decorated the store's walls.

"It's good to see you, Olivia," Lady Orwin responded.

"Indeed. Who's this handsome young man with you?"

"My name is Wolf—" Wolfgang stopped himself before he could finish; it wouldn't be good if people here found out who he was. "Uh, I am a guest of Lady Orwin."

"What an odd fellow." Olivia laughed. "Well, what can I help you with?"

"I'd like to purchase some lavender and vinegar if you have any."

"Of course, I'll be right back!" Olivia said as she stepped away to fetch the items.

"Lavender smells wonderful, dear. Vinegar also helps keep pests like termites away," Lady Orwin told Wolfgang.

***

After getting the plants, they departed the shop and continued their errands. The two visited several other shops, including a baker and a butcher. By the end of the day, the carriage was full of groceries and they headed back to the manor. Wolfgang looked out the carriage's window, still unsure of what he'd seen. The island wasn't full of bloodthirsty pirates like he thought. Surely pirates were there, but it felt like a normal village.

"I grew up here," Lady Orwin began. "My father was a pirate, and my mother was a working girl. She died while I was young. I had to learn to survive on my own."

"But I haven't seen any pirates," Wolfgang replied.

"Looks can be deceptive. Pirates are human, too. Of course, many pirates left after that initial attack a few days ago." Lady Orwin smiled. "My husband was a pirate. But he rescued me from my life as a street urchin."

"What happened to him?"

"He died many years ago, in a battle on the high seas, like many pirates do, like all pirates should. He was a great man, but like all men who seek war, he was foolish, and therefore he died a fool's death."

"I'm sorry to hear that."

"Don't be sorry, dear. Just heed my words."

The carriage stopped. They were back at the manor. Julian and Wolfgang unloaded the carriage and brought everything inside. He thought about the things he'd seen in the village. It reminded him of home and of his family. He wondered about Otto's whereabouts and hoped everyone was okay, but while he was at the manor, there was no way of knowing. Still, this manor felt like an oddly peaceful place.

Chapter 26

Wolfgang had gotten used to the manor's routine. He'd wake in the morning and either Julian or Niva would greet him with a bowl of soup. He'd then change and walk the grounds, often looking at the sea. Around noon, Wolfgang would help Julian or Niva with various maintenance tasks around the manor.

Julian led Wolfgang down a stone path behind the manor.

"This path leads to the garden. As you can see, it's in a state of... disrepair," Julian said as he pointed at broken stones along the path. He then pointed to a small handcart next to the path. "I have several stones and a pick in that handcart. Dig up the broken stones and replace them."

"You want me to replace all these stones? I'm still injured, you know," Wolfgang complained.

"Not all, just the broken ones. Those stones only weigh a few pounds. Consider this healthy exercise to help you recover," Julian laughed, walking back to the manor.

Wolfgang grabbed the pick out of the handcart and got to work. He dug a broken stone up and replaced it with a new stone. It didn't quite fit, so he grabbed another one, then another, until he found one that fit. He repeated that process for several hours.

***

Exhausted, Wolfgang sat against the handcart to catch his breath. He heard humming in the garden. It was a beautiful sound. He stood and walked toward it to see who was singing.

As he entered the garden, he saw a woman in a blue dress kneeling by some flowers. For a brief second, they looked almost like Elise, but it was Lady Orwin. She looked at him and smiled.

"Hello, dear. Fixing the garden path, I see," she said.

"Oh, yeah. I didn't see you enter the garden," Wolfgang replied.

"I've been here for a few hours. I really enjoy being in the garden. What's with that look on your face?"

"Look?"

"You look surprised, dear."

"Oh, sorry. I, uh, well, you just reminded me of someone."

"Someone special, I hope," she said as she stood.

"Yeah, she's really special." Wolfgang paused. "Hey, thank you for taking care of me over this last week, but I'm going to have to leave soon. I need to find—" He stopped as Lady Orwin raised her hand.

"I know you can't stay forever. I'm sure people are worried about you. But you mustn't leave so soon. I'd hate for you to return to the world when it's so full of violence."

"But hasn't the world always been full of violence? It's just the way of things," Wolfgang replied, somewhat confused by Lady Orwin's suggestion.

"Not always. Humans weren't made for violence."

"Not made for violence? I don't understand."

"I believe humans were made for love, dear. To be with one another, to be happy with each other. Doesn't that sound nice?"

"I guess. But if that's the case, then why is the world so full of violence?" Wolfgang asked, still confused.

"Why indeed? Maybe men prefer war to love. After all, killing your foe is easy, but loving him is a trial." She paused. "Sorry, dear, just the ramblings of an old woman. You said I reminded you of someone special, right? Who might that be?"

"A girl, the same age as me, from back home. Her name is Elise. I want to marry her someday. That's why I'm out here, to fulfill the promise I made."

"You're out here fighting because of a promise? Is it a promise that's worth the blood of many?"

"I don't understand," Wolfgang responded, scratching the back of his head.

"Look at these lilies. They are beautiful this time of year, aren't they? Truly, life is something special." She stopped. "Sorry, I'm rambling again. I think I'm going to head inside. Niva is starting supper soon. I'll have Julian fetch you when it's ready."

She left for the manor and Wolfgang returned to his work. As he replaced stone after stone, he dwelled on Lady Orwin's words.

"She isn't making any sense." he said to himself. "I'm a noble. I must fight. It's what we're supposed to do."

Chapter 27

Wolfgang awoke to a loud bang, with several other bangs following in quick succession. Cannon fire. He threw off his sheets and tried to get out of bed, only for the pain of his injuries to stop him. He grunted and got up, running to the window. The sun hadn't risen yet, so it was hard to see. Still, he could make out ships firing at the village. They weren't just any ships either, they belonged to the merchant's war fleet.

Wolfgang squinted to get a closer look. Rowboats were deploying from several ships. They were attacking Deadman's Cove, and it was his only chance to get home. He quickly dressed and threw open his door. Standing in front of him was Niva.

"Lady Orwin figured you'd be up, master. She's in the dining hall."

"Huh? I don't have time for this," Wolfgang said as he ran out of the room.

"She won't let you leave until you see her. You owe her that much."

"Fine."

Wolfgang rushed to the dining hall. Lady Orwin sat at the end of the table wearing a black dress and sipping tea out of a small ceramic cup. She smiled as Wolfgang entered.

"Hello, dear. I'm sure you've heard the commotion outside," she started. "You probably want to leave, but I implore you to stay."

"I can't. I need to go," Wolfgang yelled.

His gaze landed on the poleax hanging on the wall. He moved to grab it.

"Stop there, Crimson Wolf. That's what they call you, isn't it?"

"How did you know that?" *Has she known the entire time?*

"You may try to hide your name, but you cannot hide your eyes. Word from merchants and travelers mentions a deadly karl with red eyes called the Crimson Wolf. They say he fights like a vicious animal. There are all kinds of rumors about you."

"Really?"

"Yes. Some say you're the spawn of the devil, others you're an old king reincarnated. In a short time you''ve made quite the name for yourself, but I suppose that's natural considering your disposition. It's hard to discern the truth from the fantasies. Many don't believe you exist. I didn't until I saw you on the shore. You didn't look like a grand warrior or devil. Just a young, confused boy."

"Looks can be deceiving."

"Yes, they can." Lady Orwin smiled. "But I've seen your heart. You're not bad, just confused. A boy faced with a complicated and violent world. Despite the world, you have the freedom to choose. You can choose peace."

"I'm sorry, but I can't. The brothers that I've fought with—bled with—are in that battle. My path to Elise is in that battle. I must go."

Wolfgang grabbed the poleax off the wall. As he did, Lady Orwin stood and tried to stop him. She tugged on his arm, and he pushed her off. She fell and hit her head on the corner of the table.

"I'm sorry, are you—" An unsheathing sword cut him off.

Julian stood in the hallway, stalking toward him.

"How dare you harm Lady Orwin, after she's shown you such kindness," he said.

"No, I didn't mean to. I'll come back with medicine, and I'll bring back the—"

"Quiet, insolent fool. You've made your choice."

Julian swung his long sword from his upper right. Wolfgang raised his poleax in defense, deflecting the blow.

"I don't want to fight you!" Wolfgang shouted.

"You've made your decision, now parlay."

Julian swung his sword from his lower left. Wolfgang swung his poleax and deflected the blow. He backed up toward the wall to create space between them. Julian pressed the attack, swinging again. Wolfgang defended himself with a counter, swinging his poleax from the opposite direction and meeting the sword in the middle, forcing it to the ground. Wolfgang twisted around and pushed Julian back.

Julian fell and knocked over a small table with an oil lamp on it. The oil spread over the ground, catching the wall on fire.

Julian stood and took up a guard, continuing the fight. Wolfgang did the same, but was hesitant to attack. Julian thrust his sword forward. Wolfgang swung the flat side of his poleax, hitting Julian in the head. Julian dropped his weapon and fell backward.

The fire consumed most of the dining hall, spreading through the manor. Lady Orwin climbed to her feet. Wolfgang turned to her. She stood on the other side of the inferno.

"Are you okay?" Wolfgang asked. "You need to get out before the fire spreads—"

"Quiet, you. Go, just go, devil child—go back to the slaughter. Pay your promise in blood."

Wolfgang ran out of the manor toward the village as the blaze consumed the manor.

***

It took Wolfgang nearly an to reach the village. He ran past burning buildings and people rushing to the outlying farms and homes for safety. Wolfgang made his way toward the village's center. He stopped in front of the flower shop he visited a couple days before. A stick and ball sat next to the door. Then a man shouted at him from down the street.

"You! Come with me. Those merchants are attacking the harbor. We can't let them break through!" He must've been a pirate.

Wolfgang made his way toward the harbor, running past buildings reduced to rubble by the merchant's opening barrage. Among the rubble were pirates and merchants fighting one another. The battle was chaotic, and Wolfgang couldn't discern who was who. As he scanned the battlefield, he saw Francis on the ground, pinned by a pirate, struggling to break free.

The pirate pinning Francis was trying to shove a dagger through Francis's visor. He missed as Francis moved his head; the dagger scratching the visor's sides. Wolfgang approached from behind and swung his poleax at the pirate, slicing his neck open. Wolfgang's injuries burned. He stopped for a moment to recover.

"Wolfgang?" Francis was surprised to see him.

"Are you alright? Where's Otto?" Wolfgang asked as he helped Francis up.

"He is on the *Regent*. The last battle wounded him. We thought you were gone."

"No, I'm fine. Thank you, Francis."

As Wolfgang spoke, a pirate ran at him, swinging a longsword. Wolfgang stepped back and used his poleax to deflect the blow, forcing his opponent's blade to the ground. He then stepped forward and swung his poleax up the pirate's leg. The pirate fell to the ground, holding his wound.

"Wolfgang, we will retreat soon. The aim was to rattle them and burn their town. Make your way back to the docks."

"You're sure?"

"You are clearly wounded. No one would want you to injure yourself further. I will keep fighting for a while."

"If you say so."

***

As Wolfgang made his way through the battle toward the docks, he spotted Alphonse standing firm with a long sword, squaring off against the pirates. They certainly outmatched Alphonse.

"Alphonse!" Wolfgang shouted as he ran over to him.

"Huh?" Alphonse turned from the pirates.

As he did, one lunged forward. Alphonse quickly raised his blade to block the blow. Another thrusted his sword at him. As the blade drew near to his neck, Wolfgang pushed his poleax between them to deflect the attack.

"Looks like you owe me," Wolfgang said sarcastically as he positioned himself back-to-back with Alphonse.

"Ha, I saved you from that dire wolf, remember? This makes us even. Glad you're still with us," Alphonse replied.

Alphonse pushed his opponent back. They each had a foe to fight. Wolfgang acted first, rushing his opponent. He thrust the point of his poleax forward. He had reach, but the pirate was fast. The pirate side-stepped to avoid the attack, then swung his longsword at Wolfgang's left side. Wolfgang planted his left foot on the ground and twisted toward his opponent, holding his poleax parallel across his chest. The pirate's sword bounced off the staff of Wolfgang's poleax. Wolfgang swung his weapon, catching the pirate's side. He pressed the ax into his enemy until they couldn't stand.

Meanwhile, Alphonse waited for his opponent to make the first move. The pirate had a small frame. Alphonse could surely overpower him. The pirate likely realized that, and was on the defensive. Alphonse was tired of waiting, and made the first move.

He opened with a forward sword thrust. The pirate responded by raising his weapon. Their blades met, and the pirate pushed Alphonse's sword up, successfully parrying his opening attack. Alphonse tried to recover as the pirate swung his sword from above. Alphonse staggered. The pirate's blade bounced off Alphonse's chainmail hauberk, giving him the opportunity to press the attack. Alphonse rushed forward with his sword at his side. He swung it down, catching the pirate's blade as he tried to block. Alphonse pushed, using his overwhelming strength to force his opponent to the ground. He then shoved the tip of his blade into the pirate's neck, finishing him.

Wolfgang walked over to Alphonse, both heaving from their duels. Alphonse balled his fist and held it out. Wolfgang smiled as he bumped his fist against his friends. He then noticed something. A pirate with a bow pointing an arrow at Alphonse's back. Before he could say anything, the pirate released the string. Wolfgang shoved Alphonse aside—although he wasn't strong enough to push him completely out of the way, so he positioned his body in front of Alphonse. He did so just in time to protect Alphonse from the arrow, but he couldn't protect himself. The arrow pierced his shoulder. He fell to the ground, writhing in pain.

"Wolfgang!" Alphonse shouted. "Why did you do that?"

The Wolf's Song

"I don't know—I didn't want you to be struck by the arrow," Wolfgang said, bleeding on the ground.

Before he knew it, everything went dark, and he passed out.

Chapter 28

Wolfgang drifted in and out of consciousness. He saw men loading him into a rowboat and taking him to the *Regent*. He woke briefly to witness Tuferan performing surgery.

Wolfgang woke up in the barber-surgeons quarters. It was dark, but a single candle illuminated part of the room. He could barely move, and he felt exhausted. His eyes traced the darkened room until they met a figure sitting next to him.

"For the greatest love of all is a love that sacrifices all. And this great love is demonstrated when a person sacrifices his life for his friends," the figure murmured kindly; the wandering priest. "You've sacrificed much and shown love to your comrades, my son. You've been through a lot. There's time for you to reflect on your choices, as not everything you've done is good or beneficial- not for your spirit, or for those around you."

As the wandering priest spoke, Wolfgang thought about the past two years. He'd seen much of the world, but he'd also seen how the world was twisted and broken. Wolfgang thought about the young girl shackled in the bowels of the ship. He thought about the men he killed in Oustliut and Cleovet. He thought about the boy on the pirate's galley he'd slain at the lighthouse, and Lady Orwin. A great sorrow overcame him. Tears fell uncontrollably. Just as his sorrow turned into a deep depression, a warm calmness filled him. It was joy mixed with sorrow, creating a longing melancholy. The wandering priest placed his hand on Wolfgang's forehead.

"The time for reflection isn't now. You've been tested, and many tests remain. Soon you'll understand this world deeper than most, of that I'm sure. We all must bear the shame of our sins. Tis' the cross we carry on our shoulders. I can see that the cross you bear weighs heavy on your heart. In the coming years, a mirror shall be held to your soul, and things will be made clearer. But now is not the time for reflection. Now is the time for rest. Go to sleep."

***

As daylight broke, the sailors awoke began their duties aboard the *Regent*. Otto stopped by the barber-surgeon's quarters to visit Wolfgang. Tuferan was checking his pulse as Otto stepped in.

"He's a strong one. Still has a good pulse. But his injuries from the battle are severe. Broken ribs and internal bruising. I've bled him and done what I can to re-balance his humors. Now it's on him to survive." He turned to Otto. "But don't worry. This kid could probably survive a fall from Mount Vestala."

"Yeah, he's resilient. I'll be heading up to clean my cannon and check its bore. Just wanted to make sure everything is alright."

"Yeah, of course. I'll let you guys know when he wakes up."

Otto left to perform his duties on the upper deck. As he scrubbed down the bore of his cannon, Lindermann approached.

"We'll be heading to Norsica. The most damaged ships will limp to the Rikedome of Svenland. We'll stop in Uotguard before returning home. I know you guys never wanted to sail, so you can leave when we make port. You could stay with us until Grosshenburg, too." Lindermann paused. "I wouldn't mind it if you guys stayed. You all make fine sailors."

"Thank you, Captain. But we still have our own quest to

complete. We need to make it to Etalia and pluck an eidelwiess from the mountains," Otto said.

"I suggest you get off at Norsica," Arthur suggested, approaching the two with guitar in hand.

"Why there?" Otto asked.

"Stirrings of a war, brewed by a madman in a pot of violence! The once ostracized executioner is now leading an army!"

"None of what you said made any sense," Otto replied.

"I heard about it from merchants in Grosshenburg. The king of Uotguard, who ruled several small dutchies, was killed. Last I heard, the dukes that murdered him were planning a revolt."

"How did you learn all that from a merchant?" Otto asked, arching a brow.

"I said merchants, with an s. That means more than one. I'm a bard and an adventurer. I always keep my ear to the ground and listen to the machinations of the world. If Norsica doesn't suit you, how about Angland? I hear the new king of Albion is seeking to reunite the Anglish Isles. We could go to Kaspia, sip some fine wine and olive oil while enjoying the excitement of battle."

"You don't even fight. Besides, why are you so obsessed with war?"

"Clashing swords create heroes and villains, and many pretty widows. Perfect for making songs recalling the tales of adventure and heroism… and to make coin."

"I've had enough of war. We just want to finish our quest and return home."

"You say we, but you mean you. What of you, Alphonse the Ox?" Arthur turned his attention to Alphonse scrubbing the deck with a mop.

"Don't call me that," he sighed. "But if you're asking me about war in Norsica, I think it would be a great chance to test our mettle. Besides, Otto, don't forget Wolfgang needs that dowry, or whatever. We won't get that if we can't make coin."

"I suppose that much is true," Otto grumbled.

"Then it's decided! I shall join you when we make port!" Arthur shouted.

"Join them?" Orion yelled from the sterncastle. "If you leave, who will lead our crew in song? I swear, nothing will get done if these men aren't entertained."

"Toby is more than capable of taking up my station."

"So, am I to lose my shantyman, along with five skilled fighters?" Lindermann asked.

"Don't fret, people come and go. It's the way of things." As Arthur spoke, he noticed several members of the crew staring at him. "Ah, now's not the time to be sad, lads! Come on, don't despair, let us sing a goodbye song! For we all must depart some day!"

Arthur strummed his guitar and led the crew in song.

I thought I heard the Old Man say

"Leave her, Johnny, leave her,"

Tomorrow ye will get your pay

And it's time for us to leave her

Leave her, Johnny, leave her

Oh, leave her, Johnny, leave her

For the voyage is long and the winds don't blow

And it's time for us to leave her

Oh, the wind was foul, and the sea ran high

Leave her, Johnny, leave her

She shipped it green, and none went by

And it's time for us to leave her

Wolfgang awoke to singing echoing throughout the ship. He looked around the barber-surgeons quarters. It was empty. Daylight shone through a small porthole.

"What was that? I remember something... a dream? Did someone visit me?" he asked himself. Tuferan opened the door and stepped inside. "Everything feels... hazy."

"You're awake? Wow, I thought you were a goner this time. Are you sure you're human?" Tuferan laughed.

"What? Tuferan?"

"You're aboard the *Regent*. Do you remember? Taking an arrow in the shoulder, being covered in injuries."

"Oh, yeah."

"Well kid, you're still in the land of the living, it seems. I think you'll be fine, but you need to rest—for a while. We're headed for Norsica now. Should be about six weeks until we arrive, at least according to the shipmaster."

"Norsica?"

Wolfgang tried to sit up, but the pain caused him to fall back into bed.

"Now, now. Don't try getting up. You'll probably be mostly healed when we get there, but even then, take it easy. I really mean it this time. You're way too reckless. Your luck will run out one of these days."

"Luck? I don't believe in luck." Wolfgang rubbed his eyes.

"Ha! Could've fooled me. Maybe you have a guardian angel looking out for you," Tufern laughed. "I'll have the cooks make you soup. They always refuse when anyone asks for anything but breakfast and supper, but they won't refuse the guy that gives everyone nausea medicine after eating their terrible food."

Tuferan left and Wolfgang laid in bed. His whole body ached; he could hardly move. Even breathing was slightly uncomfortable. But he was alive, and he was back with his family.

The crew sang and sang as they drifted toward Norsica. Through every storm and every battle, they'd seen it through to the other side and made their mark on history. The tales of most men would end there. Having their fill of adventure, they'd go home to relinquish their tales as warriors and become the most famous person in their village. But the group is in the Age of Heroes. Otto the Scholar, Alphonse the Ox, Francis the Kind, Jurgen the Swordmaster, and Wolfgang the Crimson Wolf—those names will be etched into the walls of history, uttered for generations to come. This is an era of unprecedented strife and conflict- but like the time of the Wolf King, the conflicts that are to come will shape the destiny of mankind. The seeds of the future have already been sown in Oustilüt and on the high waves of the Sea of Ice. On the cold snowy fields of Norsica, in the frozen fjords and the rocky mountains, these boys will make history once again. They didn't know it, but soon, they would be known to the world as heroes.

Thank you for reading *The Wolf song: a Blood of the Wolf King Novel*. I hope you enjoyed it! Our heroes will return in the sequel: *Blood, Spice, and Iron*. As a thank you for finishing the book, please enjoy a special bonus song! Scan the QR code below.

Made in the USA
Columbia, SC
14 June 2024

b1c35060-bc23-4400-9e43-d50dbd2601f0R01